A Bride's Guide to Marriage and Murder

Dianne Freeman

KENSINGTON
PUBLISHING CORP.

www.kensingtonbooks.com

KENSINGTON BOOKS are published by

Kensington Publishing Corp.
119 West 40th Street
New York, NY 10018

First Kensington Hardcover Edition: July 2022

ISBN: 978-1-4967-3167-8 (ebook)

ISBN: 978-1-4967-3164-7

First Kensington Trade Paperback Edition: June 2023

10 9 8 7 6 5 4 3 2 1

Printed in the United States of America

Books by Dianne Freeman

A LADY'S GUIDE TO ETIQUETTE AND MURDER

A LADY'S GUIDE TO GOSSIP AND MURDER

A LADY'S GUIDE TO MISCHIEF AND MURDER

A FIANCÉE'S GUIDE TO FIRST WIVES AND MURDER

A BRIDE'S GUIDE TO MARRIAGE AND MURDER

A NEWLYWED'S GUIDE TO FORTUNE AND MURDER

Published by Kensington Publishing Corp.

A Bride's Guide to
Marriage and Murder

Chapter One

London, February 1900

Family, like a rich dessert, is a treat best enjoyed in small portions. One may love it and want to indulge in great quantities, but too much of either can lead to such a noxious experience one might be prompted to avoid it—or them—forever.

Well. Perhaps just my family.

My mother invaded—I mean, arrived—at my home four months ago for my sister's wedding, then stayed on to plan mine. Since that time, I'd gone from considering elopement to contemplating a move to the Outer Hebrides, but since the Gaelic language eluded me, I stayed home and endured the invasion—I mean, visit, for four months.

Four. Long. Months.

The single refuge left to me were my thoughts. Daydreaming had become my escape. It might appear that I was enjoying breakfast with Mother and Aunt Hetty while they reviewed the final—please let it be the final—list of wedding details, but in my head, I was in the church, saying my vows.

I smiled. The dream would be a reality in a little more than twenty-four hours.

I, Frances Helena, do take thee, George—

"Ahem!"

And just like that, the dining room came back into focus. The altar transformed into the table, draped with a white cloth and littered with handwritten notes and forgotten breakfast plates. The candles that had glowed in my daydream were replaced with the gas chandelier, and the choir turned into rattling china as Mrs. Thompson, my housekeeper, brought in fresh plates.

The reverend's voice was replaced with my mother's.

"Do you intend to drink that coffee, Frances, or simply admire it?"

It took another moment before her ice-blue stare came into focus. "I beg your pardon?"

"You've been gazing into that cup for at least ten minutes now and haven't heard a word I've said."

That was rather the point.

She drew her brows together. "What's wrong with you?"

Where to begin? I had a house full of relatives. My mother was organizing my wedding like a military campaign, while I attempted to coordinate a move to my new home during the coldest February in my recollection. And now I'd been distracted from a lovely daydream. Of course, I could tell her none of that.

"Nothing's wrong." I pasted on a smile. "What were you saying?"

"I've just heard from the florist." She tossed a note card onto the table. "He can't manage the pure white roses for the wedding. Now what am I to do?"

I shuddered to think. It was quite possible that poor florist's head would roll.

Aunt Hetty sought refuge behind the morning paper. I took a long drink of my coffee for fortification. "If they're the pinkish color, they should be just fine," I offered. "Rose is wearing pink." Rose was my eight-year-old daughter and only attendant. She was also the one person Mother didn't argue with. To her, Rose could do no wrong.

She sighed and sank back into her chair. "I can't risk the flowers being the wrong shade of white. I'll have to call at the shop and have a look at them myself." She gave me a pointed look. "That means I shan't be able to accompany you to your dress fitting."

Somewhere in the heavens, a choir of angels sang.

I covered my grin with my cup. An afternoon without Mother's harping was akin to a miracle. For a few hours, I'd be in control of my own life while she scoured London for the perfect white flowers.

This was my second marriage, so I don't know that white *everything* was appropriate, but neither was it worth the argument. Besides, I'd prefer to forget my first marriage. Ten years ago, my mother had orchestrated that one, too. She had even chosen the groom. I'd gone along with her plan, so I can't really lay all the blame at her door. But Reggie Wynn had been a poor choice. At the time, he was the heir to the Earl of Harleigh and was experiencing financial distress. Thus, he met Mother's criteria: a man who needed my money and could give me a title. For my part, I was relieved he wasn't in his dotage, as were many of the eligible aristocrats that season. At thirty-three, he was fifteen years older than I'd been, but he was dashing, and his devil-may-care attitude made him seem much younger.

Rose was the only positive result of that marriage. I was actually surprised by my willingness to try it again, but I had an excellent inducement in George Hazelton. He was the furthest thing possible from Reggie. First and foremost, George loved me, not my money—a good thing since I had very little of it left. He loved my daughter, and we loved him. More importantly, I trusted him. He had a very progressive attitude about women, or at least me. Though George occasionally practiced law, his true profession involved a variety of clandestine assignments for the Crown. That he never spurned my assistance told me I needn't worry about being left at a crumbling country estate like some unwanted baggage, which was an apt summary of my first marriage.

"Good morning, ladies," my father said, joining us in the dining room. He and my brother Alonzo had arrived from New York the previous evening. "Alonzo's still sleeping, is he?" He rounded the table and bussed my cheek before slipping between the back of Mother's chair and the sideboard to pour himself a cup of coffee.

"Good morning, Franklin," Mother said, still studying her wedding notes. "You've been up for hours. Where were you?"

"In Frankie's library," he replied. "I had some cables to send. Your kitchen boy took them to the telegraph office for me. I hope you don't mind the liberty."

"This is Aunt Hetty's house now," I pointed out. "He works for her." Since Rose and I were moving to George's home next door, Hetty had offered to purchase the lease on this snug little house. I couldn't imagine a better neighbor and was delighted to sell it to her.

Hetty waved a dismissive hand at my father. "Please, make yourself at home."

"But you are meant to be on holiday, Frankie," I replied. "Can't your business wait?" To my siblings, Franklin Price was Father or Papa, but I had never called him anything but Frankie, and he called me the same. After all, I was named for him. It was clear to both of us, we were the only ones who had not grown weary of the affectionate moniker, but it was one of the few things I shared with him. Perhaps the only thing. As a child, I knew the back of his head better than his face since that was my view of him as he left for his office. The last time I saw Frankie was at my previous wedding. I hoped I wouldn't have to marry a third time in order to see him again.

He pulled out a chair and seated himself between Mother and Aunt Hetty. "Business never waits, my dear."

Hetty lowered the paper, and I was struck by the image of brother and sister side by side. They could not have looked more alike—thick, dark hair; brown eyes; tall, sturdy build. Frankie now sported a few more lines than I remembered and a face full of whiskers. Aunt Hetty, happily, had neither of those things. Nor did she wear spectacles. Alonzo and I both looked more like our father—tall, regular features, and dark hair, though there was some of my mother's pertness to my nose and I had her blue eyes.

"Now, remind me," Frankie continued. "Why won't Lily be at the wedding? I thought she lived here now." He took a sip of his coffee and sighed in satisfaction.

Mother gave him a long look, cocking her brow before deigning to answer. "Lily's father-in-law sent them to France. Her husband is working on"—she waved a hand—"something or other."

"It's business, Franklin," Hetty added. "Since you missed her wedding due to your business, I would have thought you'd approve of her keeping Leo's nose to the grindstone."

"I don't disapprove, but France is not that far away. Just a short trip to attend her sister's wedding."

Mother placed a hand over his. "It's too far for my daughter to travel when she's with child."

In truth, Lily had been with child when she married Leo four months ago. Her decision not to attend my wedding was to keep anyone from noticing that her pregnancy was perhaps a bit further along than expected. Once the babe was born, she could claim it was early. I wasn't sure if my mother was aware of the circumstances.

I certainly hadn't the nerve to tell her.

"You'd know better than I about that, but I'd hoped to see her. Imagine, Daisy. Our youngest is soon to give us another grandchild." He pulled off his spectacles to wipe them with the napkin while he studied Mother's profile. "You look far too young to be a grandmother."

"Why, thank you, Franklin." Mother looked positively flustered. Was that a blush?

"I suppose you'll want to go to her and stay until the child is born," he added, taking another sip of his coffee and fogging his spectacles once more.

Mother's smile faded. "Perhaps I will," she snapped. My gaze flitted between Frankie and Mother. That went wrong quickly.

Aunt Hetty folded down the corner of her newspaper to glance at my father. "Do you know Peter Bainbridge, Franklin?"

Frankie tapped his index finger against the cup he held. "One of the Bonanza Barons. Made his fortune in silver. Now he has a financial interest in nearly everything west of the Mississippi."

Hetty released a tsk. "I meant personally."

"I might have met him at a business dinner back in New York," Frankie said. "Why do you ask?"

"He arrived a few days ago for a visit to his London home. Yesterday someone broke in and vandalized his office."

"I'll give you three guesses as to who is responsible for that, and the first two don't count," Frankie said. "Does the article lay blame on anyone?"

Hetty lowered the paper. "No, but who else could it be but James Connor? He's also residing in London at the moment, and I can't imagine a better suspect."

"Why James Connor?" I asked.

They both threw me a look of scorn. "Because of the feud," Hetty said. "Haven't you heard of it?"

I'd have to be dead not to have heard of it. Both men immigrated to America—Connor from Ireland, Bainbridge from England—many years ago. They had been business partners early in their careers, but had fallen out. Since that time, they'd gone to great lengths to spread shocking and scandalous stories about one another, using the newspapers.

"It's not by chance they're both in London. Word is, they're interested in purchasing the same company," Frankie said. "Connor is trying to scare Bainbridge off, I'd wager."

"His office was the only part of the home damaged and nothing was stolen," Hetty added. "It's the type of petty act they've both participated in. From what little I've heard of him, petty describes Connor quite well."

The truth of her last statement was disheartening. Mrs. Connor was a friend. Her husband, whose fortune was also founded on silver, had a lamentable personality. He was loud, vulgar, and his humor was always at someone else's expense. As much as I enjoyed Willa Connor's company, I avoided Mr. Connor whenever possible. Fortunately, he didn't care for society, so that wasn't difficult.

"Petty, you call it? It's a criminal act." Mother tutted in disgust. "This feud of theirs has everyone in London believing Americans are daft. It's an embarrassment, and I blame Mr. Connor. The Bainbridges wish to put an end to this constant baiting of one another, but Connor refuses to cease."

All three of our heads swiveled in her direction. She turned her round, blue eyes on each of us and held up her hands. "What did I say?" She looked as innocent as a china doll, and even more lovely. Her flaxen hair was drawn back from a perfect oval face, devoid of a single wrinkle, blemish, or freckle. She worked very hard to keep it that way. Maintaining her beauty was part of Mother's very being. Having such intimate knowledge about robber barons like Connor and Bainbridge was not.

"How are you so familiar with the matter?" Hetty asked.

Mother wavered. "I don't suppose I am, really. The Bainbridges are friends of mine. What I know about this so-called feud, I have heard from them." She shrugged. "One-sided, I suppose, but they have told me they'd like to call it a draw and have an end to this nonsense."

My father chuckled and rose to fill a plate at the sideboard. "I imagine they do. That way, Gladys Bainbridge can offer to buy up all the prominent landmarks of Paris and no one will be the wiser."

Mother gave him a quelling glare. "That was years ago, Franklin. She is not such a rube anymore. I think it's horrible of Connor to have someone spying on her and reporting her every move to the papers."

"Everything they do to one another is horrible," I said. "The newspapers are the sole beneficiaries of this feud. Mr. Connor pays them to publish every foolish thing Mrs. Bainbridge does, while Mr. Bainbridge digs up unsavory details of the Connors' lives. It wasn't long ago I read a story about Mrs. Connor's humble origins. They have a daughter making her debut this season. A story like that might ruin her chances for a good match." I let out a tsk. "What do these men have against one another?"

Hetty shook her head as she moved to the sideboard for more coffee. I tried my father. "Frankie, do you know?"

"No idea," he said. "As long as I've been aware of their existence, I've been aware of the feud. I barely know the men except by reputation, and Connor's isn't good. An enormous fortune and a lack of principles is a dangerous combination. I've done no business with him and hope I never have to."

"It may not be business, but you will have to put up with him for one day, at least." At his inquiring gaze, I continued. "The Connor family is coming to the wedding."

Hetty, having returned to the table and her newspapers, looked up in surprise. Mother gasped. "You've added someone to the guest list? Without consulting me?"

I'd given up reminding Mother this was my wedding. Judging from the look on her face, she saw my inviting the Connors as an egregious act of defiance.

"I added the Connors two weeks ago at Alonzo's request. You must have missed their names on the guest list."

"Why on earth would he want them at your wedding?" My mother's eyes narrowed as suspicion formed. I wished Alonzo had dragged himself out of bed to deliver the news himself.

"I think he's quite taken with Miss Madeline Connor. They met in New York. She told him she'd be here for the upcoming social season." I picked up my fork and returned to my now-cold eggs, hoping I'd sounded casual.

"I thought she was here to catch a duke or an earl," Hetty said. "Someone with a distinguished title."

"That's certainly possible. Her father could provide an enormous dowry for some lucky lord. However, as with the Bainbridges, you can't believe everything you read about the Connors." I shrugged. "They accepted the invitation."

Mother grumbled as she rifled through the wedding notes. Probably looking for the seating chart.

My father returned to the table with a full plate and a grim expression. "I must have a chat with Alonzo," he said. "The girl may have the face of an angel, but her father would be the devil to deal with. He'd do better to find someone else. I don't even like the idea of that man at your wedding."

"If you don't like it now," Mother said, scribbling on the seating chart, "you'll positively hate it when I tell you Mr. Bainbridge will be there as well."

"You invited the Bainbridges?" It must have been after she'd taken over the guest list. It was one thing for me to add to the numbers, but quite another when Mother did. This was my wedding, after all. "This was meant to be a small affair, with close family and friends. I don't even know them."

"I suppose you are close friends with the Connors?"

"I'm well acquainted with Willa Connor. Alonzo must have

a friendship with Miss Connor. And Graham is hosting the wedding reception at Harleigh House, which happens to be next door to their home. Thus, they are neighbors to my brother-in-law."

"As if that counts for anything." Mother lifted her chin. "The Bainbridges are my friends. With Gladys in Paris, Mr. Bainbridge is alone, so I invited him. And a good thing too since you've invited an extra lady. Now the numbers will be even."

"But he doesn't know the Connors are also attending, does he?" I asked.

"Of course not. I just found out myself."

My father grinned as he glanced around the table. "Two parties to a feud at your wedding, Frankie. You may well end up with fireworks."

I set off for my errands that afternoon with a lighter step and my maid, Bridget, cheered by the thought that in one more day, I'd be sailing off to the south of France on a wedding trip with my husband. Ten days alone with George at the luxurious Villa Kasbeck. The owners of the villa, Russian grand duke Michael Mikhailovich Romanov and his wife, Sophie, Countess de Torby, were involved in our last investigation. They felt George and I had done them a service, and I suppose we had, but I was stunned when they'd offered us the use of their home.

Upon our return, I'd live next door to my former house with George. Mother would stay with Aunt Hetty, or return to New York with Frankie and Alonzo, or travel to France as Frankie had suggested, to be with Lily. Whatever her decision, we'd be in separate houses, making for a much better relationship.

Bridget and I alighted from the cab on Bond Street, where despite the heavy gray sky, ladies and gentlemen crowded the pavement, moving briskly from shop to shop while ragged boys with brooms rushed ahead of them to clear their paths of slush, mud, or any other unpleasantries. Our destination was just a few steps away—one of the most expensive dress shops I'd dared to enter since becoming a widow. I'll confess that while I've never been the reckless spendthrift my late husband was, I paid little attention to the price of anything until he was gone, and the bills landed on my desk. That was a gasp-inducing surprise. From that point on, I became utterly parsimonious when replenishing my wardrobe—having gowns restyled, hats refurbished, and only buying new when it was absolutely necessary.

Until now, such a purchase had not been necessary. But Mother had bought my wedding gown, so I felt emboldened to splurge on my going-away dress. I wanted something special. Something new to start my new life. Madame Arquette's clothing was nothing if not special. I couldn't wait for this final fitting.

A bell jingled when Bridget opened the door, causing two ladies to glance our way as we stepped inside the cozy receiving room of the shop. Of all people to meet here! Mrs. and Miss Connor. Bridget took my coat and slipped away to join another maid in one of the chairs against the wall, while I approached the ladies with a smile and a "good day."

"Such a surprise to see you here, Lady Harleigh." Mrs. Connor spoke with the slow, lilting accent that placed her origins somewhere in America's South. I'd always wondered where, but then the embarrassing gossip about her background had come out, marking her as working-class before her marriage to Connor ten or so years ago. Though my own family had solid middle-class beginnings, I sensed asking about her past might cause her pain, something I was loath to do. She was a bright, handsome, middle-aged woman, small of stature with dark hair and eyes and currently dressed in a fashionable red suit. Regardless of her history, she seemed to have landed on her feet. Yet she always had a tense look about her, as if she were waiting for the other penny to drop.

"I would have thought you'd be busy preparing for the wedding tomorrow," she said. "Are there not a hundred things to do?"

"Ah, but this is one of those many things, the final fitting of my going-away gown."

Madeline Connor perked up at this. "Where are you spending your wedding trip, Lady Harleigh?"

"Cannes, primarily. But I hope to see a bit of the French countryside, too."

"That sounds lovely." Mrs. Connor's face took on a dreamy look. "I'm afraid we're here for the rest of the winter. Mr. Connor has some business to take care of, and we need to outfit Madeline for the upcoming season."

"Assuming Papa allows me to have one." The young woman's tight lips and the glint in her eye warned of rebellion.

Mrs. Connor, easily four inches shorter than her stepdaughter, reached up to stroke her cascading brown curls. "Your father would not deprive you of a debut. But the season is not all about parties and dancing, you know." She turned back to me and smiled. "Madeline has a new suitor, and Mr. Connor seems to think he's prepared to offer for her hand."

That would be bad news for Alonzo. I schooled my expression so as not to show my disappointment. "Perhaps you should make him wait for an answer, Miss Connor. You may have many suitors once the season begins."

Mrs. Connor's brow furrowed as she twisted her fingers together. "Madeline wouldn't want to cause him any anxiety, would you, dear?"

Before the girl could answer, Madame Arquette stepped up to fetch Mrs. Connor. "I shall be with you in the briefest of moments, Lady Harleigh. We are a bit short of staff this morning."

"I could not have better company," I said. Linking my arm through Madeline's, we moved to a comfortable settee hidden by a table piled high with bolts of sumptuous fabrics. Never one to pry into another's personal business, I dearly wished to learn the name of her new suitor—for Alonzo's sake, of course. At eighteen years of age, she looked impossibly young to me, but I tried to see her through my brother's eyes—heart-shaped face, rosebud lips, half-moon eyes that tipped up at the corners. About average height, she'd come up to Lon's shoulder and glance up at him through her long eyelashes. Oh, yes, Lon would be lost.

While I struggled for a suitable way to return to the subject of her suitor, Miss Connor took charge of the conversation. "Has your brother arrived in town yet, Lady Harleigh?"

"Yes, he and my father arrived yesterday."

"Yesterday?" Her eyes rounded. "Golly, a spot of foul weather, and they might have missed the wedding altogether. I assumed they'd been here for days now."

Despite her professed concern, I noticed a small smile. Had she thought Alonzo was in town for *days now* and not called on her? "Not even one day yet," I said. "My father was up and about this morning, but Alonzo was still sleeping off the effects of travel."

"I see." She turned on her end of the settee, facing forward. Then, with a tip of her head, she glanced at me from under the brim of her hat. "May I speak in confidence?" she asked. "I don't wish to impose, but because my stepmother mentioned a suitor, I'd like to explain."

It was as if she'd read my mind. I nodded my encouragement.

"It's Daniel Fitzwalter."

Heavens! Her family was aiming high. Viscount Fitzwalter was the first-born son, and heir, of the Marquis of Sudley, a powerful and influential member of the House of Lords. His was an old and lofty title. The only one higher would be that of duke. To top it off, Fitzwalter was young. He'd recently finished his studies at Oxford, so barely over twenty. If she were title-hunting, I'd have offered her a "well done," but her expression told me she was not pleased with this outcome. Her unhappy face was turned to me. Waiting for a reaction.

"I sense you are less than thrilled with the potential match," I offered.

She heaved an exaggerated sigh. "I'm so pleased you understand."

I blinked. Understand what? She'd told me nothing. "I'm afraid I don't."

"My father is overjoyed at the mere possibility of such a match, but I have no interest in titles or pomp and circumstance. I hardly know Fitzwalter, but my father is bribing him with an enormous dowry, and I'm worried the viscount will propose to me. If he does, I don't see how I can turn him down."

As I listened to her lament, I realized she wasn't looking for advice so much as a messenger. I was meant to deliver this information to Alonzo, which I would, but I wished he had told me what his intentions were toward Madeline. Did he care enough to fight for her, or would he give her up to Fitzwalter? Without that knowledge, I had no idea what to say.

"If you object to Fitzwalter," I ventured, "but you don't want to reject him, why not tell your father, or Willa, how you feel?"

"My father would be furious with me, and I don't believe my stepmother would try to sway him. I'd much rather speak to your brother."

That's what I'd feared. She wanted Alonzo to rescue her. That almost never worked. Not to mention that any assistance he provided Madeline might bring on the wrath of her father. And none of us wanted that. "I'm sure the two of you will speak soon, Miss Connor."

A motion at the back of the shop caught my eye. Willa Connor had finished her business and was coming our way along with Madame. "At some point, you will have to make your preference known to your father," I continued. "Though you fear he won't like your decision, in time he may adjust his opinion. You might gain that time by discouraging Fitzwalter's suit. In delicate matters such as this, it's best to proceed with caution."

I rose as Madame beckoned to me. After saying goodbye to Mrs. Connor, I turned to bid Madeline a good day and was struck by the bleakness of her gaze. There was clearly something she hadn't told me, and now I doubted my advice would be sufficient for her needs. I hoped she and Alonzo wouldn't do anything rash.

Chapter Two

The dress fit to perfection and was ready to be delivered to my house that very afternoon. Bridget had left to pick up my new matching gloves. Thus, I was wreathed in smiles when Fiona Nash stepped into the shop. Fiona is George's sister and my dear friend. She was here to accompany me to Harleigh House, the London home of my brother-in-law, the Earl of Harleigh, to check on the preparations for the wedding reception.

Fiona's chestnut hair, which was often styled into a veritable tower, was today more of a plateau. All the better to balance a hat that looked like a red platter holding a frosted and flower-strewn cake. Perhaps it was her stature, or her willowy form, or her long, aristocratic face and nose, but only Fiona could carry off such a hat.

Just looking at it made me hungry.

She crossed her arms and leaned back to observe me, an indulgent smile on her face. "Ah, young love."

"Hardly that," I said. Once I'd fastened my coat, I took her arm and led her out of the shop, stopping once we reached the pavement to pull my collar tighter against the chill. Fiona nodded in the direction of her carriage and we moved on.

"Fine. Call it new love then, will that do?" Fiona's driver opened the carriage door and let down the steps. We climbed in, eager to escape the cold, damp air.

"I'm not sure we qualify for that either," I said, sinking into the soft leather seat. "George and I have known each other for years."

"But the love part is new."

I couldn't argue with that. Though I'd met George Hazelton many years back, he returned to my life less than a year ago when I moved into my new home and discovered he was my neighbor. The love part, as Fiona dubbed it, came soon after. A shiver ran through me that had nothing to do with the weather. "New or not, it is quite the best feeling."

Fiona settled in next to me and squeezed my arm. "That's the response I was looking for. For a moment I thought you might dash my hopes."

"I fear I did that to someone else a short while ago." Fiona's comment had brought Madeline Connor to mind. In fact, the girl's desolate expression had barely left my thoughts while I had my fitting. I met Fiona's expectant gaze with a shrug. "I'm afraid I must keep the details in confidence. Suffice it to say, a young lady confided in me on a matter of romance and I fear she was quite disappointed in my response."

"Looking for an agony aunt, was she? Young people have no idea how difficult it is to advise the lovelorn."

"I'm not certain the matter was about love." I flashed her a grimace. "It sounded more like desperation."

"I'm sure you advised her admirably." She patted my hand. "You can't help everyone. At least not today. We have your wedding to think of."

"Indeed, we do. I still find it hard to believe Graham offered the use of his home for the reception, but I'm so grateful he did. Even this small celebration would be too much for my house, or Aunt Hetty's as it is now. George's might have done, but with us leaving for our wedding trip tomorrow evening, we'd be chasing the guests out of the house so we could be off."

"It's a shame the wedding is in February," she said. "Cannes would be much more pleasant in a month or two."

"The longer we waited for the wedding, the longer I'd be living with my mother." I raised a brow.

"Good point. How was it to see your father again? It's been years, hasn't it?"

I nodded. "He didn't come when Rose was born, nor to Lily's wedding. I understand that his work is demanding, but if he doesn't step away from it now and again, he'll become a stranger to his family. I daresay that's why Mother has stayed with me so long—for the company." I couldn't imagine spending months at a time away from George, though that was exactly how my first marriage had gone. My late husband had little interest in me beyond my dowry. I hoped my parents still had some interests in common.

"Regardless of the lapse of time," I continued, "he seemed much the same as I recall him—endlessly involved in his work. He is a little grayer, a little heavier."

"Yet your mother never ages," she remarked. "She should extend her magic to her husband."

"She keeps to a strict regimen. I can't see my father willingly submitting to it."

We arrived at Harleigh House and waited for the driver to hand us down. Fiona glanced out the window. "Isn't that Inspector Delaney?"

I stretched my neck to see around the wide brim of her hat. "At Harleigh House?"

"No." She leaned back and tapped on the corner of the window. "At the door of the Connors' home."

She still blocked my view. "Fiona, they do make hats that are not three times the size of one's head."

"You've missed him anyway." She cast a glance at me as the

driver opened the door. "I enjoy being tall for the very reason that I can carry off such a hat."

We walked briskly up to the door where Graham's butler, Crabbe, bowed us inside the dim entry hall. I greeted him and asked about his lumbago. He took our outerwear and replied at length about a new salve he was using, then left us in the drawing room while he informed Graham of our arrival.

"What made you think the man you saw was Delaney?" I asked Fiona.

"He's rather unmistakable, wouldn't you say? That shapeless brown coat and his unruly hair."

She was right. Delaney's hair, and his eyebrows, for that matter, were a combination of wavy brown and wiry gray that seemed almost alive, certainly beyond his control, and very distinctive. "I wonder what business he has with the Connors? Oh, hello, Graham."

The last was said to my brother-in-law, the Earl of Harleigh, who had just stepped into the drawing room from the hall. Something looked different about him. He wore a gray morning coat over a dark waistcoat and striped trousers. His very light brown, not quite blond hair waved back from his forehead as usual. He'd been experimenting with various styles of whiskers over the past few months. The current version was clean-shaven with a mere suggestion of mutton chops along the outer corners of his jaw. I was pleased to see his mustache was gone—wait, that was the difference—Graham was smiling. A responding smile tugged at my own lips.

"Good afternoon, Frances. Lady Fiona." He nodded to Crabbe, who remained in the doorway. "Please ask Mrs. Rimstock to join us."

"Very good, sir."

Graham turned back to us, no longer smiling, but wearing a pleasant expression. I was so used to his face being pinched and disapproving he rather looked like a stranger, but one I could become used to very quickly. "You are looking very well today, Graham."

"Am I?"

Heavens, there it was again and this time with a flash of teeth.

The exchange caught Fiona's attention. She turned from surveying the room to examine him. "Frances is right," she pronounced. "Whatever you've changed, it suits you."

"Thank you, ladies." He gestured toward a sitting area. "I shall inform my valet that whatever he's done to me, should be continued."

I had a feeling his valet had nothing to do with this improvement to his looks. Such a change had to be the result of improved spirits and outlook. I suspected a lady was involved, but unless he chose to open the subject, I wouldn't intrude. It hadn't been quite a year since his wife died, and while I was pleased that he might yet find happiness, he wouldn't consider it seemly for such news to be public.

"I've asked the housekeeper to join us in case you wish to make any changes to the present arrangements. Since it's a small affair, I think we'll get by with the dining room, for the luncheon, and open up the doors between the east and west drawing room. Since the weather's been so blighted cold, we can keep the doors to the winter garden closed." He nodded toward the end of the spacious drawing room where a smaller room, filled with potted plants, looked out to the back garden. "Still have a pretty view."

"That should be perfect, Graham. I've brought the guest list for Mrs. Rimstock. It's up to twenty-two now, but we should have plenty of space to mingle."

"I've had the library cleared out for the photographer." He led us across the entry hall and threw open a set of doors to reveal a bright, largely empty room. "It had far too many tables with far too many bits and bobs," he continued. "He'll need an open area to set up his equipment and there's good light in here, don't you think?"

"Indeed," I replied. "It seems you've thought of everything, Graham."

"Will it feel strange, Frances, to be celebrating your wedding here?"

Fiona's question was one I'd asked myself, and George, several times. After all, when I was married to Reggie, this was my home, though I'd spent no more than a few months here each year, and usually without Reggie.

"No, I quite like the arrangement," I said. "It's familiar yet without too many memories attached to it. And those I have are good ones." I turned to my brother-in-law. "Thank you for offering it."

When Mrs. Rimstock arrived, we spent a few moments chatting about some of those good memories before turning the conversation back to the practical. I handed over the seating chart, discussed the placement of flowers, and reviewed the menu for the luncheon. The term *wedding breakfast* was a misnomer, in my opinion. The wedding itself would take place at the church at noon, with a light luncheon, and of course, wedding cake, to follow here. Mrs. Rimstock assured me Cook was delighted to bake the elaborate confection. It might have been my imagination, but she seemed to give Fiona's hat an assessing glance.

"We're all so happy for you, my lady," she whispered as we took our leave. There was the suggestion of a tear in her eyes that warmed my heart and caused me to squeeze her hand, but it did not make me wish for the old days. My life with Reggie, while not completely miserable, was hardly filled with fond memories either. I cherished my new life and was looking forward to even happier days with George.

As we waited in the entry hall for the carriage to be brought round, Graham caught sight of something outside and scowled.

There was the expression I'd always associated with him. "What the devil is going on next door?" he asked.

I peered through the side light. "You were right, Fiona. It's Inspector Delaney. I've been hoping to speak with him."

We took a hasty leave of Graham and made our way to Delaney, catching up with him as he was about to climb into a waiting cab. Fiona called out, and he turned, stepping back down to the pavement. He pulled his hat from his head when we approached.

"Lady Harleigh. Lady Fiona. Good afternoon."

"Good afternoon, Inspector," I replied, restraining myself from inquiring as to his business with the Connor household. While clearly none of my concern, it filled me with curiosity, nonetheless. Instead, I broached the subject of my wedding. "I received your regrets last week, but I'm hoping I can persuade you to change your mind and come to the wedding tomorrow."

He frowned, drawing his caterpillar-like eyebrows together.

"My lady, while I am happy for you and Mr. Hazelton, it wouldn't be right for me to attend your celebration. I wouldn't mix in with that crowd." He forestalled any debate with a raised palm. "And as it happens, I have a shift to work tomorrow and would not be able to attend in any event."

I sighed. Delaney might have felt uncomfortable mingling with aristocrats at a social event, but he was an integral part of my life with George, odd as that may seem. We spent a great deal of our time working on cases with him. "Your absence will be felt," I said. "But I shan't argue with the Metropolitan Police."

A rare smile played about his lips. "They'll be relieved to hear that, ma'am."

I gave him a wry look, but before I could make any comment, Mr. Connor emerged from his front door and stomped across the frosted lawn to us. The man was above average in height, and bulky. He loomed larger the closer he came, his handlebar mustache bouncing with each step, his face mottled red from both exertion and the cold. Or, perhaps, anger. Fiona and I stepped back—unnecessarily, as it turned out. He completely ignored us and came nose to nose with Delaney. If that wasn't officious enough, he poked a finger into the inspector's shoulder for good measure.

"You tell Bainbridge, I don't appreciate him sending the police over. Not one bit. If I had been responsible for it, he wouldn't be around to file a report."

Delaney, hardly a small man himself, looked down at the poking finger, then back up at Connor's face. When his brows drew together, Connor removed the offending digit. "Have a care, Mr. Connor," Delaney said, his voice almost too calm. "That sounded very much like a threat."

"And what if it was?" Connor's voice held the slightest Irish lilt, which, oddly, made the words sound even more menacing.

"I'm not familiar with the workings of the police in America, sir, but here, you are not above the law. It would behoove you to watch your step. We will get to the bottom of this matter."

"You'll find I had nothing to do with it. As if I'd stoop to vandalism." Connor curled his lip and turned on his heel. After a few steps, he twisted back, as if he'd suddenly realized Fiona and I had been there all along. He poked a finger in the air at each of us in turn. "Lady Fiona. Lady Harleigh." His voice had lost the sneer but it could hardly be called friendly.

"You have indeed identified us, sir," I said. Were we expected to applaud his effort?

The finger moved back and forth again. "Lady first name. Lady title. Born posh. Married posh." He grinned. "You see? I'm learning how you do things around here."

Clearly, he'd missed the lesson on tact.

"One may be aware of these things, sir," Fiona said, "but one rarely discusses them."

He made a noise of impatience and turned his attention to me. "Your brother has an interest in my daughter, Madeline, I believe. Tell him from me that he should direct those interests elsewhere."

"Well!" I bristled with umbrage. The man was not just tactless, he was rude.

Delaney stepped forward. "You had better not be about to utter a threat, sir."

Connor raised his hands to signal he meant no harm and headed back for the house.

"Goodness," Fiona said. "What a positively odious man. How can Mrs. Connor allow him out of the house?"

"Odious, and apparently a vandal." And invited to my wedding. I sighed. "I do wish you'd reconsider coming, Inspector. Both Mr. Connor and Mr. Bainbridge are expected to attend."

Delaney reminded me he'd be working. "Let's hope I don't have to show up in my official capacity," he said. "Those two together could be trouble."

"That's precisely what I'm afraid of."

Fiona and I stopped for tea, so it was early evening when I arrived home, delighted to learn that George was in the library with my father, Alonzo, and Aunt Hetty's new beau, Mr. Gilliam.

Though I hadn't been particularly fond of Gilliam when we first met a few months ago, he changed my opinion quickly by having the good taste to admire my aunt. When I learned she returned his regard, I decided he was the best of men. The owner of two theaters, he was smart and ambitious, but his business didn't consume him as it did my father. I hoped the two of them would become friends.

The four gentlemen were enjoying Aunt Hetty's brandy and a crackling fire, and seemed to be getting on famously when I poked my head around the door. To my left, Frankie sat behind my desk. Gilliam and Alonzo relaxed in the guest chairs,

and to my right, George, tall and lean, lounged against the bay
window, one hand resting on the seat fitted beneath it, the
other holding a snifter of brandy. The late sun glinted on his
dark hair. His smile crinkled the corners of his eyes and drew
me to his side.

"Wait." My father came half out of his chair. "Isn't it supposed to be bad luck for the bride and groom to see each other
before the wedding?"

I waved him back to his chair and settled into the window
seat. "If we hadn't seen each other before the wedding, it's
highly unlikely we'd be marrying at all."

Alonzo laughed. "I assume you don't subscribe to supersti-
tions."

Gilliam's mustache twitched with his smile. "Plenty of those
in my line of work." Gilliam was broad-shouldered, dark, and
adventurous. And a decade younger than Hetty, which gave
her a few qualms, but not enough to give him up, thank heaven.
"I believe it's the night before the wedding when the groom
should make himself scarce," he added.

George pulled out his watch and checked the time. "Ah, then
strictly speaking, we still have an hour or two." He beamed a
smile at me. "How was your day? Everything shipshape at
Harleigh House? Still planning to marry me?"

"My day was very interesting. Graham has everything under
control. And yes, I am, so you had better show up at the church
tomorrow." I shook my head. "It seems so silly we aren't going
together."

"Some occasions require a nod to tradition," he said.

"Hazelton was telling us about the plans for your wedding
trip," Gilliam said. "Two weeks in Cannes at the Romanovs'
villa. I hope the weather cooperates for you."

"I'm confident the weather won't bother us at all."

He chuckled. "No, I expect it won't."

"You said your day was interesting," George said. "In
what way?"

"In a way that has to do with Lon, though I'm not entirely sure how much." I eyed my brother. "Nor am I sure you'd want me discussing it in company."

"Now that you've baited my curiosity, you must go on." Alonzo shifted his chair around to take me in, crossing one long leg over the other. I marveled at how much he resembled our father, or rather how Frankie would have looked at twenty-three. They both had longish faces, high foreheads, and earnest brown eyes, but Alonzo's hair was nearly jet black, curly, and clipped close to his head. He also had a young man's energy and a ready smile where our father was more serious. "We're all family here," he said, "or close enough anyway. What happened?"

"All right, then, but you must stop me if this becomes too personal."

He raised his brows. "Come now, Franny. Are you going to tell us or not?"

"Fine. I came across Mrs. and Miss Connor this morning."

Alonzo's expression brightened, a sight that made my father's brow furrow.

"Have you and Miss Connor any sort of understanding?" I asked.

"Well. No, not exactly. She's aware of my interest and I feel she's encouraged it, but I'm not officially courting her yet."

"Yet?" My father's frown grew deeper.

"Yes. That's why I've asked Frances to invite the Connors to the wedding. I hope to gain their approval to call on Miss Connor. She's a lovely girl, isn't she, Frances?"

My father didn't wait for my response. "Be that as it may, Lon, her father is something of a shady character. Some of his business practices are unethical to say the least. Association with him would ruin your reputation."

"But we are not in the same line of business at all. What has mining to do with trading on the stock market?"

"He has his fingers in many pies and he's so notorious that it doesn't matter what business you're in. You'll be judged by his actions."

"I'm afraid my news might make that a moot point," I said. "Apparently, Madeline has a new suitor and her father approves of him. In fact, it sounds as though he likes him more than Madeline does."

"Just as well." My father rose to his feet. "I don't mean to sound unkind, Lon, but hers would be a difficult family to marry into." Placing a hand against his back, he stretched. "I'm going up to ready myself for dinner. Had an enjoyable day, Hazelton. Good to meet you, Gilliam. Looking forward to tomorrow."

After he ambled out of the room, George reached for the brandy, conveniently waiting on the table near the fireplace. "Still an hour or so before dinner. Frances? Gentlemen? Another splash?" He shot a glance at me and pulled a guilty face. "Apologies, Frances. I ought to consult you before offering your brandy."

I waved a hand. "Aunt Hetty keeps us supplied with spirits and I'm sure she wouldn't mind. Which reminds me, why are you all crowded in here rather than with the ladies? I assume Mother and Aunt Hetty are in the drawing room?"

Gilliam laughed and shook his head when George presented the bottle. "They were deeply engrossed in a discussion of their wardrobe plans for tomorrow. We slipped out somewhere around the mention of hats. I doubt they noticed."

Alonzo held out his glass, which George duly filled, then turned back to me. "By the way, a delivery arrived from your dressmaker." He lifted a brow. "What might that be?"

"Never you mind." My gaze drifted to Alonzo, who had slipped into silence. "Are you terribly disappointed, Lon?"

"Actually, I'm not. I now have fair warning about Connor and will keep that in mind. If things progress with Miss Connor, I'll be sure to keep my dealings with her father on nothing more than a personal level." He narrowed his eyes. "Who is this new suitor? Anyone I should know?"

"I doubt it. His name is Daniel Fitzwalter."

George whistled. "I take it what Connor approves of is the man's future title."

"One would assume so." In response to my brother's blank gaze, I clarified. "His father is the Marquis of Sudley. Fitzwalter will one day inherit the title."

To my surprise, he brightened. "That means Miss Connor would have to live in England and she's told me many times she prefers America." Alonzo grinned. "This may not be so difficult a battle after all."

"Mr. Connor told me in no uncertain terms to keep you away from her."

George touched my hand. "You saw Mr. Connor today too?"

"It was a separate encounter." I gave them an abbreviated version of the event. "That's when Connor gave me Alonzo's marching orders," I concluded, and shifted my gaze to my brother. "Would you still consider him as a father-in-law?"

"Admittedly my imagination hasn't taken me quite that far yet. I want the opportunity to court her and find out if we suit as much as I think we would. If it comes to marriage, perhaps our best action would be to stay far away from her father."

"That's the spirit!"

I turned to George in surprise. "You are encouraging him?"

"Indeed, I am. If I hadn't accepted your mother's dismissal, I wouldn't have had to wait so long for you."

I had no answer for that. Though I'd forgiven my mother for chasing George off once she'd set her sights on Reggie, I would not be so forgiving had George married someone else in the intervening years. I was grateful he waited, but when I thought of my daughter, Rose, I couldn't completely regret those years with Reggie. Perhaps George and I were meant to be together, but not at that time.

"I must throw my support to the pursuit of romance as well." Gilliam came to his feet and lifted his glass. "What say you, young man?"

Alonzo angled his lanky frame from the chair in imitation of Gilliam. "Hear, hear!" he said. "I may not win the fair Madeline, but I will fight for her right to make her own choice. And in the interest of romance, Gilliam, we should leave the happy couple alone. I must change for dinner anyway, and you can seek out the ladies."

When they departed, I was left with a sense of frustration that Lon had completely dismissed all warnings about Mr. Connor. "I wish you hadn't encouraged him, George."

He moved to sit beside me and took my hand. "He's in love, Frances."

"Is he? I'm not at all sure of that. It almost seems as if the challenge of winning Miss Connor's heart is more important to him than the prize itself."

He brought my hand to his lips. "They both need the opportunity to find out if the prize is worth the pursuit. If your brother gives up, they will never know what might have been."

The longer his lips whispered against my wrist, the more his premise made sense. Or at least, the less it mattered. I was alone with my fiancé. We were to be married tomorrow. I'd worry about Alonzo another time.

Chapter Three

My wedding day had finally arrived! Heavens, had I been this excited when I married Reggie? No. In truth, I'd been terrified—for good reason, as it turned out. This time was completely different. I couldn't sit still and checked the time every few minutes, had Bridget, my maid, restyled my hair twice, ultimately returning to the original style, and misplaced my gloves no fewer than three times.

Fortunately, Bridget had had the foresight to dress for the wedding early, or my antics would surely have made her late. Her blond hair was topped with a stylish hat. The blue plumes perfectly matched the two-piece tailor made I'd handed down to her and highlighted her peaches and cream complexion. The moment she finished my hair, I put her in charge of Rose while I chose my jewelry for the day.

Rose wanted some pearls woven in her hair to match the bracelet George had given her. She was to be my sole attendant, and I was delighted to have her with me as we prepared. "Mummy, why do you call Grandfather Frankie, when Uncle Alonzo calls him Father?"

I wrapped a bracelet over my gloved wrist and struggled with the clasp. "Because I'm named for him and it's a private joke we share—well, more endearment than joke, really." I gave up on the bracelet and gave her my attention. "Are you wondering what to call Mr. Hazelton when we are married?"

She gave me a cautious glance. "I don't want to call him papa."

No, of course, she didn't. Reggie had been her papa, and aside from being absent for much of the time, when he was home, he treated her like a beloved daughter. I didn't want her to forget him.

"May I call him Georgie?"

I tested the word. "Georgie." It brought to mind an image of George as a boy. Admittedly, it was no more youthful than the name Frankie, and my father had put up with that for the whole of my life. In fact, I'm quite sure he cherished it. George might love the idea. I crossed the room to her side. Bridget had drawn her dark hair back and was weaving a string of tiny pearls into the twists.

"I think you and Mr. Hazelton should have this conversation, but you might want to have a few options at the ready that the two of you can choose from. There are plenty of alternatives to Papa." I'd said the word as she had, placing the accent on the second syllable as many of the British did. Though I've lived in England for ten years, I'd rarely pronounce a word as my British friends did, or my daughter, for that matter. It was natural she'd have British speech patterns. She was born and raised here, after all. But every now and then she'd pronounce a word as I would, and I'd raise a silent cheer of victory that my voice had some small influence.

"You are half-American, Rose. When we pronounce the word, we put the accent on the first syllable. We say, Pa-pa. Is that different enough?"

She frowned while she mulled it over. "There's Father, too. But what I like about Georgie is that he could call me Rosie."

I blinked to keep my eyes from welling. "You've given this a bit of thought, haven't you?"

"I want us to be friends." She spoke the words like a vow.

"So do I, dearest." Heavens, I didn't want to start crying again. "I suggest you make him the offer."

As eager as I was to get to the church, naturally I misplaced an earring at the last moment that took a full ten minutes to find. My father had hired a carriage for his stay in London and everyone was inside it and waiting for me by the time I rushed down the stairs and out the door. The servants' cab waited right behind ours and would take them to the church as soon as they locked up behind me.

I squeezed in next to Mother and Aunt Hetty. My father, his nose in the paper, and Alonzo were opposite. "Where's Rose?" I asked.

"She rode with Hazelton, who left a full five minutes ago." Mother turned her frown of disapproval on me. "What kept you?"

I bounced against the seat as the horses lurched forward, then straightened my skirts. "A misplaced earring."

"Frances can't be late, Mother." Alonzo gave me a grin. "As an essential part of the ceremony, they can't begin without her."

"We aren't late yet, anyway. George simply left early. We'll be fine." Even if we weren't, I had no intention of allowing my mother to unnerve me today of all days.

"Will the Connors be at the church, Frances?" Alonzo asked.

"The Connors? I have no reason to believe otherwise." I noted the lines between his brows. "Do you?"

"I called on Mr. Connor this morning and Miss Connor wouldn't let me see him."

"Before noon?" Mother was aghast.

I patted her hand. "The world will keep turning, Mother."

"I wasn't his first caller," Lon continued. "Miss Connor told me he was closeted with Mr. Bainbridge in his office. Their raised voices carried all the way out to the vestibule."

"He was closeted with Mr. Bainbridge?" Mother shook her head. "I can't imagine why he would give Mr. Connor the time of day."

"Heed my warning, Lon," Frankie added. "Her father is trouble."

"He may be, but I have not given up on Miss Connor. Hazelton encouraged me to fight for her."

My brother the tattletale.

Frankie's whiskers turned downward as he leveled his gaze at me.

"I am not Hazelton," I said. "Glaring at me will not stop him from advising Alonzo."

Mother let out a tsk. "They are barely tolerated in New York society, dear. You could do so much better."

Alonzo cocked a brow. "We are barely tolerated in New York society, Mother. And that is largely due to Frances and her title. Considering my competition, Miss Connor could do much better than me."

"Indeed?" she said. "Who is this exalted competition?"

"Someone who's to become a duke someday," Lon grumbled. "I don't recall his name."

"Viscount Fitzwalter," I said. "He will not be a duke."

"I say let him have her." Frankie shifted his paper.

Mother ran the name through the copy of *Debrett's Peerage* she kept in her head. Her nostrils flared when she landed on the proper entry. "The heir to the Marquis of Sudley is available? What a wonderful catch for some enterprising young woman." She redirected her sour expression from Lon to me.

She could not be serious. "Must I remind you we are heading to the church where my groom awaits? This is not the time to throw Fitzwalter or any other man into my path."

She sighed. "Yes, I suppose it's too late for you."

I suppressed a sigh of my own. "It is most definitely too late. And I'd like you both to stop arguing with Lon, too. We are celebrating my wedding. Let's all be happy, shall we?"

My father forced a smile. Lon grinned. Mother pouted, but finally let out a grudging "fine." Aunt Hetty squeezed my hand, reminding me she'd always be on my side.

"And look. Here we are." Thank heaven, we'd arrived. I didn't want to hear one more bickering word. Once the door opened, Mother took charge, sending my father and me off to an anteroom near the entry and out of sight of the guests who were starting to arrive. I caught Fiona's eye and tipped my head toward my mother, silently imploring my friend to stop her from organizing everyone. I wouldn't be surprised if she had a replacement groom waiting somewhere in the church—just in case. When Fiona gave me a nod, I turned back to where I'd left my father, but barreled into Madeline Connor instead, nearly knocking her off her feet. She clutched at my shoulders to steady herself.

"Forgive me, Miss Connor. Have I injured you?" Indeed, she looked quite unsteady until her stepmother took hold of her arm.

"She's fine, Frances," Willa assured me.

I wasn't so sure. Madeline looked pale, but perhaps it was her gown. That shade of green didn't suit her. Willa touched my shoulder and I gave her my attention. "I know you have much to do," she said, "but I wanted to tell you that Mr. Connor sends his regrets. He was unable to break away from some business. Fortunately, Viscount Fitzwalter volunteered to escort us." She gave me an awkward smile. "I didn't want to leave you with an odd number at the table."

She motioned to my left, where the viscount stepped forward, bowed, and said something I'm sure I would have considered gracious if I'd been listening. Instead, I was imagining the adjustment to the seating chart and the fact that Lon would be rather upset to see his rival here today. Since Fitzwalter was far more congenial than Connor, I found it to be an excellent trade. I assured them that it was no inconvenience at all and excused myself.

Unfortunately, I stepped backward and into another guest. Mr. Bainbridge took hold of my shoulders from behind before I could knock him down. He waved off my apology, and I finally headed into the church.

Perhaps we should have eloped.

Rose was waiting in the room when we arrived. A widow who remarries normally would not have any attendants. I suppose those of us who managed to catch a second man were expected to consider ourselves lucky, marry quietly at home, and leave all the pageantry to the young maids. That would have been fine with me, but this was George's first—and hopefully only—marriage, so I wanted to do something ceremonial. Thus, the church and the traditional wedding breakfast. And Rose was such an important part of our lives together that I wanted her involved in the proceedings. She was already disappointed she couldn't come on the wedding trip with us. She became much less so when I offered her the role of maid of honor.

She took her duties seriously, brushing the small wrinkles from my skirt and fluffing up the lace trim. Before I knew it, the organist was playing, the choir began "The Voice That Breathed o'er Eden," and a church attendant poked her head inside to say they were ready.

The butterflies swarmed to my stomach.

Rose gave me a quick kiss, then headed off to take her walk down the aisle.

"I believe it's time, Frankie."

My father held out his arm, ready to escort me to George. I took a deep breath and the butterflies settled. Still there, but quiet now. "I'm ready."

I was surprisingly calm as we walked down the aisle. I took note of the pinkish white roses in Mother's flower arrangements nestled among potted palms and even looked out at the guests, all of them smiling benignly. Well, not all of them. I caught sight of Madeline Connor with red-rimmed teary eyes. She might be one of those people who cry at all weddings, but for heaven's sake, it had barely started. Fitzwalter, to her left, looked equally confused by the show of emotion. I let my gaze move along. There was Mr. Bainbridge, sitting behind Mother. I sent out a silent thanks to Fiona for making her take a seat. Alonzo seated next to her, twisted around and glared at Fitzwalter. Could my family not control themselves for the length of a wedding?

Then I saw George waiting at the steps of the chancel, in his gray morning suit, holding his silk hat in one hand and Rose's hand in the other. He gave me his crooked smile, and everything else faded away.

It faded so thoroughly, I barely recall exchanging our vows, though we must have done. My left glove was in my right hand and a gold band nestled up against my engagement ring. Organ music rang out. A smiling Rose returned my bouquet. When we turned to face our guests, I wore the most ridiculous, giddy grin. Then George tucked my hand in his arm, and I fairly floated back up the aisle.

Here we were, husband and wife after all these months— years if you go back to when Mother chased him away. I was so glad he came back. We waited in the vestibule to thank our guests for attending. Shaking each hand and smiling into each face. Most of them would come to Harleigh House to celebrate, including Bridget and George's valet, Blakely. The other servants, both mine and George's, would return to his house for a celebration of their own. Bridget was completely overcome when she came through the line, which started me crying. Fortunately, she was the last to leave.

After a run through a pelting of rose petals and a sprinkling of icy rain, we settled into George's carriage. Mother had taken custody of Rose, so at last we were alone, for the next few minutes at least. George seemed to read my mind. He settled in beside me wearing a silly grin of his own.

"I have you alone at last, Mrs. Hazelton."

"Indeed, you do. What do you plan to do about it?"

Those were the last words I said for quite some time. The next thing I knew, we were at Harleigh House and I definitely needed to straighten my clothing.

"Back to reality, I'm afraid," George said. "But in a few hours, we'll be leaving for Cannes, and it will be just the two of us for the next two weeks."

George opened the door and helped me down. I brushed off my skirts, fluffed the lace at my shoulders, and caught sight of a small spot under the lace trim. "What on earth happened to me?" I picked up the lace and twisted my neck to look closer at my sleeve.

"With the trim down, you can barely see it."

"I know, but it's my wedding gown. I hate to think it's ruined before the day is even over."

George leaned over and lifted the lace for closer inspection. "It looks like blood. Have you injured yourself?"

I held out my arms. "Everything I'm wearing is white. If I somehow managed to injure myself, I'd be unlikely to bleed in one single spot on my sleeve."

"Must have been one of the guests." He frowned. "It's not bad luck, is it?"

I couldn't help but laugh at the absurdity of the question. "To find blood on one's wedding dress? I've never heard, but I doubt it's a good omen."

Chapter Four

We arrived at Harleigh House amid cheers from our small group of guests. Graham approached us at the doorway, ready to guide us into the drawing room, but I forestalled him.

"I'm afraid I'm in need of my maid's assistance before I can do anything, Graham." I told him about my dilemma and he directed me to a room at the top of the stairs and promised to send Bridget to me directly.

George squeezed my hand before letting me go. "I'll mingle while you see to your repairs. Look for me when you come back down so we can make our rounds together."

Bridget popped into the borrowed bedchamber mere minutes after I did with her sewing basket. After a brief assessment, she determined the spot was indeed blood, which could not be cleaned without a significant amount of time and the removal of the dress. Fortunately, she was a genius with a needle and quickly turned the flounce at the shoulder into something more of a cap, tucking the spot inside a fold.

In less than fifteen minutes I proceeded back downstairs where I heard the hum of voices and the strains of a violin and cello. Mr. Bainbridge was in the hall, handing his coat off to a footman. Mother appeared behind me to greet him, then escorted him into the drawing room where the rest of our guests were gathered.

I paused in the doorway. Decorated in shades of red and deep blue with paneled walls, it was generally dark in here, but with both chandeliers blazing and the sunlight pouring through the doors of the west-facing winter garden, it looked positively cheerful.

"There you are, Frances."

George waited just inside the drawing room, holding out a hand to me. He stood next to Fiona and a man in uniform who resembled George nearly to a T. Both men smiled at me when I stepped up and took George's proffered hand. On closer inspection, I saw the other man had brown eyes and a slightly heavier build. "This must be your brother, Colin," I remarked. "I'm delighted to meet you at long last. George was so hopeful you'd be here today."

Colin Hazelton was four years older than George. A military man, he'd been stationed in India for almost as long as I'd been in England. It was a happy chance he'd been reassigned and was in London temporarily awaiting his next orders.

He gave me a toothy grin while he tipped his head toward George. "Did you hear that? She's already speaking for you, old chap. Soon you'll be referring to her for all your opinions."

George shook his head. "Spoken like a confirmed bachelor."

"If you're trying to frighten him off, Colin," I said, "you are about an hour too late."

There was mischief in his eyes when he brought my hand to his lips. "Then allow me to express my joy at seeing my brother happily married at last. You have all my good wishes for a wonderful life together. And welcome to the family." He tipped his head to the side. "Am I the first Hazelton to say that?"

Fiona let out a tsk. "I've been welcoming Frances to the family for simply ages. It was about time the two of them took my hint."

"I was attempting to introduce Colin to your family," George said, "but halfway through we ran out of members. I couldn't find your mother or brother."

"Funny, I saw Mother just a moment ago. And there's Alonzo across the room."

George and Colin followed my gaze. "That looks dangerous," George muttered.

Indeed, it did. Though they weren't making a scene, Alonzo and Fitzwalter were clearly having words while Madeline, looking uncomfortable, attempted to placate them.

"I suppose I should do something about that before it gets out of hand. I do hope we have another chance to speak this afternoon," I told Colin. "You can tell me all of George's misadventures as a youth."

"Delighted to oblige you, Mrs. Hazelton."

The name sent a little thrill rushing through my veins. Mrs. Hazelton. Though I was still Frances, Countess of Harleigh, I was no longer Frances Wynn. Yes, that thought was worthy of a thrill.

Fiona came with me to confront the terrible trio. We barely arrived in time to keep the men from pulling Miss Connor in two. I sidled up to Lon.

"What do you think you are doing?" I kept my voice low while I took him to task. "Can't you see the two of you are distressing Miss Connor?"

"It's not me, it's him. The man's acting as if he owns her." He cast a glance at Fitzwalter, who was now chatting with Fiona, while Madeline looked on. Viscount Fitzwalter had an athletic build, blond hair, and reasonably good looks. But it was his future title that made him the quarry of every debutante this season. All save one, that is. Madeline appeared less than charmed by the young man. In fact, she looked about her as if checking for an escape.

Alonzo gave me a nudge. "Leave off, Frances. Now's my chance."

"Mind your manners, Lon. Don't pester Miss Connor. Come along with me instead."

"I'm not leaving her with him."

I met his stony look with equal stubbornness. "Fine." I stepped around Lon and took Madeline's hand. "Miss Connor, might I borrow you for a moment? There's something I'd been meaning to ask you."

Lon huffed, but Madeline, looking grateful, came with me across the hall and into the dining room. It was currently empty of guests and set up for the celebratory feast to come. The crystal and silver gleamed against the mahogany table and the chandelier cast a happy glow over everything—except Madeline. "My dear, you should not let those young men upset you so. You always have the power to walk away."

"Golly, I didn't think of that." She drew a mighty breath. "I'm afraid Fitzwalter's presence here has rather annoyed your brother."

Though she lowered her head, I could hear her sniffles and imagined tears were not far behind. "My brother's behavior is inexcusable. He should not blame you for his disappointment."

"I tried to explain, but it was difficult with Fitzwalter there."

"Perhaps later we can find a way of distracting him so you and Alonzo can speak. But you shouldn't go back out there in your present distress. Would you like me to find your step-mother?"

She shook her head furiously. Fortunate, because I didn't recall seeing Mrs. Connor in the drawing room either. Where had everyone gone? I put my arm about her shoulder when the tears began in earnest. This was not merely the result of two young men fighting over her. "Can you tell me what is wrong?"

"I simply need to collect myself." She patted her sleeve and turned her red eyes to me. "Have you a handkerchief?"

I handed her mine. "That will not do." I drew her out to the hallway that led to the entry hall and the stairs. "Go on upstairs. The first bedchamber is available. I'll send my maid up to set you to rights."

I stayed by the stairs until she made the turning, then peeked into the drawing room once more. I still didn't see Mrs. Connor. With a sigh, I stopped a passing footman and asked him to get a message to Bridget. She'd take care of Madeline. At least I could count on her.

I found George again easily. This time he was with Charles and Lottie Evingdon, my cousin by my former marriage and his wife. After a short chat we moved on. "Shouldn't we be getting on with things by now?" George whispered.

"Yes. We ought to be eating. I'm famished. Graham was directing everything, but I don't see him anywhere." I scanned the room. "Nor do I see—wait. There's Mother. I'm sure she'd love to take charge."

"Undoubtedly," George muttered.

"Be nice. She's going to move everything along." I held up my hand before Mother could walk right past me. "Have you seen Graham?" I asked.

She frowned. "Not since we first arrived. Why?"

"Because we've been here for nearly an hour and I think we are all ready for luncheon at this point."

She looked remarkably nonplussed as her gaze traveled the room, finally settling on my father, who was in conversation with Mr. Bainbridge. Her lips twitched downward when she turned her attention back to me. "You're right," she said.

"Have another glass of wine, and I'll have a word with the butler. We should definitely be serving luncheon by now."

I watched her drift away before turning to George.

"Good Lord, who was that woman you were speaking with?" he asked.

"I barely recognize her myself. She seemed almost reluctant to take charge."

George took a glass of champagne from a passing footman and offered it to me. I shook my head. "If I have another before eating, I'll surely become tipsy and someone in this family needs to keep a clear head."

His eyes sparkled with mischief. "This is your wedding day. You do not have to be the responsible party this time."

"That's a very good point. I should be allowed to relax a bit." I took the glass just as the butler stepped into the doorway and announced that luncheon was served.

Everyone was once more in attendance when we all adjourned to the dining room for luncheon. My father made a toast, as did George's brother. All the strangeness of an hour ago seemed to fade into good cheer. Even Madeline Connor was back and in good spirits. A quick change of place cards had her sitting next to Alonzo. I'd changed Mr. Connor's card to read *Fitzwalter* and moved it to the other end of the table with Charles and Lottie. Since that was appropriate due to his rank, it was perfectly natural to make the switch.

After our meal, the cake was wheeled out—a thing of beauty and far too much for everyone here. But slices would go to the Wynn servants and some sent home for ours and Aunt Hetty's. Once George and I cut the ceremonial first slice, the footmen stepped in to box up the rest for our guests to take home, and Graham escorted us to the library at the front of the house for our photograph. Both George and I were excited about this session. Neither of us had wanted to take the time and trouble to sit for a portrait, but we wanted something to commemorate the occasion.

"I do hope you know how much we appreciate this, Graham," I said. "It's such a thoughtful gift on top of hosting our reception."

Graham grinned from ear to ear. "Delighted to do it. Mr. Wilson has been one of my instructors, so I'm certain you'll be pleased with the results. His use of light and shadow is incomparable."

"Here's the happy couple, as promised." Graham waved us into the room and made the introductions. Our photographer was a surprisingly young man for an instructor. He was no more than thirty years of age and somewhat Bohemian in his style, dressed in shirtsleeves, waistcoat, and trousers. A mop of dark curls brushed his collar and a full beard adorned his chin.

"Excellent," he said. "And you were correct, my lord. The light is perfect right now."

"Ah, you made use of my studio then?"

"I did. Two plates by the fireplace and two by the window. I developed them not five minutes ago in your darkroom and I'm quite satisfied with them."

Graham took note of our confusion. "Wilson typically works from his own studio where he can control the lighting. Since that wasn't possible today, a couple of test images were in order."

He clapped his hands together. "I'd love to stay and watch the session, but guests must be seen to." He strode to the door. "I'll leave you to it, then," he said, and stepped out.

"This is considered good light for a photograph?" I glanced at the windows where the weak sunlight tried valiantly to make an entrance.

Wilson chuckled and moved over to his camera, a wooden box atop a larger wooden box in the center of the room. "It's the best I've seen so far this afternoon. Lord Harleigh requested a photograph of you standing near the fireplace, which should add some interesting shadows to the composition. However, you might prefer a pose near the window."

"Since this is the best light you've seen, let's try Graham's plan first, shall we?" George and I stepped up to the fireplace and stared at one another, then at the photographer, who affixed a sort of cape to the back of the smaller box.

"Perhaps one of you might sit?" he suggested.

"Very well." George pulled a chair over and invited me to sit, then stood behind me with his hand on my shoulder. Wilson was tucked under the cape where I assumed he watched us settle into a pose through the lens of the camera. He emerged from under the heavy cape and moved beside the apparatus. His hand reached for the brass lens cover.

"I'm not sure I like this pose," I said. "Wouldn't it be better if we were facing one another?" I tipped my head back. "I can't even see what you're doing behind me."

"What could I possibly be doing? I'm standing behind you, staring at the camera."

"Are you smiling?"

"No. Why would I be smiling?"

"Because you're happy?"

He squeezed my shoulder. "I am indeed happy, but I'd rather not look like a grinning idiot for all eternity in this photograph."

Mr. Wilson cleared his throat. "The camera is focused. Are you ready?"

I straightened my spine, folded my hands in my lap, and gave him a nod.

"Then please be so good as to stay very still."

He removed the lens cover and focused on the watch in his hand, holding one finger in the air. I wished I'd thought to ask him how long we were to remain still as my nose truly wanted a scratch. Fortunately, he replaced the lens cover before my eyes crossed. George stepped over to the camera and asked Wilson to show him how it worked. After scratching my nose, I rose to take a look myself.

Mr. Wilson invited me around back and allowed me to look through the lens. He showed me how he centered the subject and ensured everything was in focus. Once that was done, he replaced the focusing glass with a photographic plate. "At this point," he said, "when I remove the lens cover, the image is captured on the plate."

It was fascinating, but Mr. Wilson was clearly ready to move on and so should we be. Our next pose was near the window. It looked out to the lawn between Harleigh House and Mr. Connor's home. It was not particularly green at the moment and unlikely to make much of a background, though the draperies were a lovely deep blue. This time we both stood, facing each other and holding hands. As Mr. Wilson pulled off the lens cover, a movement caught my eye outside the window.

It was reflex. I turned my head.

Wilson groaned and replaced the cover.

"It looks as though Mrs. Conner is going home," George observed.

"How odd that Madeline isn't with her."

"Perhaps she's checking on her husband."

"Whatever she is doing, she will forever be a ghost in that photograph." Mr. Wilson slipped a new plate in place.

"A ghost?" I asked.

He nodded. "There should be a slight blurring of your face because you turned, but the two of you will still have a fairly normal image. She was in the frame for the length of a few seconds, and moving, so she'll either appear as a blur or as a ghost."

"How positively amazing." George and I stared at each other as if we'd discovered something wondrous. Apparently, we presented an image Mr. Wilson wanted to capture.

"Don't move," he commanded.

It was almost impossible not to laugh, but we didn't have to hold still for very long. Perhaps ten seconds or so before Mr. Wilson replaced the cover. "I think you'll like that one," he said.

I sighed. "We shall if Mrs. Connor doesn't show up as a ghost again." I directed George's gaze to the window where we both saw Willa slip around the corner of the house.

"That answers our question, doesn't it? She must have been checking on Connor, or something else at the house."

I turned to Mr. Wilson. "Perhaps we should take another."

"I'm happy to take as many as you like," he replied.

The second attempt was managed without interruption and Wilson suggested we pose seated once more. This time George sat in the chair and I perched on the arm with his arm around my back. It felt so intimate, I knew this was not a photograph I'd share with anyone else, but treasure all the same.

"Damnation!" George's curse caused me to jump and Wilson to sigh.

"I must say, the two of you are very energetic," he said.

"Apologies. There's another guest crossing the lawn. Where in creation are they all going?"

I glanced out the window to see Mr. Bainbridge this time. He was headed to Harleigh House, but could only have been coming from the Connor residence. I glanced wistfully at the camera. "Do you suppose we'll have one decent photograph to show for this sitting? I feel almost as if we're wasting your time."

"Nothing like it, ma'am. Anyone who shows up in that window can be removed from the finished plate. You needn't worry. I'd like to retake that photograph, since Mr. Hazelton is apt to be blurry. And maybe one more—something a bit more formal."

George and I agreed and returned to our places. After a moment or two of giggles, we settled into the pose and as we gazed into each other's eyes, I never even noticed the passing of time until Mr. Wilson replaced the lens cover. "I have a feeling that one will be special," I told George, who nodded in agreement.

Wilson brought us both to our feet for the last pose. He instructed me to look out the window, ironic since that was what we had both been trying not to do. George stood at my back, looking down at me. One hand rested on my shoulder, the other on the drapes. Wilson then moved the camera so that we were not quite in profile, not quite facing him. The way the sun warmed my cheeks, I had the sense this would produce the shadow effect he'd spoken of. And miracle of miracles, we remained still throughout the photograph.

When Mr. Wilson replaced the cap and pulled the plate, I leaned my head back against George's shoulder. I became Mrs. Hazelton today, and everything was wonderful. I closed my eyes a moment. When I opened them again it was to see Alonzo walking across the dormant lawn to Connor's home. And Madeline was not far behind him. I sighed and nodded to the sight. "My father warned me about fireworks today," I mused. "We may be about to see them."

We thanked Mr. Wilson and encouraged him to stop at the kitchen and partake of the feast once he'd packed up his belongings. George stayed behind to make arrangements to see the photographs when we returned from our wedding trip, while I said a tearful goodbye to Rose and left her in the custody of her doting grandmama. Then I slipped upstairs to ring for Bridget and change for our travels. I'd hate to be late and miss our train.

Fortunately, Bridget had kept better track of time than I and was waiting for me when I stepped through the bedchamber door, my traveling dress at the ready.

She raised her hands when she saw me. "Here you are, my lady." She turned me around and began working on the buttons on the back of my gown.

"Did you find time to eat?" I asked her.

"Yes, ma'am. We're feasting below stairs. I don't recall his lordship ever running to such extravagance with a luncheon menu before."

"Funny, I don't recall a thing I ate. I suppose weddings are like that. There's so much planning beforehand and the actual event passes by in the blink of an eye. Are you and Blakely ready to leave for the train?"

Bridget had finished with the buttons on the back and was now working on the sleeves. "As soon as we get you changed, I'll hand this gown off to the housekeeper and I'm as good as ready. I've asked her to send it on to your aunt's house, ma'am, as I'm sure Jenny will know how to clean it."

Since Jenny had been my maid before she worked for Aunt Hetty, I was quite familiar with her skills and certain Bridget was right. "Well done, Bridget. What about the bags?"

The baggage is already loaded on the carriage. Everything is ready and waiting for us." She peeled the sleeves off my arms and I stepped out of the wedding gown.

"I'll need to say goodbye to the guests. After that, I'll be ready to leave, too. It's been years since I've had a trip."

"Don't I know it." Bridget laid the gown out on the bed and picked up my traveling dress. "Are you planning to throw your bouquet, ma'am?"

"I hadn't thought of that. If there's anyone left to throw it to. The whole time we were with the photographer, guests were traipsing back and forth between here and the Connors' residence. I can't imagine why." I turned to see myself in the mirror as she began fastening the dress.

"That color is perfect for a trip to the south of France."

She was right. It was a blue-green that brought to mind the sea and warm, sunny climes. And it fit to perfection. It was worth every penny I'd scraped together.

The new kid gloves matched beautifully. I sat down to button up the left hand while Bridget fastened my shoes, then buttoned up the right for me. She handed me my bag and bouquet. "This is it," I said, nearly bursting with excitement. "I'll meet you on the train."

Bridget smiled up at me. "Yes, you will, Mrs. Hazelton."

George awaited me at the foot of the stairs. I wanted to skip down them, take him by the arm, and be on our way. The doorbell sounded over the hum of voices in the drawing room. George looked at me, shrugged, and opened the door, admitting Inspector Delaney.

"This is a surprise," I said. "How lovely you've decided to come and celebrate with us after all. What a shame we're on our way out."

Delaney glanced around, taking note that we were the only ones in the entry hall. "My felicitations to you both, but I'm here in my official capacity."

I moved slowly down the stairs, fighting a sense of dread. It was never a good sign when the police showed up at one's wedding.

"Is something wrong, Inspector?"

He cleared his throat. "Do you have a relative by the name of Alonzo Price, ma'am?"

"Yes." Fear kept me frozen in place. "He's my brother. Has something happened to him?"

"I'm afraid he's been arrested."

"Arrested?" George echoed. "Whatever for?"

Delaney heaved a sigh. "For the murder of James Connor."

My legs began to wobble and I reached for the bannister, dropping my bouquet. It bounced down the remaining steps, leaving sad remnants behind until it settled in a heap at George's feet.

Chapter Five

❧

Mr. Connor, dead.

Alonzo, arrested.

I should have known we couldn't have a normal wedding.

A burble of laughter from the drawing room broke through my shock and drew my attention. It was unlikely anyone else had heard Delaney's announcement over the flow of genial conversation. But if we lingered here much longer, the guests might take note and join us. I'd prefer to learn the details in private. George must have been of the same mind. He picked up the bouquet at his feet and placed it on a table near the door. Then he took my hand and motioned for Delaney to precede us into the library the photographer had recently vacated.

When George closed the door behind us, I took hold of Delaney's arm. "What do you mean Alonzo's been arrested? Why would you do such a thing?"

George detached my hand from the inspector's arm and drew me to his side. "Tell us exactly what happened," he said.

"I arrived on the scene only a few minutes ago and have very little information at the moment." Grim-faced, Delaney pulled his ever-present notebook from his coat pocket and thumbed through it until he found the page he sought. "According to the constable who responded to the call, Miss Connor and the butler found your brother standing over the dead man, holding a knife, which we believe to be the murder weapon."

"There must be some mistake." I shook my head. It was inconceivable that my brother could take someone's life. "That's impossible."

George, bless him, remained calm. "Is Mr. Price still next door? May we speak with him?"

Delaney stiffened his posture. "Constable Timmons took advantage of the availability of a telephone. He had someone from the precinct take your brother in for questioning before I arrived with the coroner. I'd have preferred to have made that decision myself." He blew out a breath as if frustrated. "He's a young lad. New to the job and a bit too eager. But he's on the case now, and I ought to return to the Connor home before he arrests the lot of them." He pocketed the notebook. "I also came to inform you that I'll be sending Constable Timmons over here shortly to take statements from your guests. I ask that you keep them from leaving until they've each provided one."

"Our guests? Why should you need a statement from them?" I asked.

"The ground outside is a bit damp. Judging from the footprints we observed, there seems to have been a significant amount of traffic between this house and the Connor home. If your brother did not commit the crime, someone else among your guests may have done so."

"We saw a great deal of that traffic." I waved my hand toward the windows.

George nodded. "We were in here for perhaps half an hour.

In that time, we saw several people pass to and from the Connors' house. It was quite the parade. Perhaps your constable can make heads or tails of it. Mrs. Hazelton will ask the earl to ensure everyone provides a statement. As for myself"—he heaved a sigh—"I shall provide my statement at your precinct after I see to the welfare of my client."

I was caught between relief and despair. Alonzo would be in the best of hands with George standing for him. But we would miss our train, our boat, and our wedding trip. I gave myself a mental shake. My brother had been arrested for murder. How could I think of myself? I turned to George. "Do you leave right now?"

"The sooner the better, I'd say."

"I'll tell Bridget to have the carriage unpacked." I held on to his hand as he made to leave. He raised a brow in inquiry. "Thank you," I said.

His smile felt like an embrace. "He is my brother now too."

When George stepped out, Delaney moved closer. "Nothing has been determined yet, my lady. At least let us investigate before you lose heart."

"Thank you, Inspector," I replied, though in truth, I barely heard him. My mind raced in a dozen directions at once. Perhaps Graham might help in informing the guests while I gave the news to my parents and—heavens, Mrs. Connor must be informed.

Delaney seemed to realize he'd lost my attention and cleared his throat. "I must get back if I'm to learn anything from the coroner's initial observations. I'll send the constable over."

"Yes, of course. Someone will escort Mrs. Connor home. She'll want to be there before you question her stepdaughter." I opened the door and followed him into the entry hall, spotting my bouquet on the table. Sadly, that jolly tradition must give way to something quite the opposite.

*   *   *

I spotted Graham as soon as I'd closed the door on De-laney's departing figure. Catching his eye, I crooked my finger. I hoped my expression said urgency rather than panic.

He excused himself and sauntered over to me with a cat-in-the-cream smile, which vanished when I yanked him into the library and closed the door. "I'd say that went off rather well." He tipped his head to the side. "I suppose you and Hazelton are on your way now?"

"No, Graham. Unfortunately, there's been a change in plans. A complication." His brows lowered as he looked at me in confusion. Hardly a surprise as I couldn't manage to get the words past my lips. "It's your neighbor, Mr. Connor. I'm afraid he's dead."

He stretched his head forward, blinking rapidly. "I say, what was that?"

"Mr. Connor is dead."

"Whatever happened? Did his heart give out?"

"I suppose it did, ultimately. But prior to that, he was stabbed."

He took a step back. "That's a bloody complication, all right."

"It's worse than that. The police have arrested my brother for the crime."

"Your brother? What has he to do with it?"

"It appears he was at the wrong place at the wrong time." I drew in a calming breath. "And he was holding the knife."

Graham put a hand to his forehead. "Frances, please tell me that's the last of it."

"That's all I know."

He drew me over to the chair and I sat. "This feels like a bad dream," I said. "George has gone to the precinct to see to Alonzo and represent him if necessary."

He patted my hand. "There must be some mistake about his arrest."

"Delaney didn't have all the details, but he understands that Alonzo was found with the deceased Mr. Connor, and the murder weapon."

"Deuced bad luck."

"Indeed." Graham's gift for understatement kept me from succumbing to tears. "Now I have to tell my parents and poor Mrs. Connor."

He nodded. "I can send in your parents, but why don't you leave Mrs. Connor to me?"

"That's kind of you, but a constable will be here soon to question the guests. Delaney asked that you make sure everyone provides a statement."

"They're going to question the guests? A policeman? Questioning my guests?" Graham sounded more concerned about the imposition to his guests than Alonzo's arrest, or the murder itself.

I sighed. "Yes, it's simply outrageous, Graham. But murder is a heinous crime, and they'd like to get to the bottom of this. Several guests traveled back and forth between here and Connor's home. One of them may have killed him."

He gave me a sharp glance. "Everyone? They want to speak with everyone?"

"Sadly, yes." I came to my feet. "I expect the constable here at any moment, so if you can work with him, I'll go and find my parents."

"No."

I drew a bracing breath. "Graham, we can't simply allow the guests to leave as they please."

"I understand, but then Mrs. Connor will hear the news along with everyone else in the house. We can't have that."

That threw me off balance. I'd been prepared to argue, but he was absolutely right.

"Let me tell her," he said. "I'll ask someone else to watch for the constable and monitor the guests. Perhaps Evingdon."

"Cousin Charles? You want *him* to take charge? He couldn't organize a pair of cufflinks, for heaven's sake." I scoured my brain for another likely candidate. Fiona? George's brother, perhaps. Then it hit me. "Mr. Gilliam, Hetty's friend." Graham looked doubtful, but I persisted. "He runs a theater and organizes an entire cast of players. He'd be perfect. I'll collect him along with my family and set him to the task."

"Fine, fine, but we had better make haste or the constable will arrive and reveal the news himself."

It didn't take long to gather my family. I quickly found my father, staring at the curiosity cabinet with a look of distaste. Since I knew it contained boards filled with a variety of impaled insects collected by the fourth earl a good sixty years ago, his expression was understandable. Once I had him by the arm, I waved to Aunt Hetty and Gilliam, tucked behind a potted palm, and gestured for them to join us. Decorum be damned. This was an emergency. Finally, I spotted Mother speaking with Mr. Bainbridge. We swept her up and since we were closer to the library, we met there.

The four of them took the news with varying degrees of emotion. Frankie pounded his fist on the table, then prowled the room, stroking his whiskers while he pondered his next move. Mother lowered herself slowly into a chair. "I knew that man would be trouble. You should never have invited him, Frances."

Hetty, leaning on Gilliam's arm, made an impatient noise. "He wasn't even here, Daisy."

Mother flapped a hand toward Hetty. "I simply mean everything the man does causes trouble for someone else—even his death."

"Why the devil did the police arrest Alonzo?" A vein pulsed in Frankie's brow. "I thought they'd treat someone of his standing with more caution." He gave me a questioning glance. "Or is that treatment reserved for British aristocrats?"

"Aristocrats are typically handled with care. Wealth may grant some privileges, too. But in this case, I'd suspect anyone caught holding the murder weapon would have been arrested."

Frankie conceded the point with a shake of his head. "Nevertheless, I must go see to his release. Where have they taken him?"

"He's at the Chelsea precinct. George has gone there to sort everything out. You can be assured Alonzo is in the best of hands. George will do everything he can to ensure his release as soon as may be."

"What was Alonzo doing there in the first place?" Aunt Hetty asked.

I raised my hands, palms up.

"You can be sure it was about Miss Connor," Mother said with a tone of disapproval.

"I told him to leave the girl alone," my father replied with a growl.

"You ought not to speculate, particularly when you speak to the police," I said. "A constable will be here soon. In fact, he may already be here to take a statement from everyone."

"A statement?" Frankie snapped. "Why would they need to do that?"

Goodness, Frankie was in a state. I reminded myself his son was in danger, and adopted a conciliatory tone while I repeated what Delaney had told me. I assumed the explanation would calm him. The result was quite the opposite. "I can't imagine what the police expect to learn from me about who murdered Mr. Connor."

"One never knows what may be helpful in an investigation," I said.

"That makes good sense," Gilliam said, speaking in a soothing voice that had no effect on my father, who let out a snort.

"They can take my statement at the precinct. I'm going to fetch my son."

I didn't bother stopping him as he stormed out of the room without so much as a backward glance at my mother. With luck, George would calm him down when he arrived at the precinct.

Gilliam glanced around the library. When his gaze finally settled on the desk, pushed against the wall for our photography session, he followed it. Opening the drawers, he rifled through them until he found paper and pencils. "Who is organizing this inquisition?"

"In truth, I was hoping you would. The earl is giving Mrs. Connor the news, and I'd like to go to her directly."

"Then I am at your service, ma'am. Leave everything to me. I shall organize and act as secretary."

"What are you up to, Herbert." Hetty eyed him suspiciously.

He swept the sheets of paper before him as he executed a bow. "I plan to record every word from each of the guests as they give their statements." He pulled open the door and strode out.

Hetty once informed me Gilliam had never been an actor himself, but that exit was worthy of an ovation.

Mother came to her feet. "Surely the constable won't let him take notes, will he? And in any event, how does that help Alonzo?"

Hetty stepped up and took her arm. "He's very good at this sort of thing, Daisy. I suspect Gilliam will pull it off admirably." She glanced at me. "And it may help with Alonzo's defense."

"She's right, Mother. Anything we learn could be useful."

"Yes, of course." Mother glanced at me. "Hetty and I will be fine. You should see to Mrs. Connor."

I complied, moving briskly past the drawing room, where our guests spoke in hushed voices. When I reached the dining room, the door opened and Graham emerged, looking solemn. His gaze landed on me and we closed the distance between us.

"Mrs. Connor is inside," he said, indicating the dining room. "I told her about her husband's death."

"How did she take it?"

"Rather stoically, I'd say." I detected admiration in his tone. "How is your family dealing with the news?"

"Quite the reverse, but their situation is different." I glanced across the hall at the group in the drawing room. "Everyone seems a bit on edge. Has the constable arrived yet?"

"He arrived right as I caught up with Mrs. Connor. I sent him with the housekeeper for a cup of tea to give us a little time. I expect him back at any moment." He tipped his head to the right. "There he is now, with that Gilliam chap."

The two men were coming down the hallway from the servants' stairs, chatting amiably. Delaney hadn't exaggerated. Constable Timmons was very young. Of average height, but thin enough to appear gangly. His hair, dark brown and very curly, made me imagine Delaney as a young man. I returned my attention to Graham. "When you speak to the constable, don't let on that Gilliam has anything to do with Alonzo's family."

"You want me to lie to him?"

"No, but there's no need to offer any information. Don't explain who he is and allow him to act as secretary. He'll reveal himself in the end and give his statement, but this way he can hear the statements of everyone else." I changed the subject before he could argue. "Will you be escorting Mrs. Connor back to her home?"

"Actually, I suggested you accompany her. I hope you don't mind."

"Not at all. She should have someone with her and I'm sure

she's anxious to get home to her stepdaughter." I tapped lightly on the door and stepped into the dining room, leaving Graham to deal with the guests and the police. To think, less than thirty minutes ago, we were celebrating a wedding here.

Mrs. Connor was staring vacantly down at the table as if she never heard me. I stepped to the bellpull to call for a servant, then cautiously approached her, placing a hand on her shoulder. "Willa, dear, I'm so sorry."

Her watery eyes met mine. She reached up and patted my hand. "I'd like to go to Madeline now."

"Of course you would." A tap sounded at the door and a footman stepped inside. I instructed him to fetch our coats. "I'll come with you, dear. Unless you prefer to go alone."

She bit her lip. "I would greatly appreciate your support."

I heard raised voices outside the door in the hall. Much louder than the polite level one would expect at such a gathering. I told Willa I'd be right back and slipped out the door. Mr. Bainbridge and Gilliam were alone in the hall, nearly nose to nose.

"I'll be damned if I'll submit to this inquisition like some common criminal." Bainbridge poked Gilliam in the shoulder. His brow was drawn and angry. "Fine way to treat your guests."

Bainbridge would not get away if I had anything to say about it. The feud he and Connor carried on put him high on my list of suspects. I stepped between the two men. "I regret the necessity, Mr. Bainbridge, but a man has been murdered. Since the police have erroneously arrested my brother, I would appreciate your taking the time to answer their questions so they may apprehend the real murderer."

At least he had the grace to look chagrined. "I'm sure I have no information that could help them in that endeavor."

Taking his arm, I guided him back to the drawing room.

"Come now, Mr. Bainbridge. If everyone took that position, the police would never solve a case. It should take no more than a moment of your time."

I left him in the drawing room with the other guests and turned to see Gilliam grinning at me. "Well done," he said before returning to the constable to record the guests' statements.

I wasn't entirely confident my insistence would keep Mr. Bainbridge from slipping out, and considering his relationship with Connor, he was my prime suspect. I flagged down a footman, a young strapping man.

"Yes, my lady?"

"I believe some of the guests may attempt to leave without giving a statement to the constable," I said. "Please station yourself here. If anyone comes to you for their coats, check with his lordship first. If he says they may leave, then you can provide their outerwear."

"Yes, ma'am." He didn't bother hiding the twinkle in his eye at the prospect of holding the toffs to the letter of the law.

When I returned to the dining room, the other footman had arrived. He helped us with our coats, and escorted us to the door. Fitzwalter called out to us before we reached the front steps. "Please accept my condolences, Mrs. Connor, and allow me to accompany you home. Miss Connor must be beside herself with grief."

When he extended his arm to the lady I nearly backed off, but Willa held tightly on to me. "Thank you, no, Viscount Fitzwalter. Lady Harleigh is with me as you see, and my stepdaughter needs a mother right now, not a suitor."

She turned with a swish of her skirts, leaving Fitzwalter on the stoop clearly baffled. He wasn't the only one. Since the young man had accompanied them here, it was only natural he'd want to escort her home. But Willa left me no time to question her. I had to step lively or be dragged. "I don't think he's very happy at the moment," I said.

"He's likely to remain that way. Madeline will surely cry off the match now."

Cry off? Had there been an understanding between them? Something more definite than Madeline had implied? If so, she should never have encouraged Alonzo. This was very confusing. And very interesting.

Chapter Six

The first thing we encountered when we entered the Connor house was Madeline's piteous weeping from somewhere nearby. With a gasp, Willa straightened her spine and rushed to her stepdaughter's aid. The tap of her slippers on the marble-floored entry was muted by the carpet in the parlor as if in reverence for the grief inside the room.

I followed her at a slower pace, handing my coat to a waiting footman. Stopping at the entrance, I turned up the gas on the sconces along the wall. They cast a soft glow across the small room. Madeline was seated on the edge of a wingback chair, her elbows on her knees and her face in her hands. When Willa bent to stroke her hair, Madeline lifted her head and I caught a glimpse of haunted eyes before she sank into the older woman's embrace.

Her grief tore at my heart. The poor dear must have been very close to her father. I turned as a motion to my right caught my eye. Inspector Delaney exited the room across the entry hall. I shuddered wondering if that was Mr. Connor's office. The inspector closed the door and gestured for me to join him.

I followed him down the wood-paneled hallway. We passed the open drawing room and paused below the first landing of the grand staircase.

"Is she still weeping?" he asked in a soft voice.

I nodded. "She's quieted now that Mrs. Connor is with her, but I doubt she'll be calm enough to provide anything resembling a coherent statement for you today."

Delaney sighed. "I'm afraid it's imperative that we hear from her. It's possible she could exonerate your brother." He raised his brows.

"I see. It would behoove me to help things along, would it?" It was my turn to sigh. "Perhaps some tea."

"An excellent suggestion."

The double doors across the hallway from where we stood were closed. "That must be a dining room. I'll ring for someone there."

Delaney pushed through the doors and turned up the lights on a room covered with more dark paneling. I found the bellpull and rang for a servant. "Have you spoken to the staff here?" I asked. "Did they have anything to contribute?"

He eyed me, and I knew he wondered how to respond. I was helping him for the moment and it wouldn't serve to antagonize me, but he clearly felt uncomfortable giving me any information. "You know Hazelton is representing my brother. Won't he eventually have access to anything you've learned today? How can it hurt to enlighten me now?"

Two heavy steps brought him to the long table where he rested his hands on the back of a chair and leaned forward as if to ease an ache in his spine. "The butler's statement does not help your cause. He believes your brother murdered Connor in cold blood."

"Heavens! What did he witness?"

"As it turns out, not much. He happened to be in the entry hall when Mr. Price and Miss Connor arrived. He stopped

Miss Connor long enough to ask her a question. Your brother forged ahead, and after a knock on the office door, he walked in. The door closed behind him. The butler states he heard a shout from the office whereupon he and Miss Connor ran to the door, pushed it open, and saw Mr. Price standing beside the body of Mr. Connor. The deceased was slumped forward over the desk, a knife plunged into his back. Your brother's hand was on the knife."

I sank into the nearest chair. This did look bad for Lon. While I recovered myself, a footman came to the door in response to the bell. Delaney ordered tea to be delivered to the small parlor. That done, he returned his attention to me. "The coroner is in Connor's office now, though I don't expect any information from him until the morning. But he should be able to tell us if it's possible that your brother murdered the man."

"Meaning he'd be able to tell how long Mr. Connor has been deceased."

Delaney wobbled his hand. "Within a reasonable range of time, yes."

"Then it would be wise to speak with Mrs. Connor, too. I assume she and Madeline were here with him until they left for the wedding."

"I'll need a statement from Mrs. Connor regardless, but yes, it would be good to learn everything that happened in this house before they left it this morning." He pulled a watch from his pocket. "We'd best get on with it." He frowned. "I'm sorry your plans were cancelled."

"So am I. But I could hardly go off to France and leave my brother in such straits. Perhaps Hazelton and I can leave in a day or two." I rose to my feet. "As you say, we'd best get on with it."

A maid brought the tea at the same time Delaney and I crept into the room. Willa had taken a seat at the end of the sofa nearest to Madeline and held her stepdaughter's hand. I seated myself next to Willa and took charge of the tea service. Neither of the ladies seemed to notice us until I addressed them.

"Will you take some tea?" I asked. "It might help with the shock."

Willa accepted the cup and saucer absently, then blinked a few times as if forcing herself back to the here and now. "Yes, yes, of course." She straightened her posture and took in her surroundings. "Inspector—Delaney, is it? Won't you take a seat? I assume you have questions for us."

The room was small and the furnishings were grouped close together, aiding our conversation. Delaney seated himself across the low table from us and pulled out his notebook. "You have my deepest condolences for your loss, madam. I appreciate your willingness to speak with me and shall endeavor to keep this as brief as possible."

Madeline lifted her head for the first time since we entered the room. Her face was wet with her tears, her eyes red and swollen. "I don't know what sort of information I can provide, Inspector, but if it will help save Mr. Price, I too will answer any questions you pose."

"Mr. Price?" Willa's tone was sharp. "Mr. Alonzo Price? Why would he be in need of saving? Was he not with you, when you found your father?"

Delaney interceded. "Mr. Price was taken to the precinct for questioning based on what your butler, Mr. Parker, told the constable. I would like to hear what you have to say, Miss Connor. Can you tell me exactly what you and Mr. Price did from the moment you left Harleigh House to come here?"

"And why did you leave?" I asked, earning me a scowl from Delaney. This concerned my brother. Had he expected me to keep quiet?

Madeline turned to me. "I apologize, Lady Harleigh. It was terribly rude of us to leave your celebration."

I waved a hand. "I didn't mean to imply any wrongdoing."

"Lady Harleigh." Delaney's voice held a note of threat. "Perhaps you'd like to return to your family now."

"Oh, no, Frances." Willa reached out a hand to stop me, which it might have done if I'd had any intention of leaving. "Please stay with us."

"Of course, Willa. I wouldn't dream of leaving you." I glanced at Delaney and gave him a nod to continue, which he met with a look of annoyance before redirecting his attention to Madeline.

"What made you and Mr. Price decide to come here?"

"Viscount Fitzwalter had accompanied us to the wedding and the reception. He stayed quite close to my side throughout and made it difficult for Mr. Price and me to speak—on a personal matter."

Delaney narrowed his eyes. "Was he protecting you from Mr. Price?"

"Not at all. I did wish to speak with Alonzo, I mean, Mr. Price. We finally had a chance when Fitzwalter left to fetch some punch for me. When he returned, he overheard some of our conversation and took Mr. Price to task for what he perceived as a slight." She heaved a sigh. "Then they argued."

Willa frowned. "I don't understand. What did they have to argue about?"

Though I suspected the subject of the argument was Madeline, I caught a glare from Delaney that encouraged me to remain silent.

"Mr. Price wanted to ask Father's permission to court me. He called on him this morning, but Father was occupied and I sent him away. Fitzwalter overheard Mr. Price asking when he should call on Father."

Delaney frowned. "Am I to understand that both men were vying for your affection?"

Madeline nodded.

"And perhaps you preferred Mr. Price to Viscount Fitz-walter?"

She cast a quick glance at Willa. "I should have preferred a chance to become more acquainted with both gentlemen," she said.

I had to admire Delaney's patience. Madeline was doing her best to reveal nothing. "That seems like a reasonable request," he said. "Was that not possible?"

"I had hoped it would be, but Viscount Fitzwalter said he and my father had already drawn up a marriage contract."

Willa drew in a sharp breath. This must have come as a surprise to her.

"And Mr. Price objected to that," Delaney prodded.

Madeline swiped at the tears on her cheeks, then looked straight at the inspector. "I objected to that. Since I was unaware of this contract, Mr. Price suggested it didn't exist. He wanted to speak to my father immediately."

"How did the viscount react to that?"

She tossed her head. "He obviously felt quite secure. He told Mr. Price to go right ahead and do so, and that my father would set him straight."

"That explains why he came here," Delaney said. "But why did you?"

Fresh tears spilled from her eyes. Willa cooed and pulled her into her embrace. After a protracted moment of silence, it was clear Delaney would wait as long as necessary for an answer. She pulled away from Willa's arms and wiped her eyes. "My father was set on Fitzwalter and I feared he would reject Mr. Price out of hand. I wanted the chance to speak with Father first."

Delaney scribbled in his notebook. "Did you come here together, or did you follow him?"

"We left together. When we entered the house, Parker stopped me. He asked me a question about dinner, or some such thing. I can't even recall what. Mr. Price went on to my father's office. I think he knocked first. I saw him enter. Then he shouted."

She lowered the handkerchief, her eyes imploring Delaney. "He shouted, 'Dear God!' He was shocked at seeing my father, in that state. Does that not prove his innocence? He was in the office for no longer than a minute or so. Barely long enough to look around and realize what he saw before he shouted. Parker and I ran to the office immediately. He had no time to stab my father. It's not possible."

Delaney was writing in his book. Madeline turned to me, desperation in her eyes. "He couldn't have done it," she repeated, though I needed no convincing.

"What happened then?" Delaney's voice called us both back to the moment. Madeline looked confused. Delaney, not unkindly, persisted. "After you and the butler entered the office, what did everyone do?"

"Parker went to the entry hall and called for a footman." She shook her head. "I don't know who answered, but whoever it was, Parker sent him to fetch a constable." She paused and looked down at her hands folded in her lap. "I must have been in shock. Mr. Price came to me and led me here to sit and recover myself. Parker returned and directed him to step away from me. That's when I realized Parker thought Mr. Price had murdered my father. But you can see it was simply not possible."

A soft knock sounded at the partially closed door. A man holding a hat and coat gestured for Delaney to join him. The inspector excused himself and stepped into the foyer, leaving the door open. Since I didn't hear their voices, I assumed he crossed the entry hall to Mr. Connor's office. Willa was encouraging Madeline to drink some tea, so I slipped quietly to the door. Delaney was actually a step or two outside the front door speaking to the man. The coroner, perhaps?

I had no desire to view the corpse, but since George was currently attending to my brother, he might have no opportunity to examine the room in which the crime had taken place until after it had been cleaned. I crept across the hall and pushed open the office door to take a peek.

What a shambles! Items had been swept off the desk and the bookshelves and lay scattered on the floor. One of the heavy club chairs from the guest side of the desk was overturned. I let my gaze travel over the room, which was identical in size to the receiving parlor across the entry hall. The first wall held three small paintings with a sofa under them and low tea table in front of that. Close to the table were the guest chairs facing a large desk of some exotic-looking wood, dark in color and polished to a high sheen.

What I didn't see was a body, for which I was grateful. The coroner must have already had Mr. Connor removed. Something I did see, which set my mind wondering, was a second door across the room. Based on the frontage of the house, and the window farther along the wall, it must be an exterior door. To my mind, that definitely complicated matters. Anyone might have entered through that door to murder Connor.

"I thought your purpose here was to provide comfort to the bereaved."

A peek over my shoulder revealed Delaney half a step behind me. "It can hardly surprise you that I'd want to give Hazelton a description of this office." I nodded to the door across the room. "Might someone have entered through that door, caused this damage, and murdered Connor while they were about it? It certainly looks as though the guilty party was searching for something."

Delaney shook his head. "I suspect this mess is staged. As if someone wants us to believe Connor was murdered during a break-in." He cocked a fuzzy brow. "Shall we return to the ladies?"

I stepped back so he could close the office door, then preceded him into the drawing room. Willa looked up. "Are we finished here, Inspector?"

Delaney resumed his seat. "Just a bit more, ma'am. I've a few questions left. Can you take me through your morning? Before you left for the church. Did either of you have any exchanges with Mr. Connor?"

"We did," Willa said. "Connor was working all morning. I thought it was to free up time to attend the wedding, but he called us both in about half past nine to tell us he'd not be going. He'd already asked Viscount Fitzwalter to act as our escort."

"Busy, was he?"

Willa shook her head. "Always."

"Why would he have asked Fitzwalter? Is he a longtime friend?"

Madeline spoke first. "Father wanted Fitzwalter and me to marry. He will one day be the Marquis of Sudley. I suppose Father thought a title in the family would improve our standing in society. Lately, he'd tried to throw us together whenever the possibility arose."

Delaney scratched a few lines. "Was that the only time you saw him this morning?"

"We saw him for a few minutes at breakfast," Willa said. "After that he went into his office. He had a meeting with Mr. Bainbridge about ten. It's likely on his schedule in the office."

"Is that also when Mr. Price called?"

"Yes," Madeline said. "Father was in with Mr. Bainbridge. It sounded as though they were in a rather heated argument, so I sent Mr. Price away."

"Arguing, were they?" Delaney raised his brows. "Any idea what that was about?"

"I'm afraid Connor didn't discuss his business interests with us," Willa said. "You'll have to ask Mr. Bainbridge."

Mr. Bainbridge was shaping up to be my suspect of choice. He had two opportunities to murder Connor. I wondered what Delaney thought.

"So, the viscount called for you here," Delaney said, "escorted you to the church, then on to Harleigh House, is that correct."

They both nodded.

"Neither of you stopped off at home first, and you were at Harleigh House until you, Miss Connor, came back here with Mr. Price. Does that sound correct?"

They agreed that it did, which confused me. I chose not to speak up at the moment. Delaney had yet to take my statement. I could tell him what I'd seen then.

Finally, he closed his notebook and came to his feet. "I thank you for giving me your time, ladies. I think I have all I need for the present. Again, please accept my condolences. I shall be in touch when we know more."

I rose with him. "Willa, is there anything else I can do for you?"

"Frances, thank you so much for your kindness. You must go back to your family. Heavens, we've taken you away from your husband on your very wedding day."

My husband was currently at Delaney's precinct with my brother. But I was eager to get back with my family and eventually to George.

Delaney and I took our leave and collected our coats. Once out of the house, he offered his arm. "If you'd oblige me, ma'am, perhaps I can take your statement while I escort you back to Harleigh House?"

I was grateful for his arm as dusk had fallen. Though both houses were illuminated, the light didn't extend to the patch of lawn between them. As we crossed, I gave Delaney a summary of my day and that of Alonzo's, at least while he was in my company. When he asked what I knew of my brother's relationship with Miss Connor, I demurred. "Alonzo has been at my house for less than two days. Two days in which I was either preparing for a wedding or in the process of being wed, followed by a celebration with our closest friends and family. I did not have much time to spend with him."

The inspector made some innocuous sound. "Are the Connors a part of your closest friends and family, then?"

He had me there. "Willa Connor is a good friend, but the family were invited at the request of my brother about two weeks ago."

"So, he had some acquaintance with Miss Connor before he came to England."

"One could assume as much." I glanced up in time to catch his scowl. "While I admit I prefer not to give you any rope with which to hang Alonzo, the truth is, I know nothing about his relationship with Miss Connor. Anything I say would be conjecture."

"Did you happen to note the argument between your brother and Fitzwalter?"

"No, but I saw that their behavior toward one another earlier had made Miss Connor uncomfortable. As any hostess would, I needed to remove one of them from the conversation. I chose Miss Connor."

"Did you observe anything else I should know about?"

"I did." I told him about the photography session in the library and that we saw Mr. Bainbridge, Mrs. Connor, and Alonzo and Madeline pass by the window on their way to and from the Connors'. "I'm no longer certain of the order in which we saw them, but Alonzo and Madeline were the last."

I could see Delaney calculating.

"Mrs. Connor neglected to mention that," he said.

"She did. Not that I think she murdered her own husband, mind you. But you should know Alonzo was not the only person who was in that house this afternoon. Surely, you haven't forgotten about the feud between Connor and Bainbridge?"

We had reached the front door of Harleigh House, and Delaney applied the knocker. "There are definitely other suspects on my list, ma'am, including Bainbridge. I can't forget he and Connor hated each other with enough passion to spread rumors and slander one another. But this case is far from over. Your brother is not off the hook."

Chapter Seven

My family were gathered in the drawing room when I returned, surrounded by the usual detritus of a celebration—empty glasses on tables, plates with pastry crumbs. All the things usually cleared away in an instant by the staff, left to wait until the room was unoccupied.

Every head turned my way when I paused at the doorway, including one belonging to a person I hadn't expected. "Viscount Fitzwalter. What a surprise to see you still here."

He stepped away from his post at the fireplace and ambled toward me. I moved into the room and we met halfway, where Graham leaned against the back of the sofa, chatting with Gilliam. They stopped their conversation when Fitzwalter spoke.

"Ma'am. May I assume your return means the police are finished next door?"

"For today, yes. But surely, you don't intend to call on the ladies?"

The young man seemed absorbed in straightening his cuffs. "Indeed, I do. I'd like to assure myself they are in need of nothing."

Graham's expression clouded over. "Go home and save it for the morning, Fitzwalter. Right now, the Connor ladies need the solace of each other more than well-intended callers."

Fitzwalter stiffened at the comment. "I am merely showing the interest of a friend. I shall accept part of your advice, however, and take my leave of the present company."

Graham signaled to the footman who was standing nearby. "The viscount is in need of his hat and coat," he said. "And have his carriage brought around." While we waited, Fitzwalter bid us all a good evening, something that was so unlikely with Alonzo in such straits, it was darkly humorous. Though, like Graham, I hoped he'd leave the Connor ladies alone, I was even more eager for him to leave us. Finally, the footman brought his outerwear and Fitzwalter left us in peace.

"I do hope he allows the ladies their privacy tonight," Hetty said. "I wondered why he was lingering so long. The young man seems to have no sense of when he's unwanted."

"As a young aristocrat and heir to a marquis, he's unlikely to have felt the sensation before. I suspect he's knocking on their door as we speak." I took a chair near the fireplace and Graham stationed himself next to me. A glance at the clock told me it was half past six. "Would you like us to leave as well, Graham? I'm sure we're keeping your servants from their dinner."

"Not at all. Please stay at least long enough for a cup of tea. I'd like to hear what you learned next door."

Mother, Hetty, and Gilliam all leaned forward in interest, so I conceded. Graham ordered tea and told the butler to have the servants take their own dinner.

I spent the next half hour relaying everything I recalled from Delaney's interview with Mrs. and Miss Connor. Then added what I had gleaned from viewing Connor's office. "I feel confident Alonzo's arrest was an error made in haste," I said, mostly for my mother's benefit. "There wasn't sufficient time for him to make such a shambles of the office. With the butler accusing

Alonzo, and Madeline in tears, the constable simply acted rashly. Delaney said he was new to the job."

"Then they should release Alonzo immediately," Mother said. "We should go to this place where they are holding him and see to it."

The Metropolitan Police might not survive a visit from Daisy Price. "Frankie is already there, Mother. And Alonzo could not have a better advocate than George. If anyone can arrange to bring him home, they will."

Hetty took Mother's hand and squeezed it. "I'd be surprised if we don't have Alonzo home by tomorrow."

I hoped she was right. "What transpired here? Did Constable Timmons obtain a statement from everyone?"

"I believe he did," Graham said. "He left shortly before you arrived."

"We missed one person." Gilliam frowned and shook his head. "I don't know how he slipped away, but Bainbridge never gave a statement, and when I looked for him, I learned he'd been gone a good hour."

"That's unfortunate. Delaney will have to catch up with him tomorrow." I had to admire Gilliam's commitment to his task. "Did you manage to record everyone's statements?"

He grinned, and behind me I heard Graham snicker. "I am an excellent secretary, I'll have you know. Of course I took down the statements."

"Constable Timmons allowed Gilliam to manage the entire process," Graham said. "He's a bit green, I think, and would have been lost without some assistance. He became rather confused when finally it was time for Gilliam's statement and he learned he was actually a friend of the family and not a member of my staff."

"Speaking of staff, he will likely return tomorrow to interview them," I said.

The grin fled from Graham's face. "Why would he do that? No one on my staff would have any reason to harm Connor."

"They see everything that happens in a household," I said. "They'll be asked for their observations."

Graham raised a brow. "Indeed? Everything?"

"Most definitely. You can hide nothing from them no matter how discreet you may think you are." I turned back to Gilliam. "I assume the constable took all your work with him, did he not?"

"He did, but I recall the gist of it. I'll prepare further notes and have them ready for you and Hazelton tomorrow, in case it's needed for young Mr. Price's defense."

"Did you learn anything that might lead us to another culprit?"

"Hard to say until I put everything together. Most of the questions tended toward everyone's whereabouts throughout the afternoon. People were coming and going quite a bit for a short afternoon event." Gilliam furrowed his brow as he thought. "Even you were absent for a stretch of time." He nodded to Graham. "I believe you told the constable you were instructing the servants, so you'll have people to vouch for you. Thus, you're off the hook, my good man."

Graham flushed and pulled at his collar. "Ah, yes. Those people who observe everything."

"Delaney interviewed the Connor ladies while I was there. Madeline's statement seemed about right, but Mrs. Connor neglected to mention a few details."

Gilliam stroked his beard as his gaze drifted upward. "A few people noticed her absence shortly before the luncheon, if I remember correctly. No one recalled seeing her."

"She left the house again after the luncheon," I said.

"No, I'm quite certain she was in either the drawing room or the dining room all afternoon," Graham said.

I turned to him. "You were absent here and there yourself, so she might have left while you were elsewhere. I was looking for her on Madeline's behalf quite early on, and couldn't find her in either room."

"Once Delaney has Constable Timmons's notes," Gilliam said, "I'm sure he will follow up with her about her movements today."

"Now that I think of it, Fitzwalter was looking for her right before the luncheon," Hetty said. "I didn't see her anywhere in the house."

"There you have it," Mother said. "She could have slipped home and murdered her husband."

"Could have and did are two very different things, Daisy." Aunt Hetty looked at my mother as if she didn't quite recognize her. "We mustn't jump to conclusions. Mrs. Connor must be given a chance to account for her whereabouts."

"And I tell you, she was here the whole time," Graham said. "You are both mistaken."

Now I was certain something was wrong with Graham. In the normal course of his life, he concerned himself with issues, items, and people that directly affected him or his family, and was oblivious to everything else. For him to proclaim that he paid such close attention to the movements of his guests at this gathering tested my level of credulity.

"I believe Mr. Bainbridge went missing for a time, as well," I said, so as not to linger overlong on the subject of Mrs. Connor.

"And he slipped out without providing a statement to the constable." Gilliam was still rankled about that.

"Don't forget he and Mr. Connor were in the midst of a feud," Hetty added.

Mother let out a huff of impatience. "Shouldn't we get along home? For all we know, Alonzo is there already. I believe we have imposed on the earl enough for one day."

"True enough, Mrs. Price." Gilliam stood and offered Hetty his arm. Before she stirred herself, I came to my feet.

"If you can give me a few more minutes," I said. "I'd like to thank the staff for all their hard work today on my behalf." I turned to Graham. "Would you mind taking me down?"

Graham glanced around the room as if I might be speaking to someone else. "Um, certainly."

We walked out to the entry hall and would have turned toward the dining room to take the service stairs, but I pulled Graham in the other direction to the library. Far enough from the drawing room to keep anyone from overhearing.

He glanced at me in confusion. "I thought you wanted to speak to the servants?"

I waved my hand. "I've already done that. It's you I want to speak to. Why were you so insistent that Mrs. Connor never left this house?"

He frowned. "Whatever are you implying? I wasn't insistent, simply stating what I saw."

"And you saw Mrs. Connor here all day?"

"Indeed, I did." He flicked a bit of lint from his sleeve. "I can't imagine why you'd question it."

I leaned into an offensive posture, wondering if my gambit would work. "You forget that I was with Inspector Delaney when he interviewed Willa and Madeline. I've already heard her statement."

His brows shot up. The man looked positively terrified. Good heavens, what had he done? He narrowed one eye in suspicion. "She never told you where she was."

"Didn't she? A police inspector was questioning her in relation to the murder of her husband. Of course she told him where she was. Now, I'd like an explanation about why you were lying for her."

With a growl, Graham sat back against the desk. "Come now, I could hardly blurt out the truth, could I? Tell your family—tell you—that Willa and I were together. In fact, I can't believe she spoke of it in front of you, police inspector notwithstanding." He let out a tsk. "One simply doesn't kiss and tell."

I found myself speechless. Graham? Graham and Willa? I'm

quite sure my jaw hung slack as I took in the information, which was long enough for him to realize this was indeed news to me. He stepped away and slapped his hand against the padded back of a chair. "She didn't tell you." He sighed and turned to face me, shaking a finger. "You tricked me."

"Would you have told me otherwise?"

"Of course not!"

While I attempted to gather my thoughts, Graham's expression changed from outrage to shamefaced regret. "And now you think ill of me for dallying with a married woman. You must think me a monster."

Monster was a bit much. Cad would do, rather like his brother, my late husband. "I certainly don't approve your behavior, but I'm more inclined to wonder about your sanity. Of all the women you could choose to dally with, as you phrase it, you chose the wife of James Connor? For heaven's sake, don't you realize he employs men who would happily drop by to break your legs, or arms, or anything else you would prefer remain whole? What were you thinking?"

Rubbing the back of his neck, he groaned. "To be honest, there was not a great deal of thinking involved. I've held on to the belief that since Connor didn't value his wife, he didn't care what she did." He gave me a cautious glance. "Would he really have done such a thing?"

I gawked in amazement. "He had Mr. Bainbridge's office vandalized because they were competitors for a business deal. History is full of men who didn't value their wives, yet fought duels over such an insult to their own honor."

"He couldn't have known. We were very careful." Graham's furrowed brow belied the confidence of his words.

I wasn't so sure about that but didn't see the point of spending any more time on the matter. "Regarding Willa's absence, she said nothing about it in her statement, and Delaney took note of that. He intends to question her further, and soon.

Once she tells him, it will look very odd that you said you saw her all afternoon."

He compressed his lips, then gave me a reluctant nod. "I see your point."

"You can expect Delaney to return here to question you."

He wiped his hand across his forehead. "What a mess."

"It's always best to tell the truth, Graham."

"Not, perhaps, in this case," he muttered. "If the police find out Willa and I were involved, they will likely suspect us of Connor's murder. Gad, what a scandal that would be."

"Yes, this does give you both a motive, but that is not evidence of a crime." I paced in front of the desk. Time was ticking away. I couldn't keep my family waiting all evening while Graham and I resolved this. "If you told the constable that you had your eye on Willa all afternoon, you will want to correct your statement."

"I didn't actually see her leave."

"I did. You can account for the time she spent with you, but I also saw her crossing the lawn to her home while George and I were in the library with the photographer."

His face registered his surprise.

"It doesn't mean she murdered Connor," I continued, "but don't cast suspicion on yourself by lying for her."

I left Graham recovering from his shock and headed back to the drawing room to collect my family. Surely this day had been longer than twenty-four hours already. In the hallway I encountered a footman. While asking him to bring our things and order the carriage, recognition dawned.

"Aren't you the footman I asked to guard the door earlier?"

"Yes, my lady."

"I understand Mr. Bainbridge managed to slip out without giving a statement to the police."

The young man looked confused. "That's not what I was told, ma'am. I remember the gentleman asking for his coat and hat. When I went to check with his lordship, an older woman told me he'd already provided a statement. If that's not true, I'm sorry, but I didn't want to call the lady a liar."

An older woman? Mrs. Connor was forty, but even if the footman considered her "older," she had already left by that time. The only other women who fit that category were my mother and Aunt Hetty. Why would either of them have lied for Mr. Bainbridge? "The woman? Was she fair or dark?"

"Very fair, ma'am."

"I see." I told him everything was fine and sent him back to his task, though in truth, I didn't understand it at all. Mother had lied for Mr. Bainbridge. How very strange.

The carriage let me down in front of George's house—*our* house, that is. His—*our* butler, Jarvis, met me at the door.

"Welcome home, my lady," he intoned, assisting with my coat. Jarvis had the address and bearing of a gentleman, a manner that would brook no nonsense, and a rather small stature for a butler. Certainly no more than forty, he also lacked the typical years of experience. It was unlikely he rose from the rank of footman to attain his current position. One day I'd have to inquire about his background, but this was not that day.

"Thank you, Jarvis. Right now, home may be my favorite word."

"I understand things didn't go according to plan today."

"Not at all. We've rather thrown a spanner in your plans, too. You weren't expecting us to be here this week."

"Good staff are always prepared for the unexpected," he said.

"Has Mr. Hazelton returned home?"

"He has and he awaits you in your bedchamber."

Goodness, that sent a little shiver of delight through me. It was still my wedding day, after all. I was headed for the stairs when it hit me. "I'm afraid I don't know where my bedchamber is, Jarvis." I'd visited George at home frequently and been all over the public rooms. It never dawned on me to ask for a tour of the whole house.

Jarvis bowed. "I'll take you, my lady."

"Thank you. And Jarvis, while I've kept my title, in this house, I'm Mrs. Hazelton."

He nodded and I saw a hint of a smile. "Of course, ma'am."

I followed him up the stairs and waited while he tapped on the first door on the right, then pushed it open for me. Couldn't he simply have told me it was the first door on the right? I took in the room with a glance—sage-green paper on the walls, dressing rooms off to either side, a large bed to my left, a bureau next to the nightstand, and George, seated at a writing table tucked under the window that must overlook the back garden. My survey of the room ended there. He came to his feet as I stepped inside and, oh my, this room wasn't the only thing I'd never seen before. His valet had clearly been here already and taken George's coat, tie, cufflinks, and shirt studs. His hair was tousled, his shirt open at the neck, sleeves pushed up, all revealing far more of him than I'd expected to see. I barely resisted sighing like a young maiden.

Then he gave me his cockeyed smile and said, "Mrs. Hazelton."

I sighed like a young maiden.

Jarvis cleared his throat and we both turned his way. "Is eight o'clock acceptable for dinner, ma'am."

I glanced at George in his casual attire. "I asked for dinner to be served up here," he said.

How indulgent. "Eight will be fine, Jarvis."

With a bow, he left, and I turned to George. "As much as I adore being Mrs. Hazelton, I prefer the sound of *Frances* from your lips." I stepped into his waiting arms. "Or darling, dearest, my love, etcetera."

"Etcetera is far too vague." The words whispered in my ear sounded much more romantic than they ought. "How about Frankie? I rather like that for you."

I pulled away and stared in horror. "Not Frankie. That will only bring my father to mind."

"Then Frankie is definitely off the list."

"Good."

"First things first." He threaded his fingers in my hair, sending several carefully placed pins tumbling to the floor, and brought me close for a toe-tingling kiss that left me breathless.

"I hope that will be first, second, third, and so on."

"As eager as I am for the 'so on,' I must admit I'm also famished." He leaned back, squinting at me. "Did you manage to eat anything today?"

"Perhaps one bite at the reception, and nothing before that."

"I couldn't eat this morning either. Too nervous."

Somehow, I found it endearing that he'd been nervous about the wedding. "I'm in desperate need of sustenance," I confessed. "And I'd like to hear how Alonzo is faring."

"And I'd like to know how the interviews came off." He drew me over to the table where, based on the closely written notes, he'd been working on before I arrived. To my surprise, the desk also held a bottle of wine, a decanter, and two glasses. "Dinner will be here shortly," he said, "but I think we have time for one glass. We'll have to mix business with pleasure."

"Before I engage in either," I said, leaning against the bedpost, "I simply must ring for Bridget to take down my hair." I gave him an apologetic smile. "The pins are poking my head and it's been rather a long day."

"Say no more." He pulled out the chair from the writing table and gestured for me to sit. "I told your maid you wouldn't need her tonight."

"You want to take down my hair?"

He waved a hand toward the chair.

I approached it with caution and lowered myself slowly. His fingers deftly removed pin after pin. "You are aware that there is more than just my hair piled up there, aren't you?" I waved my hand vaguely at my head.

"It is quite a sculpture." He leaned over my shoulder—his voice a low hum in my ear. "Is this where you store your valuables, madam?"

"No, but there are a few supports in there. It's not all my hair."

He straightened and returned to his work. "If you are referring to those muslin-wrapped parcels of hair you ladies use, I believe it is yours. What are they called again?"

"Rats."

"Yeoww!" He flung one of them onto the table in front of me. "There's one now."

Laughing, I reached back and stroked his arm. "You really are absurd, but you have a wonderful touch, so I'll forgive you for teasing me." I sighed as his fingers removed the last of the rats and pins. Once it was loose, he ran his fingers over my scalp and through the strands in a way that was simply hypnotic.

He seemed to agree with me. "Mesmerizing," he said, then let out a sigh. "I'm afraid we must return to business, my dear."

When I lifted my head, he was back at the table. With a sigh of my own, I stood and joined him there.

While he decanted the wine, he gave me a summary of Alonzo's statement. It sounded exactly like Madeline's. "Did he mention his earlier visit to the Connor house?"

George filled our glasses. "He mentioned that he didn't get to see Connor. Is it important?"

"There's an outside entrance to the office. Though Alonzo called at the front door, and was refused an audience with Connor, he could easily have walked away from that door, and entered Connor's office through the other."

He pondered the idea. "Assuming the door was unlocked, that's true of any of the suspects." He gave me a sharp glance. "Please tell me there are other suspects."

"There are. I think Willa Connor is among them."

"His own wife?" George looked ill.

"Wives have been known to murder their husbands."

He clutched at his chest. "And you tell me this on our wedding night?"

I made a dismissive motion. "You probably have nothing to worry about."

"Probably?" His voice rose on the last syllable.

I patted his hand reassuringly. "It's difficult for me to imagine Willa as a murderer, but I'd be surprised if Delaney doesn't suspect her."

I relayed the details of the interviews with Madeline and Willa Connor, including the fact that Willa had neglected to tell Delaney she'd returned home during the wedding reception. "Gilliam is compiling notes from the interviews of all the other guests, with one exception. Mr. Bainbridge managed to slip out without giving the constable a statement."

George took a sip of wine. "And we saw him head over to Connor's house this afternoon."

"Considering their feud, he must be a strong suspect. There's one more interesting bit I learned today. Connor's office was—well, vandalized might be too strong a word, but it was a mess. Chairs tipped over, papers strewn about. That sort of thing. Delaney suspects that it was done to make it look as though someone had been searching for something, whether or not they were."

George stroked his chin. "Interesting. From all reports, Alonzo was alone in the office for less than a minute or two. That detail should help his case."

"Exactly. He didn't have enough time to make that mess. But he was also there in the morning." I paused as a thought occurred to me. "I don't recall if it was Madeline or Alonzo, but one of them told me Connor was in a meeting with Bainbridge when Alonzo called. He couldn't have entered the office through the exterior door, unless he waited for Bainbridge to leave."

George nodded. "Alonzo mentioned that in his statement. Bainbridge's presence gives your brother an alibi for that point in time."

"Willa said she and Madeline met with Connor in the morning." I frowned and cursed my memory. "I don't recall if it was before or after Alonzo called."

"That should be in Delaney's notes. They definitely don't have a strong case against your brother. In fact, if it weren't for the filing of paperwork, I believe they'd have let your father take him home tonight. As it is, I expect he'll be released tomorrow."

"But will he still be a suspect?"

"Probably, but a very unlikely one. Chances are he won't be let off the hook until they arrest someone else."

"What of the state of Connor's office? Doesn't that make you think of Bainbridge?"

"That actually makes me suspect him less. Particularly if Delaney is correct and the mess was staged. Considering Bainbridge's office was recently vandalized, and allegedly at Connor's instigation, the police would naturally suspect him. He wouldn't want that."

"But someone else might," I said.

"The question is, who?"

Our gazes met across the table and he gave me a look that reminded me we were newlyweds. "I appreciate your coming to Lon's rescue," I said. "And I'm terribly sorry about the wedding trip."

He raised a hand. "I don't for a moment believe your brother murdered the man, so this is all a matter of circumstance and no one's fault." He took my hand and stroked my knuckles with his thumb. "Perhaps the wedding trip isn't completely out of the question. We have use of the villa for a fortnight. If Delaney wraps this case up in a day or two, we could still go."

"Wouldn't that be lovely? Do you know what we should do?" I came to my feet and moved close to him, leaning against the arm of his chair. "I think we should forget all about murder for tonight and very selfishly act like newly married people."

He reached up and touched a curl beside my cheek. "I like that train of thought. I'm very new to marriage, you know. Tell me, how are we meant to act?"

I smiled. "It's been some time, but I daresay it will all come back to me." I drew him to his feet and into my arms.

"But what about dinner?"

"Are you hungry?"

"Not anymore."

"Then lock the door. We'll eat later."

Chapter Eight

I woke to the sound of activity in the room and forced one eye open in time for Bridget to push back the draperies, flooding the room with far too much daylight. Rolling over, I felt for George but found nothing but bedsheets.

"Over here."

I rolled back to my other side and there he was, standing beside the bed, buttoning his waistcoat and smiling at me as if I were the woman of his dreams—tangled hair, sleepy eyes, and all. I returned his smile. "Why are you already dressed? It feels so early."

"Yes. Earlier than I'd planned," he said. "It's just gone eight, but I'm told your father awaits me in the breakfast room. I'm going down to meet him."

"What?" I pushed myself up onto my elbows. "It's the day after our wedding!"

George snapped his fingers. "Crikey, that's right! I knew something momentous happened yesterday."

I gave him a wry smile. "I'm delighted that you remember, but it doesn't seem as though my father does."

"He's anxious about his son, and I don't blame him. He and I shall have a quick breakfast and head to the precinct to see to Alonzo's release."

"I understand his anxiety, but I think he might have been able to wait another hour."

He placed his hands on the bed, one on either side of me, and leaned forward—to kiss me, I thought. Instead, he lowered his voice and said, "He caused quite a disturbance when he joined me at the precinct yesterday. I don't want him going there without me, or I may have two Price men to extract from a cell."

"We can't have that."

George frowned. "What is this third degree he kept going on about?"

"It's a brutal method of extracting a confession from a suspect. I understand the New York Metropolitan Police are famous for employing it—or at least the threat of it."

"That explains his concern." George straightened, and I threw back the sheets, calling for Bridget to find a tea gown.

"Are you coming down?"

"I might as well." I leaned in close and stroked his cheek. "There's nothing for me up here."

"That's it. I'm sending your father home." He waggled his brows. "I'll be right back."

Chuckling, I tugged on his arm as he made to leave. "I'm not quite that selfish. A kiss will satisfy me for now." He complied, and I sent him off to my father, telling him I'd join them shortly.

Bridget helped me into the gown and set about untangling my hair. "How disappointed are you to still be in London today?" I asked.

She compressed her lips while she combed my hair into sections. "I'm surely not as disappointed as Mr. Alonzo is to find himself still locked up today. You and Mr. Hazelton know your way around a police investigation. He needed you to stay and lend him your expertise."

"That's very altruistic of you, Bridget, but this is me you are speaking with."

She caught my eye in the mirror and allowed her mouth to sag into a pout. "I so wanted to see Paris, my lady—I mean, ma'am. And Cannes is supposed to be quite beautiful. Do you suppose you'll go some other time?"

"If we can move through this investigation quickly, and remove Alonzo from the list of suspects, we may still go soon."

Her blue eyes rounded. "Truly? There's a chance?"

"I wouldn't rely too heavily on it, but yes, there is a chance. The Romanovs gave us use of the villa for a fortnight, so perhaps we may be able to go for a week or ten days." I raised my hands helplessly. "I still have a little hope."

It was good to see her perk right up. "Lovely. Then I will, too."

Ten minutes later, I was dressed and walking into the breakfast room. I've loved this room since I first visited George here. It was rather a thrill to know it was now mine, too. If there was even the slightest suggestion of sunlight outside—a single ray peeking out from behind a cloud—it found its way into this room and cast everything with a golden glow. On this occasion, that glow was countered by the two thunderclouds seated along the side of the oak table with George—my father and mother.

Before nine o'clock in the morning.

On the day after our wedding.

I gave myself a mental shake. George was right, their concerns were of an urgent nature. Besides, the aromas of coffee and sausages were calling to me.

"Good morning." Slipping behind their chairs, I greeted them both with a kiss on the cheek, then stepped over to the marble-topped table under the window. It was laden with a wide variety of breakfast fare but all I wanted at the moment was coffee. I poured myself a cup. "Mother, are you going to the precinct with Frankie and George?"

Her glance at my father ought to have covered him in frost. "I'd intended to do so, but it seems they both think it's a bad idea."

Hmm. I glanced at the head of the table to see George and Frankie avert their gazes, looking anywhere but at Mother or me. I took a sip of coffee and considered. Mother did have a rather demanding nature. I suspected the men had their own plan for obtaining Alonzo's release and wanted nothing of her interference or dramatics. That's how I felt about it last night, but we might all be a bit short-sighted. Mother's attitude tended to garner results. I'd parted my lips to impart my opinion on the matter when Jarvis stepped into the room to announce Inspector Delaney's arrival.

"We'll see him in here, Jarvis." George glanced at me. "Does that meet with your approval, Frances?"

"Of course." I took a seat between George and Mother at the table. "I always believe feeding a man makes him much more amenable."

"I certainly hope he's brought Alonzo with him."

I squeezed Mother's hand. "Jarvis would have mentioned it if he had." I leaned in closer to her. "But now you can find out firsthand what is happening with him rather than waiting for Frankie to return and give you the details."

"I don't need the details," she said. "I need to have my son back. Why they thought it necessary to arrest him in the first place is beyond me." She placed a hand on my father's arm. "When that inspector comes in here, you must demand that he release Alonzo."

"I made my demands last night and you saw how far that got me," Frankie grumbled. "The police here operate somewhat differently from those in New York." He shrugged. "Perhaps Hazelton knows better how to approach them."

George was saved a reply by the arrival of Jarvis and the inspector. At my invitation, Delaney took a seat at the table between George and myself—probably the safest spot. "I apologize for calling so early, but I assumed you'd want to hear about Mr. Price as soon as possible." He glanced down the table at my parents and frowned. "I hope I'm not intruding?"

"You assumed correctly, Inspector," George said. "And it's no intrusion. I don't suppose you've met Mrs. Hazelton's parents, Mr. and Mrs. Price." He cocked a brow. "You have their son in custody."

Both my parents gave Delaney a deadly glare. "We'd like to know when you plan on releasing him." Mother uttered the words with an expression that said she was ready to go to battle with Delaney and the entire police force if necessary.

"That's one of the reasons I'm here," Delaney replied, staring warily at my mother. "Mr. Price should be ready to go home shortly—no more than an hour, I'd say. There's a bit of paperwork to complete and he'll be released. I thought you might want to go to the precinct yourselves to collect him."

That rather took the wind out of Mother's sails. She was momentarily speechless. Frankie gave Delaney a shrewd look. "Does this mean he's no longer under suspicion?"

"It means he's now one of several suspects, but I see no reason for us to detain him. However, he will be expected to stay in London until he's cleared of all suspicion."

"That's some comfort, I suppose." I poured and handed Delaney a cup of coffee.

"A very little comfort." Mother wasn't ready to give up her resentment yet. "Are you saying he must wait around in case you wish to arrest him again?"

"There's little likelihood of that happening, Mrs. Price," George replied. "Alonzo had nothing to do with Connor's murder, and with Delaney's skills, the police are sure to flush out the culprit. However, as the case progresses, they may need to question Alonzo further." He waved a hand. "Nothing for you to worry about."

Mother actually smiled at George. "Now, that's all I needed to hear." She sighed as she glanced at my father, then glared at Delaney. "You should know better than to come in here frightening a mother like that."

"That was not my intention, ma'am." Delaney spoke with great patience.

"Nevertheless."

Frankie took her hand. "Now, now, Daisy. I'm sure the inspector didn't mean any harm." He turned to Delaney. "My money is on Bainbridge or someone else involved in Connor's business. I'd guess he simply cheated the wrong man."

"We'll be looking into every possibility, I assure you."

"I understand Bainbridge managed to slip out yesterday without giving an account of his time," Frankie added.

"Good heavens, Franklin," Mother said. "You seem to have the man tried and convicted. As you said, it might be any number of Mr. Connor's business associates."

While I was more than a little amused that my father was attempting to run Delaney's investigation, I wanted some information from the inspector and couldn't risk my parents chasing him off. "Does Alonzo's release have anything to do with the coroner's examination?"

George's smile told me he'd been thinking along the same lines.

"In part, yes. He hasn't completed his examination yet, but he has somewhat of a range for Connor's time of death. Mr. Price couldn't have killed him at the time he was found holding the knife. The man would have been dead for at least an hour by that point."

Mother drew in her breath in a gasp.

Delaney turned to George. "Perhaps we should discuss this at another time."

"No." George and I spoke at once.

"Frankie, hadn't you and Mother better call for the carriage so you can fetch Alonzo?" I slipped around Delaney, ready to escort them out. "You certainly don't want to leave him waiting on the street, do you?"

I could see Frankie was loath to leave the discussion, but eager to have his son back in the fold. At the mention of Alonzo, Mother was on her feet. "You are right, dear. We should be off."

"Yes, we should." Frankie rose from the table, eying Delaney. "I highly recommend you investigate his business transactions. That's where you'll find the guilty party."

"I'll keep that in mind, sir."

Frankie gave him a nod and followed Mother and me to the front door, where our footman, Frederick, waited with their coats. "I'll stop by to visit Alonzo once he's back home," I told them, then fairly pushed them out in my haste to return to the breakfast room. Delaney was speaking when I rounded the corner.

"—keep your father-in-law from interfering in a police investigation."

"He's worried about his son, Inspector." I entered the room and returned to my seat beside Delaney. "You're a father. Tell me you wouldn't do the same."

He gave me a level look. "I would not attempt to bribe an officer to release my son."

I turned my horrified gaze to George.

"That's what started the disturbance I mentioned to you earlier," George said. "He offered to make a large donation in exchange for Alonzo's release. I gather the police are more flexible in New York."

"Perhaps, in small matters, but I doubt my father has ever dealt with the police regarding a murder before." I glanced at Delaney. "I'm sure he meant no harm. Money has usually solved his problems in the past."

"See to it that he doesn't try it again or he will find himself with very grave problems indeed, and he will not be able to buy his way out."

We both nodded contritely and I offered him breakfast.

"No, thank you. I must be off."

George inched forward. "Wait. Can you tell us nothing more about the coroner's examination?"

"And who the other suspects are?"

Delaney heaved a sigh. "I suppose the two of you plan to launch an investigation?"

"We'd prefer to be on our wedding trip, but since your constable arrested Alonzo so hastily yesterday, we are now working to prove my brother's innocence. And Hazelton is his legal counsel. It's not as if he won't eventually obtain this information."

George sat back and grinned. "I couldn't have stated it better myself. Unless Mr. Price is no longer under suspicion, we still have an interest in this case."

Delaney pulled out his notebook. "Your brother may not be our only suspect, but he is still under suspicion. He wanted to court the Connor girl. Her father refused to hear of it and as much as promised her to someone else. Alonzo Price has a motive. While Connor was already deceased at the time Mr. Price was found with the knife, he did pay a call on the man earlier in the day." He held up a hand as I was about to speak. "I'm aware he didn't gain admittance at the front door, but there was a second entrance. No one can confirm the time he left your home to make this call or what time he returned, since you were all preparing for the wedding."

"But, as you said, there are other suspects," George added. "Bainbridge recently had a run-in with Connor. They also had a long-standing feud between them, and he was very cagey yesterday in slipping away without providing a statement."

"He was also late to the reception," I added. "If he had come directly from the church, he'd have arrived with everyone else."

"And we saw him head to Connor's home when we were with the photographer."

"That's something I wanted to check with you about." Delaney flipped back a page or two in his book. "Mrs. Hazelton stated you saw four people cross the lawn to the Connor residence. About what time was that?"

I glanced at George. "It was probably three o'clock when we saw Mrs. Connor walk by. How long is this range of time the coroner gave you?"

"It's a little tricky. He has only done a preliminary examination so far, but in addition to the knife wound, Connor sustained two head injuries—one to the back of his head, the other to the temple. He wasn't sure yet, what came first. Considering Connor was found bent forward over his desk, it isn't likely he was stabbed first, then sustained the injury in a fall."

"But if he was sitting at his desk, someone could have bashed him in the head, then stabbed him."

Delaney gave George a nod. "Yes, both strikes may have come at roughly the same time. The earliest part of the range would have been four to five hours before we discovered him."

"Late morning, then?" I gasped and clutched at George's arm. "Heavens, I'd completely forgotten about the blood on my gown."

George rubbed his chin, thinking, while Delaney leaned forward, with a wary look. "Tell me about it," the inspector said.

George nodded for me to go ahead. "After the ceremony, we waited in the vestibule of the church to greet out guests as they came out to wish us well. As soon as we arrived at Harleigh House, I noticed a smear of blood on my sleeve. It wasn't there when I dressed, and I had no injury, so I must have acquired it at the church."

"What time did the wedding begin?" he asked.

"Noon." I suddenly felt rather ill. "That might have been Connor's blood."

Delaney's head jerked up from his book where he been writing. "You are speaking in the past tense. Did you clean the blood off?" He closed his eyes for a moment. "I don't recall seeing blood on your sleeve."

"You didn't see me in my wedding gown. I was already wearing my going-away dress when you arrived. I left it at Harleigh House. Graham's housekeeper will send it on here and leave any necessary cleaning for Bridget. If it would be of any use to you, I can have it sent to you as soon as it arrives."

"I would appreciate that."

George refilled his coffee cup. "Considering the potential timing of the murder, and the fact that Connor had an outside door to his office, your suspect pool must widen," he said. "Mr. Price is not wrong when he suggests Connor's business associates."

Delaney came to his feet. "I'll keep that in mind, but for now I'll concentrate on those already on my list." He pocketed the notebook. "First up is Mr. Bainbridge."

Chapter Nine

After Delaney left and George and I were finally alone, I filled my plate from the sideboard, settled into the chair next to my new husband, and made a confession.

"I just withheld some information about the investigation from Delaney." I worried my lip with my teeth while I watched for George's reaction.

His face took on a wary expression. "Something that implicates your brother?"

"No! Nothing like that. It's something Delaney ought to know, but I shouldn't be the one to tell him."

His brows rose. "Are you planning to tell me, or am I to guess while you talk your way around this—something?"

I blew out a breath. "Graham and Mrs. Connor are romantically involved."

He closed one eye and drew back. "Graham? Your brother-in-law? Lord Harleigh?"

"Yes, to all three."

"Mrs. Connor? I'd have thought Harleigh had a stronger sense of self-preservation."

"My thoughts exactly." I lifted my shoulders. "Apparently, we're both wrong."

"Did Connor know?"

I scoffed. "If he had, I suspect it would have been Graham's body we found, not Connor's. He doesn't strike me as a man who would turn a blind eye to that sort of thing, which makes this all the more astonishing to me. Neither Graham nor Willa is reckless or impulsive."

"Love makes people do strange things."

I spread marmalade on my toast, feeling better now that I'd shared my secret. "I'm not sure love had anything to do with it, though that might be because I can't imagine anyone madly in love with Graham."

"You're probably right about Connor's reaction, but whether he knew or not, this still makes Graham a suspect. Mrs. Connor, too. How long have you known?"

"I learned of it yesterday evening." I picked up my fork and tucked into my breakfast. "Graham was making strange claims about Willa being in the drawing room all afternoon when I knew she hadn't been. He was quite insistent she never left the house. I finally pulled him aside and asked him why he was lying for her. I might have implied that Willa had already told me everything." I snuck a glance at George and was relieved to see him smiling. "That's when he confessed. I advised him to tell Delaney the truth before he found out on his own."

"Good advice." George followed my lead and returned to his breakfast. "Delaney will consider him a suspect either way, but lying about it would definitely make matters worse."

"The same could be said for Willa, don't you think? Delaney is already suspicious of her."

He took a sip of coffee. "I'm not as familiar with Mrs. Connor as you. Is she likely to have stabbed him?"

"No more likely than any other wife." I laughed at his horrified expression. "I'm teasing. All I meant was that Willa doesn't seem any more lethal than every other woman I know. Less, in fact, since she's so mild-mannered." I considered my assessment of the woman. "Of course, she'd have to be or she'd never tolerate the man. He was a good twenty years older than her, particularly unpleasant, and quite the tyrant."

George raised his brows.

"I don't see either of them as having done it," I added. "They are two more people with a motive, but Graham wouldn't have had much opportunity. Other than the time he was sequestered with Willa somewhere, he was in plain view of the guests throughout the length of the party."

George leaned over the table and put his hand on mine. "Wait. Are you telling me he and Mrs. Connor disappeared for a time during the reception, and they are each other's alibi?"

I froze. "When you put it like that, it does sound nefarious. They had better hope a servant saw them slip away."

"And saw precisely where they went." His expression was stony.

"Heavens, this is a predicament for them. I didn't get the sense that Graham saw any future for the two of them, but neither did I ask. It's hard to believe they snuck away and murdered Connor. For their sake, I hope Delaney feels the same."

George squeezed my hand. "Take heart. The coroner may determine the murder took place before the wedding."

"If so, Graham should be safe. He was preparing for the breakfast. I'd imagine the servants can account for every minute of his time."

"Nevertheless, he shouldn't keep this from Delaney."

"I daresay he hopes to protect Willa's good name."

George raised his hands helplessly. "This is a murder investigation. He can't ignore that in favor of her reputation."

We were interrupted by the entrance of Jarvis carrying a note on a salver. He extended it to me. "The maid next door just delivered this for you, madam."

I placed the note beside my plate. "Well, it can't be from Mother, so it must be from Hetty or Rose."

"You could simply open it and find out."

I thought I heard Jarvis chuckle as he left the room. I shrugged. "It seemed rude to do so, since we were in the middle of a conversation, but if you don't mind?"

He grinned. "Perhaps Rose has some information about the case."

"Ha, ha," I said, already scanning the note. "Not information exactly, and not from Rose. Aunt Hetty says Gilliam plans to call on her this evening and will bring his notes from the police interviews. We are welcome to join them if we like."

He gave me a cautious glance. "It's our first full day as newlyweds, but would you mind if we stopped by?"

"I must confess, I'd like to see his notes, too."

He pulled the napkin from his lap and placed it on the table. "Since our evening is settled, and Alonzo is taken care of for now, why don't we go over to Harleigh House and speak with your brother-in-law? I'm not certain I trust him to give Delaney his full story."

I nodded. "He may need further convincing. I could also pick up my wedding dress if the housekeeper hasn't sent it on yet."

"Excellent. The sooner we put this case to rest, the better our chances of taking a wedding trip."

"My thoughts exactly."

When we arrived at Harleigh House, Crabbe put us in the east drawing room to await Graham. It wasn't quite as cold now that the west room was closed off but it was chilly enough for me to choose one of the Queen Anne chairs near the fire. George stepped right up to the hearth when something on the mantel caught his eye.

"What is this?" He held out a small framed watercolor.

Without looking, I knew why he asked. "The fifth countess fancied herself an artist," I said. "It could be a flower or a house. It could be Graham as a baby. No one knows. There is nothing recognizable in any of her work."

He drew it back and squinted at the image. "Yet it has pride of place on the drawing room mantel?"

"The frame is lovely." I shrugged. "Her lesser works decorate the nursery. I had to face them to the walls when Rose used the room. They frightened her."

He returned it to the mantel when Graham joined us. Before I could inquire about the wedding dress, George asked him about Willa.

Graham cut his gaze to me, a look of betrayal on his face. "I told you about that in confidence."

I let out a tsk and crossed my arms. "It's not as if I told the police. George is my husband, and I thought he might do a better job of convincing you to explain your circumstances to Inspector Delaney."

Graham wandered over to stare out the window. "I'm having second thoughts about that. You said yourself our relationship gives us both a motive to do Connor in." He turned around to face us. "If you think so, how much more likely is it that he will?"

"Very likely," George conceded. "Which is why you will have to account for your time. Motive or not, if you had no opportunity to harm the man, you won't be a suspect."

Graham still looked doubtful.

"Connor might have been murdered as early as eleven and as late as half past three," I said. "Can someone vouch for you during that time? You were at the church for the ceremony. Here for the reception. Before that, I assume you were either with your valet or instructing your servants."

"I suppose that's true, but what is Mrs. Connor to do? Admit she was involved with a man other than her husband?"

"That happens to be the truth," George said baldly.

Graham moved to the other Queen Anne chair and sank into it, drumming his fingers on the arm.

"I understand your desire to protect her," George added, "but I suspect she'll have servants who can vouch for her, too. The point is, if you are caught in the lie, it will look all the worse for you. And for her."

"Her husband is—was a brute." Graham straightened and jabbed a finger at each of us in turn. "And this I tell you in the strictest of confidence. Willa has such a sweet, accommodating nature. She would never stand up to him." He dropped his gaze to the floor. "I've heard him belittle her, shout at her, and I suspect he laid hands on her—in a violent way."

I drew in a sharp breath. "Are you saying he struck her?"

"I'm more inclined to believe he struck her repeatedly."

George and I stared.

"Sometimes she'd flinch if I reached for her and she wasn't expecting it. I've seen bruises on her arms." He let out a low growl. "I'm certain she didn't kill Connor, but she is better off without him."

Though Graham had no actual proof, I found myself believing him. Willa did her best to maintain a perfect façade, but I often thought Connor intimidated her. He was loud, and gruff, and ruled his family as if they were employees. She rejected gowns if she thought Connor wouldn't approve of the style, or left a luncheon before it was over if she thought she might be late getting home.

I've wondered—now and then—how she found the patience to stay with such a man. But did she have any choice? Willa was alone in the world. Her livelihood, her very life depended on Connor. Where was she to go if life with her husband became unbearable?

But Graham was only speculating. I hoped he was wrong. If he was right, then she was better off without him and that did give her a strong motive. "I thought I knew her reasonably well," I said. "I can't imagine her murdering Connor."

"Nor can I," he said. "And I desperately hope she has an alibi. When everything comes to light, if it comes to light, everyone will think her guilty."

"Have you called on her today?" I asked him.

"No, I've deliberately stayed away, for propriety's sake."

Once we gained Graham's agreement to tell Delaney about his relationship with Willa, we had only to ask about my wedding dress, which, it turned out, had already been sent on to our house. After that, we collected our coats and took our leave. When the door closed behind us, I glanced up at George.

"What now?"

"I've been thinking I ought to go by the Chelsea precinct to follow up on the contingencies of Alonzo's release. Things like not leaving London. After the bribery incident, I fear your mother and father will disregard little details like that."

"I have to admit my father's disdain for police authority rather took me by surprise." We walked down the cobbled path to the street, our breath clouding in front of us as we spoke. "If you don't mind going alone and coming back for me, I'd like to check on Willa and Madeline. They are friends after all."

"That should be fine. I doubt I'll be much more than an hour. Shall I walk you over?"

"I can manage, but do hold the carriage until I'm let in. They may not wish for company."

We separated at the pavement. I walked up to the Connors' door while George headed for the carriage. I rang the bell, then turned to smile at him. How nice it was to have someone waiting for me.

The door opened, revealing a butler with a rather harried expression. Behind him, two men seemed to be in an argument with an even more harried Willa Connor.

"This is not the best time, ma'am," the butler intoned.

"I believe the opposite may be true." My ire up, I stepped right past him and up to Willa's side. "What do you two think you're doing?" My arm rounded her shoulder instinctively, and we faced down the men together. They appeared to be workmen of a sort by the look of their simple garments—loose trousers, shirts open at the neck, where knotted kerchiefs didn't quite fill the opening, and heavy, shapeless overcoats. The larger of the two wore a soft cap while the smaller man, who was still significantly bigger, and brawnier, than me, wore a bowler atop his tawny hair. As he moved, I thought I saw a crumble of dried mud fall from his coat to the white marble floor. Both men stared at me and seemed at a loss for words.

"How dare you come here and disturb Mrs. Connor. Do you realize her husband passed away less than a day ago? She is in mourning." I cast a glance at Willa, who glanced up at me in amazement, then back to the two thugs. I hated to make a snap judgment about two men I'd never met, but considering their size, their general lack of cleanliness, and their threatening manner, there was little else to call them.

The large one opened his mouth to speak, but I hadn't finished. "You are in the presence of two ladies, and you are indoors. Why are you still wearing your hats?"

Both men snatched the coverings from their heads.

"That's better. Now, I suggest you leave your card with—" I glanced at the butler.

"Parker, ma'am."

"Leave your card with Parker and allow Mrs. Connor her privacy." I made as if to escort Willa to the drawing room, when one of them cleared his throat. I glanced at them over my shoulder.

"We don't have no card, ma'am," the smaller man said. "And our business can't wait until Mrs. Connor is up to visitors."

"If this has something to do with Mr. Connor, I suggest you contact his man of business. I'm sure Parker here can provide his name and direction."

"We been there. He won't see us." He fixed his gaze on Willa and bobbed his head in her direction. It might have been meant as a gesture of respect, but from one so large, it simply looked awkward. "I apologize, ma'am, if our manners caused you any alarm." His words were halting as if he were carefully choosing from an array of unfamiliar phrases. His eyes lit when he landed on the word *alarm*. "Why don't we start again and talk this out genteel-like?"

I glanced at Willa, wondering if she planned to take control of this meeting at some point. Parker looked like a capable man, but I doubted his ability to remove both of these lugs from the house. It was certain Willa and I couldn't. It seemed the best way to move forward was to take care of their business. Whatever that entailed.

Connor's office remained locked under order of the Metropolitan Police but there was the small parlor across the entry hall. That might do. "Willa, perhaps you should allow these men to explain their business."

"Do you think so?"

"I think if you don't, they are likely to become permanent fixtures right where they stand." I gestured to the parlor. "Gentlemen, perhaps we can all sit and discuss this sensibly. Whatever the problem is."

The two men turned and lumbered into the room before I'd even finished speaking, so Willa had little choice in the matter. "Would you prefer to speak with them alone?" I asked.

Her eyes widened and she clutched my hand. "Definitely not. Please come with me."

"Of course." I lingered long enough to instruct Parker to wait in the foyer and perhaps call for a footman to assist him should we need rescue. Then I followed Willa, who now seemed somewhat less apprehensive, into the room, drawing the door partially closed behind me.

"I'm not sure what we can accomplish here," she said. "I've

already explained that Mr. Connor's office has been locked by the police. I have no way of writing you a draft."

"Is that why you are here? You are owed payment for something?" I asked. "Who are you, by the way?"

The larger man spoke. "Name's Higgins. I'm Archie. This is my brother, Sidney." He pointed to his associate and the man nodded to us both. "We did a job for Mr. Connor. He gave us half the payment up front. We were to come to his office yesterday and he'd pay us the rest. Except he wasn't there. Today we heard he's dead."

"Condolences, ma'am." Sidney Higgins nodded at Willa.

"As I were saying"—Archie cut a glance at his brother—"we heard he was dead and asked ourselves, what do we do now? The kind of work we do for Mr. Connor, he don't put on the company books, if you catch my meaning."

The expression on Willa's face as she turned to me was ashen and more than likely matched my own. "I'm sure we both catch your meaning," I said. "Why don't we all take a seat?" I wasn't particularly concerned about their comfort, but I needed a moment to think. They'd called on Connor yesterday. Had he refused to pay them? Had they in turn walloped him over the head, then stabbed him in the back? It sounded as though that was an exercise that might fall within their purview.

They shuffled to the sofa and Willa and I took the chairs opposite them. "You say you called on Mr. Connor yesterday at his office. Here in this house?"

"He don't have no other that I know of."

"He has no other office," Willa confirmed. "When we are in London, he conducts all of his business here."

"Did you call at his office door?"

The man nodded. "He didn't like us to bother the staff. We was here at half past two. Sharp like."

"You mentioned he was gone. Did you enter the office?"

"That woulda been rude, ma'am." He shrugged. "Besides, the door was locked."

"So you left?" Odd. They seemed more likely to knock down the door. Since it was still standing, I supposed I must believe them.

"As it happens, we had some other business to take care of. Came back about five. Saw the constable here with a plain-clothes man and figured it was best to postpone our business. Then we heard the news."

I glanced at Willa, who still stared at the men in disbelief. "What exactly was this job Mr. Connor owed you for?" she asked.

Sidney Higgins narrowed his eyes. "We did some work at Mr. Bainbridge's office the other day."

Willa truly looked ill now. Understandable, under the circumstances. Connor actually paid these men to vandalize Bainbridge's office. And it sounded as though he employed them on a regular basis. So far, they'd been minding their manners. That and the knowledge that Parker, and perhaps a burly footman, waited on the other side of the door, made me feel secure for the moment. But I had no idea how long that moment would last. It was time to send them on their way.

"Willa, where might I find pen and paper?"

"I believe there's some in that table." She still looked rather dazed.

I crossed the room to the small writing table in the corner. There was indeed paper and pen in the drawer. Willa told me her husband's man of business was one Mr. Winston. I proceeded to write him a note. "What is the amount Mr. Connor still owes you?" I hoped they wouldn't state a number that was too outrageous.

"Ten quid."

That didn't seem too high. Perhaps there was honor among thieves after all. Though it's not as if I knew the going rate for a spot of vandalism. I wrote out the instruction for the agent to pay out the sum to the Higginses and asked Willa to come over and sign it.

"We're going to pay them?" she whispered.

"I think it's the best way to get them out of your house, don't you? Parker might be able to throw them out, but without their payment, they will likely come back. And they may not be as agreeable next time."

She signed the note, and I handed it over to the larger Mr. Higgins. "This is Mrs. Connor's authorization to pay you. If you take it to Mr. Winston, you should have no problem."

The man grinned, and thankfully, they both stood, apparently ready to leave. "It was a pleasure doing business with you, ladies." Archie Higgins turned at the door and bowed graciously. "Please accept our condolences on your loss, Mrs. Connor. If you ever need our services, we're happy to help. Everyone knows where to find us."

I hoped "everyone" included no one I knew.

With that they sauntered from the room. I held my breath until I heard the front door shut behind them. Parker popped into the parlor. "They've left, ma'am."

I sagged against the desk. Were those men Connor's killers or were they telling the truth? Killing a man who owed you money didn't seem like a good way to obtain payment. On the other hand, they had found a way to obtain it, hadn't they? Was a man's life worth no more than ten pounds?

It seemed a poor motive for murder to me, but they certainly had opportunity. I would definitely bring these men to the attention of Inspector Delaney.

Chapter Ten

Once Parker backed out of the room, we both sank into the sofa as if our knees had given out. Poor Willa may have learned more about her late husband in the past twenty minutes than in the entire length of their marriage. Most of this newly gained knowledge was likely unwelcome.

"That was rather terrifying," I said.

"You didn't look frightened at all." Willa stared at me with rounded eyes. "You stood your ground, took charge, and sent them on their way."

I chuckled. "With a promise of payment."

She waved aside the thought of money as only a wealthy person could do. "That hardly matters. I'd have given them ten times that amount to make them leave, but I didn't know what to do. You swept in and took care of everything." She reached across the sofa and squeezed my arm. "Thank you, Frances. I'm both grateful for your presence of mind and terribly embarrassed you had to witness that scene."

I gave her a smile. "You might consider hiring someone to deal with such people for you. I don't want to pass judgment on your husband, but if he associated with such rough types, you may receive calls from more of them."

She nodded. "A good suggestion, but I have no idea how to go about finding someone like that."

"Your husband's agent could help you."

"You must think me a simpleton. I know nothing about Connor's business and little more about his life in general."

"Once the police let you into his office, you can set about learning all that."

She drew in a shuddering breath and wrapped her arms about herself. "I'm not sure I want to learn."

I completely understood, or at least thought I might.

"Please don't think too ill of Connor. It's clear to me now that he was responsible for the damage at Mr. Bainbridge's office. He had a ruthless streak and hadn't always behaved ethically in his business dealings, but there was goodness in him."

Her head rested against the back of the sofa and the way she snapped it to the side to meet my gaze made me wonder if I'd unknowingly made some sound of derision. "The rumors Gladys Bainbridge spread about me are true, you know," she continued. "My first husband died and left me to fend for myself in a camp full of miners. I had nothing. Even to scrape up enough money to get to San Francisco would have taken months of sewing and laundry. I couldn't believe my luck when Connor came along."

"He rescued you," I suggested.

"That he did." Her tone indicated she meant this sincerely. "He was a widower and already quite well-to-do. There was a Catholic church in the nearby town and the priest told Connor about my situation. First, he hired me to tend to Madeline while he went about the business of his day. She was the sweetest little one. Not seven years old yet. It wasn't long before he bought a home for the two of them, and I became his housekeeper, then his wife." She shook her head. "At the time I had no idea all this"—she waved her hand—"was on the horizon."

"I suppose we never know what life has in store for us."

"Connor offered me security, and I accepted it gratefully. I could once again live without the fear that at any moment I might be evicted from my rooms. That's all I wanted, but he gave me so much more. I've never been able to grow into the position of the grand lady, or the stylish hostess he wanted in a wife. I've disappointed him—time and again."

The way she spoke the words sounded like a refrain; as if she'd heard them "time and again." "I'm sure that's not true. You loved his daughter and he had to love you for that."

"Who wouldn't love Madeline? She and her father were very close, too. Truth be told, I'm worried about her. She has yet to leave her room and every time I check on her, she's crying."

"Poor dear. She's had quite a shock." I was concerned for Madeline, but I wasn't ready to leave the subject of Connor yet. "Do you suppose one or both of the Higgins men might have had something to do with your husband's murder?"

"This is the first I've ever heard of them. Connor did not share anything about his business dealings with me. Even so, I'd have to be blind and deaf not to be aware that much of what he did wasn't entirely respectable."

She stood up suddenly. "I'm in need of some refreshment, aren't you?" She rang for the butler before I could stop her, and requested tea. George would be here within thirty minutes or so, but I suppose that was time enough for tea.

Willa returned to the sofa. "Now that I've told you my entire life story, the least I can do is feed you." She gave me a rueful smile. "Though I wouldn't be surprised if someone from Connor's business life is responsible for his death, I know so little about that part of him, I can't really provide any direction. The only business colleague I'm familiar with is Mr. Bainbridge. The two of them would probably fight to the death to be king of the hill. It's as if there wasn't room enough in the world for both of them."

"How did that come about? Weren't they associates at one time?"

"Mr. Bainbridge was Connor's legal advisor on one or two projects. They didn't work together very long. A few years after they parted ways, Bainbridge was interviewed by the *Morning Call*—a San Francisco newspaper," she added upon seeing my blank look. "Connor's business enterprises had grown tremendously by then and he'd created quite a name for himself, so it wasn't surprising that the reporter asked Bainbridge about his dealings with him. In his response, he implied Connor's ethics were questionable."

She shrugged. "He wasn't wrong, but the article sent Connor into a rage and he never recovered. From that moment on, anything he could do to disrupt Bainbridge's business, he did. Then it came to the point of hiring detectives to follow the Bainbridges around and report to the newspapers about every strange thing Gladys Bainbridge did. Nothing was too small. If it made them look bad or foolish, or harmed their reputations, Connor was overjoyed. Eventually, the Bainbridges fought back, which is how my history came to light."

With a warning tap on the door, a maid stepped in with the tea service. We remained quiet while she arranged everything on the table in front of us and silently left us alone. Willa busied herself pouring.

"Considering all the animosity between them, perhaps they should have settled matters in the boxing ring."

Willa chuckled. "They did that, too. It wasn't in a boxing ring, but they did come to blows in the office of a bank in San Francisco. Caused a tremendous scene—two prominent, middle-aged men pummeling each other. It was in all the newspapers in America, but perhaps not here."

"Are you quite serious?" I took the cup she handed off.

She nodded and placed a few biscuits on a plate. "Men can be so childish. I'm not saying Mr. Bainbridge had anything to do with Connor's death, but it wouldn't surprise me. Connor would never give in, and Mr. Bainbridge may have had enough of their feud."

Though Willa had told me quite a bit about her life with and without Connor, I didn't sense that she had any fear of him. Of course, he was gone now, which might make all the difference. I couldn't help but notice she'd never mentioned love in relation to her husband either. As Graham had said, she was taking his death quite stoically.

"Why did you come back here yesterday?" I asked. "Had you forgotten something?"

"No, I merely hoped to convince Connor to come to the celebration. Like those two ruffians said, he didn't answer the door to me either, and I never enter his office without permission." She gave me a curious look. "How did you know I came home yesterday?"

"Hazelton and I were having a photograph made and we saw you cross the lawn."

She smiled. "And you wondered why I didn't mention it to the inspector when I recounted my day."

"I . . . well—"

She waved a hand. "The inspector wondered, too. He stopped by not long before you arrived, and I corrected my statement. I suppose between the shock of Connor's murder and my concern over Madeline, it simply slipped my mind."

"Understandably," I said. Perhaps it had been merely an oversight, rather than a deliberate omission.

Willa set her cup in its saucer with a decided chink and turned sharply to me. "Now I recall something else that slipped my mind," she said. "Your brother. Forgive me, Frances. How is he? Have the police released him yet?"

"This morning. He should be home by now."

Relief flooded her expression.

"I do hope you know he had nothing to do with Connor's death." My inflection turned the statement into a question.

"I never thought for a moment he did. Madeline is so fond of him. I was sorry Connor felt so strongly about Fitzwalter. Madeline and Mr. Price would have been more compatible in my opinion." She smiled. "I can't imagine your brother murdering Connor because he'd rejected his suit."

"Alonzo never had the chance to present it. That reminds me. Did Fitzwalter call on you last night?"

Her lips compressed into a wide line. "He did, foolish young man. Madeline refused to see him. I doubt their courtship will last much longer. Madeline is ready to be done with him."

"Do you suppose she'd be willing to see me?" I asked. "Alonzo will never forgive me if I go back home with no word of her."

"I'd be so relieved if she does, but the worst that can happen is that she turns you away. Please, go on up."

I didn't have much more time before George came to collect me, but I didn't want to squander this chance to talk with Madeline. Willa walked me to the impressive staircase and told me how to find her room. The thick runner muffled my steps as I slipped up the stairs and rapped on her door. "Madeline?" I paused. "It's Frances Wynn. No, I mean Hazelton. Frances Hazelton. Heavens, I can't even recall my own name, but will you speak with me anyway?"

The key turned in the lock and she pulled the door open enough to peer out. "Lady Harleigh?"

"Not unless this is a formal occasion, and as you see, I'm not dressed for one."

She gave me a ghost of a smile and pulled the door wide. "Mrs. Hazelton, then." She turned, and I followed her inside the darkened room, and guided her over to an upholstered bench by the window. Then I pushed aside the heavy brocade drapes to let in a little light and we both took a seat.

"Your mother is worried about you, dear." I winced at my words. Willa was her stepmother, and though I knew they were close, I didn't know if Madeline made the distinction. Nevertheless, I went on. "Sometimes grief is easier to bear when it's shared."

She nodded and stared down at her hands. In her nightclothes with her hair loosely plaited and hanging over her shoulder she didn't look much older than Rose. I stroked her hair and she dropped her head against my shoulder. "This is all my fault," she whispered.

"Come now," I cooed. "How is that possible?"

"If I hadn't fought him about marrying Fitzwalter, he'd have been at the wedding and he'd still be alive."

"I assume he wanted Fitzwalter to go in his stead so the two of you could spend some time together. Is that right?"

She nodded. "He was so set on the match. I should have given in, but I didn't want to marry him. I still don't."

"Then you mustn't. Your father could only have been thinking of your happiness. I'm sure eventually he would have realized his mistake."

She craned her head around to look at me, her tear-reddened eyes wide with disbelief.

"Parents make mistakes, too, and in doing so, your father was in the wrong place at the wrong time. You mustn't blame yourself for his death."

"What about Mr. Price? Surely you blame me for encouraging him. And now he's accused of murder."

"Ah, that's no longer the case. Locked up here in your room, you aren't privy to all the new information. Alonzo has been released. Though he's still under suspicion, the police are investigating elsewhere."

Her body expanded on a gasp. "He's been released?"

"Indeed, I expect he's home with my parents right now."

"That's such a relief to hear. With Parker accusing him and the constable arresting him, I was certain they would simply close the investigation."

"Then I'm glad I was able to bring you some good news.

However, with Alonzo free, I fear he may come by to call on you—just to ensure himself that you are bearing up, you see. But I wonder if you encouraged him simply to discourage Fitzwalter." I leaned back to look into her face. "Should I tell him not to come?"

She pulled a handkerchief from her sleeve and mopped her eyes. "I do like Mr. Price, but I don't believe I'm quite up to callers yet."

That didn't exactly answer my question. "Then I'll tell him to wait. But what of Willa? She is grieving, too."

She gave me a tentative smile. "I will clean up, dress, and go down by teatime." She found and squeezed my hand. "Thank you for making the effort of pulling me out of my sorrow, Lady Harleigh—er, Mrs. Hazelton. I'm not sure I'm worth your trouble, but I do appreciate it and your kind words."

"Nonsense. You are worth far more trouble than I've put myself to. And you are the best person to comfort Willa. She loves you so."

She nodded, and I rose to my feet. "I'll see myself out, but don't forget your promise to go down to tea."

"I promise," she said as I swept out the door. On the landing I heard a commotion below. Heavens, had those Higgins brothers returned? I descended the stairs to see men in blue uniforms enter the front door. The police?

Chapter Eleven

❧

"What is happening here?" I fairly skipped down the remaining steps to join Willa and the policemen in the entry hall. I was surprised to see George follow the last one through the door.

Willa turned a tearful face to me. "They say they are here to search Connor's office again."

Thank heaven George was on hand. The officers, two rather bold and brash individuals in my opinion, made no effort to explain why they needed to search Connor's office. They simply instructed Willa to stand back while they unlocked the door and stepped inside. Since he was at the precinct a short time ago, it seemed George knew what they were searching for. He motioned us back into the parlor.

"This room hasn't seen so much use in all the time we've been here," Willa protested. "We'd be much more comfortable in the drawing room, I believe."

"That may be so, but then we won't be able to observe these men at work." George turned back from the doorway to face us. "I can ensure that nothing they pick up finds its way into their pockets. More importantly, I can see what they take back as evidence."

"Is that why they're here?" Willa and I sidled up to George and the three of us watched the proceedings across the foyer, though Willa, with her small stature, struggled to see around us. "I'd have thought they collected all their evidence yesterday."

George blinked when he turned and saw us both at his shoulder. "The coroner has provided more information." He paused, examining Willa's face. "We needn't discuss it if you're not up to hearing this, Mrs. Connor."

Her hands fluttered to the brooch at her collar. "If this is about what happened to my husband, I'd like to know."

"It pertains to a second injury."

"The blow to the head?" I asked.

Willa's eyes appeared to lose focus. I put an arm around her waist in time to stop her from collapsing, but the dead weight of her small person nearly brought me to the floor. "George, help me!"

No sooner did he touch her shoulder than Willa flung her arms about. "I'm fine," she said, cautiously taking her weight back onto her own feet.

I kept an arm about her until she seemed steady. "Perhaps you should sit," I suggested. "And Hazelton is right. We don't have to discuss this now."

She straightened her gown and tucked her hair in place. Her face appeared flushed, but perhaps she was simply embarrassed. "Forgive me. It was a momentary shock. Are you saying the killer struck Connor?"

George watched her for a moment, then nodded as if to himself. "He had two injuries to his head, which, as you suggested, could have been from someone striking him with something. The coroner has set these men to the task of retrieving any objects that may have been used as a weapon. It may help him determine exactly what happened."

"He can do that?" Willa asked. "Determine exactly what happened?"

"He can determine the order of the events and perhaps whether Connor was seated or standing when the blow was struck. That can sometimes determine the strength or the height of the culprit." He glanced toward the foyer. "If you ladies don't mind, I'd like to sneak up to the office and take a closer look."

Willa and I followed him into the entry hall, stopping in our tracks when he rounded on us. "I can sneak much better on my own," he said.

"All right, then. We'll wait here." We returned to our post in the doorway and watched as he settled himself in between the hall table and the doorway to Connor's office, giving him a perfect view. Since he had yet to see the room, I didn't mind waiting in the background. At least not much.

I was about to suggest that Willa and I return to our seats when I noticed she was shaking. I put an arm out to steady her. "Forgive me, Willa, for keeping you here. This has been too much for you on top of an already difficult day. Why don't I take you to your room?"

"I hate to leave them alone." She gestured vaguely toward Connor's office.

"The police? Let Hazelton manage them. He'll make sure they don't overstep."

She raised a hand to her forehead. "I do suddenly feel rather overwhelmed."

"That settles it. Once I get you up to your room, I'll ring for your maid to make you comfortable." Willa leaned on my arm and directed me to her room. "I'm sure you'll feel better after a rest." I pushed open the door to a feminine, fussy room in hues of yellow and blue that clearly told me she and Connor hadn't shared the room, and settled Willa on the edge of the bed.

"I don't know what's come over me," she said with a sob in her voice.

"You've been through a great deal in the past two days and

you can only push yourself so far." I unhooked the tieback holding the draperies open and allowed the heavy velvet to sweep across the window. Looking around for the bellpull, I noticed great tears running down her cheeks. "Where might I find a handkerchief, dear?"

She pointed to the bureau. "Top drawer."

I shook out two fine linen handkerchiefs embroidered in the corner with her monogram and brought them to her. She mopped her eyes while I rang for her maid.

"I wonder if it was a thief who murdered Connor," she said in a small voice. "With everything so strewn about in his office."

"That's possible." I returned to the bed and seated myself beside her. "Did Connor keep valuables in his office? Did Inspector Delaney ask you if anything was missing?"

She gave me a helpless shrug. "I'd have no way of knowing. He kept no expensive baubles on display, but I'm not at all familiar with the contents of his desk. Perhaps he had a safe."

"It seemed to me that someone was searching for something specific," I replied. "Even if it was a safe that makes me doubt it was a random thief. The culprit had to know enough about your husband to know that was his office. That it was a room closed off from the rest of the house. And if they were searching for something, what could it be?"

"I've no idea." That brought on another round of tears. "I'm really of no help at all."

I hugged her to my side until her tears abated and her maid swooped in and took charge of her. As I took my leave she reached for my hand. "Thank you, Frances, for"—she waved a hand—"taking care of things."

"Think nothing of it, dear. Get some rest." I made my way to the door. "Oh, I neglected to tell you, Madeline agreed to come down for tea this afternoon. I'm sure the police will be gone by then and you will feel much refreshed."

That left her with a smile. I slipped downstairs to find George still leaning against the doorframe at Connor's office, watching over the police officers. "How is Mrs. Connor?" he asked when I reached his side.

"Understandably distressed. She had some callers when I arrived." I told him about the Higgins brothers and the work they did for Connor. "Then the police arrived to search again." I shrugged. "It's been quite a day, but she's resting now. What has happened here?"

"They seem to like that walking stick as a possible murder weapon." He nodded at the desk where the stick lay across its cluttered surface. It was more fashionable than functional with an embossed silver knob atop a wooden shaft that tapered to a narrow tip.

"I didn't see it on the desk yesterday. Where did they find it?"

"Across the room, under the table."

"Probably not Connor's, then?"

He shrugged. "Hard to say. The killer might have struck Connor, then given the stick a toss. Its proximity to the body is meaningless, but whoever owns it certainly ought to be a suspect." He glanced at me and his brow creased with worry. "Does your brother carry such a stick?"

"I haven't seen him with one, but I couldn't say for certain. Has the coroner determined that the blow to the head is what killed Connor?"

"The one to the temple." George pushed away from the doorframe. "And it appears these men are done here."

Indeed, the two constables quickly shooed us back to the entry hall, locking the door to Connor's office behind them. George had them leave a receipt for the items they took as possible evidence—a glass paperweight and the walking stick—and within minutes, he'd closed the front door behind them. "I believe we're done here as well, don't you? Shall I ring for Parker to bring out coats?"

I stared at him in disbelief. "I would have thought you'd want to have a look around the office yourself."

"That would be helpful, but, as you see, the police have locked the door."

"A lock hasn't stopped you before."

He stepped closer and replied in a low voice. "I have no intention of breaking in only to have the butler catch us in the act. Ah, and here he is now."

Parker was indeed striding down the hallway, our coats over his arm. "I heard the door," he said. "And made the assumption you'd be ready to depart."

"You assumed correctly, my good man." George reached for my coat.

Though I was greatly disappointed, I could conceive of no reason to delay our departure. George helped me with my coat, then allowed Parker to help him into his, and we found ourselves out on the pavement, heading for the street.

The empty street.

I stopped. "Where is the carriage?"

"Jack's been driving it around the neighborhood to keep the horses warm. He'll return by and by." Taking my elbow, he led me off the pavement to the lawn between the two houses.

"Are we to wait at Harleigh House?"

"I suppose that's an option." He guided me to the side wall of the Connor house. "Or we could make a quick stop first."

My confusion lasted only a moment. George deftly opened the exterior door to Connor's office and drew me inside. He must have unlocked it while the police were occupied with their search. "Very clever," I whispered.

He gave me a grin. "We don't have as much time as I'd like," he said, keeping his voice low. "It would look rather suspicious if one of the staff notes the carriage waiting for us ten minutes after we've left, so we'll have to move quickly. There's something I want to see for myself." He held out a hand, which I took automatically. "If you'll assist me?"

"Of course." He led me to the guest side of the desk where two club chairs ought to have sat side by side. Instead, one of them was pushed several feet away from the desk. George had me stand in front of that chair while he stood facing me with his hands on my shoulders. "I'm close to Connor in height," he said. "If he was struggling with someone, he and his assailant would have been about here."

"Which might be why the chair is pushed back."

"Exactly. Now, look at my feet. Notice the very unfortunate placement of the carpet?"

I did as he suggested and took in the bound edge of the carpet, George's height, and the distance behind him to the edge of the desk. "Connor might have lost his footing on the carpet and, in falling, cracked his head against the desk."

George eyed the space behind him. "I wasn't sure if there was enough space here for that to be possible, but it appears so. *If* he was struggling with someone." He released me and turned to examine the desk. "There is something here that looks like blood."

I moved to his side. "There's more on the floor." I pointed to a few rust-colored spots on the wood floor, wondering what all this meant. "If Connor hit his head against the desk—and it appears he hit something there hard enough to leave blood—how did he get back to his desk chair? Or how did his assailant get him there? It wouldn't be a simple task to move such a large body. And wouldn't there be a trail of blood?"

George straightened up and parted his lips to answer, but now that I'd applied a bit of logic to the situation, the questions were simply rolling off my tongue. I raised a hand to forestall him. "Why move the body in the first place? And for heaven's sake, why stab him if he was already dead?"

He lifted a brow. "Have you finished?"

"Probably not, but please go ahead."

"Hitting his head on the desk didn't kill Connor. It might have stunned him for a moment and I'm sure it hurt like the devil. But since there's so little blood, he must have got up quickly and I suspect the first thing he'd want to do is sit down until the room stopped spinning."

"That may well be, but what of the other person in the room? The one who was struggling with him? If he was trying to murder Connor, would he simply wait while his opponent had a rest?"

"It's possible that's when the other person began the search. But once realizing Connor hadn't succumbed to his injury, this would have been the point where the assailant picked up the paperweight or the walking stick and struck the fatal blow."

"Of course, the second injury."

"The one that killed him." George glanced at the clock on the desk. "Jack should be around with the carriage by now. We should leave."

"We didn't accomplish very much. What about the desk?"

George slipped around the desk and pulled open a drawer. "Empty," he said. Closing it, he quickly repeated the process with the remaining drawers. "The police must have taken the contents."

"What about these?" I bent to scoop up a handful of torn paper strips from under the desk.

"Connor's rubbish?" He held out a hand to me. "I have a much better idea of what happened now. We should leave."

"I don't think it's rubbish. It's scattered across the floor." I indicated the space between Connor's desk and the exterior door and continued collecting the scraps.

"This is a crime scene, Frances. You ought to leave that here."

I stuffed the paper in my pockets and straightened. "The police have been here twice to collect evidence and never touched these scraps. They aren't likely to come back for them now. Like you, they probably thought someone knocked over the waste bin."

"A reasonable conclusion."

"Then they shouldn't mind that I tidied up." I glanced around. "That seems to be the last of it." I could see him debating whether or not to allow my small act of thievery. "Shouldn't we be leaving?"

With a shake of his head, he waved me to the door. "After you, my little scofflaw."

"Ha! Says the man who illegally entered a crime scene." I sailed past him and out the door. Jack had just pulled up to the curb between Harleigh House and the Connor residence. George and I dashed to the carriage. I climbed in while he gave instructions to Jack, then joined me inside.

"Goodness, it's chilly in here," I said, rubbing my gloved hands together until George took them between his and finished warming them.

"Tell me, madam," he said, "what is your plan for those purloined scraps of paper?"

"With luck, I hope to reconstruct whatever document the killer tore to shreds."

He gave me a skeptical look. "You think the killer did that?"

"Possibly. Perhaps Connor used this document to blackmail someone or coerce them. The person wanted the document back and was willing to murder Connor to obtain it."

"Hmm. If so, why wouldn't the killer have taken it with him, or burned it? Why leave it in pieces at the murder scene for the police to find?"

Bother! I hadn't thought of that. "I may have the wrong idea about the document or letter or whatever it is, but I'll still attempt to piece it together. Connor didn't strike me as someone who would leave shreds of paper around his office. It may have something to do with the crime, though I'm no longer sure how."

He nodded. "You never know what may shed a little light on a case like this."

"I wonder why the killer stabbed Connor if the second blow killed him. What would be the point of that?"

George puffed a breath between my hands, gave them a rub,

and returned them to me perfectly toasty. "To ensure that he was indeed dead?" he suggested. "To throw off the investigators? Or perhaps because he truly hated Connor. For all we know there was a second person who stabbed him. One who didn't realize Connor was already dead."

"Two killers. I hadn't thought of that."

"He had enough callers yesterday."

"Now we can add the Higgins brothers to the list. They didn't seem the type to be above bashing Connor in the head. Or stabbing him."

"You think they're responsible for the damage at Mr. Bainbridge's office?"

"They as much as told us they were."

His brow furrowed as he mulled over this new detail. "I'll have to pass that bit of information along to Delaney."

I nodded and took a glance at the window. Wiping away the fog my breath made on the glass, I realized we were still in the neighborhood of Mayfair. "Are we not going home?"

"I was hoping you wouldn't mind if we made a stop along the way."

"And where might that be?"

"If your brother were well and truly out of the woods, I'd say we should go and book passage on the next ship to France, but since that's not exactly the case, I think we should talk to another suspect." He raised a brow. "Are you willing to visit Mr. Bainbridge?"

"Indeed. I've been wondering about him. Do you know he and Mr. Connor came to blows at one time? Willa told me about it."

George looked surprised so I told him the story. "To me, that makes Mr. Bainbridge a likely candidate as the person Connor was fighting in his office."

He grinned. "Assuming it all happened the way we surmise."

"Yes. I suppose that isn't a definite thing. What about the state of the room? Didn't it look like the culprit was searching for something?"

"Possibly, but the whole mess in the room might have been staged."

"That's what Delaney said." I slipped my chilled fingers under my legs. George pulled my right hand out and rubbed it between his own again. I eagerly gave him the left.

"Did Mrs. Connor explain why she returned home during the party yesterday?" he asked.

"What makes you think I asked her?"

His look of disdain was answer enough.

"She said she came back to convince Connor to join the celebration. When he didn't answer her knock, she returned to Harleigh House."

"Do you believe her?"

"I think I do. She's always eager to please, so going home to coax Connor into some revelry sounds reasonable. But because she's also quite timid, I'm not at all surprised she gave up when he didn't answer the door. She said she'd never enter his office without an invitation."

He sank into the padded back of the seat and stared upward. "I keep thinking about Graham's theory that Connor abused her. I'm certain the last thing he meant was to draw suspicion toward her, but I must admit I am now suspicious."

"If that's the only reason, you ought not to be. Plenty of husbands are brutes. Some wives are able to escape to their families. I don't believe Willa had that option, but those with nowhere to go rarely murder the husbands no matter how many people feel they ought to."

George heaved a sigh. "I've been feeling guilty for suspecting her, so I hope the killer turns out to be Bainbridge or some other business associate who'd been cheated one time too many."

"We did see Mr. Bainbridge pay a call on Connor at about the right time. And he did slip out of the house without answering the constable's questions." I glanced out the window. "We're very near his house now. What do you plan to ask him, and why should he answer our questions?"

"As Alonzo's legal representative, it's hardly strange that I might have some questions for the man. He doesn't have to answer them, but I was hoping, as a friend of your mother, he will."

We were about to find out as the carriage had come to a stop in front of the Bainbridge home, one of the largest on Park Lane. We left Jack to walk the horses again and rang the bell. A tall, imposing footman answered. Upon stating our business, he left us in a small, and blessedly warm, receiving room while he found out if the master was at home. I took a seat while George stood before the blazing hearth.

"Do you suppose he'll see us?" I asked. When George didn't answer, I glanced over to see him leaning against the mantel, holding up a hand for me to stay quiet. I quickly met him there and understood the need for silence. Apparently, Bainbridge was in the next room and this fireplace serviced both. We could hear him speaking with the footman, though discerning what they said was another matter. A female voice spoke. Then we heard footsteps.

George nodded to the seating area and we both scurried over and took our seats as the door opened and Mr. Bainbridge entered. He was a distinguished-looking man of about fifty-some years, average height, relaxed posture, and a slightly receding hairline. What remained was a dark blond with no suggestion of gray. He stopped in his tracks about two steps into the room and gawked at me, his moustache twitching.

"Lady Frances. I-I didn't realize you were here, too." Bainbridge had a deep, strong voice an orator might envy, with the occasional American vowel creeping into his British speech. He must have emigrated at an older age than Connor.

"It's Lady Harleigh," I said, coming to my feet along with George, who gave me an odd look. That's right, I was married again. I let out a nervous laugh. "Forgive me, I'm actually Mrs. Hazelton, now."

Mr. Bainbridge gave me a rueful grin and shook his head as he stepped forward. "Of course you are. My apologies for having forgotten. I was at your wedding yesterday, after all. One would think I'd remember."

George held out a hand to the other man. "I'm not as concerned about your recollection of the event, sir, as I am about my wife's."

Bainbridge chuckled and shook his hand. He and I exchanged nods. "How can I be of service," he said, perching on the edge of a chair facing ours.

We took our seats and George explained that he represented Alonzo in the matter of James Connor's death.

Bainbridge frowned. "I thought Mr. Price had been released already?"

"Did you?" George raised his brows. "How did you hear of that?"

"That inspector came around this morning to take my statement. He mentioned it."

"Ah, I'm glad Delaney came by. Yes, Mr. Price has been released, but until the culprit is in custody, he is still a suspect in this crime. As his legal counsel, it's my job to gather all the evidence in the matter. At some point, I'll be able to obtain your statement from the police, but since I'm already here, would you mind indulging me by answering a few questions? You may have observed something yesterday that you didn't realize was important." He shrugged. "And I might have questions Delaney didn't ask. This would save me coming back later."

Mr. Bainbridge glanced back and forth between the two of us as if unsure how to go on. "I suppose I can spare a few minutes. What can I tell you?"

"I understand you paid Connor a visit yesterday before the wedding. Do you mind telling me about that?"

Bainbridge crossed his arms over his chest. "I assume you've heard about the incident at my office the other day?"

"The vandalism?"

Bainbridge nodded. "Connor was responsible for that. Hired a couple of local thugs who broke in and tore the place up."

"How do you know it was Connor?" I asked.

"He readily admitted it. There's a company we're both interested in acquiring here in England. That was Connor's way of telling me to back off. The purpose of my call yesterday was to tell him I had no intention of doing so. That's when he asked if I liked what his decorators had done to my office." He shrugged. "I took that as an admission of guilt."

Having met the Higgins brothers, it was easy to imagine what Mr. Bainbridge's office looked like when they were through.

"Did you argue?" George asked.

Bainbridge snorted. "Of course. One never has a normal conversation with Connor, one argues." He stopped and lowered his gaze. "Or one did, I mean."

"Not an easy man to do business with, I take it." George adopted a sympathetic tone.

"We were not even conducting business. That's the sort of man he was—get in his way and he'll push you down—or try to."

George leaned forward in his seat, elbows on his knees. "But now Connor is out of your way."

"You mean as far as the acquisition?" Bainbridge shook his head. "A local consortium is my biggest competition in that endeavor. Not Connor. Regardless, after our conversation became heated, Connor rang for someone to show me out. The butler can attest that Connor was alive when I left."

"Glad to hear it." George's expression gave nothing away. But from my view, neither did Bainbridge's. He'd seemed a bit nervous when he first walked in, but now he spoke with confidence. "We both can attest to your presence at the church," George said.

He smiled. "I'm surprised you even took notice, considering the event was your wedding."

"We also noticed shortly after three o'clock you left the reception and paid a call at the Connor home," George added. "What was that about?"

"I left my walking stick there that morning. At least I believe I did. I didn't miss it until I was leaving for the church. Since Connor was next door to the reception, I thought I'd check."

"Did you find it," I asked, suspecting the answer.

He shrugged. "I knocked at his office door. No one responded. I assumed if he wasn't working and he wasn't at the wedding, he must be away from home."

So the walking stick the police took was likely Bainbridge's. I recalled seeing him return to Harleigh House rather quickly. If Connor hadn't answered at his knock, as he hadn't answered when Willa knocked, there was a chance he was already dead. There was one more thing I wanted to ask Bainbridge.

"Mr. Bainbridge, I believe you left the church along with the rest of us, but you were perhaps twenty minutes or so behind us in arriving at Harleigh House. Did you have a stop to make?"

"I did," he said, though the words sounded more as if he thought my suggestion a good idea rather than an honest answer. I noticed his hand had crept to his tie as if to straighten it.

"Where did you go?" George asked.

"I, ah, came back here."

"Can anyone attest to that?"

"No, no. I doubt anyone saw me."

"Indeed?" George leaned back with an expression of surprise. "Not your butler, or another servant? Surely you took your carriage. Your driver must be able to verify your whereabouts."

Bainbridge came abruptly to his feet. "I'm afraid that's all I have to say on the matter. If you'll excuse me, there's much I need to be doing."

We rose and followed him toward the door, but George did not let the subject drop. "It seems a simple matter of speaking to your driver. We won't keep him long."

Bainbridge's jaw tightened but he kept his voice calm. "No. I'm afraid that's impossible."

"But why?" I asked.

Suddenly the door leading to the foyer swung open. "That's enough from the two of you. I insist you stop persecuting this man this instant."

The female voice came as a surprise, but it was nothing compared to the shock I felt when Mother walked through the door.

"If you're looking for Mr. Bainbridge's alibi, here I am. He was with me yesterday."

Chapter Twelve

Three of us stood in stunned silence until Mother snatched me by the arm and marched me out the front door and down the walk to our carriage. George lingered in the house long enough to collect our coats. I had to give him credit for joining us in the carriage at all since I'm certain Mother's frigid welcome made him consider braving the elements with our driver. He settled himself in the rear-facing seat while we wrangled our coats on, and Jack guided the carriage into the street. Hugging her coat to her, Mother finally broke the silence.

"I don't know what you two thought you were accomplishing with that—that inquisition you were conducting back there, but you were terribly rude to Mr. Bainbridge."

Her attack finally broke through my shock at finding her at his home. Oh, no, no, no! We were not in the wrong here. "What we were doing was looking out for Alonzo's interest, or would you prefer that he rot in prison?"

"Perhaps we can better discuss this at home," George suggested.

I let out a huff. "Are you quite serious? My father is at home."

"We'll have this out now," Mother agreed. "And don't drag Alonzo into it."

George squeezed himself into the corner.

"Alonzo is the reason for our interview. If the killer isn't found, he may face an assize. We must gather all the facts and do so quickly."

"In other words, you must find an innocent man and accuse him of this crime, is that it?" She glared at George. "What kind of lawyer are you?"

Poor George. I drew her attention back to myself. "They're called solicitors here. And we accused Mr. Bainbridge of nothing. As I said, we need to gather the facts, and he never gave a statement to the police."

"He did so this morning. And why is questioning him your responsibility?" Mother's voice rose as her face grew red. "What are you, some sort of detective?"

I glared at her. "You are avoiding the primary issue at hand. What were you doing with Mr. Bainbridge yesterday—between my wedding and the reception, of all times?"

She raised a perfectly arched brow. "What are you implying?"

I heard George groan across the carriage and ignored him. "I wouldn't have to imply anything if you'd simply answer the question. And you might want to lower your voice or everyone on the street will hear you."

"It's February and it's freezing." She waved a hand at the window. "There's no one on the street."

"I wish I were on the street," George muttered.

Tears stung my eyes. I took a breath to steady my voice. "You must answer me, Mother. Are you and Mr. Bainbridge conducting an illicit affair?"

She gasped. "How dare you?" She pounced on George. "Did you hear what your wife asked me? Have you no control of her?"

George reached up and knocked on the roof of the carriage. "What are you doing?" I asked as the vehicle rolled to a stop.

"I'm getting out. It's clear you both need to have this conversation, but I beg that you excuse me." He opened the door and jumped down before the carriage had stopped completely, and before I managed to form a reply. "I'll meet you at home," he said, then slammed the door. Within seconds we were rolling again.

I blew out a furious breath. "Now see what you've done."

"You were the one who brought sex into the conversation."

I gasped. I had no idea that word was in Mother's vocabulary. "Well, if it's not that, what is it?"

"We are friends, that's all."

"Does Frankie know?"

She spread her hands as if she had no idea. "I've made no secret of our friendship. Back in New York, Mr. Bainbridge and I are both left to our own devices. Franklin is always working, or so he says. Mrs. Bainbridge travels the world looking for her place in society—any society that will accept her. She's tried establishing herself in San Francisco, then left her husband behind while she went to Boston, then on to New York. When he followed her there, she moved to Paris. It's almost as if she's running from the man." She waved her hand with a flourish. "Because of our spouses, we found ourselves attending the same events alone so frequently, we began attending together."

My heartbeat slowed from its wild pounding. Perhaps this wasn't as bad as I'd thought. "Then he's more of an escort than a friend."

"No." She set her jaw. "He's been a good friend to me and I hope I have been one to him."

"Let me ask a more specific question. Does Frankie know you were with Mr. Bainbridge yesterday?"

She glanced down at her hands. "He does not. When we arrived at Harleigh House, I told your father I needed a moment to collect myself, but in truth, I needed a moment with a friend. After your wedding, I was feeling blue at the loss of my daughter."

"The loss of your daughter?"

She looked at me as if I were an idiot. "I mean you."

"I assumed as much, but I was wed yesterday, not buried."

"It's still a loss."

Was she serious? "You married me off ten years ago and sent me to live on another continent. I don't recall you being anything but gleeful at the time. Why is my marriage to George cause for such despondency?"

"I'm not sure." She looked down to watch her fingers fluff the fur trim of her gloves. "Perhaps because the four of us were having such a lovely time together—you, Rose, Hetty, and I." She lifted her gaze to meet mine. "It was sad to see it come to an end."

Mother and I definitely took different views on our living situation for the past few months.

"You have a new life. Hetty has Gilliam." She raised her hands as if helpless. "What do I have to go back to, I ask you?"

"You have Frankie."

"Do I?" Her words were tiny chips of ice.

The carriage had stopped. I looked out the window to see we'd arrived at home. I touched Mother's hand before she could stir herself and tapped on the hatch in the ceiling. It opened and Jack peered down at me. "Please be so kind as to take us around the block," I said. "Perhaps two blocks."

"Yes, ma'am."

"Why did you do that?" Mother asked as soon as the hatch closed again.

"We're not finished here, and I don't think it's a conversation we should have where Frankie might overhear."

She sighed, but said nothing. With a jerk, we were moving once more. "The two of you are no longer starting out in life," I said, choosing my words carefully. "Can't you suggest he work less these days, so you can spend more time together?" I leaned back to put a little space between us. This was something I'd suggested before and nearly had my head bitten off.

She scoffed. "You think he's working, do you?"

Now, I was confused. "You said he was working."

"I said that's what he *tells me* he's doing and I don't believe him for a minute."

"Then what do you believe he's doing?"

"It's obvious. Your father is having an affair."

I nearly laughed out loud. Of all the possible activities my father might have indulged in without my mother's knowledge, dallying with another woman never would have made my list. "That's impossible. Frankie would never betray you like that."

Nothing could have prepared me for the look of utter outrage in her eyes. I almost expected her to growl. "Well, I. Like. That." She nearly spat the words in my face, clearly indicating that she did *not* like that. "You would believe it of me, but not your father."

I gaped, still confused.

"Not ten minutes ago you accused me of betraying your father with Mr. Bainbridge."

Dear heavens! I had, hadn't I? "In my defense," I began, "you rather presented me with a situation."

"One you completely misinterpreted to my detriment. Yet, you can't conceive that your father could act in the same manner." She let out a tsk and crossed her arms.

How had this conversation become so deranged? There was nothing else to do. "Please accept my apology, Mother. I reacted without due consideration. Of course, you'd never stray from Frankie. Any more than he'd stray from you."

"That's where you're mistaken, dear. The father you believe can do no wrong has indeed strayed."

Arguing was futile. "What makes you think so?"

"The fact that he's never home. He claims to be working, but his so-called work days can run to eight or nine o'clock at night. Even I know the stock market is not open that late."

I don't claim much familiarity with my father's business, but somehow, I doubted trading on the market involved nothing more than handing bids or bills of sale back and forth. From speaking with Aunt Hetty, I knew my father invested in budding new companies. Surely, that took some research, perhaps meetings, and, sadly, that's where my imagination let me down.

The pain in my mother's eyes told me I had better tread carefully. "He does come home every night, doesn't he?"

"Eventually."

"Has he ever come home smelling of another woman's perfume?"

She pulled a handkerchief from her sleeve and dabbed her eyes. "Once."

I froze. Heavens! I hadn't been prepared for that answer. "When?"

"The night before I sailed to England for Lily's wedding. It was all over his clothing."

"Did you ask him about it?"

"I couldn't. If I'd confronted him, I don't believe he'd lie to me. And I couldn't bear to hear the truth."

We sat quietly, while I digested this bit of information. My heart told me Frankie was not a philanderer as my late husband had been, but how well did I really know my father? Surely, Mother knew him better. Yes, I'd like to believe Frankie was blameless, but Rose likely thought the same about Reggie, and I certainly knew better. Mother's evidence was weak at best, but with little more evidence, I'd accused her of the same offense.

"I shouldn't have told you." She sniffed and blotted her eyes again. "I don't want you to lose respect or affection for your father. I thought sharing this secret would make me feel better, but it doesn't."

"You must speak with him about it," I said.

"Why, so he can relieve his guilty conscience, then divorce me for his shameless woman?"

"So, he can have an opportunity to explain himself. It may all be perfectly innocent." I held up a hand to stop her protest. "I don't know how, but it's possible."

Her expression was incredulous—and disappointed. "Can you do no better than that?"

"He works with Alonzo. Do you really believe he'd dally with another woman right under his own son's nose?"

That made an impression. "I'd forgotten about Alonzo."

"If Frankie were up to something nefarious, you'd have seen a change in Lon. He would have lost all respect for his father. Truly, Mother, you must speak with Frankie about this. I'm certain there's a reasonable explanation. You'll both laugh and put it behind you."

I saw a glint of hope in her eyes before she turned away. "Goodness, we're home again."

I hadn't noticed that the carriage had stopped. "Let's go in. You can talk to Frankie now."

"Now?" She stared at me, aghast. "No, no. I must collect myself first. I'm far too emotional right now. What time is it?"

As I had no timepiece, I had to guess. "It must be coming on three o'clock."

"Excellent. Today is Mrs. Hodges's 'at home' day and I've been meaning to call on her. Come with me."

She was too upset to speak with Frankie, but not too upset

to visit relative strangers? "Must we go now? The horses have been out all day."

"We'll walk," she said firmly. "Do come with me, Frances. It will be a distraction."

She didn't need a distraction. She needed to have a talk with her husband. The last thing I wanted to do was walk several blocks in the cold to drink weak tea and listen to gossip when my own home was merely a few yards away—where both heat and my new husband awaited.

Then I saw the look of desperation in her eyes. "Let me go in and tell George." We'd been around the block so many times, he must have arrived at home by now. I really thought marriage would have us seeing more of each other, but with my family around, it was turning out to be considerably less.

Indeed, George was at home. He met me in the entry hall and while I emptied my pockets of the paper scraps and piled them on the hall table, I briefly explained that Mother was not quite ready to face my father, and we were instead going to tea at the home of Mrs. Hodges. "Do not let Jarvis move or dispose of these," I said, indicating the scraps. "I don't want to lose them."

He agreed to guard them with his life and prompted me to ask Mother where and at what time she was in Mr. Bainbridge's company, which I did while we walked.

"Are we back to that again?" She slanted a glare at me from under the brim of her hat. "Why are you so determined to convict him?"

"I am doing no such thing. The wedding reception was a small gathering that took place across two connecting rooms. When guests are missing it's noticeable. Besides, I saw him walk in late. I simply need to know more about his alibi. And by the way, what did you tell the police about yours?"

"The same thing I told your father. I needed a moment to compose myself. I simply didn't mention Mr. Bainbridge was with me."

I resisted any comment about the propriety of her actions and simply asked, "How long were you together? And where were you?"

"There's some sort of sitting room at the back of the house, past the dining room. Mr. Bainbridge saw me head in that direction and followed me. It wasn't as if we'd planned a tryst. We spoke for perhaps fifteen or twenty minutes until I felt better, then I returned to the reception. Mr. Bainbridge left through a back door and walked around to the front of the house."

"For the sake of discretion, I suppose."

She lifted her chin. "Don't be cheeky."

The walk, much like our conversation, was cold but blessedly short—one block away on Chapel Street. And dry, thank heaven.

Once we were divested of our coats, the housemaid showed us to the dimly lit drawing room, packed with an overabundance of furnishings, from large, sturdy cabinets to wobbly, fragile-looking tables, one topped with a large birdcage covered with a fringed scarf. Half a dozen ladies awaited us, including Mrs. Hodges. I was acquainted with all of them, but wasn't particularly close to any. Most of the ladies were at least ten years older than me and had grown children, so I expected our conversation to consist mostly of their offspring. The fact that we were greeted with surprise and even a few gaping mouths reminded me that yesterday's activities made me something of a curiosity, and Mother only slightly less so. I feared we were in for a rocky half hour.

Mrs. Hodges had just handed me a cup of tea when it began. "Felicitations on your recent nuptials, Lady Harleigh." The matron seated to my left on the sofa, Constance Effington, leaned in so close to me we nearly clunked hats as she purred the words with a slow flutter of her gloved fingers.

"It was very recent, wasn't it?" Mrs. Hodges asked from across the low tea table. "Are you not Mrs. Hazelton now?"

"Yesterday," was all I managed before the lady to my right, Althea Jefferies, broke in. "She'll always be Lady Harleigh. Won't you, my dear? It's a courtesy title."

I smiled. "I'll use it when the occasion calls for such formality. Otherwise, I am very happy to be Mrs. Hazelton." Bother, that came out wrong. But why the questions? These women were British, for heaven's sake. Didn't they all know how titles worked?

"But if you were married yesterday, why are you still in town? Are you not taking a wedding trip?" Althea, a rather pinched-faced, gossipy woman, stared at me with rounded dark eyes beneath a cloud of dark fringe. She didn't fool me a bit. I was certain she already knew most of the story and I had no intention of filling in the details.

Mother had other ideas. "Haven't you heard? Mr. Connor was murdered yesterday. His house is next door to Harleigh House, where we held the reception."

All eyes focused on her. If she hadn't been one sofa's length away from me, I'd have given her a nudge. A sharp one.

"It was quite the to-do," she continued. "The police arrived, of course, but for some perfectly ridiculous reason, they arrested my son."

The intake of breath ought to have drained the room of oxygen.

"You poor dear!" Constance cooed to Mother, then turned to me. "Well, with your brother under arrest, of course you had to stay and comfort your mother."

"Goodness no." Mother waved a biscuit in the air, dismissing any suggestion of my providing comfort. "She and Hazelton are solving the crime."

I failed to repress a nervous titter. This was the end. I could not let Mother out in public again. If I hadn't been with her for the last hour, I'd have thought she was tipsy. Six pairs of eyes stared at me in anticipation. "That's not entirely correct. Hazelton is providing legal counsel to my brother, who, by the way, has been released. Clearly, the police realized their mistake."

"But how did they make such a mistake in the first place?" Constance asked.

"It was Alonzo and Miss Connor who discovered the body, right there in his office." Mother tsked and took another sip of her tea while two of the ladies visibly blanched. The hypocrites. They'd be dining on this story all week. I heaved a sigh when they all turned to me for confirmation.

With a shrug, I nodded.

"But what were they doing together?" Althea simply would not let this go. Did no one chat about the weather any longer?

"Alonzo wished to speak with Mr. Connor, and Miss Connor was kind enough to escort him. It was all very tragic." I lowered my head in respect for the deceased Mr. Connor and in the hope that these kindly ladies would relinquish this topic for good.

Mother deflated my hopes. "I didn't approve, but he wanted to ask Mr. Connor's permission to call on his daughter."

"But haven't you heard, dear, her betrothal to Viscount Fitzwalter is all but announced." Alice Clark gazed in sympathy at Mother. "In my day, a young lady made it clear to a potential suitor when she was no longer available."

"Perhaps you were misinformed, Alice," Althea countered. "Fitzwalter had his eye on her to be sure, but they may not have come to a settlement." She turned away from Alice to give us all a knowing glance. "I'd expect his family to demand a large dowry."

"I believe the marquis is in dire need of it." The eldest woman in the room, Lady Ruth, was not one to mince words. She smiled with a touch of devilment. "If you know what I mean."

We all knew what she meant. Heavens, the bird in the covered cage probably knew what she meant. This might be the most mean-spirited group of women I'd ever visited. What happened to saying nothing when one had nothing nice to say?

"I can't imagine anyone better able to provide such a dowry as Mr. Connor, do you?" Alice's brows shot up in question.

"Perhaps, but the Connors aren't even British." Constance gave me an apologetic glance. "I mean no offense, Mrs. Hazelton, but the Fitzwalter bloodlines go back simply ages and the family are quite proud of that fact. I'd be very much surprised if they didn't demand their son marry a young lady with an equally illustrious pedigree."

"That may have been their preference"—Lady Ruth gestured with her cup—"but such a pedigree doesn't always come with an illustrious bank account." The room erupted in titters.

"My understanding is that the young lady in question was not entirely in favor of the match," I said. "Perhaps she had a change of heart."

"One's heart is rarely consulted in matters such as these. I too have some acquaintance with the Connors, and I know Madeline and her stepmother were planning on a lively social season." Alice slipped her hand up to her mouth and leaned closer. "Well, I shouldn't speak ill of the dead, but we both know Mr. Connor ruled that household. Once he made a decision, the Connor ladies jumped. But in this case, a match was the ultimate goal for all concerned, so the ladies can have no real cause for complaint."

Except that one had a dead husband and the other a dead father. No, no cause at all.

I took a surreptitious glance at the clock to see that twenty minutes had passed and we could safely leave without appearing rude. It had been a long time since I'd socialized with a group of such unpleasant women. I'm not sure if it was their influence, but a rather cruel thought passed through my mind when Alice mentioned Connor's demanding nature. With him gone, the Connor ladies wouldn't have to jump any longer.

Chapter Thirteen

It may have been the longest day of my life. I felt as though I had pried into the personal secrets of far too many people—Graham, Willa, Madeline, Connor himself, and worst of all, my mother. It didn't matter that all the details were freely given, I felt like a voyeur, though that may have been the result of Mrs. Hodges's "at home." What I needed was a long soak in a tub. Those women were worse than the reporters who wrote the scandal sheets.

It was comforting to be home at last. I'd taken Mother to Aunt Hetty's door, stayed long enough to learn that Alonzo was indeed safely back, then escaped as quickly as possible to my own home, where Jarvis greeted me and took my coat. I asked him to send Bridget up to me, then made for the peace and quiet of my dressing room-cum-boudoir, sinking gratefully into the slipper chair at the dressing table. The late afternoon sun shone through the ornamental window high in the wall, making dancing patterns on the wood floor as I bent to loosen the laces of my boots.

I'd found this room by accident this morning. I'd assumed it was a typical dressing room, with cabinets and drawers to store clothing and barely enough room to change. Little did I know, George had broken through the wall to the room next door, then divided it up into a dressing room, a small sitting area where I could share tea with friends or read a book, and as the pièce de résistance—a bath. The dressing room that was original to the house was on the other side of the master's chambers and designed for George's use. That one was essentially cabinets and drawers and George said it suited his purposes.

With a soft knock, Bridget pushed through the door from the hall and stepped inside. "Are you ready to dress for dinner, my lady?"

"Dinner? I'd hoped for a bath, or at least to put on a dressing gown and read for a while first. Isn't it too early for dinner?"

Her usually pleasant features transformed into a mask of disapproval. "If you're asking my opinion, I'd say yes. But Mr. Jarvis informed me that dinner would be served at six and Mr. Hazelton usually enjoys a glass of madeira or some such an hour before." She bobbed her head on the last word for emphasis.

With a groan, I kicked off my boots and stood to allow her to unfasten my gown. "I'll have to speak with Hazelton about this schedule. If we eat at six, when does the staff eat—five? That seems rather early."

"Mr. Jarvis agrees with you on that point, ma'am." Bridget helped me out of my bodice and shook it out. "We don't eat until half past seven."

Though her expression remained neutral, she somehow managed to make half past seven sound terribly inconvenient.

"I take it that's late?"

"It's quite late, ma'am, for most of the staff. The butler, the valet, and I are up as late as you are, but the cook, the kitchen girl, and the maid are abed by ten so they can rise at five. If you and Mr. Hazelton are going out for the evening, Blakey and I might miss dinner altogether while we get you ready."

"I'll speak to Hazelton," I said, working on the buttons at the waistband of my skirt. "I should already have had a conversation with Mr. Jarvis about the schedule and the running of the household. I've been remiss in my duties."

I stepped out of the skirt and Bridget swept it up with a swoosh. "You've been rather busy all day, and it's not as if you were even supposed to be here."

We met each other's eyes and our faces drooped into twin pouts. "No, we're supposed to be in Cannes." I sighed and pulled myself together.

Bridget held up a gown for my inspection. "Will this do?"

The burgundy silk was a bit formal for dinner at home, but it was my first dinner—first dining room dinner, that is, with my husband, and it had a very flattering neckline. "Yes, that's perfect."

I waited while she worked open the buttons. "Have you had any progress in your brother's case, ma'am?"

"I saw him when I dropped Mother off. Having him back at home is some progress, I suppose." She held the dress open about knee height, allowing me to step in and turn around for her to straighten and fasten it. "I'll have to speak to Hazelton about that, too. Alonzo is still under suspicion, but the police have other suspects to investigate now." I cast a glance over my shoulder as she worked the buttons up. "In other words, I don't know if it's safe for us to leave yet."

"Of course. You wouldn't want to leave your brother without any legal help, especially since he's American. He may not understand the ins and outs of our legal doings."

I recalled my father's attempts to bribe the police and readily agreed. "Yes, he does seem to require some guidance there." When she finished with the buttons, I seated myself at the dressing table. "How are you settling in here, Bridget?"

"Just fine, ma'am. I already knew everyone from living next door." She held up two pairs of slippers for my approval.

"Those pinch my toes," I said, indicating the pair in her right hand. She returned them to the shelf and brought me the others. "Mr. Hazelton's valet is good with shoes. I'll have him look at them. Maybe he can stretch them out some."

"That would be wonderful." I sat back while she neatened my hair. "Anyway, I'm holding on to the hope that we shall sail for France within the next day or two. I have great faith in Hazelton."

Our dinner conversation consisted of little more than the weather while Jarvis and Frederick, the footman, were serving. We made their work a bit less demanding by sitting at one end of the table built to seat a dozen rather than at either end. Once the final course of fruit and cheese was laid before us, we dismissed them and I was free to offer George a summary of the conversation I'd had in the carriage with Mother. And congratulate him on his timely escape.

"I fled the carriage for a reason, you know," he warned. "I'm not sure I want to hear this."

"You are part of this family now, so I'm afraid you have no choice. Besides, you should be relieved to hear Mother is not having an affair with Mr. Bainbridge, although she was the reason he was late for the reception."

"Hmm, I don't need to know what they were doing, but where were they?"

"In the back sitting room, talking." Upon seeing his look of skepticism, I made a dismissive gesture. "It sounded completely innocent."

He carved some slices of cheese from the block while I explained Mother's sense of loss upon our marriage and her friendship with Bainbridge.

"It does sound innocent enough. Is there a problem?"

"She'd rather attend society events with Frankie. She'd rather turn to him for comfort." I took a sip of wine. "She doesn't press him, however, because she believes he's having an affair."

"No."

I waited for him to elaborate, but he simply moved the slices of cheese to his plate. "No?" I prompted.

"No. It's impossible. Inconceivable. She doesn't truly believe that, does she?" George's incredulous expression was almost comical.

"It seems that she does. And though the very idea is upsetting, it is not that far-fetched." I still couldn't account for Frankie smelling of perfume.

He let out a snort. "It most certainly is. Your father would have to have taken leave of his senses to betray your mother."

After my experience with Reggie, it warmed me to know George considered fidelity an essential part of a marriage. I still held hope that my father did, too. "Do you really think so?"

"Indeed, I do." He cut a clump of grapes from the bowl. "If your mother knew for certain your father had cheated, she'd strip him of every cent he had, tear him limb from limb, and leave nothing for the buzzards to find." He popped a grape in his mouth while I stared open-mouthed. "Any man would be insane to cross Daisy Price. Your father is not insane."

"She's quite intimidated you, hasn't she?"

He moved through a series of shrugs, head jerks, and upward glances before finally nodding and eating another grape.

"She's only flesh and blood, George."

He gave me a skeptical look, so I picked up a grape from my own plate and threw it at him. He caught it and laughed. The rascal. "Have you been teasing me?" I asked.

He held up his finger and thumb barely a smidgen apart. "A tiny bit."

"But surely you can understand that the thought of Frankie forsaking her for someone else hurts."

"Of course I do, but I also believe your mother would use revenge to salve her wounds once the initial pain had dissipated. Let us hope she's wrong and your father is blameless. I'd rather not witness the carnage."

Jarvis crept into the room, saving me a reply. Aunt Hetty and Gilliam had come to call.

"Bring them in, Jarvis." George turned to me. "Perhaps they'd like to join us, or maybe they'd prefer an after-dinner brandy."

"Chances are they haven't yet dined." That reminded me I still had to speak with him about the dinner hour, but the arrival of Hetty and Gilliam meant that would have to wait.

They swept into the room with apologies for disturbing our meal. "Frances, what is all that shredded paper on your hall table?" Hetty asked.

I'd forgotten all about the scraps of paper I'd collected from Connor's office too. This truly had been a long day. I explained my intention to reconstruct whatever the documents were. "I left them there when I went with Mother to pay a call and completely forgot about them."

Hetty's eyes grew round with interest. "Why not let me give it a try? I'm very good with puzzles."

"I've no objection. You're more likely to understand any business documentation anyway, but do let us know once you have it pieced together."

"Of course. Gilliam has a performance tonight at the theater, so I can start on it straightaway. However, that also means he must leave soon and I thought you'd like a report of the wedding guests' statements."

They seated themselves across from us when Frederick returned with two more place settings. Gilliam dug right into the Stilton while Hetty accepted a glass of wine. When the footman left us, I leaned forward eagerly. "Were you able to learn anything of interest from the statements, Gilliam?"

He brushed crumbs of cheese from his moustache with his napkin. "I learned Mr. Connor was universally disliked, but very little else. Highly disappointing, I'm afraid. No one confessed nor made any accusations. Not as dramatic as I might have wished."

"I'm afraid that's more common in theatricals," George said.

"Indeed." Gilliam produced notes from his waistcoat pocket and gave us the gist of each of the guests' statements, most of which was to be expected. People arrived around the same time, mingled and drank, then sat down to luncheon. Afterward, they returned to the drawing room to mingle and drink again.

While George examined the notes, Gilliam summarized. "Several guests went missing for a time, including Mrs. Price, Mrs. Connor, Viscount Fitzwalter, Mr. Bainbridge, Lord Harleigh, and of course, your brother and Miss Connor. With the exception of Mrs. Connor and Mr. Bainbridge, neither of whom gave a statement, each of them explained their absence. I assume Constable Timmons will check with the staff to confirm their statements."

I let my gaze drift off while I considered our information. Because of Mother's confession, we knew Bainbridge was with her. We already knew Graham and Mrs. Connor were together when they left the party, though I still had suspicions about Willa's visit to her home. Bainbridge's, too, for that matter. Who else had Gilliam mentioned?

"What was Fitzwalter's reason?" I asked.

"He said he felt ill before luncheon began," Hetty said. "He spent that time in the billiards room. I hadn't even noticed him missing."

I wondered if his absence was really due to my changing the place cards rather than any illness. Had he been angry that Madeline was seated with Alonzo and gone off to sulk?

George and I exchanged a glance. The timing was interesting, but would Fitzwalter have had a motive for Connor's murder? That called for further consideration.

"Did anyone see him in the billiards room?" George asked.

"He said one of Lord Harleigh's servants attended him," Gilliam said. "I'm sure Constable Timmons will check up on that."

The clock in the hall chimed the hour and Gilliam tucked his notes back into his pocket. "I'm afraid I must be on my way." We all came to our feet and George and I thanked them for coming.

"Sorry I wasn't more help." Gilliam looked genuinely disappointed. "There is one more thing. Your father brought up an interesting point about Connor's business associates."

"I agree," George said. "But I'm not sure we are best suited to review Connor's business transactions."

"I'll speak with Franklin," Hetty said. "Perhaps he has some idea of how to go about it."

When Hetty and Gilliam took their leave, Hetty tucked the paper scraps into her pockets, and George and I retired to the drawing room for a cup of tea, only to find Alonzo staring out the window at the now dark garden.

I pulled up short when I saw him. "Lon, how did you get in here?" I heard George groan quietly behind me.

When Alonzo faced me, his expression was glum. I thought about what he'd been through the past two days and felt selfish about my desire to be alone with George after Alonzo had suffered so much.

"Aunt Hetty told me about the back path from her house to yours." Alonzo pushed away from the window and strode up to us, his heels making staccato strikes on the hardwood alongside the carpet. "She won't see me, Franny. The butler turned me away at the door."

There was no need to ask who "she" was. I was surprised he'd found time to pay a call on her already. George blew out a breath and wandered over to a cabinet on the far side of the room that I happened to know held a nice claret. Apparently, it was to be wine instead of tea this evening.

While he poured our libation, I swept my brother over to one of the chairs by the fireplace. "She is mourning the loss of her father, Lon. I saw her this morning and it took some work to convince her to leave her room and join her mother for tea. She's certainly not up to entertaining guests."

He scowled, but said nothing.

"I was meant to tell you to give her a day or two before you called." I accepted a glass of claret from George. "Unfortunately, I was enjoined to pay a call with Mother instead. If it's any consolation, Madeline has refused to see Fitzwalter, too."

"She can't stand Fitzwalter. She told me so herself," he grumbled. "It was her father who pursued the match."

Madeline had given me no reason to believe she disliked Fitzwalter, but I allowed Lon's exaggeration to pass. "Then you should be satisfied that you no longer have him for competition," I said. "You must give her a little time. I'm sorry to put this so bluntly, but she doesn't need you right now, she needs her stepmother." I took a sip of the wine and watched for his reaction.

"I suppose you are right, but I'm worried about her. I fear that in her grief, she will let herself become ill. She's more delicate than you are, Franny."

Odd. She seemed a healthy, hearty young woman to me. I

glanced at George, who sent me a look that said he too was confused by Lon's characterization of Madeline. "I'm afraid you will simply have to worry since she has asked to be left alone."

He gave me a close look. "What if she's so upset, she doesn't know what she wants?"

I heard a choking sound from George but paid him no heed. "Now you are simply mistaking your wishes for hers," I said in a warning tone.

"She's right, Lon." I jumped as my father's voice rang out from the entry hall. I hadn't even heard the bell. Frederick's guilty face peered over Frankie's shoulder. "I was collecting the evening papers, ma'am, and saw Mr. Price coming up the walk."

George stood and gestured Frankie into the room. "Please, join us, Mr. Price. Would you care for a glass of claret?"

Frankie accepted and seated himself next to Alonzo. "I take it your sister is trying to talk you out of visiting Miss Connor," he said.

"Miss Connor made the request herself," I said. "But Alonzo doesn't seem to think she knows her own mind."

Frankie chuckled as he took the glass George offered. "If a woman tells you what she wants, you should do her the honor of believing her."

"Something else you should consider is that you are still under suspicion in the murder of Mr. Connor." Apparently, George did want to take part in this conversation after all. "Since the police consider your affection for Miss Connor as your motive, you ought to stay as far away from her as possible. At least for now."

Alonzo raised his hands in surrender. "Fine, I will leave her alone, but will you call on her tomorrow, Franny? To ease my mind?"

I gave his request some thought. I knew when Madeline said she didn't want to see anyone, she meant Alonzo and Fitzwalter, but my company might be wearing, too. "I'll pay a call on Willa. If Madeline wishes to join us, she will, but if not, her stepmother can tell me how she fares. Will that do?"

He scowled. "I suppose it will have to."

Frankie slapped him on the leg. "Come with me tomorrow instead. I have a project that might keep you from moping about the house all day."

"What will you be doing?" I asked. From his buoyant mood, I suspected Mother had not had that conversation with him yet.

"While your mother and I were at the police precinct waiting for Lon, I happened to see Constable Timmons, the young man who conducted the interviews of the guests last night."

"He's also the man who arrested me," Lon said.

"Then this will give him a chance to make up for that lapse in judgment." Frankie punctuated the last word with a nod. "As I was saying, one thing led to another, and we started discussing Connor's business associates and how he, Timmons that is, was expected to make heads or tails of Connor's files."

"I'm glad to hear it." George raised a brow in interest.

"The man cheated anyone who came within fifty feet of him. Chances are good that at least half the people he conducted business with had a motive to murder him. We have an appointment with his agent to take a look at Connor's latest contracts."

"We? How did you manage to secure an invitation?"

Frankie smiled. "The lad's completely out of his depth. Couldn't even gain an appointment with the agent until I intervened. Since Inspector Delaney is expecting him to find subtle irregularities in Connor's business transactions, the fellow's damn grateful I'm willing to lend a hand."

Speaking of irregularities. "I can't believe Delaney agreed to this arrangement."

Frankie's moustache twitched. "We're hoping he doesn't find out. Timmons can take the credit if we turn up anything."

"He's your father, all right." George's eyes sparkled with amusement.

Hard to argue with that, but I shuddered to think of Delaney's reaction if he learned of my father's involvement.

Frankie looked unconcerned. "As I said, you should come with me, Lon."

George spoke up first. "Why don't I come with you instead, Mr. Price? Alonzo is still a suspect. If you bring him along, you may both be off the case."

Frankie accepted the change of plan. The men agreed upon a time and Frankie and Alonzo left for Hetty's house and their own rooms. After George and I saw them off, we returned to the drawing room and our glasses of claret. We both relaxed on the sofa. "It seems that Mother hasn't spoken to Frankie yet about his alleged affair."

"That would be a difficult conversation to initiate," he said.

I put my hand to his cheek and looked into his eyes. "Tell me I'll never have to worry about having such a conversation with you."

"You won't, and I'll take the same promise from you, if you please."

"You have it." I slid closer and rested my head against his shoulder. "Do you think Frankie's search will produce any results?"

"It's not a bad idea. Worth looking into, but if Connor were up to any nefarious business, he'd have kept any evidence of it in the files at his home office, rather than with his agent. Perhaps I can maneuver the two investigators in that direction."

"Are you planning to tell Delaney about the blood on Connor's desk?"

"Absolutely. With any luck I can see him in the morning before I go off with your father." His fingers worked their way into my hair.

"Don't forget to tell him about the Higgins brothers."

"Remind me tomorrow," he murmured into my ear. "I'd rather not think about them tonight."

Chapter Fourteen

❱❲

If newlywed couples were meant to be granted a period of time only to themselves, clearly our families were unfamiliar with that school of thought. George's sister, Fiona, stopped by as we were finishing breakfast the following morning. George was about to leave to call on Delaney before joining my father on his quest for unsavory business deals, but I insisted she help herself to eggs and sausages and join us at the table.

"Will you ever be able to leave for your wedding trip?" she asked between bites. "Has Delaney not declared your brother innocent yet?"

"Not quite yet, Fi," George said, rising to his feet. "My hope is that we'll have that declaration within the next day or so and Frances and I can still get away." He planted a kiss on the top of my head. "But for now, I'm off to see Delaney."

"Don't forget we are to call on the photographer this afternoon."

"I remember." He gave his sister a peck on the cheek and departed. I let out a sigh. "I have a feeling George and I shall be disappointed in that hope."

Fiona poured herself some tea. "Is the case not coming along well?"

"It doesn't seem to be going anywhere." I shrugged. "It has only been one day. Perhaps Delaney's investigation has produced some results." I brightened at the thought. "What brings you here today?"

"Your welfare. I had hoped the police would have their man by now and you and my brother would be crossing the channel to the sunnier skies of France, but since that is not the case, I thought you could use some cheering up."

Dear Fi. "How kind of you. Did you have anything in particular in mind?"

"The air is brisk but the streets are dry. Perhaps a turn around Hyde Park? Or a visit to the shops if you like. I am always eager for a new hat."

That reminded me of a visit I did have to make. "I'm afraid the shops will not do for me today, but if you don't mind, I have instructions to call on the Connor ladies. I've already made a condolence call and I hate to appear to be pestering them in their time of grief. If you come with me, I can say that I'm just along with you."

Fiona narrowed her eyes. "That's hardly likely to cheer you. And did you say you have *instructions* to call on them? Who would be so presumptuous?"

"Presumptuous?" I peered across the table at her. "Have you never met my family? The Demandersons? Lovely people, but so many expectations."

"Your mother can't have asked it of you."

I shook my head. "My brother is quite carried away with Madeline Connor and asked me to confirm with my own eyes that she is not fading away from her grief." I stopped myself abruptly. "That was unkind. I don't mean to call her grief into question. She's suffered a terrible loss. But Alonzo has an image of her as a sort of fragile little flower. I find that rather infuriating."

Fiona studied me over the rim of her teacup. "You may speak freely to me and fear no judgment. I am well aware you bear Miss Connor no ill will, but I sense having much of your family nearby has been a bit wearing."

I sighed. "I love them, but they seem to be here all the time."

"I understand completely. I was delighted to welcome my brother Colin when he came to visit and happy to see the back of him four days later when he left for Risings to visit my eldest brother."

"That's it exactly. I wish George and I had more time to ourselves, but instead, he is investigating and I am checking on Miss Connor for Alonzo."

She took another bite of her eggs and mulled the matter over. "Isn't Madeline to marry Fitzwalter?"

"I've no idea. Her father was in favor of the match but she was not. Since Mr. Connor is no longer with us, it remains to be seen if she'll marry him. Alonzo seems to think she was trapped. He hoped to rescue her."

"That's very interesting."

Her tone caught my attention. "Is it? What do you know of the matter?"

"Nothing of the Connors' side, but I've heard some talk. Lord Sudley has been pushing Fitzwalter to marry an heiress. The family is in need of a financial infusion. In spite of that, he was not at all in favor of Fitzwalter's choice of Miss Connor."

"I had heard he was rather a stickler about pedigree."

Fiona nodded and sipped her tea. "However, their financial situation may be worse than the marquis realizes. By all reports Fitzwalter enjoys a game of chance and has been living in quite a grand manner since he left Oxford. His debts on the betting books are impressive."

"By all reports?"

She shrugged. "Nash and his friends."

Fiona's husband was definitely a reliable source. "How could the marquis be ignorant of his son's debt? If his creditors were unable to collect from Fitzwalter, surely they'd call on the marquis himself and attempt to collect from the estate."

"I didn't ask Nash for details, but he suspects Sudley doesn't know the half of it. What's more, Connor offered to pay off Fitzwalter's debt and provide an enormous dowry for Madeline into the bargain."

How does such private information get out? "Fitzwalter would find that difficult to resist. From speaking to Madeline, it seemed both her father and Fitzwalter were on one page, and she on another."

"Now she can write the book herself." Fiona drained her cup and set it on the table. "In any event, I'd be happy to call on the ladies with you."

I did feel ridiculous calling on the Connors yet again and hoped I wasn't making a nuisance of myself. We arrived at their home and were shown into the drawing room. I was pleasantly surprised to see Madeline with Willa. Both ladies were dressed from head to toe in unrelieved black. "How are you, my dear?"

"Much better. Thank you." She did not look better. Her face was pale. She still had shadows under her lifeless eyes as if she hadn't slept in some time. There was something different in her air, but I couldn't identify exactly what it was.

Fiona expressed her condolences and tea was ordered. I inquired about funeral services.

"I haven't heard from the police yet," Willa said. "Apparently, the coroner was not quite finished with—whatever he is doing." We all shuddered at the thought of what the coroner might be doing. "So, I haven't been able to make any arrangements."

There was no polite response for that so we lapsed into talk of the miserable weather until a servant entered with the tea service. Madeline was seated closest, so she poured. That's when the difference in her registered with me. Her left hand looked as though it weighed a good five pounds more than yesterday due to the addition of the enormous emerald and diamond ring on her third finger.

Though I was struck speechless, Fiona had no such problem. "My, what a lovely ring," she said, reaching for the teacup Madeline passed to her. The girl snatched her hand back so quickly, it was fortunate Fiona had a good grip on the saucer or the delicate porcelain would have smashed to bits on the tea table.

Willa sent a scowl to her stepdaughter. "I thought you intended to put that away for now."

Madeline covered the ring with her right hand. "I'd forgotten I had it on."

I choked back a laugh. How was that possible? The girl could barely lift her hand.

With an air of resignation, Willa turned to us. "Daniel Fitzwalter paid a call earlier this morning, and, well, Madeline has accepted his offer of marriage. I'm not pleased by the timing of this event, but it is the match her father wanted for her, so I believe he'd approve."

I was stunned. "Fitzwalter called this morning?"

Willa pursed her lips. "As I said, his timing is in rather poor taste. Though Madeline accepted, we'll be keeping this to ourselves for the next several months, so I beg you ladies not to breathe a word."

Fiona agreed readily. I glanced at Madeline, whose eyes were downcast, watching her fingers twist the ring. She did not look like a happy bride-to-be. Two days ago, Willa stated that Madeline would put an end to any understanding she may have had with Fitzwalter. Yesterday, Madeline herself said she'd never marry him. Yet here she was—engaged and looking quite miserable. What was going on in her head?

Without taking my eyes off Madeline, I addressed Willa. "I

fully understand your desire to keep this news close for now, but I do believe Alonzo deserves to hear of it."

Madeline flinched at the mention of his name and she nodded without looking up. "You are right. He deserves to know."

I did not relish being the one to tell him.

We couldn't leave quickly enough. I didn't have to work very hard to feign a headache, and Fiona followed my lead, offering to take me home immediately, making our apologies, and nearly whisking me out of the house and into her waiting carriage. When we settled into the seats, Fiona gave me a sorrowful glance. "From the look of you, I fear your brother is going to be devastated." She patted my hand. "You are a good sister to worry for him."

"My concern is for myself," I said. "He will surely strangle me when he finds out what happened."

"You? The girl changed her mind. What have you to do with that?"

"He wanted to call on her yesterday and again this morning. I advised him to wait. Madeline was adamant that she didn't want to see either Alonzo or Fitzwalter until she came to terms with her grief. I insisted he respect her wishes. So did my father and George, but I doubt that will matter to Lon." I raised my hands palms up. "Meanwhile, Fitzwalter didn't respect her wishes, called on her, offered for her, and she accepted." I clapped my hands to my cheeks. "She told me less than a full day ago she wouldn't marry him. How could this have happened?"

Fiona let out a snort. "That ring may have had something to do with it."

"That ring!" I made a show of lifting my left hand with my right. "This little bauble? I forgot I had it on." I sniffed. "That's like saying she forgot she had a leg iron attached to her ankle."

"It must be a family heirloom," she mused. "He hasn't the

wherewithal for jewels like that." She let out a gasp. "I wonder if Lord and Lady Sudley know he's given her that ring."

"One would think they must. I'm sure they'd keep such valuable jewelry under lock and key. Unless Fitzwalter managed to break into his father's safe and steal away with it, Lord Sudley must have had a change of heart." I grimaced. "Rather like his future daughter-in-law."

"Still, it was terribly bad form to propose marriage right after her father was killed. I wonder what made him rush in like that?"

"Perhaps he was worried about competition from Alonzo. You may recall they were arguing over her like two dogs fighting for a bone at the wedding reception. Or maybe Sudley finds her more acceptable now that her father is out of the picture."

"Whatever impulse he acted on, it worked." She gave me a pitiful look. "Is your brother very much in love with her?"

Her question gave me pause. "I'm not sure. He wanted the opportunity to court her, but never claimed to be in love. If she is so fickle with her affections, he might be better off without her."

Fiona raised a brow. "Do you think he'll see it that way?"

"Perhaps. Someday. But not before he strangles me."

Fiona insisted we stop for tea at Fortnum's to cheer me up. By the time we pulled up to the house, my own carriage was at the curb, and George tapped his toe beside it. I'd forgotten the photographer. "It seems I must dash, Fiona. Thank you for coming with me today."

George opened the door and helped me to the pavement. Fiona bid him good afternoon and gave me a sympathetic smile. "At least this means you won't have to face your brother for a while longer," she said before driving off.

Out of one carriage and into another, I thought, wishing I had a moment to go indoors and shake off the chill. I burrowed closer to George, who wrapped an arm around my shoulders. "What was that about facing your brother?"

I told him about Madeline's decision to marry Fitzwalter. "Mrs. Connor is not happy that he offered, or that Madeline accepted at this particular time, so they are not making any sort of public announcement yet."

George frowned. "While I'm sorry Alonzo will be hurt by this news, I almost feel he's made something of a good escape. Yesterday she was wracked with grief, today she's accepting marriage proposals. Contrary to what we said last night, I'm not sure she does know her own mind. I suppose she was over the moon?"

"You would think so, wouldn't you? I'm not certain how she feels. She claimed to have forgotten she wore the ring, and though I find that hard to believe, she did seem surprised when Fiona remarked upon it." I held up a hand while I collected my thoughts. "No, she was more embarrassed or perhaps regretful. I'm sure Willa took her to task for accepting at such a time, but since she did accept him, I'd expect her to shake off Willa's concerns and be happily anticipating her future."

"I take it that wasn't the case?"

"She looked anything but happy."

"I repeat, Alonzo may have had a lucky escape."

"I may need you with me when I tell him."

"Always at your service, my lady." He drew my gloved hand to his lips.

"Speaking of service, how did the review of Mr. Connor's business files go? Did you find anything of interest?"

"I stand by my original statement. If Connor was involved in any shady dealings, he'd have kept those files to himself. I left your father at the agent's office with Constable Timmons. They seemed very interested in the company both Connor and Bainbridge had hoped to acquire."

"Mr. Bainbridge has a clear shot at it now."

"Not so. As he mentioned, there are several British investors interested in the company. I doubt that will come to anything, but I do hope your father looks into the files from Connor's desk."

"Hmm. Did you ask Delaney about the files this morning?"

"He was already gone when I arrived, so I had no chance to speak with him at all."

The carriage rolled to a stop before I could ask when George planned to check with him again. I peered out the window. "Is Mr. Wilson's shop in his home? This appears to be a residence."

George opened the door and lowered the step. Swinging himself down, he reached back in for my hand. "I believe it's more of a workroom or studio than a shop. And it does appear to be in his home."

I stepped down and instantly felt the chill in the wind. George closed the carriage door and wrapped an arm around me, quickly guided me up the steps of the closest house, and rang the bell.

Wilson answered the door himself and after a brief greeting, ushered us down the hall, past the stairs, to a back room, similar in size to my old library. Shelves and tables lined three of the four walls, with his camera, lights, and other miscellaneous equipment stacked beside the door. A central light fixture with a conical shade hung from the ceiling.

"I believe you'll be quite happy with the plates," he said. "If you recall we took several images so you have a selection to choose from."

We watched, fascinated, as he pulled the glass plates from a stand and placed them side by side, covering the long table that stood under the window.

"May I touch them?" I asked.

He added one last plate to the array on the table, then lifted the shade over the window. "Let me show you how." Taking it by the edges, he raised one plate to eye level, in front of the window. George and I both leaned forward and stared.

And stared.

"What exactly are we looking at?" George asked, relieving me of the necessity of doing so. I honestly had no idea. They looked like little more than black swirls and swishes on the clear glass.

Wilson picked up a paintbrush and using the wooden end, pointed to one of the black swishes. "This is your dress," he said, then moved the brush up a fraction. "And this is your face. Here is Mr. Hazelton's face . . ."

And suddenly, I saw it! What was light in color was black, or a shade of gray on the glass, and what was dark, was clear. Amazing! Something of what I felt must have shown in my expression, for the photographer chuckled. "Is this the first time you've seen the negative plates?" he asked.

"Yes. I've never seen anything but the end result of a photograph." I paused in my exuberance to look away from the plate to the photographer. "This isn't the end result, is it?"

"No. I wasn't expecting to see you until after your wedding trip, so I set these aside to develop a little later. That's one of the beauties of dry plate photography, one does not have to process them immediately."

I glanced at George, who looked as fascinated as I was. "Ah," he said, "that explains your question about looking at the negatives when I asked if we could view the photographs." He laughed. "I guess I should have asked what a negative was."

"I'm glad you didn't or we might never have seen them." I turned to the photographer. "Do you wish us to choose from these, or do you plan to develop them all?"

"I definitely plan to develop them all. You should make your selection from the finished product, but you're welcome to view all of the plates if you like. In fact, didn't we have problems with people outside the window? I can show you how I'd cover that up."

He deftly lifted each plate in the row, holding them up to the light one by one and handing them off to George or me. "Not this one," he said, and handed it to George. "This is by the fireplace. As I suspected, the light didn't work for that location. Ah, here's one." He extended the plate, about the size of half a sheet of writing paper, so we could view it. "This is you, Mr. Hazelton, standing thus. And there you are, ma'am, seated in the chair."

He glanced over his shoulder to see if we were following. Squinting at the glass, we both nodded. Once again, he used the end of the paintbrush to point out an object in the image. "Here's the window, and right there is someone outside it."

"I can barely see it." We leaned closer. "It's a woman," I said, "and she's alone, so it must be Willa."

The photographer waved his free hand. "Who it is or isn't won't matter because I can make her disappear. With a few brushstrokes, she'll become a tree or a bit of shrubbery." George and I exchanged a glance while he set the plate back on the table. "Let me show you how easy it is."

"No." We both spoke at once, causing Mr. Wilson to raise a brow.

"You want this figure to stay in the window?" he asked, his confusion apparent.

"Perhaps." I glanced at George. "Do we?"

"It adds nothing to the photograph," Wilson said. "It's actually rather distracting."

George took a step back and stroked his chin with thumb and forefinger, glancing between me and the photographer. "It might be best to wait. I'd hate to lose the evidence by having you paint over them."

Mr. Wilson narrowed his eyes. "Evidence?"

"There was a crime committed next door to Harleigh House. It may have happened while you were there photographing us. These people moving back and forth across the window are all suspects."

"Good Lord!"

While they were speaking, I examined the other plates closely. "This is odd," I said. "In this one, Mr. Bainbridge is walking toward the Connor residence. I don't remember seeing him go."

The photographer took the plate from my hands and examined it. "You're looking at it backward." He flipped it over in his hands. "This is the correct image." He handed it back to me and I could see Bainbridge moving in the correct direction and George and me back on the proper side of the window.

"Much better," I said.

The photographer waved his hand over the plates on the table. "I can make more than one print from each plate. If you like, I can develop all of these as they are. Then after you've chosen those you like, I can touch up the plates if necessary, and develop that one again."

"That sounds like the perfect solution," I said.

"Yes," George agreed. "If one of them was on his way to murder Connor, I'd like to have something more solid than our memories to give to Delaney. And speaking of him, are you up to one more stop?"

Delaney had just returned to his precinct when we arrived and agreed to spare us a few minutes of his time. The three of us entered his office together and doffed our heavy coats. The inspector seated himself behind his desk and gave us an assessing glance. "A little early in the case to be checking on our progress, isn't it?"

"I'm always eager to know where the police stand on a case, particularly when my client is a suspect." George took a seat on the hard wooden chair next to mine. "On this occasion, I'm rather more interested in a sort of comparison of notes."

Though the inspector's posture remained relaxed, his eyes showed a keen interest. "I'm listening."

Choosing his words carefully, George explained that he and

I had been at the Connor home when the police returned to search for a possible murder weapon, and that he had observed their search. "They seemed to disregard the desk itself as a weapon though I noted blood on the edge along the front of it. It's possible Connor hit his head against that edge."

"He did," Delaney confirmed. "We noted that on our first examination of the office and took samples. It was indeed blood. The shape of the edge matches one of Connor's wounds, but the coroner doesn't think that blow was enough to kill him. It was the dent at the man's temple that made us go back for another search. The walking stick seems to fit the bill."

"It may belong to Bainbridge. He told us he left his stick in Connor's office when they met that morning," George said. "Though it doesn't necessarily follow he was the one to use it on Connor."

"It seems as though we all have the same information, doesn't it?" Delaney leaned back in his chair. "So much for a comparison of notes."

"Actually, we have some photographs," George said.

Delaney cocked his head.

"I'm not certain they are of any value." George went on to explain about the photography session and the plates we'd seen. "Obviously, none of the images depict someone murdering Connor, but they do confirm that Mrs. Connor and Mr. Bainbridge paid a call on Connor before Alonzo Price and Miss Connor did."

Delaney nodded. "I'll visit this photographer and take a look at them, but both parties admitted they tried to call on Connor, but insist they never entered his office."

It was beginning to look as if we had nothing to offer Delaney. Or did we? "Are you familiar with the Higgins brothers' involvement with Connor?"

A spark of interest lit his eyes. "I know they did a spot of business for him now and then. Is there something more?"

I glanced at George, who gestured for me to carry on. "They paid a call on Willa Connor yesterday while I was at her home. It seems Connor hired them to vandalize Mr. Bainbridge's office a few days ago. He'd already paid them half of the agreed upon amount. They wanted to collect the rest."

The inspector raised his brows. "It's a little late to charge Connor with the crime now, wouldn't you say?"

I sighed. "The brothers also called on Connor at his office the day he was murdered. Half past two, they told me. Should they not be considered as suspects? Perhaps Connor refused to pay them."

Delaney ran a hand across the stubble on his chin. "Murder is not exactly in their line of work, particularly one of this type. But I suppose it's worth paying them a visit. They're easy enough to find."

Well, apparently everyone did know how to find them.

He frowned. "Anything else?"

"Only another question," George said. "Since you seem to be a step ahead of us on this case."

The inspector motioned for George to go on.

"Connor's desk was emptied. Was that the work of your people?"

A rare smile spread across Delaney's lips. "I won't ask how you know that. His desk was full of files detailing business transactions. We brought them in for inspection. It may lead to nothing." He lifted his shoulders. "But might lead to his killer."

"Money can be an excellent motive," I said.

"Indeed. Young Constable Timmons has found a financial expert to help him review the more recent files from Connor's agent's office. If the man's agreeable, we hope to have him review those Connor kept at his own office."

George struggled to hide a smile. "Constable Timmons has proved useful after all."

"In this one area I must say he has. The arrangement has the additional benefit of keeping him out of my way."

"I suppose we should take ourselves out of your way as well. Don't you agree, my dear?"

I came to my feet as George extended a hand to me. "Of course. I daresay you have a great deal to do, Inspector. It's unfortunate we couldn't provide more helpful information about the case."

Delaney looked suspicious as he showed us to the door. I barely breathed until it was closed firmly behind us. Then I glanced at George. "How has Constable Timmons managed to keep Delaney from learning my father is his financial expert?"

George shook his head. "I don't know, but I wouldn't want to be that young man when Delaney does find out."

Chapter Fifteen

Though Delaney confirmed our suspicions—one of Connor's head wounds came from the desk and the other from the walking stick—we learned nothing new that would lead us to the killer. I also wondered why he'd been so dismissive of the Higgins brothers as suspects, but my curiosity would have to be satisfied another time. It had been a long day and we were happy to head home. Upon our arrival, however, we found it was not yet over.

"Your brother awaits you in the drawing room," Jarvis said as he took my coat. A quick glance through the doorway told me he was not only waiting, but had spotted me. Too late to run. Fiona was right, my family had become exhausting. True to his word, George accompanied me inside and stood beside me while I gave my brother the news.

He did not take it well.

"I knew I should have called on her myself." He pounded a fist on the back of the sofa. "Why did I listen to your advice?"

I threaded my fingers together. "It wasn't so much my advice, Lon, as it was Madeline's request. Based on that, I wouldn't have expected her to receive Fitzwalter either."

He snapped around, shaking a finger in my face. "That's because you don't know her as I do."

I batted the finger aside. "You barely know her at all."

"I know she has a kind heart. She would not have turned me away. Instead, Fitzwalter played on her kindness and managed to trap her. I should have trusted my better judgment rather than listen to you and Father. You joined forces against me."

"We merely advised that you yield to her wishes. I'm sorry you lost her, Lon, but if Fitzwalter took advantage of her emotional distress to win her hand, I doubt that he also won her heart. If you tell me that would have been good enough for you, I shall be very disappointed."

"He probably told her it was her father's wish. I'm sure that's what decided her."

For heaven's sake. In his eyes, I was to blame. Frankie was to blame. Even Connor was to blame. Everyone was guilty, it seemed, except the young woman who had actually made the decision to accept Fitzwalter.

"Well, it's not over," he said. "Not until she tells me she made this decision of her own free will."

Exhausting. That's what they were. The weight of their problems poured over me like a thick glue and smothered me from head to toe. "Lon, I don't—" A sting in my arm, just above the elbow, cut off my words. I turned to George, my mouth hanging open in astonishment.

"You must act as you see fit, Alonzo," he said.

My brother's face was set in determination. "Yes, I must." He gave me a nod. "Good evening, Frances. Hazelton."

I waited until I heard the front door close behind him before turning on George. "You pinched me!"

"Yes, I did." He grinned. "You did that to me once, and I recall it stopped me in my tracks." He cocked a brow. "You had to be stopped."

"But now he'll go to the Connors to confront Madeline."

"Maybe he will and maybe he won't. And maybe that's exactly what's needed. Whether he does or not is not your affair." His hand against my cheek took the sting from the words. "You can't take on everyone's problems as your own."

With that, the sheer weariness that had been draining my spirit eased a bit. I smiled up at him. "You might be right about that. And about your previous point—Alonzo may have had a lucky escape."

Once my brother left, there was little time to change for our six o'clock dinner, so we simply didn't bother, and for the duration of our meal, we set aside the investigation and spoke of generalities—or rather George did. With my mind still full of my family and their various problems I made only cursory replies. By the end of the third course, I couldn't say what we discussed or what we ate, but I did hear George sigh.

"I think we can get along on our own, Jarvis," he said. "That will be all for tonight."

I gazed at him in curiosity when Jarvis and Frederick left us. "Why did you dismiss them?"

"You seemed unwilling to speak while they were here." He placed his hand over mine. "Jarvis and Frederick have heard any number of topics discussed around this table. I've never been concerned that either would breathe a word of those conversations outside this house."

"I'm not worried about Jarvis and I'm well aware that Frederick is the soul of discretion." I flipped my hand over and gave his a reassuring squeeze. "It's my family that's weighing on my mind. I can't seem to stop worrying about them."

"You can't solve everyone's problems, Frances, though I love you for trying. In Alonzo's case, I think you must let him resolve his relationship with Madeline on his own. As long as Fitzwalter doesn't turn up dead, your brother shouldn't find himself in further trouble."

I gave him a wry smile for his attempt at humor while considering his suggestion. "I suppose we all learn from our mistakes. He's unlikely to take my advice anyway. However, it was my parents I was most concerned about." I heaved a sigh. "I haven't heard from Mother all day, which leads me to believe she hasn't spoken to Frankie yet."

"There's probably nothing you can do for them either. I'm sure he's innocent of her charges." He pushed his plate away and topped off our glasses with the decanter of wine Jarvis left on the table. "So many problems can be circumvented if couples speak openly about them. I'm so pleased you and I are always able to talk out our differences."

"So am I. There is one thing I've been wanting to speak to you about."

The look of horror he shot me almost made me laugh out loud. "Nothing like that, George. It's this, our six o'clock dinnertime."

"What's wrong with it? I always dine at six."

"It's too early. We've been busy the past few days, but under normal circumstances we'd have tea at three or four, as I did yesterday. Who needs to eat a mere two hours later? It also means the staff don't eat until nearly eight."

He frowned. "I wasn't aware of that. They've never complained."

"Of course not. Bridget never would have mentioned it if I hadn't asked."

George looked wary. "What time do you wish to dine?"

Hmm. This might become more of a negotiation than I'd expected. "At least seven," I said. "Half past would be better still."

"I suppose seven isn't too late."

"Seven will do," I said. "It will give the staff more flexibility in their mealtime and on a day like today when we have somewhere to go in the evening, the cook needn't prepare anything."

He straightened his back and lowered his glass. "Where are we going this evening?"

"To Graham's reception, don't you remember?"

"Clearly, I don't. How could we have accepted when we weren't even meant to be here?"

I rose from the table because whether he recalled the engagement or not, it was still time to make ourselves ready. George followed me to the stairs. "Graham sent the invitation over yesterday," I said. "Actually, it was more of a message saying that since we were still in town after all, he'd love for us to come. I left it on your desk."

"Did we say yes?" George held the bedroom door open for me to precede him inside.

"We did, but clearly you'd rather not." I heard Bridget in the dressing room getting my things together.

"I would definitely rather not," he said. "We are newly wed after all. Aren't people supposed to leave us alone during this time? Yet here we are investigating by day and socializing by night."

I leaned back against the bedpost and crossed my arms. "If I had known that's how you felt, I would have declined. But Graham had gone to so much trouble in hosting our wedding reception, I felt obligated to accept." I stepped forward and straightened his tie. "It's just a drawing room soiree—a little music, some hors d'oeuvres, and champagne. We don't have to stay long."

"Fine. As long as we leave early, I'll go."

"I'll make sure that we do. And as for investigating by day, I've done no real investigating. You went with Frankie this morning on a specific search, but anything I've learned was completely unintentional. I was simply in the right place at the right time. Even the visit with the photographer turned into a piece of investigative work."

"Perhaps we should put more effort into flushing out the killer, so we can still take our trip."

"Let's," I said. "In the meantime, I must get ready for this evening's function. If we're to leave early, we can't be late, too."

"No more evening events, do we agree?"

"This will be the last one," I said, and slipped away to the dressing room where Bridget awaited.

Ready as always, she had me dressed within minutes, then seated me in front of the mirror to arrange my hair while I pulled on my long evening gloves. "Do you know if my wedding dress made it to Inspector Delaney?"

"As soon as it came in from Harleigh House, I told Mr. Jarvis where it needed to go. He had Frederick deliver it. That was early this morning."

"Excellent. Another piece of evidence, which may turn out to be worthless. This is the strangest investigation, Bridget. So difficult to determine what is and isn't important." I gave her a sharp look. "You didn't happen to notice anything that day, did you?"

Bridget widened her eyes. "I was far too busy. Between getting you ready, getting the bags ready, and getting myself ready to travel, I barely had time to look around. You might want to check with the earl's staff. They may have taken note of something."

"I suspect the police already interviewed the staff, but it might be worthwhile."

"Maybe the Connor staff, too," she suggested.

"We'll have to count on the police for that," I said. "I have no access to them. Parker, the butler, was very forthcoming, but all he had to say was Alonzo is guilty."

"I know Mrs. Connor's lady's maid. She says it's a difficult family to work for."

"Did she say why?"

"She didn't much like Mr. Connor."

"Unlikable seems to be the consensus about Mr. Connor."

Bridget wrinkled her nose. "She didn't say anything directly, but she implied the mister was not very kind to Mrs. Connor, if you take my meaning. And her such a little thing."

"Do you mean to say he struck her?"

"All she said was that Mr. Connor bullied his wife, so I can't say for sure what she meant. A man doesn't have to raise his hand to make his wife fear him. I don't like a house like that. Everywhere I worked the mister and missus treated each other with respect."

"Someone else mentioned that to me, but he was merely speculating."

"A lady's maid doesn't have to speculate, ma'am. My guess is everyone in that household is relieved he's gone."

"Is the sentiment strong enough that one of them might have murdered him?"

"If I had to guess, my money would be on his wife. If she wanted to be rid of him, no time could be better than when he was openly feuding with Mr. Bainbridge."

"I can't imagine that. You said yourself, Mrs. Connor is such a small woman, and she's so meek and mild tempered."

Bridget shrugged as she put the finishing touches on my hair. "She might be small, but it sounds to me like she'd be motivated."

We arrived at Harleigh House in good time. It wasn't a large gathering, thank goodness, and we were able to dash up the walk and right into the entry hall. George was right, with the damp and the chill, this would have been a perfect evening to stay at home. We handed our outerwear to the footman and surveyed the gathering in the drawing room. About thirty or so finely dressed ladies and gentlemen holding flutes of champagne mingled among themselves while footmen passed trays of small delicacies. Music wafted through the room from a string quartet in the far corner. Frankly, it looked incredibly dull.

"One hour," George whispered in my ear.

"If that," I said, looking around for a familiar face. The reception was for the benefit of some cause I didn't recall. The company assembled seemed to be made up of Graham's neighbors, so some local issue, perhaps?

Then I spotted Lord Sudley and Mr. Bainbridge. Though Mr. Bainbridge kept a house in Mayfair, it wasn't as though he spent much time here. His presence was mildly interesting, but even more so was the fact that he and Sudley were clearly arguing. The latter gentleman had become quite red in the face. Perhaps this gathering wouldn't be so dull after all.

A footman approached us offering glasses of champagne. George took two flutes and handed one to me. "I'm not sure where it's safe to tread," he said.

"I wouldn't mind overhearing what Bainbridge and Sudley are discussing in such a heated manner." I tipped my head in their direction only to see Fitzwalter had intervened and was leading his father away. Bainbridge, still scowling, lifted his shoulders in a shrug and joined a couple standing by the fireplace. "Heavens, that's Mother and Frankie. I didn't know they'd be here."

"Let's stay away from your parents," George replied. "With her friend"—he waggled his brows—"so close at hand, things could become explosive."

"I told you, there's nothing between Mother and Bainbridge." I surveyed the room. "There's Lady Sudley. She may have some information about her son's engagement. Even if she doesn't, she's usually amusing."

"Look closer. Do you see the person standing next to her?"

Lady Esther. One of the most crotchety matrons I've ever had the misfortune to encounter. To her, most of us were merely whetstones on which to sharpen her wit. She'd devastated my confidence in the past, but more recently I've managed to hold my own, trading barb for barb.

"You're going over there, aren't you?" George gave me a look of abject misery.

"You don't have to join me. Perhaps some of your friends

are in the billiards room. Or you may find Sudley or Fitzwalter there. I'll speak with the ladies myself."

He perked up instantly and we went our separate ways. Lady Sudley smiled when she saw me weaving through the crowd toward her. Lady Esther merely bared her teeth. In looks, the two women couldn't be less alike. Lady Sudley, about my mother's age, was all curves, curls, and ruffles, while Lady Esther, perhaps two decades older, was a study in straight lines and severe angles. Both came from old, aristocratic families. Neither suffered fools.

We greeted each other, engaged in the usual chitchat, and I admitted that I had no idea what the gathering was in support of. "Hazelton and I hadn't planned to be in town, so I never received a proper invitation."

Lady Sudley tipped her head to the side. "Something political, I believe."

Lady Esther cast a sharp-eyed gaze toward the back of the room where the French doors to the wintergarden were closed against the chill. "Do you see that gentleman over there by the doors? He is standing for the seat in the Commons vacated by the sudden death of Harold Lawrence. I suppose the earl favors his candidacy and this evening is meant to garner support."

"If so, the gentleman should consider mingling a little more," I said.

"I should say so." The lady turned her eye back to me. "Now that you mention it, I'm surprised to see you here. Should you not be on your wedding trip?" She blinked. "Felicitations, by the way."

Lady Sudley bestowed her good wishes as well.

"Thank you, and yes, we'd be away now, but for Mr. Connor's untimely end."

"That's right." Lady Sudley's gaze sharpened. "The investigation completely disrupted your reception. Fitzwalter told me all about it. Police everywhere, asking questions as if your guests were common criminals."

"Goodness, I hope it wasn't quite that bad. I was at the Connors' with Willa and Madeline. They were both distraught, as you can imagine."

Lady Sudley compressed her lips as if weighing what she should say next. In that instant, Lady Esther saw her chance to draw blood. "Wasn't your son paying court to Miss Connor?"

"Young men can be very difficult." Lady Sudley gave me a cautious glance. "I trust as a friend of Mrs. Connor you are already aware my son has made a fool of himself over the daughter."

I pretended to search my memory, wondering if I should admit to my knowledge or feign ignorance. If I chose the latter, the lady might keep her thoughts to herself. "Madeline did mention it, but considering the circumstances, Mrs. Connor asked that it remain confidential."

She released a sigh. "The foolish boy. I'm sure he was simply overcome with sympathy for the girl. I'm pleased to hear she asked for your discretion, my dear. Perhaps she understands that Lord Sudley does not approve the match at all." She placed a hand on Lady Esther's arm. "Fortunately, since they're in mourning, they can't make an official announcement for some time."

She gave me a knowing look, then her lips parted in a rather frightening smile. "Much can happen in a year. Perhaps there need never be an announcement."

That certainly confirmed the rumors I'd heard. Lord and Lady Sudley had no interest in a connection to Connor. Perhaps they had another heiress in mind for Fitzwalter. Or as Fiona had suggested, they weren't aware of the extent of their son's debt.

Someone caught Lady Sudley's attention. When she stepped just out of earshot, Lady Esther harumphed. "She said that for your benefit, I daresay. Implying it was her husband alone who objected to the match."

"I see. Like you, she disapproves of American brides for British peers, but unlike you, she was polite enough not to say it to my face."

She narrowed her wrinkled eyes, making them almost disappear. "Tut-tut. Manners are of the utmost importance in the young, but a woman of my years places a higher value on honesty."

I tightened my lips to repress a smirk. Lady Esther only valued honesty when she was the one doling it out.

"Besides, it's been years since I thought of you as American. You've adapted so nicely to our society that if it weren't for your unfortunate accent, you might pass as British."

I paused to absorb her words. "Am I to take that as a compliment?"

"What a foolish question. How could it be anything else?" She extended a bony finger at me. "And if you raise a brow or titter, I shall be forced to take it back." She withdrew her finger and muttered under her breath. I assumed she was wondering what could possibly be better than to be mistaken for British. Since anything resembling a compliment from Lady Esther was as rare as hen's teeth, I thanked her kindly.

"As to Miss Connor," she continued. "There are American brides, and then there is the daughter of James Connor. Who in their right mind would choose to align themselves with that family? Mark my words; there will be no engagement announced. If Lord Sudley doesn't prevent it, Lady Sudley will."

I struggled to maintain my composure. "Fitzwalter may be young but I believe he's gained his majority. If he is determined to marry her, what are they to do about it?"

Lady Esther lifted her chin. Clearly, I'd presented a challenge, and she was about to rise to it. "Fitzwalter is not their only child. Nor is he their only son. Children have been disowned for lesser offenses, and I'm sure his younger brother would be more than happy to inherit the title and all that comes with it." With a nod, she wandered off.

I considered joining Lady Sudley's group right behind me, but Mother stepped up beside me. "Good evening, dear. I wasn't expecting to see you here or we might have come together."

"It was something of a last-minute decision," I said, taking her in. "You look lovely this evening." She wore a velvet gown in a shade of amber that brought out the gold in her hair.

Rather than return the compliment, Mother took note of her surroundings and released a tsk. "It's a shame you're no longer mistress of this house. Reggie's death was such bad luck."

"Even more so for him, I daresay." I glanced around. "Where is Frankie?"

"He stepped away to the billiards room for a cigar."

"I take it you haven't brought up your concerns with him?"

Her cheeks flushed. "This is not the place, Frances. What if someone should hear you?"

That was highly unlikely as the dozens of conversations reverberated through the room and combined to create an indistinguishable hum that quite overwhelmed the quartet. No sooner had I noticed the din of voices, than it was rent by a chilling scream followed by a crash.

Mother clutched my arm. "What on earth was that?"

I was already disengaging her hand from my arm. "Let me check," I said and followed the rush of people headed for the dining room, where the scream had originated. I almost ran into George in the doorway.

Since the dining room had not been in use, it lay in eerie darkness. Someone turned up the gaslight and the glow of the chandelier overhead illuminated the empty table in the center of the room and the chairs lining the walls. A weeping maid had collapsed into one of them, an upended tray at her feet. A cluster of men blocked my view of the rest of the room. A cold sense of dread settled over me at the thought of what might be behind them.

George took my arm and drew me inside and along the wall. On the far side of the table lay the lifeless form of Lord Sudley, his blood staining the carpet near his head. A silver candlestick lay on the floor beside him.

I tore my gaze away when another cry resounded and Lady Sudley fainted into a gentleman's arms. I froze when I saw the man directly behind her.

What was Alonzo doing here?

Chapter Sixteen

～

Word of Sudley's death and Lady Sudley's subsequent collapse spread throughout the house. Within minutes there wasn't a guest or servant who hadn't heard the news, yet none of them had any idea of what to do about it. George cleared everyone but Lady Sudley and my mother, who was tending to her, from the dining room, while I directed them across the hall to the drawing room. Graham, looking haggard, sidled up to me and asked what he should do.

"If you haven't already done so, you must send someone for the police," I replied.

He pulled a face. "Do we really need to do that?" His voice rose an octave on the word *really*. "The police were here the other day. I don't relish another visit. I'd imagine my guests won't either." He cast a glance at the drawing room where those guests whispered among themselves. "We should probably send them home, don't you think?"

George had just approached us and if his shocked expression was any indication, he'd heard Graham's query. "Absolutely not," he said. "You must do your best to keep them here."

I moved in closer to Graham. "One of them is likely to be the murderer."

"All the more reason to make them leave, I'd say." He pulled a handkerchief from his pocket and dabbed at his forehead.

"Enough." George sighed and threw me an I-knew-we-should-have-stayed-home look. "Frances and I shall take care of this situation. You make sure no one leaves."

Graham nodded and backed away. George caught the arm of the nearest footman. "Did you see what happened in here?"

The lanky young man looked positively terrified. "No, sir. I was out in the drawing room until I heard the first shout. Then I peeked in there and saw him." He tipped his head toward poor Sudley in the dining room. "Like that."

"Good, then I'm sending you for the police."

"Yes, sir." He made as if to leave but George drew him back and gave him instructions to go to the Chelsea division and return with Inspector Delaney. Once the footman had left, George looked at the dining room, then to our other side at the group peering out from the drawing room. Crossing his arms, he cut a glance toward me. "I believe we'll be here longer than we'd planned."

Mother had come up to my side. "It seems we can all say that." She nudged my arm. "Let us take poor Lady Sudley somewhere more private."

George nodded. "If the two of you can remove her, I'll see to keeping everyone else out."

Lady Sudley was loath to leave her husband, but I was certain the police and the coroner would object to her presence. With some encouragement, she allowed me to guide her to the rear of the house to the small parlor. Fitzwalter strode up to us in the hallway, blocking our path.

"Leave her to me," he said, his voice quiet but commanding. "I'll take her home."

"Give her some time," I said, waving him to the side. "Let her have some tea and a quiet moment. Then she can speak to the police before she goes home, if she's up to it." We worked our way around him and into the library. Fitzwalter followed closely on our heels. I had to remind myself he'd just lost his father and was likely a bit dazed at the moment himself. "Perhaps you might send someone for a cold compress," I suggested.

He blew out an impatient breath and left.

Mother eyed me. "What's the purpose of a cold compress?"

"It gives him something to do."

Lady Sudley's sobs had eased to quiet whimpers, which quite broke my heart and almost brought Mother to tears. I left them both on the chaise, Mother murmuring softly and holding Lady Sudley's hand, while I crossed the room to pour the woman a drink from whatever Graham had in the tantalus.

When I returned, I handed them both a glass.

Mother eyed it suspiciously. "I thought you mentioned tea?"

"Brandy," I said. "It's better for shock."

To my surprise, Lady Sudley threw back her head and finished it in one gulp. After a few blinks, she did look a bit more like herself, though her eyes were still unfocused and her tears flowed unchecked. "How did this happen? Who would want to hurt him?"

Bother. That's exactly the question I wanted to ask her. "Is there anyone here tonight that your husband was at odds with?"

"We still don't know exactly what happened." Mother sent me a warning glance. "The police are coming, as is a doctor. He may have had some sort of seizure, fallen, and hit his head on the table or floor."

Lady Sudley swiped at the tears on her cheeks. "But the candlestick was right there beside him."

"Perhaps he knocked it off the table when he fell."

I gave Mother an incredulous look. She shrugged. Though she was ruining my chance to question Lady Sudley, it was rather nice to see her offering comfort.

"I suppose all that really matters is that he's gone." Lady Sudley's face grew taut with her struggle to stop her tears. I placed a gentle hand on her shoulder. I had so many questions. What sort of business was Lord Sudley involved in? Who were his acquaintances? But all of that could wait. Right now, she was a woman who had just lost her husband. She must grieve.

Fitzwalter returned with the compress. His red eyes and damp cheeks had me viewing the young man in a different light. All thought of him bullying Madeline into marriage fled when he gently placed the compress into his mother's hand.

I convinced him to leave Lady Sudley in my mother's care for a moment and join me in the hallway. "Have you any idea who might want to hurt your father?" I asked as soon as the door closed behind us.

He stared at the floor, shaking his head. "I haven't the foggiest, though I am, perhaps, not the best person to ask. Since leaving for school, I've seen him a handful of times. I came to London during breaks while he stayed in the country. When he was here for parliamentary duties, I was at school." He swiped at his cheek. "His arrival in town at this time of year came as a surprise, but I never thought to ask him why he was here."

He took a few agitated steps away from me and abruptly turned around. "I know nothing of his business or personal interests or of his activities. But I know he was a good man and only the worst type of scoundrel would do this."

I had no reason to doubt Fitzwalter's assessment of his father and had nothing to add. Sudley was an acquaintance, someone I knew socially. I sat next to him at a dinner or two and made polite conversation. We certainly never discussed anything that would provide any insight as to why someone would want to murder him.

"I saw Sudley arguing with Mr. Bainbridge not long ago," I said. "You joined them briefly. What that was about?"

He shook his head. "I was nearby and heard his voice raised in a way that might draw attention. He wouldn't have wanted to make a spectacle of himself, so I simply distracted him and led him away from the source of his vexation."

"Where did you go?"

"Go?" He blinked. "Father headed off to the billiards room. I assume he wanted a cigar. I returned to the drawing room."

The young man was so clearly distraught, I decided to push him no further. It didn't sound as if he could enlighten me as to the identity of Sudley's killer anyway. We returned to the library where Fitzwalter seated himself next to Lady Sudley, and Mother and I quietly slipped out.

After closing the door behind her, Mother paused and drew a deep breath. "I can't stop imagining how I'd feel if that had been your father instead of Lord Sudley." She stared down at her hands clasped at her waist. Her voice was barely a whisper. "I don't know what I'd do without him, Frances."

I placed my hand over hers. "You must clear the air between you two. I mean about . . ."

She shook off my hand and snapped her head around to face me. I'm quite sure a tear froze on her cheek. "About his infidelity? Is that what you mean?"

"When you do speak to him, you might want to phrase it differently, rather than accuse him of infidelity right out of the gate."

"Indeed? You've been married for what? Two days now? I suppose you're an expert on the matter."

"Stop being so prickly. I had a husband who betrayed our marriage vows from the moment he stepped foot out of the church and every day thereafter, so I might actually have some experience in this."

Her expression softened. "Was he never faithful?"

She sounded so hopeful, I hated to disillusion her, but illusions were of no value. "No. Though it's not what you and I imagine when we think of marriage, the type of arrangement Reggie and I had is not that uncommon among the aristocracy. Fortunately for me, I was never in love with him. Infatuated, perhaps, but it was nothing like what I feel for George."

"Or what I feel for Franklin."

"If I suspected George had strayed, I'd tell him of my suspicions." Assuming I could keep myself from strangling him.

She shuddered. "But what if I'm right?"

"What if you're wrong?"

"I'd feel a fool," she said. "But even that is better than what I feel right now."

"In my opinion, knowing is better than living in ignorance." And since it wasn't my place to push her, I decided to leave it at that and turn the conversation. "Speaking of not knowing, did Alonzo come here with you this evening?"

"Alonzo?"

"Alonzo. Your son. My brother. Surely, you've seen him around—tall, dark, lanky fellow."

Mother pursed her lips. "Don't be impertinent. Are you saying he is here tonight?"

"He was in the dining room when everyone crowded around to take a look at Lord Sudley. Didn't you see him?"

"I didn't, and we didn't bring him. Lord Harleigh invited us quite casually, but I was certain he meant only Franklin and me. I wouldn't have dreamed of bringing another guest." She tipped her head toward the drawing room and we proceeded down the hallway. "Why don't you find out what is happening and why Alonzo is here. I'll go to your father."

I checked the clock at the end of the hallway and gaped. We'd been in there for an hour. The police should have arrived by now and I imagined Delaney grilling my brother. We stepped into the drawing room where a constable stood in a corner taking statements from a trio of guests. Their raised voices indicated they were not in agreement with one another. Fewer than a dozen other guests remained. They formed small groups of two and three, chatting nervously until it was their turn to give their statements. As I feared, Alonzo wasn't among them. Neither was George, which gave me some relief as I hoped he was keeping my brother from harm.

Mother headed directly to Frankie. Perhaps he knew where the others were. I followed her to his side. "Has Inspector Delaney arrived?" I asked.

"He has," Frankie grumbled. "I'll be filing a complaint about him to his superiors." He crossed his arms over his chest. "The nerve of the man."

My stomach clenched. "Please tell me you didn't try to offer him money."

Frankie scoffed. "What for? To do his job? All I offered was my opinion. It was summarily dismissed."

I didn't want to hear any more. "Do you know where Alonzo is? And George?"

"Inspector Delaney questioned some of us privately, in the library across the entry hall. I believe you'll find them there."

What I found was a closed door and Mr. Bainbridge waiting outside it. The chandelier hanging overhead made his fair hair shimmer as he paced beneath it. He stopped and gave me a nod when I approached him. "Your husband and brother are inside. I'm waiting my turn."

"That's interesting. Delaney has taken it upon himself to interview the three of you and my father."

"And Lord Harleigh," Bainbridge added.

"All of whom were here for the wedding reception. Do you suppose he thinks Connor's murder is related to Sudley's?"

Bainbridge raised his brows. "Two murders took place in neighboring homes within a few days of each other. It doesn't sound like a coincidence to me."

No, it didn't. That meant Delaney would want to interview me, too. And Mother, for that matter. The remaining guests were neighbors, including Lady Sudley and Fitzwalter. Which made me wonder again about Bainbridge. "Why are you here this evening, Mr. Bainbridge? I understand this soiree was meant to raise funds for a politician Lord Harleigh favors. How would that interest an American?"

His lips twitched. "I doubt that it would, but I'm not an American. I've lived there for a good part of my life. Made my fortune there. But I never became a citizen. I'm as British as your husband."

That came as a surprise. "I suppose I assumed your history was similar to Mr. Connor's. Your names are linked so frequently."

"Thus, you assumed I courted politicians, too."

"I didn't mean to imply anything of the sort."

His jaw tightened. He glanced at the closed library door, but said nothing.

If Connor courted politicians, that might explain his interest in Lord Sudley, who, while not a politician per se, was a legislator. But what was Bainbridge's interest in the man? "Were you and Sudley acquainted?"

He sighed. "I shall have to answer the inspector's questions, madam, but I don't believe I'm required to answer yours."

"I only ask because I saw you arguing with him this evening," I began, wondering how far I could push the man. "Not long before his body was found."

With one stride he was menacingly close, his eyes narrowed in anger. "Are you accusing me of something?"

Perhaps that was one push too many. I stood my ground, largely because fear had frozen me in place. I was certain he saw it in my eyes.

Our standoff ended when the door to the library opened. It had lasted no longer than the blink of an eye. When George and Alonzo stepped into the hall, Bainbridge had already returned to his post by the paneled wall.

George's gaze traveled from me to Bainbridge. He gestured to the library. "Delaney is ready for you," he said.

Bainbridge gave him a nod. The two men moved around each other like predators until Bainbridge stepped into the library and closed the door behind him.

"The two of you looked somewhat less than friendly," George said.

I nodded. "I pushed him too far and he reacted. It was nothing. I'd rather you tell me about your interview with Delaney before I must speak with him." I turned to Alonzo. "And what are you doing here?"

He squeezed his hand into a fist. "I came here to have it out with Fitzwalter. He pressured Miss Connor into marriage when she was in no fit state to make such a decision."

Personally, I thought Lon was taking his idea of chivalry to the point of absurdity. "You did realize this was meant to be a social affair among polite society, didn't you? It was not a boxing match. How could you come here with the intention of starting trouble?"

"He left me no choice, Franny. I tried to call on him at his home, at his club, even at his usual gambling haunts. He kept ducking me. Mother mentioned he'd be here tonight." He raised his hands. "So here I am."

I wanted to ask him why he thought this was his battle. Did

Madeline want him to fight for her? Did she even know what he was doing? I set all that aside to address the matter at hand. Turning to George, I asked, "How did Delaney react to Lon's explanation?"

He gave me a wry smile. "Much as you'd expect. He suggested that Alonzo murdered Sudley."

"That's not possible," Lon said. "I walked through the front door right as someone started screaming. I ran back to the dining room alongside the footman who took my coat."

"At least someone can vouch for you," I said.

"That ought to be enough," George said. "Alonzo just happened to be in the wrong place at the wrong time."

I shifted my gaze to my brother. "You seem to have a talent for that."

"Delaney raised the theory that in murdering Connor and Sudley, he was eliminating the two men who stood between him and Madeline."

Neither of them seemed concerned about the accusation. Alonzo appeared relaxed and George was smirking. "Somehow I think you must have shown him the error in his theory."

George nodded at Alonzo. "Your brother did. When Delaney told him Fitzwalter's father was dead, Alonzo thought there had been three murders. He had no idea Fitzwalter's father and Lord Sudley were the same person. He's unlikely to have killed the man if he couldn't even identify him."

"You people go by so many different names." Lon boggled his eyes. "Some use their surname, others go by their title. I honestly don't comprehend how you keep everyone straight."

"It seems that confusion is what saved you this time," George said.

"Delaney did tell me not to leave town," Lon said. "So I'm not sure I am safe."

"I wouldn't worry too much about that," I said. "Delaney's

theory has another flaw. Connor and Lord Sudley were not in agreement about this engagement. Sudley was dead set against it and furious about Fitzwalter's impetuous offer."

George looked surprised. "Where did you hear that?"

I shrugged. "It came directly from the man's wife."

"Make sure you mention it to Delaney."

Chapter Seventeen

My interview with Delaney was brief. He asked for the usual details: when I arrived, who I spoke with, when, and if, I saw the deceased. I mentioned the argument between Sudley and Bainbridge and Lady Sudley's claim that her husband had been against the match between her son and Miss Connor. Though Delaney's case against Alonzo was weak, it was not weak enough for George and me to leave town. Though neither of us wanted to admit it, the window of time for our holiday in Cannes was slowly closing.

It closed a bit more when Jarvis brought a note for me to the breakfast table the following day. It was from Graham. I quickly skimmed the contents and, with a sigh, handed it off to George.

The note requested our attendance at Harleigh House as soon as possible. Apparently, Inspector Delaney had shown up that morning with two constables to search the entire house. Graham had no idea what they were looking for, but assumed it had to do with Sudley's murder. He begged us to come and rid him of the police.

George returned the note with a disheartened look. "You must be regretting marrying into my family," I said. "I can't believe how they've turned our lives upside down in a few days."

He chuckled. "I shall never regret marrying you. It's not as if my past hasn't caused us trouble before." He took my hand and brought it to his lips. "When this is over, we shall simply have to plan another wedding trip."

"But for now, we must go to Harleigh House and rescue Graham."

"All in a day's work," he said. While he ordered the carriage, I rang for our coats and within twenty minutes, we were on our way.

"I can't imagine what he thinks we can accomplish by being there," I wondered aloud.

George waved a hand. "Advise him of his rights, I suppose. Delaney does have a certain authority to search the house since the victim was found in the dining room, but I'd think it would be limited to the public rooms."

"Graham may be exaggerating about how extensively they're searching." I released a sigh. "It feels wrong to be on the opposite side of Delaney in an investigation."

George tutted. "I don't believe we are. We've shared everything we've learned with him. We're simply defending Alonzo's and Graham's rights. I doubt he'll hold that against us. We all want justice, after all."

"True, but I doubt he'll be pleased to see us."

George nodded. "I can't argue with that."

Inspector Delaney was not pleased to see us. When Crabbe led us into the drawing room, he looked as if he wanted to send us right back out.

"Our presence was requested," George said before Delaney could have us removed. For all I knew, he might still have escorted us back to our carriage, but at that moment a constable led Graham into the room and took Delaney's attention from us.

"Ah, Lord Harleigh, there you are. I thought I instructed you to remain in this room?"

"I'll be damned if I don't have free use of my own home," Graham snapped. "I shall go where I please."

Delaney rolled his eyes and approached Graham with a scrap of fabric. "Can you tell me who this handkerchief belongs to?"

Graham blanched and took a step back. "Is that blood?"

"It appears to be," Delaney replied. Unruffled, he held it aloft and made a show of examining it. "It's a rather delicate thing, don't you think? The fancy lace around the edges makes me wonder if it belongs to a lady. And there's an initial 'W' embroidered across the face. Might this belong to anyone in your household?"

Graham threw a panicked look my way. His late wife's name was Delia and though her surname was Wynn, she'd been an excellent needlewoman. She would have been more likely to embroider the Harleigh coat of arms over an image of Harleigh Manor and thrown in the rose garden for good measure. Even from this distance, I could see the fabric was too delicate to belong to one of his servants. That left Willa. I raised my hands helplessly.

Moving around Delaney, Graham took a seat and tried for a calm posture, crossing one leg over the other. "The house was full of guests last night, any one of them might have brought it in here."

George and I moved to the sofa opposite Graham. If he planned to dissemble, this might take some time. Delaney gazed at the bloody handkerchief. "I suppose that's true, but I didn't note anyone on your guest list with a name that begins with the initial 'W.'" He paused and snapped his fingers. "Mrs. Connor." He glanced at Graham. "The lady next door whose husband was lately murdered. Her given name begins with a 'W,' does it not?"

Graham looked pained. "It might."

"Her name is Willa, as I believe you are well aware. Now the question is why wasn't her name on your guest list?"

"I didn't invite her. She's in mourning. It would have been unseemly."

"Then how did her handkerchief arrive here?"

"If it is her handkerchief," George added.

"And I don't believe it is," I said. "Willa's has a monogram in the corner. This looks like a practice piece of embroidery. No one would place a design right in the center of a handkerchief."

"It shouldn't be difficult to determine," Delaney shot back. "But since we can't come up with another name at the moment, let's assume it belongs to Mrs. Connor, and I'll repeat my question. How did it get here?"

"What makes you think his lordship keeps track of his neighbor's belongings?" George remained calm, casual, even. I was a bundle of nerves. I'd urged Graham to tell Delaney about his relationship with Willa. Based on these questions, I was quite sure he hadn't done so. Now I feared every moment that he would.

Delaney ignored George and kept his focus on Graham. "I believe you know about this particular belonging, don't you, sir?"

"Mrs. Connor was here for the wedding reception," Graham blurted. "We were using the dining room that day. Perhaps she dropped it unknowingly and somehow it came into contact with Lord Sudley. She was not here last night, so she could have nothing to do with his death."

Delaney appeared to be considering Graham's suggestion, but I had the sense he was feigning. "That's very odd. The wedding was three days ago. Wouldn't one of your staff have cleaned that room by now?"

Graham looked as if he was struggling not to wipe the perspiration from his forehead. Instead, he tugged at his tie. "Even a good maid misses things now and then."

"Enough of this." He shook the handkerchief in Graham's face. "This wasn't found anywhere near Lord Sudley's body. It was in a drawer of the desk in your library."

I suppressed a gasp. I didn't for a moment believe Graham had anything to do with the murders, but what was he thinking to hide Willa's handkerchief?

"How did it get there, my lord?"

"Now it's my turn to say, enough." George got to his feet. "I'd like to see your warrant, Inspector. I can't imagine it covers the private contents of Lord Harleigh's desk."

Delaney turned a sardonic eye on George. "Is the earl your client, too?"

"If you authorize me, Graham, I'll act on your behalf."

"But I really have no idea how it came to be there," he began, looking at George in confusion. George tore his gaze away from Delaney long enough to raise a brow at Graham, who made a move-along gesture with his hand. "Yes, yes, of course I authorize you," he said.

Delaney and George stared at one another for a moment. Then George presented his hand, palm up.

"Fine." The inspector reached into his coat pocket, removed a document, and shoved it at George. "You'll see the warrant is in order."

George unfolded the page and read through it. Since Delaney had handed it over, I was certain everything was, as he said, in order, yet George looked surprised when he'd finished reading and glanced back up at Delaney. "You knew of the existence of this handkerchief before you had this drawn up," he said.

Delaney shrugged. "We received a tip. Turns out it was right."

"If someone told you it was in my desk, they must have put it there." Graham was back to his belligerent self.

"I'm not going to play this game any longer, my lord. Why is this in your possession? Are you involved with Mrs. Connor? Did you murder her husband?"

"Gad, no!" Graham cringed and drew back into his chair.

"Did she ask you to dispose of the handkerchief?"

"No. I never even saw the blasted thing until now."

If Graham had hoped that would put an end to the questions, he was mistaken. Delaney's gaze intensified while he waited for Graham to tell all.

It didn't take long. With a sigh, he sank even deeper into his chair. "Mrs. Connor and I are involved, as you put it. Or rather we were. The death of her husband has put a pall on our relationship."

"Was this a relationship of long standing?"

"No, a month perhaps and it wasn't likely to continue. She is a lovely woman who was tied to a brute of a husband. We were both lonely. My wife is dead. She was stuck in a loveless marriage. Our relationship grew from a period of weakness."

I winced at Graham's words. "I'm sure Mrs. Connor loved her husband," I put in.

Delaney shot me a warning look.

"We became friends," Graham continued. "Then we became more."

"Did you have plans for the future? Did she intend to separate from her husband?"

"The future?" He looked confused. "We never spoke of it."

"Never spoke of it, but might she have had hope?"

"He can't know what was in the woman's mind, Delaney," George broke in.

For heaven's sake! Between the two of them, they might as well hand Willa a length of rope so she could hang herself.

"The earl had a houseful of guests that day. He didn't have a chance to steal away and murder his neighbor," George said.

"Yes, it appears you used what time you did have for a tryst with Mrs. Connor."

Graham shot a glare at me. As if I'd have said anything. He shifted his gaze to Delaney. "How do you know about that?"

"One of your servants saw the two of you sneak away to the parlor at the back of the house."

It's a wonder they didn't bump into Mother and Bainbridge.

Graham sputtered a protest, which Delaney brushed aside with a wave of his hand. "Be grateful, my lord. If no one had seen where you went, we might be charging you with murder right now. Instead, I'm inclined to agree with Hazelton. You didn't have time to murder your neighbor, but Mrs. Connor did."

"No. She wouldn't do such a thing," Graham said.

"You'll forgive me if I don't take your word for it. I'm afraid you're a bit too close to the matter." He folded the handkerchief and placed it in his notebook. "If I were you, I'd hope she provides a better defense of you than you did of her."

Graham jolted to his feet. "What do you mean by that?"

With a nod to each of us, Delaney strode from the room to the entry hall where his constables waited. Graham glanced between George and me as the front door slammed. "What did he mean by that? Where is he going?"

"Most likely next door to speak with Willa," George said, ignoring the first question.

I felt a bit more sympathy for my brother-in-law. He might be bumbling, but he wasn't malicious. "You gave Willa a significant motive to murder her husband."

He gave me a look of astonishment. "I did no such thing."

Holding up my fingers, I enumerated the points. "You called Connor a brute, said she was trapped in her marriage, and that you had no idea what she might have planned for the future.

And he clearly believes you were hiding the handkerchief, so he suspects you of being peripherally involved."

"That's ridiculous. I meant to imply she was a dutiful wife, none of the rest of that."

"He likely finds it difficult to believe a dutiful wife would betray her wedding vows." I heaved a sigh.

Graham ran a hand through his hair and seemed to be tugging at it in his frustration. Dropping his arm, he swung around to George. "What should I do? Should I go over there and defend her?"

"I'm not sure Willa could survive any more of your defense, Graham," I muttered.

"I hate to disillusion the two of you," George said, "but there is the very real possibility that she did murder him."

"Impossible," Graham said.

"I find it hard to believe myself. As Graham pointed out, the man was a brute. I hadn't really thought about it before, but once he brought it up, I recalled how Willa would act even at the mention of her husband. She always deferred to him and granted his every wish. The thought of disappointing him sent her into a tizzy. The more I thought about it, the more it became clear to me that Willa was afraid of him. Understandably so, if he was indeed given to striking her. Considering the difference in their respective sizes, I can't imagine she'd have the nerve to attack him for fear of his retaliation."

George stood, unmoved, arms crossed over his chest. "Imagine this," he said. "Let's say Willa and Connor had an argument in his office that morning. She did say she spoke with him before the wedding. We also saw her go to their home during the reception."

I nodded my agreement. "Go on."

"Assume the argument became heated. He assaulted her and she managed to push him away. He slipped and hit his head against the desk. We both saw how easily he might have tripped on the carpet. Perhaps he stumbled around the desk to his chair. Perhaps she even helped him, and in doing so, she soiled the handkerchief with his blood. Once Connor sat down, she could see that he was weakened, but still he hurled abuse at her. Might she not have picked up the walking stick Bainbridge had left behind and given him another whack?" He raised his hands. "It might have happened that way."

Graham wore an expression of astonishment that I'm certain was mirrored on my own face. But we both remained silent. I wanted to defend her, but George was right. It might have happened that way.

"Why would she have hidden the handkerchief in my desk?" Graham looked positively ill.

"She may not have realized it was soiled until she arrived here. When she saw it, she panicked." George snapped his fingers. "The blood on your sleeve. It might have come from Willa."

"If you are right and Willa hid the handkerchief in Graham's desk, then who notified Delaney about it?"

George frowned. "Someone must have seen her hide it. A servant, perhaps."

"The police were here. The servants were questioned. Why would that person wait two or three days to come forward?"

"People are often afraid to speak up," George said, though he sounded less confident in his theory.

"What about Sudley?" I asked. "Even if Willa had murdered Connor, who murdered Sudley? She wasn't here. Their murders can't be coincidence. There must be something to connect the two men."

"Their children. But I don't see how that could get both men murdered."

"Maybe my father is right. Maybe this had something to do with Connor's business. Might Sudley have been connected in some way? Or politics? Mr. Bainbridge mentioned Connor liked to court politicians. I don't know to what end, but Sudley is rather powerful in the House of Lords."

George grew thoughtful. "A man of Sudley's influence in the House of Lords could come in quite handy for a businessman, particularly one with Connor's lack of scruples. That would explain why he'd be so keen on Fitzwalter as a son-in-law."

"Would Lord Sudley have been in a position to do favors for Connor? Did Connor have business concerns in England?"

"I thought he was here to bid on some company in England. He and Bainbridge both." George moved back and forth along the edge of the carpet. Pacing meant he was deep in thought.

"It would be helpful to look through Connor's files."

"We'll have to wait and see if they make their way to my father, but in the meantime, what if we speak with his business associates?" I suggested. "The ones he calls on when he's doing dodgy business."

"The Higgins brothers." George raised a brow. "That's not a bad idea."

Sidney and Archie Higgins operated from an address in Marylebone. I was surprised to find that George, who had never met them, already knew their location. "I asked Jarvis," he said when I inquired. Apparently, the Higginses hadn't exaggerated their fame. Their business occupied the back room of a dry goods shop. When we entered and asked about the brothers, the clerk at the counter tipped his head toward a green painted door. "You'll find them in there."

A hand-lettered sign hung over the door. "Higgins Removers," I read, raising a brow at George. "If someone gets in your way, they will remove them for a reasonable fee."

"The business is a clever cover. A mover's wagon can stand in the street for some time without being obvious, while they wait for—"

"Their victim to emerge from his house?" I tsked. "Clever

criminals are dangerous. I liked them better when I thought they were fools. Delaney didn't seem to consider them as suspects in Connor's murder though."

"He was rather dismissive, wasn't he?" George hesitated, his hand poised on the door handle. "Despite that, it might be best if I have Jack take you home."

"I've made it this far," I said. "Let's proceed."

He pushed open the door to reveal what appeared to be a storage room. Boxes and wooden containers lined the floor-to-ceiling shelves. Crates, too large to fit on shelves, were stacked or scattered across the floor, leaving marks and lines in the dust.

"At least there's a desk," George observed. Indeed, there was, made of some inferior species of wood, battered, abused, shoved into a corner, and smothered by a thick coat of dust. One of the crates served as a chair. There was no sign of the brothers.

"Business must be booming," I said. "Where do you suppose they are?"

"Out on a job?" George pointed to footprints in the dust and followed them to a back door. I crept up behind him as he pulled it open. Daylight made the place look even more derelict, something I didn't think possible.

"Oye, looks like we have a customer." The voice came from the yard outside the door. George stepped out and I peered around the doorframe into a small, fenced-in yard of gravel with a view of the backs of the buildings one street over. There was no sign of any moving equipment. We did, however, find the proprietors. The Higgins brothers were seated together on a wooden bench, heedless of the cold, smoking cigars. "Wait, I recognize you." The smaller one—I had no idea who was who any longer—pointed his cigar at me.

"Yes, we met at Mr. Connor's home the other day," I said.

"That's it. Well, we owe you our thanks, ma'am. With that

note you gave us, old Otto Winston paid us everything we were due." He set his cigar in a bowl full of ash, then wiped his hands on the legs of his trousers. Turning back, he slapped his brother on the arm. "You remember the lady, don't you, Archie?"

Ah, so the smaller one was Sidney. That would make introductions smoother.

" 'Course I do." Archie Higgins blew out a perfect circle of smoke, then dropped the cigar in the bowl and came to his feet. He doffed his soft cap in a sweeping motion which, when combined with a miniscule bow, looked almost gallant. "How can we be of service, ma'am. Or, bless you, have you brought us some business?" He eyed George.

I stepped through the doorway and stood next to George. "This is Mr. Archie and Mr. Sidney Higgins. Gentlemen, this is my husband, Mr. Hazelton. In a way, he does have some business to discuss with you."

The larger Higgins looked George up and down. "Does he now? Well, I say that calls for a nip." The two men found this uproariously amusing. Slapping each other on the back, they herded us into the storage room. Archie took a seat on the crate, pulled open a deep drawer in the desk, and removed a bottle of gin, the one item in the room that didn't require a thorough dusting. He pulled the cork out with his teeth—good heavens—and handed the bottle to George.

George took a deep pull from the bottle and handed it back. Thank goodness I was apparently exempt from this ritual. Each of the brothers drank from the bottle, before Archie Higgins returned it to its place of prominence in the drawer. With a voluble exhale and a smacking of his lips, he unfolded himself to his full height and faced George. "So, what kind of business are you interested in?"

"We're quick, thorough, and very discreet-like," Sidney added.

"I understand you did some work here and there for James Connor," George began.

"Says who?" Sidney Higgins stepped into the stance of a boxer, raising his fists until his brother pushed them back down.

"Says us. Don't you remember? She helped us collect our money from Connor's man."

"If we said it, it must be true. You a friend of Connor's?"

George let that pass. "Connor and I have a mutual acquaintance. Two, in fact. Lord Sudley and his son, Daniel Fitzwalter. I believe there was an arrangement involving Connor and the younger man's debts."

Sidney Higgins shrugged. "Hardly matters now, does it?"

"You mean because Connor's dead?" I wasn't sure where George was going with this conversation.

"I mean because the daughter's gonna marry him."

"Was that the deal, then?" George asked. "If Fitzwalter married Madeline Connor, her father would forgive his debts?"

Archie Higgins stepped forward, and placing a hand on his brother's arm, he effectively silenced him. "This doesn't sound like business to me. You're asking a lot of questions." He moved his hand over his heart. "We can't break our customer's trust all willy-nilly-like. That would be . . ." He snapped his fingers. "What's the word?"

"Unethical?" I suggested, earning me a glare from George. Perhaps I shouldn't be so helpful.

Archie pushed out his lower lip. "I like that. Not the word I was thinking of, mind you, but it'll do. Sidney and me, we have ethics."

"That means," Sidney put in, "if you want answers, it's going to cost you."

"Of course," George put in smoothly. He deftly removed a crown from his waistcoat pocket. "This should serve for my meager questions. In addition, I may have a more lucrative job for you once you explain how matters were between Connor and Fitzwalter. Sudley, too, if he was involved. Without those answers, I really can't commission the job."

"Would this fabled job be related to Fitzwalter then?"

"Indeed. Is that a problem?"

George dropped the coin into Archie Higgins's outstretched hand. The man slipped it into his pocket. "You're right, Fitzwalter was in debt to Connor, but he was in even deeper to a money lender. A loan shark. You know the type? Every week the interest doubles. Toffs end up selling their estates so they can pay that debt, 'cause the alternative could be floating face down in the Thames."

I found that odd. "What is the point of killing someone who owes you money? You'd never get it back."

Sidney gave me a reassuring nod. "Oh, they'd get it back. They'd come after the wife of the poor bloke, or the family. One way or another, they'd get their money."

That was a chilling prospect.

"So, marrying Madeline Connor didn't merely cancel his debt with her father, he'd be able to pay back the loan shark, is that about it?"

"If he married the girl," Archie said, "Connor agreed to buy his debt back from the lender."

"And the bloke'd have more money that anyone could spend," Sidney added. "Though I'd be happy to give it a try."

That explained why Fitzwalter wasn't willing to wait until after a suitable period of mourning. He needed to marry Madeline now.

George blew out his breath in a whistle. "Are you sure Connor hadn't already bought the debt?"

Archie Higgins stroked the whiskers on his chin while he considered the possibility. "That wasn't the plan, but no, I couldn't be sure. Mr. Connor didn't tell us his every move."

"All right, then. Here's the commission if you wish to accept it. I want to know who Fitzwalter owes money to—be it loan

shark or tailor—and what the payoff terms are. Can you manage that?"

The brothers exchanged a look. Sidney cleared his throat.
"We're going to have to rub elbows with a dangerous group of
characters? That's going to cost you."

"I pay for results," George said. "The sooner I get them, the
more you'll earn."

"There's nothing we can't find out."

"Excellent," I said. "I'd like to know what Connor wanted
out of the bargain."

All three men stared in confusion.

"Fitzwalter is a nice enough chap, but with all this debt,
Connor must have realized the young man would be a liability.
Why choose him for a son-in-law?"

"We did some work for the man," Archie said, "but he did-
n't exactly confide in us."

George tapped his finger against his lip. "I know you don't
believe he was just title hunting, but what about our theory of
buying a politician?"

"I think it's very likely that Connor hoped to have some influence over Lord Sudley, but taking on Fitzwalter is rather a
high price to pay unless he had some sort of guarantee that Sudley would cooperate."

George nodded in understanding. He placed his hands on
the dusty desk, facing the Higginses. "Here's what I propose,
gentlemen. I'll have a bonus for you if in your investigation,
you can find any connection between Connor and Lord Sudley. Whether Sudley was involved in the marriage contract or if
they had some other business in common."

"Done!" Archie slapped his palm on the top of the desk and
drew it back sharply.

"Splinter?" I asked, but quickly saw it was actually a gash.
The large man paled and wobbled as a trickle of blood dripped
to the floor.

"Mr. Higgins, are you unwell?"

He made a gurgling noise in response. His eyelids fluttered as his eyes rolled upward. George pulled me back just as Archie Higgins collapsed on the floor with a *thunk* and a cloud of dust.

"Heavens!"

Sidney Higgins heaved a sigh and knelt beside his brother. "He'll be fine, ma'am. Just can't stand the sight of blood." His gaze traveled between us. "Appreciate it if you kept this to yourselves. It's not good for business."

Chapter Eighteen

We revived Archie, bandaged his hand, and revived him again. Then we bid the Higgins brothers good day. "I've never seen such a large man swoon before," I whispered to George as we exited the shop. "I believe the building shook when he fell."

"I suppose that's why Delaney eliminated them as suspects. He must have known of Mr. Higgins's affliction." He grimaced. "If he had bashed Connor, he'd have to have been blindfolded."

He assisted me into the carriage and we made our way home. "What do you expect a connection between Connor and Sudley to reveal?" I asked him.

"I couldn't say," he replied. "I'm not even sure what Fitzwalter's debt will reveal. Other than Fitzwalter himself, Connor was the only one in favor of the match between him and Madeline. Fitzwalter would be the last person to want Connor dead. Still, finding what the two victims had in common may lead us to the killer. At the moment, the only thing we know they had in common was their children."

"Word among my mother's friends is they needed Fitzwalter to marry an heiress."

George nodded. "Then they'd be expecting a dowry in addition to the payment of their son's debt. This match would have cost Connor a great deal of money."

I shrugged. "It might be worth the expense to have power over the Marquis of Sudley and I do believe that was the point. He wanted a connection to a powerful peer."

"But as you said, to gain that connection, he'd have to take on Fitzwalter as a son-in-law. Why would he go to such lengths? Why not move on to some other peer? Someone would say yes eventually."

I raised a brow. "I would have thought so too, but his reputation has preceded him. You should have heard Lady Esther's scathing dismissal of the Connors. Very few families would want to be associated with a man like him. It might have taken him months to find the right one. I don't see Connor as a patient man."

"It's something to consider, but while we're keeping an open mind, why are you rejecting the possibility that Mrs. Connor murdered her husband? She certainly had motive and opportunity."

"I'm not rejecting the possibility so much as questioning it. You and I may see a motive for murder, but that doesn't mean Willa would have acted on it. Whether Connor was physically abusive, or instead battered her will, she told me he saved her. She was grateful to him. As for opportunity, they were married for ten years. She had the same opportunity to murder him each and every day and never took it. What would cause her to murder him now?"

George let out a snort. "You would never stand for that treatment."

"I had a choice. My fortune may be small, but it affords me

some independence. In their marriage, Connor had all the power and Willa none. That's all too common. A man may abuse his wife, but it doesn't necessarily follow that she will kill him. I'll concede that Willa is a suspect, but if she murdered Connor, who murdered Sudley?" I held up a finger. "Before you say his wife, remember I was speaking to her just before Sudley was found."

George's face took on a look of wonder. "You were speaking to her when Sudley was killed."

"Very likely."

"And she told you Sudley was against the match between his son and Connor's daughter."

"Yes?"

"But we never heard Sudley's opinion from his own lips." He grasped my hand. "Bear with me for a moment while I play this out. What if Sudley didn't object to the match? Perhaps he was fully aware of his son's debt. Connor's fortune would have felt like a gift from heaven. All he had to do in return was, what? Make sure Connor received some government contracts? He might have seen that as a small price."

I shrugged. "All right. What then?"

"The two mothers object. They combine forces. Lady Sudley murders Connor while Mrs. Connor is at the reception. And Mrs. Connor murders Lord Sudley while Lady Sudley is innocently mingling with the other guests at Harleigh House."

My jaw went slack. "Good heavens! The ladies may have objected, but I can't imagine they objected to that degree. You cannot seriously believe that."

"It's a devious plan, to be sure, but it provides that catalyst you spoke of, that pushes Mrs. Connor to murder. It's not out of the realm of possibility."

"I beg to differ! There's a possibility that Willa might kill her husband in self-defense, but now you say she'd kill someone else in cold blood? That I can't believe. Besides, she wasn't even at the party."

"But that's the beauty of it. She was just next door. She's familiar with Graham's house and could easily have slipped in and waited in the dining room for her moment."

"No, it's impossible. And how would the death of their husbands solve the problem? Fitzwalter offered marriage and Madeline accepted."

"They probably weren't counting on that," George conceded. "But with their fathers' deaths, the couple will have to wait to announce their betrothal. Perhaps in that time, Lady Sudley will find another, more acceptable heiress for Fitzwalter."

I bit back the argument I'd been forming and nearly choked on it. "Lady Sudley mentioned that they'd have to wait a year to make an announcement, and that much could happen in a year."

He arched a brow.

"She may have been pointing out nothing more than the obvious. It doesn't mean she had anything to do with her husband's death."

"I think you're more willing to entertain the idea, though."

"I still say it's impossible, but thank you for planting that seed in my brain. I'll never look at either woman again without wondering. I hope Delaney uncovers the killer soon and that it isn't either of them."

"It wouldn't be all that difficult to learn if they each have alibis for the time the other woman's husband was murdered." He gave me a hopeful look. "If so, that would eliminate them quickly and you'd never have to entertain the thought again."

"I've paid far too many calls on Willa since Connor's death. If I haven't raised her suspicions about my motives yet, another call and a round of questions will certainly do the trick."

He settled back into the seat. "Perhaps Delaney has already questioned her. I need to speak with him about the case."

"Delaney may be weary of our questions. Do you have any information to trade?"

"He should be willing to speak with me regardless. One of his suspects is my client. Two, if he still considers Graham a suspect."

"I don't believe he even considers Alonzo a suspect any longer."

"Until Delaney officially exonerates him, I'm still your brother's counsel, and as such I'm entitled to inquire about the status of the case. Besides, I believe I do have information to trade."

"What?"

"Our new theory about Connor's interest in Sudley's legislative influence. And I don't know if he's aware that Madeline and Fitzwalter are now officially engaged."

"Now that I think about it, I don't understand why Madeline agreed to marry Fitzwalter. Her father can no longer force the issue. As his only child, I assume she is now enormously wealthy. She can either leave him to his own devices or if she feels magnanimous, she can forgive Fitzwalter's debt and send him on his way. She doesn't actually have to marry the man."

He heaved a sigh. "You have some very good questions today. I have no answer for that one."

"What about this one—we aren't going to make it to Cannes, are we?"

He gave me a sad smile. "Are you very disappointed?"

"Me? It's my family causing the delay, and probable cancellation, of our wedding trip. I'm worried about you."

"You could never disappoint me," he said taking my hand. "As soon as this is over, we'll see about planning another trip.

It won't be the Romanovs' villa in Cannes, but as long as we're alone together, wherever we go will be paradise."

"Who could say no to that?" We laced our fingers together and I glanced out the window. We were almost home. "I'd like to stop at Hetty's and check on Rose. Since we aren't on our wedding trip, I don't know why she's still there."

George laughed. "I assume they thought we'd like some time alone, but it hasn't worked out that way, has it? If you don't mind, I'll stop long enough to say hello, then go on to Delaney's precinct. That will give you some time with Rose, and with any luck, I'll come home with new information about the case, or cases, as it may be."

That arrangement was fine with me. After a short wait at Hetty's door, Mrs. Thompson greeted us effusively. "My lady! Sir! Come in. Come in." Mrs. Thompson, my former housekeeper and now Hetty's, usually comported herself with the precision and bearing of a military commander. Though not a single hair escaped from her salt-and-pepper bun and her uniform of white apron over black gown was still tidy and buttoned up to the neck, she was far from her usual placid self. She nearly pulled me out of my coat in her rush to get me situated. I couldn't remember her ever being this excited to see me.

"Is everything all right, Mrs. Thompson?" I asked while she took George's coat.

"All right? Yes, of course." She ran her free hand down her apron. "And I don't suppose you're here to see the likes of me, are you? Shall I see if Mrs. Chesney is at home?"

"Oh." I'd expected to simply walk in. These were my relatives, after all, and they'd been walking in on me all week. Would I actually have to wait in the entry hall of my old home? I blew out an impatient breath. "I'm actually here for Rose, but I suppose I should greet my aunt. First, what about you? You

seem quite unsettled. Is everything all right with the household?"

She took on a pained expression. "I'm sure everything will
resolve in time."

Now I understood. Mother was not an easy houseguest.
Nor an easy mother, for that matter. "I'm sure you're right,
Mrs. Thompson. Everything will calm down in due course. I
believe I hear Aunt Hetty in the drawing room." I turned to
George. "Why don't I pop in with you and say hello. Then I
can go up to the nursery for Rose."

"Beg your pardon, my lady, but you'll find Lady Rose in the
kitchen."

"In the kitchen? Is she disturbing you, Mrs. Thompson?"

"Heavens, no. We're having a nice coze."

She scurried off after that, and we headed for the drawing
room where we found Hetty and my father seated on the sofa
poring over some paperwork on the tea table. Gilliam sipped a
cup of tea in the chair beside them and in the chair next to him
was Constable Timmons, who gazed in something like adoration at Frankie.

My father saw me first. "Frankie! Hazelton! Do come in, we
could use another set of eyes on this matter."

We crossed the room. "It seems you have several sets of eyes
as it is," I said. "What are you working on?" The few sheets of
paper didn't look like the contents of Connor's desk.

Hetty heaved a sigh. "Your father's charts." She held up a
page of what looked like some kind of diagram. "He's attempting to solve the murder cases." She looked me up and down.
"You clearly come by it honestly, dear."

I took a seat in my favorite chair opposite Gilliam and next
to Frankie. I eyed the array of papers on the table. "Did you actually find something of interest with Connor's agent? George
told me he thought everything looked legitimate."

Frankie shook a finger at George, who stood beside my chair. "Your husband ran out of patience and left." He grinned and shuffled a few pages around. Finally settling on one, he waved it with a flourish in front of my face. "This document details what was to have been Connor's latest investment. A distillery."

"I thought he was more interested in mining," I said.

"He was quite diversified in his investments. But this was an unusual choice for him. He tended toward new enterprises in new industries. Profitable ones. This was decidedly not. However, Peter Bainbridge was interested in this distillery. They were bidding against one another."

George took the page from Frankie's hand, frowning as he perused it. "Yes, I heard they both wanted to purchase the same company."

"Not for the first time," Hetty added. "Based on what Franklin found with Connor's agent, if Mr. Bainbridge put in a bid on something, Connor followed suit. He'd drive up the price so Mr. Bainbridge must either pay more, or back out entirely."

I sighed. "Thus, the feud proceeded."

"And it grows more interesting." The twinkle in Frankie's eyes told me he was enjoying this immensely. "Guess who sat on the board of the distillery?"

George narrowed his eyes. "Surely, not Lord Sudley."

Frankie nodded. "The very same."

"Interesting, indeed," George said. "With this purchase Connor would have made Sudley very happy, while at the same time he'd manage to put Peter Bainbridge's nose out of joint."

"How did you find this out?" I glanced at the papers that littered the table. "Don't tell me his agent allowed you to remove his documents?"

"No. Sudley's role is a matter of record. Easy to discover if you know where to look. What you see here"—he waved a hand over the table—"is the whereabouts of everyone at different times during the wedding reception." He shrugged. "Considering this new information, I wanted to determine if Bainbridge had the opportunity to commit the murder."

Hetty gave her beau a warm smile. "We'd never have been able to chart everyone's movements if Gilliam hadn't come to call and provided his recollection of the guests' statements."

"Yes. Lucky you stopped by, Gilliam," Frankie said.

I cast a glance at poor Gilliam, wondering if he would agree with Frankie's assessment. He likely stopped by with the hope of finding Hetty alone. Instead, he spent his rare free time working with my father. Still, he seemed completely content.

"You might take note of this." Frankie waved one of the pages until George stepped around the tea table and took it from him. "Mr. Bainbridge arrived twenty minutes later than the rest of us," Frankie said. "Time enough to murder Connor, wouldn't you say?"

George and I exchanged a worried glance. The man hadn't actually arrived late. He'd simply slipped away with Mother before anyone saw him. We could hardly tell Frankie that. However, Mother was going to get a piece of my mind for not having spoken with him by now. I leaned back in my chair and considered the evidence. Even though I knew Mr. Bainbridge had an alibi for the beginning of the reception, he had paid a call on Connor that morning. A heated argument had ensued. But the butler had shown him out and had seen Connor alive—or so Bainbridge said.

His visit to Connor after the luncheon was brief. Had it been long enough to murder the man? If Connor was dogging his business deals, Bainbridge had a motive in addition to their general animosity. Both men wanted to buy an unprofitable distillery in which Lord Sudley had an interest. Perhaps Bainbridge wanted Sudley in his pocket, too.

I glanced up to see both Frankie and Hetty waiting for a reaction. "Bainbridge and Sudley had an argument last night at Graham's soiree. I wonder if it was about this transaction."

Frankie lowered his head to peer at me over his spectacles. "Did you hear any of it?"

"No, but I mentioned it to Delaney. Is that everything you've learned about the business deal? I understand there was also a group of investors interested in purchasing this company."

Frankie drew his brows together. "Is that so? I shall have to dig a little deeper." He brushed his hands together. "This is merely the beginning of an investigation, of course. We shall see where it leads me."

"I'm on my way to Inspector Delaney's precinct now," George said. "I'll pass this information along to him. Have you come across anything else?"

Frankie shook his head. "Nothing else of importance. Wouldn't you agree, Timmons?"

The constable furrowed his brow. "Well, there is that document."

Heavens, this was the first time I'd heard the young man speak. His loud, raspy voice came as something of a surprise.

"Yes," Hetty said. "We are still trying to reconstruct a document from those torn shreds you brought home. Constable Timmons has been assisting." She shrugged. "There are many missing pieces but it's beginning to look like some sort of contract. Just give me a little more time with it."

"Very well," George said. "I'll take myself off then. I'll be sure to tell Delaney of your findings, Mr. Price."

George took his leave and I walked him to the door. "Gilliam must have the patience of a saint," I remarked. "Whenever he wants to spend time with Aunt Hetty he is thwarted by a family emergency, my mother's complaining, or my father's work."

"Don't waste too much sympathy on him," George said as he retrieved his hat from the entry table. "He is content to bask in the brilliance that is Hetty Chesney. It blinds him to the foibles of her family."

I stroked his cheek. "George Hazleton, that was almost poetic. I hope you are right."

He laughed and pulled me close for a delightful kiss. "I know I'm right. I have the same feeling about Mrs. Chesney's niece."

With that he swept out the door, leaving me with a lovely glow, which I took back to the drawing room. Hetty and Gilliam were now seated together on the sofa, and Constable Timmons was stacking up my father's paperwork.

"Well done, all of you. You may not have solved this case, but you've given the police a new lead to investigate." I took a seat next to Frankie. "How are you finding time to do all this?" I asked him.

He shrugged. "There's not as much for me to do while I'm away from New York. I would have returned by now, but Alonzo is required to stay, and I can't leave with his fate so uncertain. As to my access to Connor's files, Mr. Winston, the agent, will be without employment once he wraps up Connor's affairs in a few months. I implied that I'd be willing to recommend him to my business associates and he's been very accommodating."

Constable Timmons nodded his agreement.

"I think Bainbridge is a good suspect," he continued. "I wonder how he accounted for his time that afternoon."

At some point, someone was going to tell him where Mr. Bainbridge was and what he was doing at that time. I hoped it would be Mother, but I feared it would be Delaney.

The sound of activity in the entry hall drew my attention. I thought it might be George returning but was surprised to see Alonzo and Madeline walk into the drawing room instead. I stood to greet them, then froze when I saw Madeline's tear-streaked face.

"What's wrong? What happened?" Hetty and I rushed to the couple and ushered them to seats. Alonzo looked grim when he sat down next to Frankie.

"It's Mrs. Connor," he said. "Inspector Delaney has arrested her for murder."

Chapter Nineteen

Madeline appeared paralyzed from shock. Hetty offered every possible assistance she could bring to hand—a doctor, a bed, a glass of brandy—but the young woman simply stared off into the distance. Her fingers tangled together. Her eyes watery from unshed tears. Finally, Hetty settled on tea and sent the housemaid, Jenny, to bring it.

After a brief exchange with Hetty, Gilliam tapped Constable Timmons on the shoulder and the two of them left us to deal with this crisis privately.

Meanwhile, Frankie pushed Alonzo for an explanation. "Inspector Delaney had already taken Mrs. Connor away by the time I arrived at the house," he said. "Miss Connor was as you see her now. I couldn't get so much as a word from her, so I imposed on the butler and Mrs. Connor's maid to tell me what had happened."

"How long ago was that? When did you arrive at the Connor's?" I asked.

"Not quite an hour ago," he replied.

"Inspector Delaney had been searching Lord Harleigh's

home this morning and found a handkerchief he suspected belonged to Mrs. Connor. He left to question her. That was late morning." I cast a glance at Madeline. "If she's been like this all that time, I think we should call for a doctor."

"I'll send a message to him right now." Hetty left the room as Jenny entered with the tea service. While I poured, I urged Alonzo to continue his story.

"You are right about the time," he said. "The butler told me she'd left with Delaney two hours earlier. The inspector said he was taking her to the Chelsea precinct and that she was under arrest. He knew nothing more. Mrs. Connor's maid had been with her when Delaney questioned her. The handkerchief—" He stopped to glance at Madeline, then at me. "I assume you know the condition it was in?"

I nodded.

"Well, I don't," Frankie said.

Alonzo leaned across the sofa, lowered his voice, and I assume told Frankie about the blood. "Once Mrs. Connor admitted the handkerchief was hers," he continued, "the inspector asked her how it came to be next door." He looked again at Madeline. "I presume Mrs. Connor and Lord Harleigh are on friendly terms and may have shared a cup of tea from time to time." He raised his brows to such heights, I assumed he was attempting to convey that he knew they shared much more than tea.

"I understand," I told him.

Frankie glanced at me in confusion. "Well, I don't."

"Let me explain later, Frankie, or Alonzo will never get his story out. At what point did he conclude he had enough evidence to arrest her?"

"When she confessed," he said.

I fell against the back of the chair, my lips shaping the word *what* though no sound escaped me. "Willa confessed? I can't believe it."

Frankie appeared equally surprised. "She wasn't even on my list," he said. "Did she confess to both murders?"

"I asked, but neither of the servants knew. After that, Delaney allowed Mrs. Connor to tell Madeline what was happening, then he took her away."

Hetty returned at that point. "I expect the doctor within the hour," she said. "And I think Miss Connor should stay here, at least for today."

"I agree." I slipped next to Madeline and took her hand. "It's ice cold. Hetty, perhaps we should tuck her in with a hot toddy to await the doctor." I rubbed her hands with my own. "Madeline, dear, I know you've had a shock." There was not so much as a flicker of acknowledgment from the young woman. "We'll take care of you, dear."

I motioned to Hetty to help me. Each of us took an arm and urged her to stand. With a huff, Alonzo stood and shooed us away. He lifted her in his arms, then glanced at Hetty. "Lead the way," he said.

Alonzo waited outside the door while we got Madeline settled and tucked into bed. I draped her clothes on the chair. "I hope to steal Rose away from you today," I told Hetty. "George and I are clearly going nowhere until this matter is settled, and you have quite the houseful as it is."

Hetty walked with me to the door. "You're taking away my only sane guest," she grumbled. "What is going on between your mother and father? I've tried to stay out of it, but he's clearly done something to earn her ire."

"It's not my place to say, but I plan to encourage her to clear the air quickly. Taking Rose away might help. She won't be able to use her as a shield any longer. The poor child has taken to hiding in the kitchen."

Hetty sighed. "With Mrs. Connor's arrest, why can't you

and Hazelton leave on your wedding trip? Alonzo appears to be out of danger now."

We paused by the door. "George will have arrived at Delaney's precinct by now. If Mrs. Connor is still there, I'm willing to bet he will take it upon himself to offer her counsel."

"Do you doubt that she did it?"

"I'm not sure what to think. He was an overbearing husband. Graham believes he abused her physically. I can attest that Connor intimidated her. Does that mean she'd never lift a hand to him? Or was fear of the man the very thing that pushed her to do it?" I shrugged. "Either way, I don't know how she could have murdered Sudley. She wasn't at the benefit. How would she have known Sudley was even there?" I pressed my fingers to my head. "There are far too many questions unanswered. Suffice it to say George would feel badly for her and offer to help."

Hetty nodded her understanding. "You go on and collect Rose," she said. "I'll stay with Miss Connor until the doctor arrives."

I opened the door to see Alonzo pacing the hallway and turned back to my aunt. "It seems you'll have some company."

As Mrs. Thompson had suggested, I found Rose in the kitchen chatting away with the housekeeper while she cooked. I feigned surprise at seeing her seated at the worktable. "Why, you're letting Mrs. Thompson do all the work! I thought you'd be an accomplished chef by now, and here you are, merely observing."

She scrunched lower into her chair. "Mrs. Thompson doesn't mind."

"I surely don't, my lady." She turned and cast a smile at Rose. "Lady Rose is charming company."

I pulled out a chair and seated myself next to my daughter. "As you see, Mr. Hazelton and I haven't been able to go away this week. Would you be willing to bring your charming company home to us?"

"Now?" Her face lit with a smile.

"As soon as you are ready you may go up to the nursery and help Nanny supervise the packing. I'll go home and send a footman over to move your things."

Rose bounced in her seat.

"You'll also need to say goodbye to Aunt Hetty before you leave," I reminded her. "Grandmama, and Grandpapa, too."

"And Mrs. Thompson," she added.

The housekeeper turned and planted her hands on her hips. "I expect to see you back here every day, else you'll never become a cook."

"I'll be back," Rose promised, then ran up to the nursery to start her packing.

I decided it was time to go home, but Frankie called to me from the drawing room when I passed by. "Can you spare me a moment?" he asked.

"Of course." I seated myself next to him on the sofa.

"What do you make of Mrs. Connor's confession today? She's a friend of yours, isn't she? Could she do such a thing?"

"I'm not entirely sure we know our friends as well as we think we do. George will likely come home with more information about her situation."

Frankie shook his head. "I was so certain it was Bainbridge."

"It still may turn out to be him."

"It may at that. I suppose I'll put all this away and see if your mother is at home or if she's out paying calls again."

"When you find her, please tell her I'm taking Rose home with me today."

"She'll be heartbroken. She may actually have to speak with me for a change." He caught me with a calculated glance. "Something seems to be wrong with her lately. Do you know what it is?"

"No?" Bother! That hadn't come out right. I'd never actually lied to my father before.

He narrowed his gaze. "You do, don't you? What is it?"

I glanced around for someone or something to rescue me. "I can't tell you, but you very definitely should ask her."

"Well, now you must tell me."

"I can't. It isn't my place. She needed someone to confide in so she told me, and I advised her to talk with you about it." I raised my hands helplessly. "That's all I can say."

He placed a hand on my wrist, forestalling my exit. "She seems very put out with me and I've no idea what I might have done." He narrowed his eyes. "I wouldn't want to end up like Connor, if you catch my meaning."

I laughed. "I'm quite sure she isn't contemplating murder." At least not yet. "You must ask her yourself."

He took a breath, then compressed his lips. I'd never seen him anything less than sure of himself. I wished I could help. "What if she won't tell me?"

I came to my feet, hoping to make a speedy escape. "If you ask her what's troubling her, and she refuses to say, tell her I already told you, and you'd like an explanation." He looked shocked at the idea of subterfuge, but knowing my mother, he might need it. I headed for the door. Halfway there I stopped and looked back at him. "But for heaven's sake, once she's told you, don't forget to confess the truth—I never said a word." I didn't want to end up like Conner either.

Just as I turned to leave, George stepped into the drawing room and caught me in his arms. "Aha! I thought I'd find you here." He glanced behind me. "But no Rose?"

"Nanny will be bringing her home shortly."

"Rose is leaving?" We turned to see Mother coming down the hall stairs. "I suppose her home is with you. But don't be in such a rush." She took George by the arm. "Come into the drawing room and visit for a moment."

I hesitated. "We really should be going, Mother."

George gave me a quizzical glance. "Surely we have a few moments. I have some news your parents may wish to hear."

That was enough encouragement for Mother. She pulled George into the drawing room. I suspected we were a means to avoid any private conversation with Frankie.

I trailed behind them. Frankie was still seated on the sofa, collecting his paperwork from the tea table. His smile for Mother faded when he saw she wasn't alone. He stood and indicated she take the chair next to him. I sat beside him on the sofa, ready to give him a poke should he attempt to question her now. George remained on his feet. Hands clasped in front of him, he rocked back on his heels.

"You'll never believe what happened at the precinct this afternoon," he said.

Wouldn't I? "I'd believe just about anything at this point."

"Delaney arrested Mrs. Connor."

"Yes? Is that it?"

His brows lowered. "Not at all. I'm simply giving you a moment to be surprised." He rolled his hand, inviting me to do so. When I didn't react, he put the hand on his hip and narrowed his eyes. "You already know."

Mother glanced between us. "I don't. Why did he arrest her?"

"For Connor's murder," Frankie said.

Her eyes widened, then narrowed as she took in the news. "Really? Her own husband?" She glanced at Frankie. "Imagine that."

Mother looked as if she were indeed imagining "that."

Frankie pulled at his collar.

I cleared my throat, causing George to tear his rather horrified gaze from her. "Yes. Well," he said. "How did you find out?"

"Madeline Connor is temporarily residing here," I said.

He lifted his gaze heavenward. "Of course she is. Alonzo brought her, I take it?"

"Yes. She was in quite a state, but Hetty has sent for the doctor. I'm sure he'll take good care of her. So, tell me what else you learned. Alonzo said Willa confessed, but he's not entirely sure what she confessed to."

"Murdering Connor."

"What about Sudley?"

"Delaney told me she claims to know nothing about Lord Sudley's murder."

"Did you have a chance to speak with her?"

"She refused my offer of representation, much to Delaney's relief. She'd already given a statement."

"Yet she claims not to have murdered Sudley." I drummed my fingers against my knee. "Just when I thought we'd uncovered something important about Connor and Sudley that might connect their murders, we have a confession from Connor's wife. Is Delaney certain she did it?"

George's expression made it clear he questioned my sanity. "Are you suggesting she confessed to a crime she didn't commit?"

I worried my lip while I considered the possibility. "Perhaps she was only responsible for the first blow to his head. Not the lethal one. She might have confessed believing she had killed him." When I glanced at my mother and father to see their reactions, they looked equally unconvinced. It was a good thing I wasn't defending Willa in court.

"Delaney is a professional. We should assume he had her explain precisely what she did." George leaned over my chair. "I hate to cast doubt on your instincts, but she very likely killed Conner."

"But then, who killed Sudley? If Willa really did kill Connor, whether intentionally or in self-defense, then your theory about her and Lady Sudley must be false."

"I don't understand," Mother said. "You had a theory about the murders that involved Mrs. Connor and Lady Sudley?"

I leaned forward to speak around Frankie. "The theory is that they both conspired to murder each other's husband."

Mother drew in a long gasp. "How positively diabolical!" I haven't seen her this excited since Reggie proposed.

George took a step back.

Frankie dropped her hand and jumped to his feet. "Daisy, we must have a talk."

"George and I were just about to leave," I said.

"We were?"

Mother wore a look of panic. "There's no need for you to leave."

"Yes, there is. Rose is likely waiting for us." I moved as swiftly as Frankie had. Taking George's hand, I led him to the entry hall. "We'll see ourselves out."

I pushed George out Hetty's door and over to our own without even bothering to collect our coats. Jarvis greeted us once we arrived in our own entry hall. "Lady Rose and her nanny have arrived, ma'am. They're up in the nursery."

"Thank you, Jarvis. I apologize for the lack of warning, but Mr. Hazelton and I were detained next door."

His face, usually devoid of expression, seemed to light up. "It was no trouble at all. And may I say how delighted the staff are to have a child in the house once more."

With a bow, Jarvis left us and I headed for the stairs. "Are you sure we should have left them alone?" George asked. "Your mother had a rather frightening look in her eye."

"Frankie will be fine. He simply wants to find out what's been bothering her, and she's been avoiding the admittedly difficult conversation. They didn't need us about."

"Hm, I hope we needn't discuss anything difficult, or at least nothing that can't wait until dinner. I'm famished."

"We can't talk about murder at dinner. Rose is dining with us to celebrate her homecoming. We'll have to speak of other things."

"You're making an eight-year-old wait until seven to dine?"

"She spent all afternoon in the kitchen with Mrs. Thompson. She's had her tea and then some. I doubt she'll do more than pick at her food."

"Well, I'm hungry." He took my hand as we climbed the stairs to our bedchamber to change for dinner. "Imagine an entire meal without talk of murder."

"Such a novelty."

Chapter Twenty

George and I enjoyed a quiet dinner with Rose. It was lovely to sit together as a family and speak of ordinary things such as what Rose should call her new stepfather. George promised to respond to any name she chose, but for some reason, Rose was too shy to suggest Georgie. For my part I worried that she might feel the odd man out down the road when she had half brothers or half sisters who called him Papa while she called him something else. Although I grew up doing that very thing and it never bothered me. I suppose time would tell.

We came to no decisions. Rose grew more and more sleepy throughout the long meal, and by its end, she was more than happy to go off with Nanny to bed. George and I opted for tea rather than brandy. We settled into the sofa at the back of the drawing room, looking out on the garden through the French doors. At least we might have been. Instead, I was pouring tea while George studied me.

I caught him when I handed him his tea. "What is it?"

"That's what I'd like to know," he said. "It's clear you don't accept Willa Connor's confession, and I don't think it's due to your friendship with her, so what is it?"

I finished preparing my own cup and took a sip. "It's not up to me to accept or reject Willa's confession, but if we believe her, we are left with a rather large loose thread."

"Sudley's murder."

I nodded. "I can't believe that both men were murdered within days of each other and one had nothing to do with the other. Frankie did find that Sudley, Connor, and Bainbridge were all involved in the sale of the distillery. Did you mention it to Delaney?"

"I did. Bainbridge had already explained the situation. He claims the argument he and Sudley had yesterday was because Bainbridge rescinded his offer."

"He doesn't want to buy the company?"

"He never did. It seems he was aware of the game Connor was playing in pushing his bids higher and higher and decided turnabout was fair play. He put in an exorbitant offer on this distillery so Connor would outbid him. Then he planned to back out of the bidding and leave Connor with a company that was worth about half what he paid for it."

I rolled my eyes. Rich men and their games.

"With Connor dead, Bainbridge decided he'd better pull his offer before he was the one stuck."

"So if it was Sudley who was angry, Mr. Bainbridge had no motive to kill him." I sipped my tea and pondered this problem. "Or did he? Sudley's anger was understandable. He was about to lose a second lucrative offer. Perhaps he was enraged enough to attack Bainbridge, who then struck him with the candlestick in self-defense." I cast a glance at George. "Is that mad?"

He looked doubtful, but shrugged. "No more so than my theory of the two wives colluding to murder their husbands."

I sighed. "This is such a muddle. Does Delaney have some idea of who killed Sudley?"

"He had nothing more to say on the matter." He raised a brow. "Does that question mean you're willing to believe Willa murdered Connor?"

I was saved from answering by a movement outside the doors in the garden. A good thing because, at the moment, I didn't know what I believed. A bad thing because—who was in our garden? A knock on the door indicated it was likely someone from my family.

Again.

Perhaps Mother had thrown Frankie out of the house.

George opened the door to admit Hetty. With no coat, she wrapped her arms around herself. "I took the back way," she said.

"I can see that. Is something wrong?"

Hetty followed George into the room and sank into one of the club chairs. "I need your help. Whatever the doctor dosed Madeline with this afternoon has worn off. She is up, walking the floor, and quite inconsolable." She heaved a sigh. "At least, I can't console her. Would you please come and speak with her?"

"Of course." I came to my feet and glanced at George. My "you don't mind, do you?" was so obviously an afterthought, I bit my lip.

Fortunately, the gesture made him laugh. "Of course not. She needs you. I'll ponder Sudley's murder while I wait for you."

After dropping a quick kiss on his cheek, I followed Hetty back through the French doors and along the path to what was now her library. Once inside, I saw Madeline, wrapped in one of Hetty's dressing gowns, curled up in the window seat, sobbing into her hands.

I sent Hetty to see if Mrs. Thompson or Jenny could make some tea, the British cure for everything, then seated myself next to Madeline. Though her sobs were heart-wrenching, I had to admit, it was better than her previous state of foggy nothingness. I pulled her into my arms and let her cry, patting her on the back and offering useless words like, *there, there*. It took some time, but eventually, she seemed to have cried herself out.

With an enormous sigh, she pushed away from my shoulder. Her unbraided hair looked wild and with her eyes bloodshot and wide with some inner panic, she looked anything but calmed down.

"I can't believe she did it, Lady Harleigh." Her voice cracked on the words. "She wouldn't hurt my father. She lived for him, for both of us. She always said she owed him her very life." She shuddered as more sobs racked her body.

"I don't want to believe it either, dear, but if not Willa, then who? Do you have any idea who might have killed your father?"

She drew a deep, calming breath. "He was not a kind man by anyone's measure. He was beastly to Willa. But no matter how badly he treated her, she always forgave him. She couldn't have done this. He must have made enemies, don't you think? And he was alone in his office at the front of the house. With the staff below stairs, anyone could have walked in and killed him."

Hetty came in at that point with the tea tray and busied herself setting it up on the desk.

Once we were all settled with a cup, Madeline returned her attention to me. "Can you help her, Lady Harleigh? You and Mr. Hazelton? I know she confessed, but she didn't kill him."

"I'll speak with Mr. Hazelton," I told her, though I had no idea how to help Willa.

Hetty stood leaning against the desk, observing Madeline. "Why would she have confessed to the crime if she didn't do it?"

"I've no idea. It's such a strange thing for her to do that I believed it for a time. Now I feel guilty that I ever thought so ill of her." She sniffed and wiped her eyes. I noticed her ring finger was now bare. Interesting.

"There's another thing we should discuss," I said. "You came home with Alonzo and are staying with his family. Does

Fitzwalter know where you are? Do you still plan to marry him? Should we send him word you are here?" I hoped this last wouldn't be necessary, for Alonzo's sake.

She laid her hand on my wrist. "Please don't. I do not want to marry him but he refuses to release me from our agreement."

Their agreement? "Dear, the details of your agreement ought to be none of my affair, but I must admit I am familiar with them. If it is the debt Fitzwalter is concerned about, you can simply forgive it, can you not? Wipe his slate clean, so to speak."

"I can, and have offered to do so, but it was not enough. He insists I honor my obligation to him."

"Nothing was announced, my dear." Hetty seated herself in a chair nearby. "You have no obligation to him."

She frowned in confusion. "He was so insistent."

Of course he was, the scoundrel. He wanted possession of her father's fortune, both to pay off his other creditors and to finance the lifestyle he desired. How dare he take advantage of a grieving and troubled young woman?

"If you do not wish to marry him, he cannot force you. You have much on your plate right now. Avoid him for the time being. Once things have been resolved with your stepmother, you should speak with your father's solicitor. He can take the necessary steps to remove Fitzwalter from your life."

"Avoid him for how long?"

"You are both in deep mourning right now. He has no business pressing you to do anything for at least six months. By then, your solicitor will have taken care of him."

She frowned, unconvinced. "You make it sound so easy."

"It should be easy." The difficult part will be proving Willa's innocence.

George had fallen asleep while I was gone. I found him sprawled against the back and arm of the sofa. I turned down the lamps, leaving the one next to him burning, and curled up beside him to watch him in repose, thinking how lucky I was to have married him. He'd joined so willingly into my life and welcomed me into his. Reggie never truly shared his life with me. Not that I wanted to take part in his gambling, drinking, and womanizing, but that also proved how perfect George was for me. I actually wanted to become involved in his investigations. I was so grateful he never tried to shut me out.

The fact that he was charming and handsome didn't hurt either. Not so handsome that other women swooned over him, at least I'd never seen that happen and I don't think I'd enjoy it if I did. I studied his face. His tousled hair covered his high forehead so I moved down the line of his nose to those perfect lips. His cheek was scrunched up where it rested on the arm of the sofa. Actually, his neck was a bit twisted, too, and his shoulder would probably ache tomorrow if left in that position.

I moved closer, leaning in to kiss him awake.

"Gaahh!"

George shot up, his arm that had dangled off the sofa swinging around so I had to duck to avoid it, then latch on to it with all my strength.

"Calm down," I whispered. "I don't intend to kill you tonight."

"Thank heaven," he said, rubbing the back of his neck. "You caught me off guard. Was I asleep?"

"Like a baby. Or perhaps I should say, like a dragon. I'll remember never to wake you again."

In response, he released a yawn, leaning back into the cushions and covering his mouth with the back of one hand. He shook his head as if doffing the final remnants of sleep, then hissed and clutched his neck. "Remind me not to fall asleep on the sofa again." He rolled his head a few times, then turned to me. "How did it go next door? Were you able to calm Miss Connor?"

I leaned back against his chest, pulled his arm around me, and gave him the details of my evening. "She and Hetty were heading off to bed when I left," I concluded. Twisting around, I glanced up at his face. "I told her I'd speak with you about helping Willa."

"She's turned me down once already, but we can try. By to-morrow she may have a change of heart. Did Madeline know why Willa confessed and what exactly she confessed to? Was she in the room when Delaney questioned her?"

"No, to all three questions."

"The handkerchief is rather damning. It would indicate she was at least near someone who was bleeding profusely, and what a coincidence her husband was doing a great deal of that before he died."

"Your original analysis of Connor's death may have been correct. If they had a fight and Connor tripped and hit his head against the desk, it would be like Willa to try to help him."

"Thus, the bloody handkerchief. One must wonder how it came to be at Harleigh House."

"If Willa is innocent, then I would think the murderer brought it to Graham's home and hid it in the desk drawer. It must have been during the wedding reception."

His eyes narrowed as he stared into the darkness that surrounded us. "Whoever alerted Delaney to the handkerchief did so the morning after Graham's soiree."

I didn't follow his line of thought. "One of the guests?"

He gave me a penetrating look. "Who attends a party and rifles through the host's desk?"

I shrugged. "Who attends a party and murders another guest?"

"Exactly!"

Not the answer I was expecting. "Exactly what?"

"The same type of person—a guilty one. No one *found* that handkerchief, they put it there."

"Yes, the murderer. That's what I just—"

"I know you already said that, but Connor's killer might have hidden that handkerchief at any time or in any place. In fact, why not leave it at the scene of the crime?"

"An excellent question. Why wouldn't the killer have left it with Connor's body? That would have implicated Willa immediately."

He twisted his lips to one side. "I actually don't have the answer to that yet. But what I do know, or think I do, is unless Mrs. Connor killed her husband, the killer was a guest at Lord Harleigh's party. And I suspect that person also murdered Sudley, hid the handkerchief, and notified Delaney."

"That narrows the list of suspects. Perhaps Willa will have some further insights to provide."

"Assuming she'll speak with us."

The following morning after a quick breakfast, George and I were in our bedroom getting ready for the day, something I was coming to enjoy sharing with him. Though I was in my dressing room, I could still see him standing by the bureau while his valet, Blakely, adjusted his tie.

Bridget was working my hat into my coiffure, pulling a few curls out here and there, when George crossed the room to check on my progress.

"What is Rose doing today?" he asked. "Do you mind leaving her when we brought her home only yesterday?"

"She has lessons today with her cousin. Since Eldon has gone off to school, she and Graham's second son, Martin, have become the best of friends. I can't imagine she'd be willing to miss her lessons with him to spend a day with us."

George chuckled. "She has no idea how exciting your days can be, though I suppose a trip to a police precinct is not appropriate at her age, is it?"

"She'd probably be fascinated, but I suggest we wait a few years."

Bridget put down the comb and handed me my gloves. "Oh," she said with some surprise. "I've forgotten to mention that Mrs. Rimstock sent along a pair of gloves with your wedding gown, my lady, but I don't believe they're yours."

"We did bring a spare pair of gloves that day, didn't we?"

"Of course. I brought a white pair. Those were not returned. Instead, she sent a green pair with stains on the fingertips. I thought you might know who they belong to."

"Not offhand." I frowned. "And you say they're stained?"

"They are. It looks like blood."

"Blood?" George and I spoke at once, making Bridget take a step back.

"It's hard to tell against the dark color of the gloves, but that's what it looked like," she said, glancing between the two of us.

"May I see them?" Bridget scurried around the wall to the wardrobe, returning quickly with a pair of wrist-length, dark green gloves. They did indeed look stained, but if Bridget hadn't pointed it out, I might not have noticed. The spots on the fingertips were faint. George stretched them out on the dressing table.

"Those aren't my gloves," I said.

"I didn't recognize them either, ma'am, but I thought I'd better check before I returned them."

"That's definitely blood," George said.

I frowned. "I wonder who they belong to."

He glanced at Bridget. "You say they came from Harleigh House with the dress?"

"Yes, sir."

"I'd say we need to pay a call at Harleigh House before we visit Mrs. Connor."

"While you call for the carriage, I'll stop next door and assure Madeline that you are going to speak with Willa."

George took my hand and brought me to my feet. "I'll meet you out front."

As I headed to Hetty's house through the back garden, I prepared myself for what I was sure would be an emotional few moments with Madeline, but as it happened, Mother was the first person I came across when I walked through the library door.

There was no preparing for that.

She rose from the window seat to her full height of five feet and scowled at me with all the disapproval she could focus in one direction. It's a wonder I didn't dissolve on the spot. I took a step back and reached for the door behind me. If escape was possible, Madeline would have to wait.

"Frances Helena Price, you stop right there."

The force of all three names froze me in my tracks, even if one of them was outdated.

She stalked up to me. "How dare you tell your father about my friendship with Mr. Bainbridge."

Three thoughts entered my mind in quick succession—I should never have come here, George and I should have eloped, and perhaps the Higgins brothers could relocate us somewhere far, far away.

I stretched out my hand in a calming gesture. "All I told him was that he ought to have a talk with you. And if you'd spoken with him as you said you would, I wouldn't have had to do that much."

Her fierce façade cracked a bit, to be replaced by that rarest of rare looks. One that said she might possibly be mistaken. "I don't know why you felt it necessary to say anything at all."

"Frankie had developed a good case for Mr. Bainbridge having murdered Mr. Connor. He was certain that's why he was late to the reception. For obvious reasons, I couldn't tell him why Mr. Bainbridge was late. If that wasn't bad enough, he asked me if I knew why you were avoiding him. He was concerned that you were cross with him. It wasn't my place to explain the matter, so I told him to speak with you."

Her expression softened. "He was concerned?"

"Considering what you suspected him of doing, you were probably unconsciously cold toward him." Or consciously, for that matter. Mother pursed her lips. She'd never admit she wasn't always in control of her emotions, but in her own mind, she might actually be considering it. I leaned a hip against the desk. "Did the two of you talk?"

"Of course we did."

After dragging me into her personal business, now she chose to be coy? "A few days ago, you told me my father had betrayed his marriage vows. That he'd broken trust with you. That he was no better than my late husband."

Mother lifted her chin. "And you didn't believe me."

My heart pounded. "Are you saying he confirmed it?"

She heaved a sigh. "I suppose you do deserve to know this. He is not involved with another woman."

"Thank goodness. You had me worried." I paused. "Did you happen to ask him about the perfume?"

Mother looked down at her shoes, then about the room. Finally, back at me. "You were correct. It was quite innocent. He had been considering investing in a perfumery at that time. He even reminded me that the company had sent me a bottle of a custom-mixed scent." She shrugged. "I'd thought it was some sort of sales campaign."

I suppressed the urge to have her repeat her first sentence. "I am so relieved. Did you tell him about Mr. Bainbridge?"

Her eyes flashed a warning. "You don't need to know everything."

"I don't need details, but I do need to know if Frankie is aware of your friendship with Bainbridge and that he didn't actually arrive late to the wedding reception. He was in the back parlor with you."

"I told him about that." She gave me a cautious look. "I think it rather hurt his feelings."

"He wants to be the man you confide in," I said. "I'm sorry if it hurt him, but he was very close to accusing Bainbridge of murder." I gave her a narrow look. "Do you think it's possible that Mr. Bainbridge murdered Connor?"

She looked shocked. "I thought Mrs. Connor confessed to it?"

"Her confession is highly suspect. Hazelton and I are going now to talk with her. Frankie did have a good point. Bainbridge was part of a contentious business deal involving Sudley and Connor."

"I don't believe he'd do it. Mr. Bainbridge is a good man."

"And Willa Connor is a good woman." I pushed away from the desk. "I'm very much afraid we're likely to learn that someone we consider a good person did this horrible thing."

Because I knew George was waiting for me, and because I felt Mother owed me something, I asked her to inform Madeline that we were going to visit Mrs. Connor. Then I slipped out the front door before anyone else could find me, and met George at the carriage.

"That took a bit of time," he noted, handing me up into the carriage. "Was she still quite upset?"

"Apologies for leaving you waiting." I arranged my skirts and took a seat while he climbed in. "In answer to your question, I don't know. Mother caught me as I entered the library and took me to task for telling my father about her friendship with Mr. Bainbridge."

He leaned back, gazing at me in shock. "You did what?"

"I did nothing. I simply told Frankie he should have a talk with her. Didn't I mention that to you yesterday?" I gave him a brief summary of the situation.

"Then why did your mother think you'd told Frankie about her and Bainbridge?"

"I might have suggested he should imply that I'd told him everything if she wasn't forthcoming."

George smiled. "Should I be concerned about this cunning side of your nature?"

"With luck, you'll never experience it firsthand." As George's eyes rounded, I continued. "My conversation with Mother went on so long, I asked her to tell Madeline we were off to see her stepmother." I patted his leg. "I didn't want you waiting any longer than necessary."

"To think we could be in Cannes right now."

"It's not all that much warmer there, is it?"

He chuckled. "I don't know. I'd wager the sun is shining, though."

"And I thought I was the light in your life."

"What does that make me, the darkness?"

"If you keep talking like that, I'll have to say yes."

We both laughed and continued the playful banter all the way to Harleigh House. When Graham met us in the drawing room, his grim affect rather dampened our high spirits. We were seated on either side of the hearth where a roaring fire toasted the room. Graham pulled up a chair between us.

"I cannot believe Delaney has arrested Mrs. Connor." He dropped into the chair and bounced his fist off the padded arm. "What was going through his head?"

"How convenient it is when someone confesses?" George suggested.

"Confession be damned. She didn't do it." He glanced from George to me and back. "And what are the two of you doing about it?"

"Don't be snippy, Graham. Defending Alonzo was all George was meant to do, but we are planning to speak with Willa today and offer to assist her."

He heaved a weary sigh. "Apologies. I have no right to ask you to do anything."

"Before we do"—I produced the gloves from my bag— "what can you tell us about these?"

"A pair of gloves?"

"I was hoping for a little more than that. Your housekeeper sent them to me with my wedding dress. Do you have any idea where they were found?"

He did not, and ringing for Mrs. Rimstock, the housekeeper, produced nothing more than a frown of concern, and the suggestion that we ring for the housemaid, Betsy. When the timid young woman arrived, she inched toward our group with hesitant steps. "Yes, ma'am?" She addressed the housekeeper from about ten feet away.

I held up a finger to forestall Mrs. Rimstock, and turned to the girl myself, holding up the gloves. "These were sent to me a few days ago along with my wedding dress. Was it you who found them?"

She rubbed her palms against her apron. "Yes, ma'am. Is there something wrong?"

Before I could answer, she continued.

"What I mean is, I know there's something wrong with the gloves. They're stained. But I thought they could be cleaned, so I hated to leave them there and let them be destroyed. Should I not have sent them to you?"

"It was fine that you sent them, but where did you find them?"

"On the coals."

"The coals?"

"Be clearer, girl," Mrs. Rimstock snapped. "Where exactly did you find them?"

The maid blinked. "In the guest room Mrs. Hazelton was using. I found them when I checked to see if the hearth needed cleaning. They were tucked in among the coals, ready for lighting. I pulled them out and brushed them off so they could be returned to her ladyship."

George, Graham, and I exchanged a glance.

"Thank you, Mrs. Rimstock, Betsy, you may leave us," Graham said before sinking back into a chair. Once they left, he pointed to the gloves. "That's blood they're stained with, isn't it?"

"It is," George said. "I was beginning to think Mrs. Connor innocent, but I can only assume she hid them in the hearth, after killing her husband, hoping no one would notice, and that the next fire would destroy them."

"That may be the case, but there's an important detail you've overlooked. These are definitely not Willa Connor's gloves. If it was Willa who hid them, she did so for someone else. And I think we can all guess who that might be."

Chapter Twenty-one

Our detour to Harleigh House put us a bit off schedule, but we finally arrived at the Chelsea precinct. We'd rung up Delaney before leaving home to ask him to meet with us. Fortunately, he awaited us in his office, though not in any mood to be civil.

He grumbled something unintelligible at us when he ushered us into his small box of an office. I took a seat on the guest side of his desk. "Trouble, Inspector?"

He waved a hand. "Don't mind me. The Connor-Sudley case grows rather wearing, that's all."

"Then we're just in time. We've brought you some interesting evidence."

"Does it exonerate Mrs. Connor?" To my surprise, he looked almost hopeful.

I glanced at George. "I wouldn't go that far," he said. "But it does indicate someone else might have been involved."

Reaching into my coat pocket, I removed the tissue-wrapped gloves and placed them on his desk.

He poked at the tissue with a finger. "And what is this?"

"A pair of gloves."

"Gloves?"

"Yes," George said. "They have something in common with the handkerchief you found yesterday."

With that, Delaney unwrapped the small parcel and spread out the gloves on the desk. In the dim light of his office, the bloodstains on the dark green gloves were less obvious, but Delaney noted them. "I see what you mean by matching the handkerchief. Where did they come from?"

"Harleigh House," I said. "More specifically, from the room I'd used for changing my gown on my wedding day. They were tucked behind a stack of coals in the hearth. Fortunately, I wasn't in the room long enough to request a fire."

"Obviously, someone was trying to be rid of them," George added.

"I can see why." Delaney examined them closely and raised a fuzzy brow. "Dare I assume they belong to Mrs. Connor?"

"They do not belong to Mrs. Connor," I said flatly.

He dropped his pencil on the desk and sat back in his chair. "How do you know?"

"You've seen for yourself how petite Mrs. Connor is." I worked my own glove off my left hand and stretched it out next to the one in evidence. "These gloves would be a bit too large for me. Willa's hands would be lost inside them."

"Hmm." Delaney let his gaze travel from me to the gloves and back. "I don't suppose you can tell me who they do belong to?"

"I have a suspicion, but I'm quite sure Mrs. Connor could tell us if you'd let us speak with her."

Delaney crossed his arms. "Hazelton tried yesterday. She didn't want any part of him."

George acknowledged this with a shrug.

"She doesn't want legal counsel. She doesn't want a defense." Delaney spread his hands in a gesture of helplessness. "I like a confession as much as the next fellow, but something about hers feels off. Still, it's a confession."

"I think she fears for the owner of these gloves."

Delaney dropped his chin to his chest and groaned. "You're not saying—"

"You are right. I'm not saying anything unless Mrs. Connor gives me permission. That's why you must let us try to speak with her. By the way, when the anonymous person contacted you about the handkerchief, did they actually tell you the monogram was a 'W'?"

He nodded and came to his feet. "Wait here while I send someone for Mrs. Connor and find a meeting room for you." He paused at the doorway. "You understand I can't make her talk with you?"

We reluctantly accepted the fact. "Do you think she'll tell us the truth?" I asked George when Delaney had gone.

"I don't know. She's spent the night in a cell. She may be ready to speak with us."

The wait felt endless, but was probably not more than thirty minutes. Delaney returned and led us to a room farther down the row of offices. He unlocked the door and pushed it open. It was about the same size as his office, but instead of a desk, a small, worn table took up the middle of the room. A defeated Willa Connor slumped in a chair on one side of it.

"Frances!" She jerked to her feet. "And Mr. Hazelton. What are you doing here?"

"I'm here to offer my legal services once more, Mrs. Connor." George strode into the room. I followed, with Delaney close behind.

She lowered her head and took her seat. "I have no need of them."

"Let me explain why I believe you do," he said. "We have some information that may help you and we want you to know about it. If you turn me down as your legal counsel, then Inspector Delaney or some other officer will take down whatever we say. If you do hire me, he will be obliged to leave us alone."

This was news to me. "Will I have to leave?"

George patted my hand. "Heavens, no. You are part of my legal team."

Delaney made a rude sound, but I focused on Willa. A glint of life shone in her eyes as curiosity battled with suspicion. "If I hire you, will you do as I instruct, even if you don't approve?"

"As long as it's within the law, I'm bound to do so."

"All right, then. You are hired."

We both turned to Delaney, who nodded. "Someone will be posted outside this door. Knock when you are ready to leave. And try to make this quick," he added as he stepped out and closed the door behind him. I heard the key turn in the lock.

Willa was leaning over the table when I turned back to her. "How is Madeline?"

"Worried, of course, and quite unsettled, but she's staying with my aunt Hetty at her home, and she is safe."

Willa chewed on her lip, nodding. "I suppose she'll have to go to my family in Cincinnati."

That came as a surprise. "If you had family, why did you never ask them to take you in?"

"I couldn't have left Madeline. Connor would never have let me take her."

"Did you fear he would hurt her?"

She looked surprised at the suggestion. "I can't imagine that. Connor loved her, doted on her. Besides, if I left him and returned to my family, I would have been penniless—a burden to them. Madeline will have his fortune. They will take care of her."

"I suggest we take care of you right now and talk about your defense," George said.

"Defense? I have none. I hit Connor and stabbed him. I've confessed. What more is there to do?"

"I don't believe you," I said.

"Don't you? She's quite convinced me." George leaned back in his chair as if he were completely relaxed. "However, there are a few details we should clear up."

How could he say that? "I thought we were here to help Willa and find the real murderer?"

He swept his hand toward Willa. "But she seems so certain." He leaned across the table toward her. "I don't suppose you killed Sudley, too, did you?"

"Of course not. I had nothing to do with his death."

"Because we were thinking the same person murdered both him and your husband."

She crossed her arms over her chest. "Think again. I didn't do it."

"You're certain?"

"What kind of defense are you planning? I didn't kill Sudley. And what about this information you had for me?"

I parted my lips to speak, but George silenced me with a touch of his hand under the table.

"We'll get to that, but first, I need to know what you told the police."

"Why?"

"Because I haven't seen your statement yet. I shall have access to that material as your counsel." His words were crisp and fast.

"I see."

"But I've only been your counsel for mere minutes. If you recall, you just hired me."

She let out a frustrated huff. "Of course I recall."

"Excellent. What did you tell the police?"

"That we argued. He slipped and hit his head on the desk, which made him even more angry. I helped him to the desk chair, where he sat and slumped forward over the desk."

"Then what happened?"

"I pressed the handkerchief against his head. Connor was still furious, shouting at me all the while. He pushed himself up from the desk and I feared for my life. I took a step back and knocked over the walking stick. I don't even remember picking it up, but I did. And I swung it at his head."

George and I exchanged a glance. Her recounting of the experience was devoid of emotion. It was more of a recitation. If the details she spoke of hadn't fit our observations of the room and Connor's wounds, I'd have thought she'd made the whole thing up. But every word had the ring of truth.

"Why did you stab him?" George asked.

"To be certain he was really dead."

Either I never knew Willa at all, or she was lying. I had one more question that might trip her up. "Willa, how did the handkerchief end up at Harleigh House?"

She turned her cold gaze to me. "I needed to get rid of it, of course."

"But under the sofa? Didn't it occur to you that someone would find it the next time they cleaned the drawing room?"

"I was rather shaken at the time. Upon reflection, it was a foolish place, but what's done is done."

"Do you have the gloves, Frances?" George asked.

I pulled them from my bag, unwrapped them, and placed them on the table. "Mrs. Rimstock sent them to me, assuming they were mine."

She drew a shaky breath. "They ended up with your things, did they?"

"One of Graham's maids found them . . . where was it that you hid them?"

She cradled her head in her hands. "Upstairs? In a guest room? I was so upset at the time, I don't recall."

I hated making her suffer like this. I caught George's eye and gave him a pleading look. With a nod, he proceeded. "I think the reason you were upset, Mrs. Connor, is because you were hiding them for someone else. These are not your gloves."

She forced herself to look at us. "Of course they are."

I reached across the table for her hand, but she snatched it back. With a sigh, I pressed on. "I don't know how you learned Connor was hit with a walking stick, but the handkerchief was not under the sofa, and these are not your gloves. I believe they belong to Madeline."

"Mrs. Connor, you are not speaking to the police right now. You are speaking to your solicitor. I am bound to keep everything between us confidential. You may speak freely and I hope you will. That's the only way I can possibly help you."

Willa made no sound as tears ran down her cheeks. Finally, she nodded. "The gloves are Madeline's."

"I believe the handkerchief is as well. The monogram is not a 'W' but an 'M,' isn't it?"

She nodded.

George observed her for a moment. "How did you know about the walking stick?"

"You left a note telling me what the police had taken as evidence. The stick sounded more logical to me, and as it happens, I guessed correctly."

That gave me some relief. "Can you tell us what really happened that day?"

Willa took a gulp of air and let it out slowly. "That morning, just before we left for church, Madeline had a disagreement with her father in his office. She wanted no part of a betrothal with Fitzwalter. They were both very passionate people. Connor could be aggressive at times. While they argued, he took hold of her arms and shook her. She tried to back away and when that didn't work, she pushed at him. To her surprise he stumbled backward and hit his head on the desk."

The look she gave us begged us to understand. "I don't believe Connor ever raised a hand to Madeline, but she was frightened nonetheless. She panicked and began to run from the room, but when she reached the door, she realized he wasn't coming after her. In fact, he wasn't moving. She went back to him, saw he was bleeding, and used her handkerchief to stop it. Once he regained consciousness and came to his feet, she grew frightened again and fled, leaving the handkerchief behind.

"Madeline left Connor's office just as Fitzwalter arrived to take us to the church. At the wedding I noticed she wasn't herself, but thought that was due to Fitzwalter's presence. After the luncheon, I drew her out to the wintergarden to ask what was wrong. That's when she told me what had happened."

I remembered Madeline being very upset when I first arrived at Harleigh House, but put it down to the disagreement between Fitzwalter and Alonzo. "Once she told you, what did you do? Is that when you went home?"

She nodded. "I rushed over to his office, worried that the blow had knocked him senseless. I imagined him lying unconscious on the floor all that time."

"Tell us exactly what happened, Mrs. Connor." George's voice was low and calm. "Try to recall every detail."

"The outside door to his office was locked, so I slipped in through the front door, then into Connor's office." Her eyes watered as she recalled the scene. "He was seated at the desk and slumped forward. His face was on the desk and his arms were flung outward. And there was a knife, plunged into his back." She swiped at her tears with the back of her hand. "And a lot of blood. I knew this hadn't just happened. And I knew Connor was dead."

She laced her fingers together on the table, trying to compose herself. "I didn't know what to do. I had to speak with Madeline and I needed time to think. So, I walked out of the office and closed the door behind me." She sighed. "And returned to the party. I suppose that makes me a terrible wife—a terrible person, but I was worried about Madeline."

I pulled a handkerchief from my bag and handed it to her. "What happened then?"

"When I returned to Harleigh House, I pulled Madeline aside."

"You told her?"

"I did not. She must have thought I was insane, though. I noticed her gloves when I took her hand. She'd tried to clean them, but they were much as you see them now. I had her remove them. I took them upstairs to the first guest room, the one you were using." She nodded at me. "When I saw that you had left a pair on the bed, I took them and hid Madeline's. I assumed I'd retrieve them another day." She heaved a sigh. "I remember now. I hid them in the hearth. What maid cleans the hearth when there's been no fire?"

"What about the handkerchief?" George asked. "Was it you who hid it?"

"I would have had I known about it. I embroidered it for Madeline long ago when she tried to teach me. It was shoddy needlework, but she treasured it." Tears filled her eyes again. "I thought I'd die on the spot when Inspector Delaney waved it at me."

"You didn't notice it when you went to Connor's office?"

"No."

George threw me a questioning look. Did I believe her? I nodded. She'd already confessed. What reason would she have to lie?

He returned his attention to Willa. "Forgive my interruption. What happened next?"

"I brought Lady Harleigh's gloves to Madeline and we returned to the party."

I tried to work out the timing of the events in my head. "Not long after that Alonzo insisted on going to speak to Mr. Connor."

Willa nodded. "Madeline still didn't know her father was

dead, but she knew it was the wrong time to visit him and tried to stop Mr. Price. She didn't murder Connor. He was up and moving when she left his office, but I don't think the police will believe that if they knew she'd been fighting with him."

George heaved a sigh. "I know this is difficult to imagine, Mrs. Connor, but are you certain it wasn't Madeline who killed your husband?"

"She didn't do it. Connor and Madeline were devoted to one another. The only reason she agreed to marry Fitzwalter was that he presented it as her obligation to her father." She reached out and grasped George by the wrist. "But do you see why you must keep this in confidence? If the police find out what I've told you, I'm certain they will arrest Madeline."

"I cannot allow you to sacrifice yourself for a crime you didn't commit," George said.

"That's my choice. For Madeline, I can do it."

"But you are not sacrificing yourself for Madeline," I protested. "You are doing it for whoever really did murder Connor. I'd like to point out that the real murderer must have found the handkerchief at the scene and hid it in Graham's house for the purpose of implicating you. If you continue down this path, that person will never be brought to justice."

"Then find that person," she said. "I will not recant until Madeline is out of danger."

After speaking with Willa, we disturbed Delaney's peace once more, to return the gloves and remind him about my father's suspicions of Mr. Bainbridge. He assured us they were still checking into Connor's business interests and asked us for anything new in relation to Mrs. Connor's statement. I hated that we couldn't tell him anything, but we had promised her.

Back out on the busy street George raised his hand to flag down Jack, who was about to take the carriage around the block once more. He maneuvered through the throng of traffic and met us a few steps farther down the street. George handed me in and paused to speak with Jack before joining me inside.

"Where do we go from here?" I asked as soon as he'd settled in.

He gave me a blank look. "To Bloomsbury, of course. Have you forgotten about our wedding photographs?"

I had. "That's today? Should we really take time away from this investigation to view our photographs? We ought to check on Frankie's progress, or speak with Madeline. Perhaps she's more familiar with her father's business than Willa."

"I think we should keep our appointment. You may be ready to continue, but I need some time to ponder what we've just learned." He lifted one shoulder in a shrug. "Otherwise, I may not recognize the significance of what your father's uncovered or know which questions to ask Miss Connor. I doubt the time we spend at Mr. Wilson's studio will make much difference. How long could it take to choose a photograph?"

Spoken like a man who'd never been shopping with me. But taking time to think made sense.

George shook his head. "I can't believe Mrs. Connor confessed to murder to save her stepdaughter. Now I feel we have no choice but to find the real culprit, even if Alonzo continues to become a less and less likely suspect."

"What sort of cruel and twisted person kills someone, then makes it look as if the man's wife had done it?"

"Someone who hopes to get away with it. I keep coming back to the anonymous informant who contacted Delaney about the handkerchief. The informant told him precisely where to find it and identified the monogram as a 'W' when it could as easily have been an 'M.'"

"The embroidery was poor at best," I said. "It would be easy to mistake the letter."

"Regardless, the informant, who I assume is also the killer, could simply have said it was a monogram. I wish I'd thought to ask Delaney if it was a man or woman who called him."

"Why?"

He raised a brow.

"You think it might have been Madeline."

"When I consider the timing, yes. Mrs. Connor was the first person we saw cross the lawn to check on Connor. He was already dead according to her. In the time between his encounter with Madeline and Mrs. Connor's visit, all our suspects were at the church, then Harleigh House." His gaze narrowed. "Unless there's a chance your mother lied about being with Mr. Bainbridge."

"Heavens, no. If she were lying, she'd have devised something far less scandalous."

"Then Madeline Connor remains a viable suspect to my mind. She was angry at her father. Her stepmother wouldn't help her. In committing this crime, she rids herself of them both and becomes a very wealthy woman."

"I'll admit I considered Madeline for a moment, but why would she have murdered Sudley? And how? And if this was all due to a young woman's attempt to have her own way, why did she agree to marry Fitzwalter?"

"Sudley's murder is the only thing that keeps me from certainty that Miss Connor is our culprit, but his case may not be related to Connor's after all. As for her engagement to Fitzwalter, she can always cry off later."

I felt a chill as I recollected Lady Sudley's words. "Much can happen in a year," I quoted.

"Indeed."

We spent the rest of the ride lost in our own thoughts, thus we barely noticed the passing of time before we arrived at the studio, where Mr. Wilson greeted us warmly and invited us inside.

"Your timing is impeccable," he said as we followed him down the hallway to his workroom. "Your photographs are ready. In fact, the inspector from the police stopped by last night. I gave him copies of those that showed people outside the window."

I thanked him, though I doubted those photographs mattered any longer.

When we entered the room, we were met with a light vinegar and sulfur odor from whatever Mr. Wilson used on these plates. He began removing the photographs from the file and arranging them on the worktable. "I'm quite pleased with how they turned out."

"Indeed, they're remarkable," I said. Though it was impossible to miss the beauty of the images, my eye was drawn to the shadowy figures in the window. "We're going to have a difficult time choosing, don't you think?"

I glanced up at George, who had turned a curious eye on Mr. Wilson. "Why was our timing impeccable?" he asked the photographer.

Wilson looked confused. "Your timing? Oh, yes. I found something in the darkroom before you arrived. It may be of interest to you. If you'll excuse me, I'll fetch it now."

We didn't remain curious for long. In less than a minute, Mr. Wilson returned with several glass plates cradled carefully in his arms. "These are the first images I took that day."

"That's odd," I said. "I thought these were the first." I indicated the images of George and me by the hearth.

"Officially, yes. But I took these before you arrived to test the lighting. That's how I knew the photographs taken by the window would work better than those by the hearth."

"Aren't they just photographs of an empty room?" George asked.

"That's what I thought." Mr. Wilson spread out three glass plates on the table next to the paper positives we'd been reviewing. "These are a little different. In order to develop them immediately, I used a wet plate and processed them in Lord Harleigh's workroom."

"I knew Lord Harleigh had a keen interest in photography," I said, "but I had no idea he had a photography room."

"He does, and I inadvertently left these there. He returned them to me today and while I was storing them away, something caught my eye that I thought might interest you."

"You have us completely enthralled, Mr. Wilson. What is it?"

He held the plates up to the window one at a time. "When I viewed them, I recalled you telling me the people we saw in the window were suspects in a murder." He picked up another plate, gazed at it, smiled, and handed it off to George. "This is the one."

I moved behind George as he held the plate up to the light and peered over his shoulder. The image was of Graham's library, very close to the west-facing window.

"There's someone outside the window." George leaned in closer to the plate to better identify the person. "What time would you have taken these?" he asked.

The photographer shrugged. "Sometime around two o'clock, if I had to hazard a guess."

George had moved away, so I leaned in closer to the plate in question. There was definitely someone walking past the window in the direction of Connor's house. It took a moment to identify the person. Once I did, I drew in a gasp.

Mr. Wilson's neighbor was a doctor with a telephone. He graciously allowed us to use it to ring up the Chelsea precinct and leave a message for Delaney about the photograph. Back in the carriage, we debated stopping by the precinct to speak with Delaney in person, but the horses had been out in the cold for much of the day, and Delaney could be relied on to call on Mr. Wilson. In the end we decided to return home.

"I confess I am more confused now than before we saw that photograph," I said.

"It makes no sense to me, either. I'm not confident that photograph means anything. It's not as if we saw him kill Connor. And I can't imagine what would motivate him to do so."

We exited the carriage and dashed up the steps to the house to find Jarvis in the hall, ready to take our outerwear. Either the man waited by the door whenever we were gone, or he moved much faster than I would have given him credit for. I had stepped up to the mirror to remove my hat when I spotted the two men in the drawing room.

"You may be about to gain some clarity on his motives," I said to George, with a nod to the partially open door.

Jarvis cleared his throat. "Yes, sir. These men have been waiting to speak with you." He stepped closer to George and lowered his voice. "I was giving them another ten minutes before I called Frederick to help me escort them out."

"You needn't do that, Jarvis," George said. "We definitely wish to speak with them." He held out an arm to me. "Shall we?"

"Of course." The Higgins brothers stood when we walked into the room. George moved to the tantalus and poured out four glasses of brandy.

"Gentlemen. I assume you're willing to join us. If not, I hope you don't mind if we indulge. Her ladyship and I have been out in the cold much of the day." He handed me a glass and held out the tray to the brothers.

"Don't mind if I do, guv." The men lumbered over and took their glasses.

The three men quickly finished their drinks, but I merely took a sip before seating myself. "I assume you're here because you've some information for us."

Archie Higgins's answer was a five-minute recitation of the difficulties they ran into in uncovering this highly confidential information which must be extremely valuable to us. As soon as he ran out of trials to regale us with, his brother jumped in with tribulations.

George finally held up a weary hand to stop them. "Enough.

We've already agreed upon a price for your information. Either tell us what you learned, or leave without your payment. It's your choice."

"It's not that simple, me lord." Ah, George had been elevated from *guv*. "We think we're entitled to a fee for—ah, incidentals."

George stepped over to the bellpull. "Your fee is set. If you don't wish to share your findings, Frederick and Jarvis will see you out."

Mr. Sidney Higgins elbowed his larger brother aside, a sight in itself. "You drive a hard bargain, but we'll get on with it," he said. "Viscount Fitzwalter's got hisself in a mess of trouble."

Chapter Twenty-two

"Turns out Fitzwalter was involved in some high-stakes gambling," Archie Higgins continued. "Now, he's in some hot water. And with the wrong sort, if you take my meaning. They'll get him to pay up one way or the other."

Mr. Higgins the Larger proceeded to explain at length about horses and types of bets and specific people who collect debts. Much of it I didn't understand, but when he mentioned the total amount the young man owed, my head reeled at the magnitude. "And was Mr. Connor expected to pay off that amount?"

"That was the general understanding. 'Course, word got out quick that Connor was no longer in any position to pay off anything. As for the terms you asked about, Fitzwalter has five days to come up with the payment."

"Five days," I repeated. "How on earth is he to come up with that kind of money in so short a time?"

"He promised to put up some of it from the family estate, but I can't tell if his lender is willing to negotiate. Sounds to me like he needs to get that heiress to the church. And fast."

George blew out a breath. "So he had to go to his father. Did you learn anything about Sudley?"

"Only that Fitzwalter's creditors know who he is." The smaller brother shrugged. "Sometimes there's nothing to find."

"Very possible," George agreed. "I'd say you earned your payment. If you'll give me a moment, I'll see to that."

I stared at the two men after George left to fetch their payment. "What will happen if Fitzwalter doesn't have the money within five days?"

The men shifted uncomfortably and averted their gazes.

"They wouldn't really kill him, would they?"

"Maybe. Maybe not. They could hurt him enough to make him wish he were dead, though." Archie Higgins sighed and shook his head, expressing his opinion that this was a regrettable, but common, fact of life.

If Fitzwalter had murdered Connor, as I'd suspected the moment I saw him in the photograph, he perhaps deserved what might happen to him. I recalled the drink in my hand and finished it off in one swallow.

"Here we are," George said as he returned. Sidney Higgins held out his hand and George gave him the money.

"Keep us in mind if we can help with anything else, guv." With that the two men tipped their hats and showed themselves out.

When they rounded the corner, George took me in with a glance, frowned, and extended his hand for my glass. "You look as though you could use another."

"Please."

He refilled my glass and joined me on the sofa. "Evidence seems to be stacking up against Fitzwalter, don't you think? The photographer's plate shows he visited Connor before the others. And unlike the others, he had plenty of time to murder the man."

"We already knew about the arrangement to pay his debts but now we know the extent of it, and that his creditors are not the type to be kept waiting." I shuddered. "He must have been frantic to marry Madeline immediately."

George narrowed his eyes. "I'm not sure that second part is evidence against him. If he needed Connor to pay his debts, why kill him?"

"Yes, that bit has always made me consider Fitzwalter an unlikely suspect, but what if Connor changed his mind? Madeline and Connor were close. She wasn't agreeable to the match. That's what their argument was about. Might Connor have backed down?"

"He didn't strike me as the type to back down to anything, least of all to a disobedient daughter."

I raised a questioning brow.

"I'm not expressing my opinion, but what I expect his would have been."

"Willa told us Connor adored his daughter. Their argument meant she at least hoped to change his mind."

George resumed his pacing. "We have no way of knowing if the man had a change of heart, but we should get this information to Delaney, in any event. I don't know how thoroughly he questioned Fitzwalter, or what the young man told him."

"Delaney will see it as you have. Why would Fitzwalter have murdered the man whose money would have saved him?" I took another sip while considering our next move. "It was Constable Timmons who questioned Fitzwalter. Gilliam gave us the gist of his statement." I glanced at George. "The only thing I noted about Fitzwalter is that he was arguing with Alonzo before luncheon. That would have been before he went to visit Connor."

George nodded. "The photographer would have taken that image of him about the time we were all sitting down to luncheon."

"Fitzwalter and Lon were arguing about Madeline, then instead of joining us in the dining room, he went off to pay a call on Connor. You were with Alonzo when he gave his statement to Delaney. Did he provide any details about the argument?"

"Nothing that registered with me."

My mind was tripping over thoughts so rapidly I couldn't make sense of them. We should have worked more closely with Delaney on this case, though George's representation of Alonzo made that difficult. He had information we didn't have and vice versa. "Gilliam said Fitzwalter felt unwell and spent that time in the billiards room. We now know that's not true, but wouldn't Delaney have questioned the servants to confirm his claim?"

"Normally, I would assume so. But again, I say we should pass our information on to him in the event he hasn't."

"Let's go next door first. Before we pass anything on to Delaney, I'd like to gain some context and I think Alonzo, and even Madeline if she's able, could give us that."

"Excellent idea." We both drained our glasses and headed for the back passage to Hetty's house. We found Hetty, Gilliam, Mother, and Frankie all in the drawing room enjoying tea. At least three of them appeared to be doing so. Frankie was seated at the card table, poring over his charts and muttering to himself.

Mother greeted us with a smile and scooted over to make room on the sofa.

Wonder of wonders. Had something happened to restore balance to the world today? Rather than working, Frankie, while not exactly socializing, was at least suffering company, and Mother appeared to have actually forgiven me. Things were looking up. Even having Gilliam here was a bonus.

George and I took the seats next to Mother and after accepting a cup of tea from Hetty, I turned my attention to Gilliam.

"I wanted to ask you about the notes you took for Constable Evens, or rather your recollection of their contents."

He tipped his head from side to side. "What would you like to know?"

"When the constable questioned Fitzwalter about his movements that day, I believe you told us the gentleman claimed he didn't join us for luncheon because he felt unwell. Is that correct?"

Gilliam closed his eyes and sighed. "Yes. A momentary illness. A bout of nausea or something of that nature. Said he recovered quickly enough, but he didn't want to disrupt the gathering by joining us."

Hetty huffed. "I assumed he was pouting because Alonzo was seated next to Miss Connor and he was placed near Charles and Lottie."

Mother frowned. "Why was Alonzo seated there? It's not how I arranged the table."

The conversation was veering off on a tangent, but ignoring Mother was not an option. "I switched the place cards. Now, Gilliam—"

"After all my work, you changed the arrangement?"

"Good heavens, Daisy," Hetty said. "There's no need to feel affronted. It was only a minor shift."

I bit back a sigh of impatience. We should definitely have pulled Gilliam aside for these questions. "The guest list changed, Mother. We were expecting Mr. Connor but he was replaced with Viscount Fitzwalter. Order of precedence required that I place him where he rightfully belonged." There. Argue with that.

"No need to be so huffy," she said. "I simply wanted an explanation."

I returned my attention to Gilliam. "Did Fitzwalter mention anything about visiting Mr. Connor?"

"Connor? No. He never mentioned it."

George and I exchanged a glance. Not only did he visit Connor, he lied about it. George leaned forward to look at Gilliam. "He and Alonzo were arguing before luncheon. Did he say what that was about?"

"He was not very kind about it." Gilliam shook his head. "He said Alonzo was flirting with his betrothed and he put a stop to it."

"He called Madeline his betrothed?"

"If that was the case, she should not have encouraged Alonzo," Mother said. "Nor should she be encouraging him now."

"I think Madeline is far too busy grieving her father and fearing the fate of her stepmother to concentrate on encouraging Alonzo," I said.

"Just the fact that she's here is enough. If Fitzwalter is her fiancé, why isn't she at his family home?"

"Because they are grieving a loss, too," Hetty said. "The poor dear wanted to be around friends."

"Sudley was against the match," I said. "I suspect Lady Sudley was as well. It would have been very uncomfortable if Madeline had gone there." Particularly since Madeline was against the match, too.

With the scrape of his chair against the floor, Frankie stood. "I've come to the conclusion that it wasn't Mrs. Connor," he announced. His words were so close to my own thoughts, I wondered if he'd been reading my mind. Then he tossed his charts back on the table and lumbered over to our group.

"So, we finally piqued your interest, Franklin. Did you find anything that would actually remove her from suspicion?" Hetty asked.

"She has no motive for Lord Sudley's murder and if his murder isn't related to Connor's, well then, I just don't know anything about odds. In this case I'd say they're about eight to one in favor."

George looked stunned. "You calculated the odds of the cases being linked?"

"Why not? We were looking into suspects and it's helpful to determine which are long shots and which are likely. The odds of two prominent men dying by someone else's hand, in neighboring homes, a mere two days apart are fairly straightforward."

He went on to explain how one would calculate those odds until my eyes glazed over.

George and Gilliam glanced around the room in hope of an escape.

Mother gazed at him in adoration. When he finally ended his lecture, she sighed.

He glanced around the group. "I know a great deal about odds and probability."

"Of course you do, Franklin," Mother said in a breathy voice. "No one would doubt your knowledge."

"All right, then." George stepped eagerly into the lull in the conversation. "Let's assume the murders are linked. The victims had two things in common that we're aware of—the purchase of the distillery and the betrothal of their offspring. We've managed to learn quite a bit about Connor in the past few days, but very little about Sudley that wasn't already public knowledge."

"He argued with Bainbridge earlier in the evening," I said.

Frankie harrumphed. "I heard him arguing with someone in the dining room right before he was done in."

I blinked in astonishment. He'd heard someone arguing with Sudley just before the man was murdered and rather than tell us that, he'd chosen to regale us with the wonders of calculating odds? "What exactly did you hear?" I inched forward in my seat.

"Who was he arguing with?" George asked.

"No idea." He looked taken aback by our sighs of exasperation. "I'm sure it was a man. I'd have thought it was a business associate. Whoever it was, I'll lay you odds he was the one who thumped Sudley in the head."

"Let's leave odds out of the discussion, shall we? Did you mention this to Delaney?" I asked.

"Of course I did. And as I told you that evening, he wasn't interested in my opinions. He was certain the voice I heard was Alonzo's. As if I wouldn't recognize my own son's voice."

"Alonzo was entering the front door when the maid who found the body screamed."

"There you have it. Couldn't have been him."

George's lips thinned as he held his frustration in check, but he persevered. "Did you hear any of the argument? Could you tell what it was about?"

"Money. I was returning from the billiards room and passing the dining room, so I didn't hear much, but I heard words to the effect of 'what they'll do if I can't pay.'"

I choked on my tea and fumbled for a napkin.

"Oh, Frances," Mother said. "For heaven's sake!"

George jumped to his feet. "Are you certain those were the words?" he asked.

Frankie took a step back. "Those might not be the exact words, but I understood the point. The man was having trouble covering a financial obligation."

I caught George's eye. "Fitzwalter."

"Fitzwalter? Frances, no!" Hetty's voice was scornful. "You think he'd kill his own father?"

"What's all this about Fitzwalter?" Alonzo strolled into the room and picked up a tiny, crustless sandwich from the tray before plopping into the chair next to Hetty.

She handed him a plate and napkin. "Frances thinks he murdered his father."

Alonzo pulled a face. "The man's a bounder and a cad, but even I wouldn't accuse him of that."

"Fitzwalter needed Connor alive," George reminded me. "He had no motive."

"Perhaps we're focusing too much on motive," I mused. "Fitzwalter had an opportunity during the luncheon."

"We don't know that he called on Connor," he said. "We only saw him outside the library window."

"Yes, when he told the police he'd been in the billiards room. If he simply stepped outside for some air, why would he lie? And as to needing Connor alive, he's done very well with him dead, wouldn't you say? He still managed to convince Madeline to marry him."

"He told Miss Connor he and her father had come to an agreement about the marriage," Alonzo put in. "Said they had a contract."

Gilliam made a noise of disgust. "A contract sounds so impersonal."

"Madeline mentioned something about that. Is that what you and Fitzwalter argued about at the reception?" I asked.

"That's when he brought it up," he replied. "He said I should stay away from his fiancée. Madeline said nothing was settled yet, and that's when he mentioned the contract. It definitely took her by surprise."

"Madeline had told me she had an obligation to him," I mused aloud. "That she must marry him."

"That's absurd," Frankie said. "Unless she signed the contract, she's under no obligation, and it sounds like she didn't even know it existed."

George cocked a brow. "Perhaps it doesn't."

"It does." Hetty rose slowly to her feet, drawing our attention. "There is a contract. I've seen it. At least, I think I have."

Understanding dawned on me slowly. "Is it the document you're reconstructing? May we see it?"

"Your father's notes and Connor's documents are in the library." Hetty caught my hand in her eagerness and summarily pulled me out of the room. George followed. "There are actually two documents. One is a letter. The other may be the marriage contract. It's definitely an agreement of a sort and has Fitzwalter's name on it."

The three of us hurried through the hallway, stopping upon seeing Constable Timmons seated outside the library door. "Constable," Hetty said. "I thought you were taking a meal in the kitchen."

"I was, ma'am. When I came back, I found Miss Connor inside looking through the paperwork. I know these are her father's things, but she might have slipped out with something important. I'll be sure not to leave these documents unguarded again."

"Then you ought to join us," she said. "This might be of interest to Inspector Delaney."

Timmons opened the door for us. George and I followed Hetty inside and to her desk. "This is the document I was speaking of." With her hand she indicated the blotter which held a few sheets of paper pieced together like a puzzle, or rather, mostly pieced together.

George and I bent over the desk scanning the partially reconstructed documents. There were chunks missing from each page, but what I could read indicated this was a marriage settlement. And Fitzwalter's signature was affixed at the bottom of the third page.

"So there was a contract," George observed.

"But as Franklin said, it isn't enforceable on Miss Connor," Hetty said. "Particularly in its current state. Perhaps Connor changed his mind."

I straightened, wondering what to make of this. "Madeline had argued with her father that morning. She didn't want to marry Fitzwalter. It looks as though she managed to convince him."

"Or she's the one who tore this up," George said.

"But Alonzo said she was surprised to hear of it when Fitz-walter mentioned the contract. She couldn't have torn it up if she didn't know it existed." We stared at each other, ignoring Hetty and the constable, both of us searching for the answer in the other's eyes.

I took my mind back to the wedding reception. "Fitzwalter didn't join us for luncheon. He went to Connor—perhaps to complain about Madeline's flirtations or to seize that contract and wave it in Alonzo's face. But when he arrived at Connor's office, he found the man had changed his mind. Perhaps he even tore up the contract before Fitzwalter's eyes."

"Considering his situation," George said, "I can see how that would cause him to panic. He was about to lose millions of pounds—possibly his life."

I heard a gasp and glanced up to see Mother standing in the doorway with Frankie, Gilliam, and Alonzo crowded behind her. "So, he killed Connor?" she asked.

"I think he did," I said. Though I couldn't be sure, I didn't need Frankie to calculate these odds. "He would have been maddened by rage and fear of what would happen if he couldn't pay his debts. He swept up the walking stick Bainbridge had left behind and swung it into Connor's head as he sat at his desk." I sank into Hetty's chair. "Then stabbed him to ensure he was dead."

George nodded his agreement. "Then he makes a mess of the office to make it look like a burglary. He may have gathered some of the scraps of paper as so many seem to be missing. Then he finds the handkerchief he believes to be Willa's, takes it, and returns to Harleigh House in a matter of minutes."

"Wait." Alonzo held up a hand. "What about Lord Sudley? Why would Fitzwalter kill his own father?"

"Because Lord Sudley objected to the match. He planned to

make Fitzwalter wait a year before they even made an announcement, hoping they'd both grow tired of each other. Lady Esther suggested Sudley might even disown Fitzwalter and leave the title and estate to his younger brother." I tried to picture the scene. "After he'd taken the risk of murdering Connor, his father stood in his way. That was the argument you heard, Frankie. Fitzwalter is in debt to some rather ruthless loan sharks. He needed to marry Madeline as soon as possible."

"Lord Sudley!" Hetty moved the pieces of paper around on the desk. "There were pieces of a letter here, too. It was from Sudley." She glanced at Timmons. "It's gone."

"Sudley wrote to Connor?" That was unexpected.

"Do you recall any of the content?" George asked.

Hetty looked flustered. "It was fine stationery, with Sudley's name and crest, but there were only a few pieces."

"From what I could make of it," Timmons put in, "the writer refused to take part in a scheme."

I glanced at George. "Do you suppose Sudley understood what Connor was up to? That in bailing Fitzwalter out of his troubles, he expected to have Sudley in his pocket?"

"If Sudley refused to cooperate, it would hardly be worthwhile for Connor to take on the trouble of Fitzwalter."

"Perhaps Madeline has the letter," Hetty said.

"Madeline!" I clutched George's hand and turned to Constable Timmons. "You said she was in here when you returned after your meal. She must have seen this contract. And she very likely has the letter."

"I don't know how she could miss it, ma'am."

Hetty tutted. "Did she appear upset?"

He nodded vigorously. "She did indeed, both when she ran upstairs and a few minutes later when she stormed out the door."

"She left?" My stomach knotted.

"She's probably gone to the police, Frances." Hetty's words did not reassure me.

"A policeman was right here." I indicated the constable. "I fear she did something more impetuous."

I looked at George and he nodded. "We should find her."

Chapter Twenty-three

"Find her?" Alonzo pushed past Mother and into the room. "Why? What do you think has happened?"

"I hate to imagine," I said. "We've managed to put everything together. I must believe upon seeing this, she has done the same."

"But you have more information than she does," Hetty protested. "Perhaps she simply went back to her home."

"That would be a relief, but this contract alone is enough to tell her Fitzwalter tricked her into a betrothal. I think she's clever enough to realize he murdered her father. I fear she's gone to confront him." I looked around the room wondering whom I could trust to do what.

"Constable Timmons," George said, "will you go to the precinct and explain all this to Inspector Delaney?"

"Sir, I'm not certain I underst—"

Hetty cut him off. "We'll go with him. Gilliam can drive us in his motorcar, and I'm quite sure I can explain everything."

"I'll go with them," Alonzo said.

"No, I want you to come with us to her home," George said.

"If she's at home, we'll contact Delaney to inform him that she's safe."

"If not," I added, "George and I shall go on to Sudley House and Alonzo can telephone Delaney and have him meet us there."

"Agreed," he said.

"What about us?" Frankie was standing behind Mother with a hand on her shoulder.

"Wait here in case she comes back?" I suggested.

"That's not much of an assignment," he grumbled.

"It will be fine, Franklin," Mother said. "They know what they're doing."

"We need to leave now." George was on his feet and holding out a hand to me. "Come, we'll stop at home and collect our coats. Alonzo, meet us outside."

I put my hand in George's and followed him down the hall and out the back door. We made our way through the back gardens and into the drawing room. By the time Bridget fetched our coats, Alonzo pounded on the door. I waved Jarvis away and opened it myself. "Where's your carriage?" he asked.

"That will take too long." George helped me into my coat and we joined Lon on the step. "It's a block over to Grosvenor Street. We can find a cab there faster."

Indeed, we found one almost immediately, and before Lon's anxiety rose to a boiling point, we were knocking on the Connors' door. It was answered by a rather harried looking Parker.

"I'm afraid Miss Connor is away from home at the moment," he said in response to our inquiry.

Alonzo pushed his way inside. "Do you know where she's gone?"

The butler stiffened. I threw Lon a glare and addressed Parker. "Miss Connor had been staying at my aunt's home and she's been in a very distressed state. She left for a walk a little more than an hour ago and given the weather and her state of mind, you can imagine we are a bit worried about her." Yes, it was something of a fib, but it was for a good cause.

His expression softened. "Of course, my lady. Miss Connor did return home. In a cab," he added. "But she left again a few moments ago."

Alonzo began speaking again, but George's well-placed elbow cut him off.

"You saw her leave yourself? Did she take her maid with her?" I asked.

"She did not. She simply said she had some business to take care of and left in the family carriage." He narrowed his eyes. "Is she in some sort of trouble? Everything has been a bit irregular in the household lately."

Leave it to a butler to understate the case. "I'm afraid she will be if we don't find her," I said, and turned back to George.

"I think we had best check at Sudley House," he said.

We made arrangements for Alonzo to telephone Delaney to inform him that Madeline was not at home, and George and I were headed for Sudley House. With luck, he would meet us there.

"I'm rather surprised that she stopped at home," I said once we were in the cab and on our way. "Perhaps she's calmed down and gone to the police after all."

"Considering she had a telephone at her disposal, I don't feel quite so optimistic. But we'll soon find out." George nodded out the window to Sudley House. The Connors' carriage waited in front. He paid the driver, and we headed up the walk to the door.

"Do you have any idea how to explain our presence here?" I asked after he knocked.

"A condolence call, perhaps?" he replied. "Or we simply demand to see Miss Connor."

The butler opened the door, but before we could do more than draw breath, a shot rang out inside the house.

George pushed the older man aside and ran in. I followed. We both hesitated in the entry hall, uncertain where to go. The butler, still holding on to the doorknob, tipped his head to the left. "It came from in there."

"Stay here," George said, before pushing open the door.

Foolish man. I stayed behind long enough to tell the butler to send for the police and rushed into the room.

I stopped short at what I saw. Madeline was indeed here. She and Fitzwalter struggled with a revolver on the far side of the drawing room.

George assessed the situation far more quickly than I did. He pushed me behind a sofa before diving back there himself. "It's over, Fitzwalter. We know what you did. The police are on their way."

"What I did?" His voice wavered in his struggle. "She shot at me!"

Bang!

Another shot rang out, followed by a crash. To our left an oriental vase shattered into a thousand pieces. I noticed George's head was above the line of the sofa and pulled him back down.

"It's all right," Madeline called out. "I have the revolver. It's my father's Colt, and I assure you I know how to use it."

There was nothing reassuring in that statement.

George and I rose by inches until we could see over the back of the sofa. Madeline did indeed have the revolver and it was trained on Fitzwalter, who stood by the hearth, shaking and holding out his hands as if to ward off the danger she presented. Considering there wasn't so much as a table or chair for him to hide behind, I understood his fear.

"Madeline, please don't shoot him." I struggled to keep my voice steady and calm. "We know what he's done and we've already told the police."

She drew a deep, shuddering breath, never moving her gaze from her quarry. "You can't know the extent of it. You can't know how he tried to fool me. My father changed his mind about the betrothal. He gave in to my wishes." She drew in a shaky breath. "These past few days I thought he was a tyrant. That he locked me into some sort of obligation to marry this . . . this . . . bounder."

"Your father and I had an agreement." Fitzwalter fairly growled the words. "He didn't back out because of your wishes, but because my father wouldn't play along." He cast a furtive glance our way before returning his gaze to the firearm Madeline held. "He left me no choice."

"You chose to murder him. You let the police think Alonzo did it. When that didn't work, you made them think my step-mother killed him." A sob shook her body. "You even made me believe it. How will she ever forgive me?"

"Oh, please! Stop pretending," he said in a mocking voice. "Your poor stepmother. Your poor father. He showed me the knot on his head. I simply finished the job you started."

How a man could sneer at a woman who held a gun on him amazed me.

"Stop goading her, Fitzwalter, or you're likely to find your-self with a gaping wound." George rounded the sofa and, mov-ing slowly, held out his hand. "You don't have to shoot him, Miss Connor. The police are on their way. They'll arrest him and set Mrs. Connor free."

"The hell they will!" Fitzwalter lunged for Madeline, who instinctively jumped back. He latched on to the pistol and her hand.

"Stop!" I shouted as I came around the sofa.

George reached out for the pistol.

Another shot rang out.

George fell to his knees, clutching his shoulder.

Both of the young people froze in place as they stared at him.

I never missed a step. I threw myself at Fitzwalter just a beat before Madeline did the same. He went down with a thud, or perhaps that was the sound of the door banging open when Delaney and two constables ran in.

My ears were ringing as one of them pulled me off Fitzwalter and took him into custody. I pulled up my skirts and crawled over to George. Dragging him into my lap, I cradled his head.

"Gah!" He growled through gritted teeth. I had no idea I was crying until I saw Delaney's face through a haze of tears.

"We're sending for a doctor," he said. "You damn well better hold on, Hazelton."

"We haven't even taken our wedding trip yet." I wiped his brow with my handkerchief and realized George had lost consciousness.

Lady Sudley stirred herself to the point of coming downstairs in time to see the constables hauling her firstborn from the house. I left any explanations to Madeline and the police. George absorbed all my efforts and attention for the moment. Delaney was kind enough to lend a hand. Kneeling beside me, he produced a knife and we cut and tore away at the fabric of his overcoat, jacket, and shirt near the wound, which we found by following the largest stains of blood on his coat.

"Bandages!" Delaney barked out orders to the butler. "And a basin of water. Carbolic acid too if you have it."

I pressed a piece of fabric torn from George's shirt against his shoulder to stanch the flow of blood. Thank goodness he was unconscious. I can't imagine him enduring the pain I was likely inflicting. Though it felt like hours, it wasn't long before the butler escorted the doctor in to take over from our ministrations. He'd brought an assistant of his own and pushed both Delaney and me aside while he set to work on removing the bullet.

Though I was left with nothing to do but pray, I hovered by his side. I have no idea how long it took, but his wound stopped bleeding, the doctor removed the bullet, and bandaged him up.

"He's still unconscious," I stated, as if the doctor couldn't see that fact for himself.

"I gave him some chloroform. He should come around any moment. He'll be in quite a bit of pain, so once you get him home, he should have some laudanum. I'll check on him tomorrow."

"But he'll be all right?"

"It will be a good long while before he's using that arm again, but yes, I think he'll recover fully."

Thank heavens! All that was left was to take him home.

The following morning Inspector Delaney paid me a call. I gave him the happy news that George was on the mend, and in turn he told me that Alonzo was officially cleared of all suspicion. Fitzwalter, through all his rantings, had essentially admitted his guilt in both murders. "Though he claims killing his father was an accident," Delaney said in conclusion.

"How does one hit a person over the head with a candlestick by accident?" I asked. We were standing in our drawing room since Delaney, in a rush, had declined any refreshment or even a seat.

"Yes, he may have some trouble with that defense. His father refused to advance him funds from the estate to pay off his creditors. Even threatened to disinherit the young man if he married Miss Connor. I'd say Fitzwalter had plenty of motive."

After promising to stop next door to give Alonzo the good news, he took his leave, only to be replaced by Madeline Connor, who called to inquire after George and thank us for our assistance to her and Willa.

"I think I must have gone a little mad yesterday," she said. "When I saw the torn pieces of that contract and the letter from Lord Sudley, I immediately knew what Fitzwalter and my father had been planning. It also became clear that Fitzwalter had killed my father. Even worse was that he made me believe, or at least made me come close to believing, that my stepmother had done it."

"I'm sure she'll forgive you," I said, keeping to myself the fact that both George and I had suspected Madeline as the culprit. I wasn't so sure she'd forgive us. When she handed me a bank draft for our assistance to Willa, I decided my lips would remain sealed on the matter.

She lowered her head. "I loved my father, but I know he had many faults. He was cruel to Willa, and yet she would never leave him because she couldn't leave me. He loved me, but Willa has always been my true parent." She blotted her eyes and sat up taller. "Families are strange things, aren't they?"

"Indeed. I'd imagine Lady Sudley would agree with you."

"Poor Lady Sudley." Madeline's gaze traveled off to the distance before returning to mine. "With Fitzwalter likely to end up in prison, do you think his creditors will torment her?"

"I'm afraid there's a good possibility they will."

"Perhaps there's something I can do about that. She's suffered enough." Madeline came to her feet. "I should be on my way. My stepmother is at home packing and I should be doing the same. I just wanted to thank you for helping to prove her innocence."

"I'm relieved we were able to do so." I walked with her to the door. "What will you do now?"

"We plan to return to America. We need some time alone to grieve and I'd rather do that at home. I will, of course, come back and bid farewell to Mr. Price before we leave."

Poor Alonzo might be heartbroken, but I completely understood. She and Willa had some healing to do.

A few days later, the ladies did go back home, leaving both Alonzo and Graham a bit lost. Both of them had taken up the habit of visiting George and me frequently. As did my parents and Aunt Hetty and Gilliam. After two long weeks of my family coming and going, I longed for some time alone with George and Rose, or perhaps I should say Georgie and Rosie as they agreed to call one another.

George was healing. The wedding was long over. Did my family ever plan to go home?

I mentioned the possibility to my father one evening when he, George, and I were enjoying a brandy in our drawing room. "I'm surprised that you've stayed here so long, Frankie. I've never known you to take this much time away from business."

"I'm actually planning to take even more time." His eyes sparkled. "Your mother and I are traveling to Egypt. For a month."

Heavens! While this was an answer to my prayers, I couldn't imagine them traveling across Egypt. For a month. Together.

Frankie was clearly unconcerned. "We won't live forever, you know."

Such a trip might well ensure that.

"It's been years since Daisy and I traveled together." He continued. "We must enjoy ourselves while we still can."

George raised his glass in a toast. "I'm certain it will prove to be a memorable trip. Don't you agree, Frances?"

A smile broke across Frankie's face. "Here's a thought. Why don't you join us?"

"Join you?" I clutched George's hand in a viselike grip.

"Yes. Since you've had to cancel your wedding trip, why not come along?"

"It would hardly seem like a wedding trip if you and Mother are with us."

"Bosh!" Frankie batted away my objection with a wave of his hand. "You'll have years to spend alone with each other."

George extracted his fingers from my fist and leaned closer. "What do you say, Frances?" His voice rumbled next to my ear.

The very thought of an extended trip with my parents induced panic and palpitations. I'd spent enough time with my family to see me through the next year. But Frankie looked so jolly at the prospect of us joining them. I worried my lip, glanced at George, who looked rather pale himself, then gave my father an honest answer. "I'm afraid we'll have to decline, Frankie. George and I would like to spend some time alone, even if it's only here at home."

Frankie looked dejected. Then a smile slowly crept across his lips. "I see how it is. But I still owe you a wedding gift. Perhaps I should set aside some funds for you to take a trip—on your own."

"That would be lovely, Frankie," I said. "We accept with gratitude."

"Excellent, but don't leave too soon. Your mother and I will want to stop in for a short visit after returning from Egypt."

"We'll be happy to have you," George said.

I agreed. As long as the emphasis was on *short*. Small portions, I reminded myself. My family was best enjoyed in small portions.

Author's Note

This book is a work of fiction, but I was inspired by the real feud between Charles Bonynge and John MacKay. Both amassed a fortune through their dealings in the silver industry and the men worked together for a time. But their relations became sour when Bonynge spoke out against MacKay, accusing him of various schemes to bilk the public. When both families decided to conquer London society, the bad blood between them led them each to drag the other through the mud in a social rivalry that delighted the gossip columnists. The mystery writer in me couldn't help but believe if one of them should happen to be murdered, the other would surely be a suspect. Thus, my feuding families were created. There are several biographies of both men, but the feud itself is well detailed by Anne De Courcy in *The Husband Hunters*.

Acknowledgments

I'm so grateful to the friends and family who helped make this book a reality, librarians and booksellers who have championed the Countess of Harleigh series, and readers who have enjoyed it. Many thanks to Mary Keliikoa, my wonderful critique partner, and Barb Goffman who came to my rescue with her editing skills. I'm very grateful to Dave Wilson of the Victorian Photography Studio in Gettysburg for his detailed information about photography and cameras of the late Victorian era.

As always, thank you to my wonderful agent, Melissa Edwards, my editor, John Scognamiglio, and the excellent team at Kensington Books. And most of all, thanks and love to my husband, Dan.

The newly married Frances Hazelton, formerly Countess of Harleigh, should be planning her honeymoon. Instead, she's unmasking a murderer among the upper crust . . .

With her new husband George busy on a special mission for the British Museum, Frances has taken on an assignment of her own. The dowager Viscountess Winstead needs someone to sponsor her niece, Kate, for presentation to Queen Victoria. Frances—who understands society's quirks and constraints as only an outsider can—is the perfect candidate.

Kate is charming and intelligent, though perhaps not quite as sheltered as she might first appear. More worrying to Frances is the Viscountess's sudden deterioration. The usually formidable dowager has become shockingly frail, and Frances suspects someone may be drugging her. The spotlight falls on Kate, who stands to inherit if her aunt passes, yet there are plenty of other likely candidates within the dowager's household, both above and belowstairs.

Joining forces with her beloved George, Frances comes to believe that the late Viscount, too, was targeted. And with the dowager seeming to be in greater danger every day, they must flush out the villain before she follows in her husband's footsteps, directly to the grave . . .

Please turn the page for an exciting sneak peek of

Dianne Freeman's next Countess of Harleigh mystery

A NEWLYWED'S GUIDE TO FORTUNE AND MURDER

coming soon wherever print and ebooks are sold!

Chapter One

⚛︎

April 1900

"**Y**ou are right, Jarvis. We couldn't fit so much as a hatpin in here." From the edge of the attic, I peered through a haze of dust that floated in a patch of sunlight at what must be generations of Hazelton cast-offs—old trunks, boxes, and furnishings, both assembled and in pieces, covered with sheets, which in turn were covered with dust and even more boxes.

"Where did it all come from?" I glanced at Jarvis, our butler. He was exactly my height, and I caught him in profile. Apart from a hawkish nose, the surface of his face was quite flat until his lips curved in a smile, pushing round cheeks up and forward.

"When Lord Brandon took over the house," he said, "most of the old earl's furnishings were sent to the attic, as were Lord Brandon's things when Mr. Hazelton moved in."

"Then Rose and I moved in with our things and more furniture was relegated to the attic." Mr. Hazelton—George—was my husband of two months. Rose was my eight-year-old daughter. For at least two generations, this house was home to the heirs of the Earl of Hartfield, but the last heir, George's elder brother, Brandon, had moved out when he inherited the title, and the earl's town home. Since the next heir, Brandon's son, was only ten years old, he would not be needing this house for several more years.

George took over the lease on the house a year ago, and I moved in when we married. I'd just spent the last hour searching for a room to claim as my office. The third floor was a schoolroom and bed chambers for Rose and Nanny. George had sacrificed a bedchamber next to ours to create a boudoir and bath for me, something of a surprise wedding present. I needed a place to work but felt a bit guilty attempting to lay claim to yet another space. And moving furnishings from that space to the attic was clearly out of the question.

I glanced at Jarvis. "Any ideas?"

"Why, yes. I do have a location in mind." Jarvis had a voice like the rumble of distant thunder. It gave his words a gravitas that had made me trust him from our first meeting—even if there was mischief in the hooded eyes that looked back at me.

"Do tell."

"Allow me to show you." He made for the narrow staircase and preceded me down to the third floor, where we passed through a baize door that took us through the sunlit nursery and schoolroom. Rose, however, took her lessons with her cousin at my brother-in-law, the Earl of Harleigh's, home. Our steps echoed through the mostly empty room. I wondered if I could close off a corner for myself up here. But Jarvis led on.

I followed him downward to the main floor, wondering where this mythical location could be, until he stopped at the open door to my husband's library and I realized what he was suggesting. "No, no, Jarvis. This won't do."

"You asked my opinion, madam, and I believe this is the perfect place."

"The perfect place for what?"

I peeked into the room. George stood and leaned over his desk to see what we were doing hanging about in the doorway. His dark brows raised with curiosity and the genial curve to his lips tempted an answering smile to my own. "It's nothing, darling," I said. "Don't mind us."

"But I must hear the answer." George had come around the desk to the doorway and leaned his tall frame against the wall. "What is this the perfect place for?"

"It's the perfect place for a cup of coffee," I said and glanced over his shoulder. "I see you have a pot at the ready."

His gaze darted to the butler and back to me. "You needed Jarvis's opinion on the matter?"

"What?"

"He said you asked for his opinion."

"You misunderstood," I said.

"Just a figure of speech," Jarvis said at the same time.

The butler and I exchanged a glance. "I'll just fetch another cup," he said before turning on his heel and nearly sprinting away.

"What the dickens are the two of you up to?" George watched me through narrowed eyes as I brushed past him to the guest side of his desk and took a seat.

"Just looking for a likely spot where I can set up my own office and allow you to use yours in peace." The library had been carved out of what had been an enormous drawing room. With doors on two of its walls, one could access it from the drawing room or the hallway. Bookcases covered a third wall filled with George's law tomes, some volumes on horticulture and travel, the works of Shakespeare and two cricket bats. Two wingback chairs framed the window overlooking the back garden. George's desk backed up to the wall of books. I'd been using it for the past two months while he recovered from being shot shortly after our wedding. While a gunshot wound wasn't something one would expect a proper British gentleman to sustain, George was no ordinary gentleman.

It had been a great relief to learn the bullet had hit him in the upper arm and wasn't fatal. He recovered quickly, though he still lifted weights to regain the strength in his arm. Actually, he'd built more muscle in his arms and shoulders to the point where he had to take his suits to the tailor for alterations. I heartily approved of his new look, though it would always be his crooked smile and the twinkle in his green eyes that made my heart beat faster. Along with his ability to make me feel like the most beautiful woman in the room.

In truth, I was tall—almost as tall as George, slender enough that a good corset could make me fit for any fashion, and fortunate to have thick, dark hair. Otherwise, I was quite ordinary—pert nose, average complexion, and blue eyes—oh, and an American accent. But in London, Americans had become rather ordinary too. Nevertheless, in George's eyes, I was a goddess.

He rounded the desk to take his seat, and I noticed the open newspaper. "Anything interesting in there?"

"Nothing interesting enough to compete with you." He folded the broadsheet and set it aside, giving me his full attention and the benefit of that crooked smile.

"A very clever answer," I said.

"I must be clever to keep up with you. You'd never suffer a fool for a husband."

"Certainly not a second time. Though I suppose I wouldn't have called Reggie a fool, exactly."

George lifted a brow. "Philanderer? Wastrel? Ne'er-do-well? Good for nothing?"

Reggie had been my first husband. He and my mother had decided that his family's title and our family's dollars were a perfect match. Our marriage had no effect on his bachelor ways. After ten years, he'd died in the bed of his latest lover. Consequently, all of those words fit him. In my opinion, anyway.

I placed a hand over George's. "He was also Rose's father."

He smiled. "Yes, yes, but I like to think she takes after you, my dear. However, for Rosie's sake, I shall refrain from speaking ill of the man."

Jarvis popped in with a coffee cup, and George filled it for me. "What are your plans for today?" he asked.

"Tea with the Viscountess Wingate and her family."

He grimaced and faked a shudder. At least I thought it was fake. "Why would you do that to yourself?"

Augusta Ashley, Viscountess Wingate, was an extraordinarily cantankerous older woman. The type of person I would not normally seek out, but her husband's family owned a neighboring estate to Harleigh Manor, my late husband's country home, where I spent much of my marriage and all of my mourning period. Lady Wingate was in residence during most of the latter, and while I wouldn't call her pleasant company, compared to my in-laws, she was a welcome relief. And she'd been kind to Rose.

"Lady Wingate has asked me to sponsor her niece for presentation to the queen."

"Just her presentation? What does that involve?"

"Not a great deal—ordering the correct gown, practicing a court curtsey, and learning how to back away from Her Majesty while wearing a nine-foot train. And of course, spending an afternoon at Court."

"Why isn't Lady Wingate presenting the niece herself?"

"I'm sure she would if the family weren't still mourning her husband's death. Don't you recall Lord Peter passed away right after Christmas? None of the family will be taking part in social events for another seven or eight months."

He raised a brow. "But the niece will? Does she have a name, by the way?"

"Katherine Stover. She's related to Lady Wingate, not Lord Peter." I frowned. "It seemed like a good idea at the time. You were still recovering, and I needed something to do with myself. But Miss Stover was delayed coming to town from Devon, so we missed the queen's first drawing room. The next one won't be until late this month and with the family in mourning, they may ask me to take on more than just the presentation and actually organize her social season."

"Is that a problem?"

I gave him my sweetest smile. "I was hoping, now that you are fully recovered, we could make plans for our wedding trip." A family emergency had put an end to our original wedding trip. To make up for it, my father had gifted us with a large sum of money, but George had been surprisingly squeamish about using it.

"Yes, well, a wedding trip will have to wait just a bit longer, I'm afraid." He gave me a sheepish grimace. "I've accepted an assignment and I'm not sure how long it will take to accomplish, or where it will take me."

My disappointment was momentary, and easily overcome by the delight I saw in his eyes. George did "something" for the government. The Home Office, to be specific, but that's as much as I knew. "That is wonderful news. I felt you were fully mended, and it seemed to me you were becoming restless. Can you tell me anything about your assignment?"

"I'm to investigate the disappearance of a rather unusual and valuable artifact." He waggled his eyebrows. "I can't really describe it further."

"I see. Something old then, I'd imagine."

He laughed. "I cannot say."

"Everything is such a secret." I let out a tsk. "One would think that you could at least confide in your wife."

"Don't take offense. I can't tell you because they haven't told me what it is yet."

"Then I suppose it's just as well that I'll have an assignment of my own. When do you begin?"

"I plan to meet with my contact today to find out what he knows of the matter. I ought to be leaving now."

"All I have to look forward to is tea with Lady Wingate," I said.

He grimaced. "I suspect your assignment will be much more onerous than mine."

Eager to meet with his contact, George left almost immediately. I dealt with some correspondence, reviewed the week's menus with our cook, enjoyed an early afternoon walk with Rose, and was just readying myself for my engagement with Lady Wingate when Jarvis brought a visitor's card upstairs to my dressing room.

I took it without moving my head since Bridget, my maid, had my hair firmly gripped in one hand and piping hot curling tongs in the other.

"Lady Esther is here?" I asked, though since her card was in my hand, the answer was obvious.

"Yes, ma'am. I put her in the drawing room while I determined if you were at home."

I considered for a moment if I wanted to be at home to Lady Esther. Though she wasn't quite as unpalatable as Lady Wingate, to deal with two such women in one afternoon was to ask a great deal of my patience. Still, Lady Esther was not one to call for the sake of calling. I consulted the clock on my dressing table. There was time enough. "I shall see her."

"Very good, ma'am."

Jarvis left to inform the lady I would be down directly, and Bridget finished my hair faster than I would have liked. Thus, there was no reason for me to linger in my room except to gather my fortitude. I drew a deep breath and ventured down to the drawing room.

Though I'd moved into George's house, the drawing room was exactly as I'd have furnished it. A long, narrow room, it had dark oak floors, paneled walls painted a warm ivory, and three distinct areas that flowed from the dining room to the back garden—tea, games, and conversation. The elderly Lady Esther was seated in the last of these, by one of the doors that opened to the garden. The deeply cushioned club chair nearly swallowed her up. Not that she was petite. She was of average height, but remarkably thin, which made all her angles—shoulders, elbows, hips, even her cheekbones and chin—look pointed and somehow dangerous. Her tongue was indisputably the sharpest instrument in all of England.

"Good afternoon, Lady Esther," I said upon entering the room. "How kind of you to call."

"And how kind of you to receive me." She rested her hands on her walking stick and smiled.

I froze in midstep. I'm quite sure I've never seen the woman smile before, though she occasionally bared her teeth. This was different. This smile appeared genuine, and while not exactly engaging, it made her look almost approachable. It took a moment to gain my bearings.

The smile slipped into a scowl as if it couldn't do so quickly enough. "Stop looking so shocked," she snapped. "I can be pleasant when I've a mind to—when I'm around someone worth the effort."

Ah! There was the woman I'd grown accustomed to. I took a seat in the matching chair on the other side of the window. "Goodness, are you saying I am worth the effort it takes for you to be pleasant? I'm flattered."

"You are meant to be." She narrowed one eye. "Though I was not entirely sure flattery worked with you, I suspected it wouldn't go amiss."

Instinct told me to be wary. "What is it you are hoping to achieve?"

"I wish to join you for tea."

"I'm so sorry, but I'm expected at the Ashleys' for tea. In fact, I should be leaving soon."

She rapped her stick on the floor, causing me to draw back.

"I'm aware of that," she said. "I wish to join you. Lady Wingate is an old friend of mine, and I heard you are considering sponsoring her niece. I want to accompany you, in part, to ensure that you take her on."

I couldn't say what surprised me more—that Lady Esther knew my business, or that Lady Wingate had a friend. And of all people, it was Lady Esther. Apparently, what they say about birds of a feather is true. "What is your interest in this matter?"

"I simply wish to make myself useful."

She smiled again. The woman was clearly up to something. However, since she'd asked so directly, it would be very ill-mannered not to invite her to join me. I suppose I'd find out eventually just what she was plotting.

When she was ready to tell me.

"Well, if we're to be on time, perhaps we should be off now."

We took Lady Esther's carriage and from the moment I sank into the soft leather seat, she kept up a stream of chatter—about the weather, an upcoming ball, and the differences between my neighborhood of Belgravia and Mayfair, where we were headed. Every time I attempted a word—*rap, rap, rap*—she tapped her wretched stick on the floor of the carriage and interrupted me. If I spent much more time with her, I'd be in danger of developing a twitch.

We were almost to the Ashleys' home before she drew breath. I leapt on the opportunity to change the subject. "How long have you known Lady Wingate?"

"A good fifteen years now. I met her at her wedding to Lord Peter. She didn't take part in society when her previous husband was alive."

That was because he was a banker and not of the aristocracy—the same reason I required a sponsor to bring me into society prior to my first marriage. Yet, here was the very proper, blue-blooded Lady Esther seeking the company of both of us. Interesting.

"Were you a friend of Lord Peter then, before his marriage?"

She slanted a glance at me. "Before his second marriage, you mean? No, merely acquaintances. His first wife didn't suit me, but Augusta and I struck up a friendship upon our first meeting."

"I'm surprised she didn't ask you to sponsor Miss Stover."

Her countenance turned to stone. "Are you quite serious? I'm far too old for such tomfoolery."

We'd come to a stop. A quick glance out the window told me we were at the Ashley residence. The groom jumped down and opened the door for us. I watched as Lady Esther stepped out sprightly with just a light touch of her hand on the groom's. Though I found it hard to believe she considered herself too old for anything, I wouldn't be at all surprised to learn there was indeed tomfoolery involved in this situation.

The Ashleys were a prominent family in society. Lord Peter, the late Viscount Wingate, was quite the gadabout up to and well after his first marriage fifty-some years ago to Mary Sinclair, the fourth daughter of Lord Pomerance. Ever the dutiful wife, Lady Mary gave the viscount two sons before she promptly died of scarlet fever. Lord Peter, as usual, was off exploring some archeological sites in Egypt, and the boys were safely shielded from the disease by their nurse, so Lady Mary left this earth causing the least amount of inconvenience to her family. It's doubtful any of the Ashleys gave her another thought.

With two sons, Lord Peter felt the title was secure and remained single for more than thirty years, leading one expedition after another in Egypt and Sudan until he became famous for finding the most interesting and exciting artifacts at his extensive excavations. Then he surprised everyone when, at seventy years of age, he made a different but possibly more treacherous trip—down the aisle to the altar at St. George's. He married Augusta Fairweather, the childless, and very wealthy, widow of a banker. The lady herself had already attained her sixtieth year and enough wealth to live out the rest of her life doing whatever she pleased. That she chose instead to enter the married state once more made the match something of a double surprise.

Particularly to his children.

The wedding had taken place fifteen years ago, and people still speculated on the reasons for the match between the outgoing, adventurous aristocrat and the always ill-tempered commoner.

Since Lord Peter had spent a mere handful of months in England with his bride during the length of their marriage, my guess was money.

Lady Esther and I were led into a large, open drawing room with dark paneled walls, where I was not surprised to see several Egyptian artifacts, including an obelisk clock in the corner and an enormous vase on a bronze pedestal, both heavily carved with Egyptian motifs. It did come as a surprise to find all the Ashleys gathered around a low tea table. I suppose after four months of mourning, any visitors were a welcome relief.

Two members of the family I knew well. The late viscount's second son, Simon, and his wife, Violet, who always referred to themselves as Si and Vi, had been chums of my late husband. They rose from their seats on the sofa and greeted me like an old friend.

We were not old friends.

Regardless, I took Vi's hands when she offered them and kissed the air near her cheek. When she released me, Si took my hand and offered his condolences. It took a moment for me to realize he was referring to Reggie's death, which had happened more than two years ago. They hadn't come to his funeral, and I suppose this was the first I'd seen of him in the intervening time.

They were as near to a matched pair as two unrelated people

could be. Both blond and blue-eyed, though now that they'd reached their forties, Si's hair was thinning and Vi had dark shadows under her eyes. Their faces bore a matching set of lines, making me wonder if they were still engaged in the exhausting effort of entertaining the Prince of Wales.

"Lady Harleigh."

I repressed a sigh and turned to face Jonathon Ashley, who drew in a dramatic gasp and momentarily covered his mouth with his hand, displaying a signet ring on his little finger. "My mistake. It's Mrs. Hazelton now, isn't it?"

His voice was as unctuous as I remembered it from more than ten years ago when he hoped to offer me marriage. Mother put an end to that hope quickly. I returned his smile.

"And I am now Viscount Wingate," he continued. "Isn't it amusing how our fates can change in a heartbeat?"

Since it had been his father's heartbeat, or the lack of one, that changed his fate and put that ring on his hand, I was rather appalled by his use of the word *amusing*. Typical Jonathon. Thank heaven Mother had rejected him as a suitor for me.

He must be about fifty. Also blond, but with dark eyes, he was stockier and wore a mustache and a neatly trimmed beard. It would be difficult to find two brothers so completely opposite. One wanted nothing but amusement, while the other didn't know the meaning of the word. Jonathon had married young and lost his wife perhaps a dozen years ago. One presumes she died of boredom.

He introduced his son, Andrew, a young man of about seventeen, the image of his father but with darker hair and no whiskers.

I was taken aback when my gaze landed on Lady Wingate. She was dressed appropriately in an afternoon gown, with her white hair styled up and away from her lined face, but her brown eyes looked empty and her mouth drooped open as she slouched in a convalescent chair, wheeled up beside the short end of the tea table. She lifted her head in response to our greetings, tightened her grip on her teacup, and coughed gently, causing her shawl to slide off one shoulder. Though she was well into her seventies, I hadn't expected her to look so fragile and ill.

Lady Wingate fixed her gaze on Lady Esther and appeared to be attempting speech. Before she could force words to her lips, her hand holding the cup trembled. She stretched it out as if she wanted to place it on the table, but dropped it instead. Lady Esther and I jumped back as the tea splashed to the floor, joined in the next instant by Lady Wingate, who slipped boneless from her chair, making no attempt to break her fall.

Heavens! Had the woman just died?

Visit our website at
KensingtonBooks.com
to sign up for our newsletters, read
more from your favorite authors, see
books by series, view reading group
guides, and more!

BOOK **CLUB**
BETWEEN THE **CHAPTERS**

Become a Part of Our
Between the Chapters Book Club
Community and Join the Conversation

Betweenthechapters.net